IN LIKE FLYNN

Pirates of King's Landing - Book 2

LAUREN SMITH

This book is a work of fiction. Names, characters, places, and incidents are the product of the author's imagination or are used fictitiously. Any resemblance to actual events, locales, or persons, living or dead, is coincidental.

Cover design by Carpe Librum Book Design

ISBN: 978-1-952063-80-0 (ebook)

ISBN: 978-1-952063-81-7 (print)

PROLOGUE

"Dear God," Captain Thomas Buck gasped as he wiped rain from his eyes and pushed his wet hair back from his face. He peered through the storm-ravaged sea toward the looming mass of a galleon caught upon the rocks near a reef. It was a beautiful prize, with towering decks and gilded woodwork at the stern of the ship. Lightning cut across the sky, flashing over the ship in distress.

"Cap'n?" A young Scotsman named Joseph McBride joined him at the railing of Thomas's own ship, the *Sea Serpent*. At twenty-five he was young for a captain, but his short life had given him plenty of experience on taking command. Every man aboard his ship knew he would sacrifice himself to save them if it came to that.

The *Serpent* was the fastest sloop in the West Indies, and her crew was proud to plunder under her sails. Even though they were pirates, Captain Buck and his men held themselves to the seaman's code to aid any ship in distress. They were simply more aggressive as to what cargo they took by way of thanks for their efforts in assisting another ship.

"Drop a boat in the water, Joe, and ask for volunteers. A ship like that is bound to have some riches—and any survivors can be taken on as crewmen or released at the nearest port if they do not wish to serve on board."

"Aye, aye, Cap'n." Joe called out for a boarding crew, and Thomas checked his belt for his cutlass and pistol before he helped the others lower a boat into the water.

They rowed across the raging sea, and he squinted at the distant tropical island that was half-shrouded in the rain behind the reef. Perhaps whoever was on this doomed vessel had managed to take a boat ashore to safety. If so, they could canvass the island to help any survivors. If not, they could salvage any goods on the ship once the storm died down, assuming it didn't sink right away from a hull ripped open by a sharp reef. Captain Buck was not like most pirates. He was an Englishman with an Englishman's honor, and he wouldn't leave anyone to die on a lonely stretch of forsaken beach.

Thomas gripped an oar and rowed alongside Joe as he and four others fought the waves to reach the other ship. Once they reached it, they could see the hull smashed and hung up on the rocks. The ship was rocking dangerously as the waves battered it. They had only a short time before it sank. Using grappling irons, they lashed their small boat against the galleon.

"Be careful, men! Search for survivors and get back as fast as you can. She'll be underwater soon." Thomas grabbed one of the dangling ropes that draped from a broken mast over the side of the ship. He scaled up the side of the listing ship to the deck.

He dropped down onto the quarterdeck and saw loose bits of broken masts rolling back and forth, bumping into a few bodies that lay there. Thomas stopped at the first and rolled the man over. There was a bloody gash across his head, and it looked as though he'd been struck by a beam or washed into something hard enough to kill him. All the masts had snapped off. He could imagine the wave that had swept over the deck and knocked this man into a spar, which had broken his now lifeless body. No doubt many of the crew had been swept overboard.

"Anyone alive?" Joe asked.

"Not here. Check belowdecks." Thomas stood and crossed to the waist of the ship and took the companion ladder down into the belly of the vessel.

"Anyone down here?" he called out.

A distant shout came from the passageway. "Help!"

He rushed in the direction of the sound. There was a cabin door, locked, at the far end of the ship.

"Hello?" Thomas pounded on the door.

A man's hoarse voice came from the other side. "Help us! Please!"

Thomas drew back and slammed against the door. The door shattered beneath the impact, and he barreled into a cabin. There was a small bed with a beautiful woman stretched out on her back, her head propped up on pillows. She was deathly pale. The blankets around her were damp and her legs were bent up as she let out a scream of pain.

Beside her, a man clutched one of her hands, watching her face with worry. But as Thomas got a better look, he realized the man was in far worse condition than the woman. He held a hand to his side, and blood was oozing from his fingers around a large and deeply embedded splinter of wood.

Thomas knelt by the man and examined his injury. "What happened?"

"I was aiding the men on deck when a wave hit . . . took out our mainmast. It shattered before our eyes. I took a blow." He nodded weakly down at his wound. "The others . . . swept overboard. I came back down to help my wife . . . the babe is coming."

He nodded at the woman on the bed. Thomas turned his face toward the woman, who suddenly convulsed and screamed.

A moment later she collapsed on the bed, and Thomas saw a tiny baby slip from her body into the sheets, covered in blood. He rushed toward the end of the bed and picked up the bloody baby, wiping it with part of the bedclothes. The babe wriggled and then hiccupped before crying shrilly in the cabin.

It was a girl. Her green eyes opened briefly between her cries as he held her, and she stared deeply into him—*through* him. Her tiny wrinkled fingers curled and uncurled as she fought for her first breaths. What a strong little creature she was, boldly facing the uncertain future that lay before her. It reminded him too much of when he was a lad and how he used to shout into the wind, daring it to hold him back.

"Please," the woman whimpered. "My baby . . ."

Thomas removed his blade and deftly cut the umbilical cord, the way he had once seen a midwife do in Port Royal a few years ago. He stripped part of the bedsheets from the bed and wrapped the tiny blood-soaked babe in it. He had to give her to her mother—a woman knew best what to do with a babe. He knew little of children and nothing at all about babies. When he moved to hold it out to the woman, her husband spoke.

"Please . . . take our child to safety." The man's face had drained of all color, but his green eyes were bright and almost feverish. "I fear we aren't long for this world." The man brought his hands together and removed a signet ring from his pinky finger. "Take this. Give it to our child. It's the truest proof of who we are."

Thomas took the ring and tucked it into the pocket of his waistcoat. Whoever this man and woman were, the weight of that ring warned him that they were people of consequence. He wouldn't leave them here.

"I'll be back for you both," Thomas promised before he rushed up to the deck. The ship swayed ominously beneath his feet. The babe went eerily silent in his arms, as though she sensed the danger they were in.

"Cap'n. No one else is alive. Many of the crew must have been washed overboard. There isna much to salvage, either." Joseph came up beside him and gave a jolt at the sight of the precious bundle in his arms.

"Is that a wee bairn?"

"It is. Take it to the boat for me. The parents are still below, both injured. I must help them." He pushed the bundle into Joseph's arms before returning to the cabin below.

Thomas halted at the sight of the babe's father's sightless gaze upon the doorway where Thomas stood. The woman on the bed drew in a shaky breath, and Thomas moved toward her, intending to scoop her up and carry her to safety. As he leaned over her, the woman raised a frail hand to touch Thomas's cheek.

"Is it a boy or a girl?" she asked in a whisper.

Taken aback by her question, he had to think about what he'd seen in those few moments before he'd wrapped the child up. "It's a girl. A strong little lass."

The woman's worried expression softened, but the weariness in her warned Thomas she wasn't going to last long.

"Brianna, then . . . after my mother." The woman smiled. "A strong name for a strong daughter."

Thomas slid his arms around her back and under her legs, but she pushed weakly at his chest.

"Let me stay with my husband. Please. I won't make it . . . too much blood." She shifted in the blankets, and he saw to his horror the blood still pooling on the bed.

"But, my lady . . ." He didn't want to leave this woman here to die alone, not when she had an infant to care for. To live for.

"It's all right," the woman said gently. "Promise me you'll love her as your own. Find her uncle. He will take care . . ." She didn't finish her sentence.

Thomas was lost in her stunning gray-blue eyes and in that moment could deny the beautiful stranger nothing.

"I'll love her as my own," he vowed to her.

Why he agreed to that, he'd never know. He wasn't married, had never even thought of children, but he wouldn't break his vow to this woman, or the man who'd died protecting her and their child. The moment Thomas had held that child in his arms, invisible threads had wound around his heart, connecting the two of them in a way that could never be broken. He would do anything for the little girl.

The woman closed her eyes and reached for her husband's hand, holding it, and let out one last slow breath. Then she was still.

Thomas searched the cabin, seeking anything he could find of value that would identify the couple in case the ring wasn't enough. A pack of letters and a few lovely gowns were all he could find. He wasn't sure why he grabbed one of the gowns, but he shoved it, along with the other personal items, into a tar-coated bag that would be protected from water before he whispered a prayer for the poor souls of this ship. Then he headed back on deck and tossed the bag down to the small boat waiting on the water below. Joseph assisted him in the climb down, and they rowed back toward the *Sea Serpent*.

"Where's the child?" he asked his first mate.

The Scotsman pulled a bundle out for him to see. He had put the baby in a wicker basket he must have found on the ship somewhere.

Thomas examined the baby. "Is she all right?"

"*She?*" the Scotsman choked. "We're bringing a *lassie* on board the *Serpent*? 'Tis bad luck, that is."

"She's an infant, Joe. What harm can she do?" Thomas asked. He'd never held with silly superstitions about women on board ships. The real trouble came not from superstitions but from men hungry for the touch of a woman, and it often led to jealousy and fights among the men. But tempting fate? That was nonsense.

"Wee bairn lassies grow up to be *womanly* lassies, Cap'n, and those are always trouble."

"It's not as though she's going to be a member of my crew, Joe. We'll find a nursemaid for her, and she will have a nice life in Saint Kitts. Perhaps even marry a tea planter or some other decent fellow." But even as he said this, the little babe seemed to protest with a wrinkling of her face in a mightily fierce expression for one so small and new to the world.

"Ah, well, that's good, then. Give the lassie a nice life and she'll bring us no trouble," Joe agreed, seemingly mollified by Thomas's response.

Thomas gazed down at the child, finding himself smiling at her face. She yawned, her little pink mouth forming an *O* shape, and she squinted at the storm around them, looking adorably furious. He used a bit of the bedsheet to wipe her face clean of some remnants of blood. The rain misted over her tiny cheeks, and she let out a primal cry that startled the rest of the crew on the boat.

"Keep rowing, lads!" Joe barked. "We need to get away from this storm."

Behind them, the galleon groaned and slipped off the reef, slowly tilting into the towering waves that soon swallowed her whole. The babe let out another shrill cry, as if she knew she'd lost her parents.

But she wasn't alone in the world. She had him now. Thomas had vowed he would raise this child as his own. He couldn't help but fall in love with the dear little girl.

"A female," Joe muttered again in that Scottish burr of his. "Terrible idea."

"She's not just any female. She's going to be my daughter. I vowed to take care of her."

His *daughter*. The daughter of a pirate. And what a bonnie wee thing she was.

It was said that all pirates craved treasure, but in that moment Thomas realized that not all treasure was silver and gold.

CHAPTER 1

Port Royal, Jamaica

1741

"WISHING YE HAD A DIFFERENT LIFE, LASS?" A VOICE WITH a deep Scottish burr asked.

Brianna Holland pulled her gaze away from a trio of beautiful women in fine gowns as they paraded through the market of Port Royal on the arms of their gentlemen. The women's parasols were poised perfectly to keep the sun off their pale skin.

"No." *Yes,* she silently amended.

Joseph McBride—or Joe, as he was more often called—was forty-eight to her mere twenty years. He was three years older than her father, Thomas. The two men were like brothers, so Joe had become an uncle to her. And he knew her so well that he often knew when she lied to him.

"It's all right ta want things in life, lass. Even *pretty* things. 'Tis yer right, as a *pretty* lass." He nudged her arm with his elbow and nodded at the genteel ladies she had been watching.

"But I'm not simply a pretty lass, Joe."

"Ye are pretty—for a pain in me arse, that is." He chuckled when she scowled at him.

"I'm *more* than that." She'd spent her whole life proving to everyone around her that she wasn't a silly creature in a skirt. She was a force to be reckoned with. A pirate, and the daughter of a pirate king.

"Aye, lass, ye certainly are more. No man who knows ye would believe ye were anything less. That being said . . . What's a pretty dress now and then if'n it pleases ye?"

Brianna's hands adjusted her leather waistcoat and trousers, more aware than she had been in a long time of her masculine disguise. It had become second nature to her to dress and act like a man. When she'd been younger, it had been harder for her. She'd had to do everything twice as well or twice as hard as any man. But over time it had become natural to her, and she'd grown confident in her life and the challenges she faced. Such as now, strolling about a market, playing the part of a young man.

The short brown wig that covered her hair was tightly pinned into her blonde tresses, concealing her feminine appearance. The wig itched, but she put up with the irritation because she couldn't bring herself to cut her hair to complete her masculine disguise. If she didn't have to pretend to be Captain Bryan Holland around everyone but her own crew, she could have ditched the wig, but in a public port like this, it was important that she go unnoticed. And a woman in men's clothing would *always* be noticed if she didn't care to hide her figure with wrappings around her breasts and either cut or hide her hair beneath a masculine wig.

She had a few frocks on her ship, but she had rare occasion to wear them, and she owned nothing so fine as what these women were wearing. She couldn't help but wonder what it would be like to drift through the market while on the arm of a handsome gentleman. She'd feel as elegant and beautiful as a butterfly. She imagined her attractive escort would be wearing a colorful frock coat trimmed in gold embroidery, and he would bow to her and offer his arm. She would smile, bat her lashes, and demurely raise her parasol against the bright Caribbean sun. He would gaze at her with admiration and desire, and she would lean in and—

Oh, what nonsense. To be a caged creature whose only purpose in life was to be a man's shadow who birthed children and eased his physical needs. No, that was no life for her. Brianna loved her freedom as the daughter of a notorious pirate. She could go where she wished and do as she pleased. What did it matter if she never had a fancy gent moon at her with stars in his eyes? She had her pick of pirate lovers, if she ever so chose. They, at least, would understand her and her seafaring life, whereas fancy gents would not.

"There's a seamstress's shop, if'n ye want ta pick that pretty frock now, lass. Ye've got the gold. Why not treat yerself?" Joe suggested. "I'll be over there, seeing ta our rations." Joe nodded in the direction of the warehouses that stored food and barrels of water. The two of them had slipped into Port Royal on a jolly boat before dawn to secure supplies for the *Sea Serpent*, still the most beautiful eighteen-gun sloop to sail the Spanish Main. Yes, it was more than twenty years old, but her father had taken excellent care of it before passing it on to her, and as far as she was concerned, the old beauty was still the best ship between here and England.

Brianna glanced around the marketplace, taking in the various stalls and the vendors selling fresh fruit and vegetables. Everything on the island was bright and beautifully colored. The scent of spices, salted meats, and the natural perfume from the bouquets of flowers in the stalls made the market Brianna's favorite place in Port Royal. The stone structures of the houses and shops behind the stalls added to the cozy feel of the market. A seamstress stood in her doorway, waving goodbye to a plump woman in a cream-colored gown that fairly dripped with pearls.

Slipping her hand into her trouser pocket, Brianna cupped her purse, which was fat with Spanish doubloons. It was her share of the spoils from a Spanish merchant ship they'd stopped last week. Their cook, a man named John Estes, had happily claimed the choicest food belonging to the captain and the higher officers for their pirate crew. Then they had left the ship and its crew to find their way to a port. It was the best way to pirate, in Brianna's view. Take what you want, but leave the crew alive and with the means to get home. It was why her father was considered a gentleman pirate.

"He wouldn't begrudge me one dress, I suppose," Brianna muttered. Her father had never insisted she follow in his footsteps as a pirate, but he hadn't discouraged her either. He'd allowed her to be whoever she wanted to be—woman, pirate, even a *womanly* pirate.

She crossed the market, dodging the occasional chicken or goat who'd wandered in from a nearby yard. She straightened her shoulders and entered the dress shop. A pair of women were in the back, looking at fine kid leather gloves. The seamstress was watching them with a keen interest, given their expensive looks.

The young woman sighed and rubbed one of the fine gloves against her cheek. "Oh, feel how soft these are, Mama."

"Kid gloves always are, my dear," the older woman said. Brianna guessed they must be a mother and daughter. The girl couldn't have been much older than she was.

She wore a frosty green gown with a stomacher embroidered with brightly colored chrysanthemums and leaves. The bodice of the gown came together with a beautiful gold cording that crisscrossed over the stomacher. It was not an overly elaborate gown, but it spoke of class and wealth. The girl's mother's gown was done in much the same style. Their full taffeta skirts were iridescent and created an almost fairytale splendor as the women moved about the shop. Brenna had never had a gown like that. Hers had always been slender things, more suited to running about than the stately, graceful drifting these ladies seemed capable of.

"May I help you?" The sharp voice broke in on Brianna's study of the ladies' clothes. The seamstress, hands on her hips, one toe tapping impatiently, was staring at her, clearly thinking she didn't belong here.

"I . . ." She cleared her throat and deepened her voice to that of a man's. "I should like to buy a gown for my sister."

"I see." The seamstress's sharp gaze focused on Brianna's tanned hands and the dirt embedded in her nails. Lord, she should have bathed last night, but she hadn't planned on coming into a shop like this.

Digging out a few gold coins, she opened her palm and almost chuckled when the seamstress gasped. The light caught on the gold galleons, making them gleam. There was not a person on earth who could turn down the glitter of gold.

"Your sister?" The seamstress's scowl softened to a polite coolness. "I don't suppose you know her . . . measurements?"

Brianna gestured to herself. "About my size, but a slightly larger bosom. We're . . . er . . . twins." She held out her hands in front of her chest to where her breasts would be when corseted. Currently, her breasts were bound flat to her chest, allowing them to be hidden in the loose white shirt and vest she wore. The seamstress made a little huffing sound as she took her measurements. She made quick work of poking, prodding, and circling the tape around Brianna, all the while muttering about the unorthodox act of measuring a young man for a woman's dress. Brianna knew the woman assumed there was no sister and that she might fancy wearing dresses. She wouldn't be the first man to do that behind closed doors.

Suddenly feeling eyes on her, she turned to the young woman watching her from behind a set of hats displayed on wire stands. The girl blushed, and her doe-brown eyes widened as she realized she had been caught spying on Brianna. Given her fair looks, she was rather used to ladies believing she was a handsome young man.

This, however, was the first time a young woman had reacted with such innocent desire to her, and it only made Brianna feel more alone. The attention she wanted wasn't from a genteel young lady, but from a man. The few times she'd found lovers it had been far away from the protective reach of her father and Joe. Those heated nights had been all too brief, but she couldn't ask for more from any man, not so long as she wanted to remain free.

"Come and view my selection of silks, sir." The seamstress waved Brianna toward the wall at the back of the shop, which had several bolts of silk fabrics and an array of colors.

"We have a beautiful orange and blue . . ." She unfurled two sets of silks on the counter, and Brianna examined them but didn't dare touch them with her soiled hands. The seamstress pulled a few sketches out from a leather portfolio. "What would she think of a robe à volante in blue, a stomacher, and underskirts in orange?"

"I believe she'd like that one." Brianna pointed to the pattern she preferred which was labeled a robe à l'Anglaise.

"Excellent choice, sir. I can have the gown made for your sister in two weeks."

"Thank you." Brianna paid extra to have the seamstress hold it for her if she was not back in two weeks to retrieve it.

"My sailing schedule is a tad unpredictable," Brianna explained.

"Yes, yes, quite understandable." The seamstress nodded, accepting the explanation readily. She had the gold in her hand and was happy to do whatever Brianna asked of her.

Brianna continued to ignore the moony gazes from the young woman clutching her new kid gloves. The girl began to move toward the door and artfully tossed one of the gloves upon the ground near Brianna's intended path of departure from the shop.

Having every intention of ignoring the obvious ploy,

Brianna had to halt when the girl threw herself in Brianna's path.

"Oh, thank you for retrieving my glove, sir." The girl shot a pointed look at the glove resting on the floor between them when Brianna made no move to touch it. It was clear the girl thought she was flirting and wanted to have Brianna play the courtly gentleman.

She let out a long-suffering sigh and bent, retrieving the glove. She tossed it at the girl, who fumbled to catch it, and then Brianna, with the barest politeness, moved the girl out of her way so she could leave.

"Well, I never!" the girl scoffed, and Brianna almost giggled.

She strode through the market, spotting Joe at the far end, but as she passed by a stall with onions and potatoes, she stopped abruptly. A bit of parchment nailed to the wooden post in front of her bore a face she recognized all too well. It was Joe's face. His likeness had been printed on the notice. It read: *"Wanted for Piracy – Apprehend on Sight."*

"Bloody hell," she hissed.

At that moment, a small patrol of British soldiers in bright red uniforms marched through the market toward the distant naval fortress that rose out of the landscape like a wolf standing proudly in defense of all that lay behind it. They would soon cross paths with Joe, and his picture was likely to be posted in the fortress. Brianna started toward Joe, keeping calm, not wanting to attract attention until the right moment. Joe was coming toward her now, and he would soon be facing the soldiers head-on. She had to act fast.

She passed by a fruit stand and picked up a juicy red tomato, testing its weight in her hands. This was a damned risky move, but she had to do something. The penalty for committing piracy was hanging, and she was not about to let that happen to Joe.

She waited until the soldiers were a dozen feet away from her, then wound back her arm and threw the tomato, aiming for the chest of one of the men in front. Unfortunately, her aim was off, and the tomato smacked the man right in the face.

The response was instantaneous, as the soldiers started shouting in alarm, then in anger as they realized they weren't being attacked but that the projectile thrown at them was actually a tomato and it had been thrown in the way of an insult rather than as an attack. The man who'd been struck wiped the tomato off his face, only to make it slop down the white lapels of his uniform. He snarled in fury.

Brianna had an instant to meet Joe's startled gaze before she bolted.

"Catch him!" the officer covered in tomato shouted. She'd unfortunately hit the *captain* who was leading the patrol.

Brianna was quick on her feet as she wove through the marketplace, leading the men on a merry chase in the opposite direction of Joe. She stumbled right into the young woman from the dress shop and without a thought shoved the girl in front of the soldiers, who rushed to catch her before she could fall and be trampled.

Brianna leapt over a cart full of vegetables and ducked into a nearby tavern. She knew Port Royal well enough to plan out a clever escape route. She dodged around the tables and drunken men to reach the staircase. She took the steps two at a time and ran until she found the first unlocked door.

"Oi!" a rotund man in a shallow bathing tub snapped as she burst into his chamber.

"Pardon me!" She flung the bathroom windows aside and noted the stout rope that hung between the tavern and the next building. It was a clothesline, but no clothes were currently hanging from it.

She could hear the shouts below as the soldiers searched the tavern's ground floor. Without another thought, she leapt out of the window to catch the rope. She dangled from the rope a dozen feet over the street as she moved across hand over hand, until she could swing her legs up and into the open window of the building opposite the tavern, landing nimbly on her feet.

Brianna raced through the empty chamber and across the hall as she searched for another window to open. The next building in her path was only one story with an open roof. She stepped around the iron railing of the balcony and then hung down over the roof of the next building before she dropped.

Landing in a crouch, she took a second to catch her breath before sprinting across the roof. Someone shouted close behind her. She cast a glance over her shoulder to see the faces of two men in the window she'd just vacated.

"There he is!"

Brianna leapt off the roof onto a cart of hay and immediately burrowed deep. The sound of approaching soldiers had her holding still, trying not to breathe. Her heartbeat slowed, but the thuds were so loud in her ears that she could barely hear what was happening just outside her shelter of hay.

"He moves fast, Captain. He must've gone that way."

Brianna waited a very long time for the voices and the clanking of weaponry to grow distant before she shifted the hay away from her face to see if she was safe. Then she kicked herself free of the hay and hopped off the wagon. She chuckled as she brushed herself off and removed bits of hay from her wig.

Everything around her seemed quiet as she rounded the corner of the building, but she skidded to a stop. Five soldiers had their rifles aimed square at her. They'd been waiting for her to reveal herself.

Damnation.

She stepped back, ready to run again, but another six soldiers ringed around the only exit behind her. One of the men, the captain, still had bits of tomato on his face and chest. He glared at her as he stalked forward.

"All this for a tomato?" she murmured, stunned that they'd spent so much effort on what they should have believed was nothing more than a harmless prank.

"Just who are you?" The captain wiped the last of the tomato off his uniform. He was handsome, but a cruelness lingered around his mouth and eyes that warned Brianna of the sort of man he was. She knew plenty of men like him.

"I'm nobody," Brianna replied.

"A nobody who throws tomatoes at an British officer? I highly doubt that." The captain lifted up a piece of parchment. "Someone said you were looking at this just before you attacked us." It was the wanted sign for Joe.

"Attacked? Tell me, how injured are you by that one silly tomato?" Brianna shot back. "If the mighty English army could be felled by tomatoes, the French and Spanish would be running the West Indies," Brianna retorted with a smirk.

The captain's face turned as red as the tomato she'd hit him with, and a vein in his temple pulsed ominously.

"It was just a bit of harmless fun," she added weakly. "I didn't mean to hit your face. I figured it would wash out of your uniform easy enough . . ."

"Fun? I think a few days in a cell will be more *fun* than you can handle, boy." He nodded at several soldiers, who now closed in on Brianna.

She raised her fists. "Like that, is it? All right." If there was one thing she was better at than running, it was fighting. She'd learned from the best men in Tortuga.

The nearest man who made a move to grab her caught a blow to his jaw that sent him to the ground hard. The next two weren't so eager.

"What are you waiting for?" the captain snapped. "He's just a boy. Grab him."

The two men shared a look and then lunged for her at the same time. She ducked and dove forward between their arms as they closed in. Their heads collided and then they fell back, both men groaning. Brianna laughed and then kicked the next man who came at her right in the dangly bits. He clutched his groin and doubled over, wheezing in pain.

Brianna whirled around to face the next attacker, but the captain had moved in, and he swung his pistol before Brianna could dodge it. The blow caught her on the temple.

She blinked, her ears ringing as she gave her head a little shake. When the sunlight above her was suddenly blotted out, she looked straight up into the face of the captain. His cold smile sent her stomach plunging to her gut.

"Now you'll see *my* idea of fun."

A second later, his booted foot rushed toward her face, and everything went black.

❧

WHEN BRIANNA CAME AROUND, HER FACE AND HEAD HURT like hell. She groaned as she sat up and gingerly touched her forehead. The skin was swollen and hot to the touch. All around her she could hear voices in other cells, the clang of bars, and the shouts of soldiers. Dread filled her as she realized that she was trapped in a British Army jail cell.

Her father was going to kill her. She fell back on the straw-filled mattress on the ground and stared at the ceiling of the cell. At least Joe was free. He may not know she'd been captured, though, and he might wait at the jolly boat hiding spot for her. It left him exposed when he needed to get back to the *Sea Serpent*. Her life wasn't worth the crew of the *Serpent* or her father's.

Blast and damnation!

She sat upright again and got to her feet. There was a small window in her cell, and she casually tested the iron bars to see if there was even the slightest give. There wasn't. She opened her mouth, making her jaw move a bit, and winced at the pain.

"Ah, you're finally awake. Good," a cold voice said.

She turned to see the captain she'd hit with the tomato watching her. He still wore his red-and-white uniform, which bore hints of tomato on the white lapels. His dark hair was pulled back into a queue and tied with a ribbon at the nape of his neck. Except for the stained uniform, he looked the part of a perfect English captain. He fingered a fine British

Army blade that was tucked into his belt as though he longed to use it upon her.

She hated him. It was the sort of loathing that was instantaneous, like a mongoose and cobra facing off for the first time. She'd seen a fight between two such creatures once in Cádiz, and she'd never forgotten it. Neither could live while the other was nearby. Such was the fate of natural enemies. She and this man were such enemies.

Brianna stared back, openly defiant. He wasn't the first man to look at her like that, with the promise of pain in his eyes. She had stared down a pirate once in Tortuga who had been quite literally mad. One English officer could not scare her nearly so much as that crazed pirate wielding a cutlass.

"All this over a bloody tomato?" she snorted. "You must have nothing better to do."

The officer ignored her jibe and held up the parchment with Joe's likeness printed on it.

"I think it's time we talked about your friend. He's a known associate of the pirate Thomas Buck. That makes *you* an associate of Buck's, as far as I'm concerned."

For a second Brianna couldn't breathe. Thomas Buck was her father's pirate name. He'd kept his true name of Holland a secret from all but her and Joe. It was why she'd been christened Brianna Holland rather than Buck, not that anyone but Joe knew her father's real name was Holland. He'd told his crew it was merely to protect her with a false name. It was ironic that real name was one more way to protect her. She'd have to think fast to get around the captain's questions about her father.

"Oh? 'Ow do ye figure that, Cap'n?" She purposely

slipped into an accent that her father would have chastised her for to antagonize this man.

"I *figure* it, as you say, because when one finds a rat eating what doesn't belong to it, there are usually more rats nearby. Pirates are nothing but rats, and anyone in the company of a pirate is most likely a pirate as well."

Following his logic, she couldn't help but grin. "And that would make you a pirate . . . since you're in my company. Or a *rat*, I should say."

He'd set himself up so perfectly and hadn't seen it coming. The only evidence of his rage was the flare of his nostrils.

"You have one chance. One. Tell me about Joseph McBride and Thomas Buck or you will be hanged, drawn, and quartered."

"And if I talk?" she asked, even though she had no intention of talking.

His lips curled in a sneer. "We'll give you a merciful quick drop and a sudden stop, but we'll leave you in one piece."

She would face a far worse fate if the man learned she was a woman. It was *always* worse for women.

"I think I'll keep my mouth shut, thank you very much, Cap'n." She turned her back on him.

"You'll change your mind soon enough." His words echoed as he left her alone.

She stared out the window and recognized with creeping dread what she'd failed to see earlier while she was testing the bars. A gallows had been erected in the middle of the fort's yard in clear view of all the jail cells. The empty noose swayed in the island breeze. Death and paradise had always been closely entwined in her life, but she'd never wanted them to be *this* close.

Brianna shuddered. It was time to find a way out of this cell, or she'd need to convince them to hang her before they tortured her. She was not about to let them discover she was a woman. Far better to face that quick drop and sudden stop. Brianna curled her fingers around the bars and inhaled the scents of the island as she closed her eyes.

Lord, she was suddenly homesick for her cabin on the *Sea Serpent*. She missed her father and her crew and the feeling of the breeze against her skin, unspoiled by the smells of a city or prison yard. She opened her mouth and sang a song her father had taught her when she was but a wee child as she watched the noose swing.

"Come all you young sailormen, listen to me,
I'll sing you a song of the fish in the sea,
And it's windy weather, boys, stormy weather, boys,
When the wind blows, we're all together, boys."

CHAPTER 2

The cell door clanked sharply, pulling Brianna out of her sleep. Before the interruption, she'd been in the midst of the most wonderful dream. She had been back on the quarterdeck of the *Sea Serpent* as it approached Jamaica. The water was a pure light cerulean, and as the ship coasted through it, she could see down to the ocean floor, spotting colorful fish darting about. Small sharks and rays drifted lazily over the sandy bottom. Ahead of her, Emerald Island was a glittering jewel.

"On your feet, pirate," came a cool voice that she recognized with dread.

Brianna blinked and slowly sat up on her straw cot. She yawned, stretched her arms back over her head, and then finally stood. She couldn't let this man know that she was frightened of him. The captain glared at her. So torture day had arrived, it seemed. She'd had little sleep in the last three days, and now she was to face whatever would come next. She could only hope to hide her gender from them. As much as she didn't want her neck stretched from the gallows, it would be a better fate than being discovered as a woman beforehand.

She took note of the two soldiers on either side of the captain.

"I don't suppose I could have a bit of food and water to break my fast?" The last time she'd eaten had been moldy bread the night before, and she'd rejected the water offered from a bucket coated with a layer of scum. It hadn't been safe to drink, and now her lips were parched.

"Thirsty, are you?" The captain's voice turned almost silky.

Brianna was no fool. That was not a tone she could trust.

"No, no, thank you. I'm fine," Brianna replied nonchalantly.

"Take him to the yard," the captain snapped, then began to walk down the corridor ahead of them. So the hanging was to begin already? A flutter of nerves stormed the battlements of her belly, but she went willingly with the soldiers. If there was a chance to escape, she would take it, but she would not waste her energy now.

"Chin up, lad," a fellow prisoner called as they passed the row of other inmates.

"That's right! Show them how a real man faces the end," another shouted. She almost laughed at that.

"Let the Jolly Roger fly!" a third man said before he spit upon the soldiers' faces as they passed. One of the soldiers slammed his gun against the bars of the man's cell. The prisoner backed up worriedly.

"Don't worry about me, lads!" she replied to the prisoners. "I'll make Captain Morgan proud." That was code.

Captain Morgan had died a little over fifty years before, but his legend had carried on from ship to ship. Port Royal had been his land before a mighty earthquake had swallowed two-thirds of the city forever beneath the sea. Now the British were in charge. A call to make Morgan proud was a final act of defiance to anyone putting a pirate to death. None cared that Morgan had once enforced antipiracy laws when he'd served as governor of Jamaica. He would always be a hero to their kind.

She had sat on her father's knee as a tiny child growing up with the legends of the great pirates and privateers. It was years later that she'd realized her father was one of them. Thomas Holland, or Thomas the Buccaneer, was now the Shadow King of the West Indies. Untouchable by any navy, he'd cheated death time and again. She would do him proud now and face whatever came, but she would not betray him.

She blinked against the bright light outside in the fort's parade ground. The captain stood waiting by a trough of water that was used to quench the thirst of military beasts in the fort. One of the soldiers shoved her forward when she halted, and she fell to her knees at the captain's feet.

"I believe you said you were thirsty," the officer sneered, and that was Brianna's only warning.

He gripped her by the back of her neck and dragged her a few feet toward the trough, then shoved her face into the water. Brianna had only a second to inhale before she was submerged. Panic and natural instinct made her flail at the sides of the trough, but her hands were soon jerked behind her and bound together.

A moment later her head was released, and she gasped for air as she broke the surface.

"Are we having fun yet?" The captain's laugh was as sharp as a whip.

A split second was all she had before the captain shoved her once more into the cold water.

Flashes of white and black danced behind her closed eyelids. She thrashed against her restraints and the hard hand still in a viselike grip on her neck, but she had no choice but to hold on. This was no different than holding her breath during hurricanes when winds whipped the seas to a fury. In such storms, she had but an instant to breathe before the waves knocked the breath out of her lungs and tried to drown her.

She was hauled up again and she gasped, her lips feeling the sweet, warm Caribbean air. She blinked away the water and stared up into the sneering face of the army captain. Her body trembled with both fear and rage.

"Now . . . Joseph McBride. We searched everywhere. Where would he hide?"

Brianna tried to collect her scattered thoughts. Nearly drowning had a way of tossing her mind about like a storm-battered ship.

"I don't know what—"

Her head was shoved back under the water. Again, she fought off the waves of panic and tried to stop fighting. She let herself go limp and focused on the last remnants of her dream, the one with the clear blue water and Emerald Island. She finally relaxed, only her lungs felt tight. She saw now what some sailors meant when they imagined death as a quiet dark sea and a flash of pain as they inhaled water. She didn't want that death. She held her breath, fighting off the need to open her mouth and breathe.

She was jerked out of the water and tossed onto the ground on her side. She was so stunned by the sudden reprieve that she didn't immediately breathe.

"You killed him," a new voice growled. "I told you this was not the way, Captain Waverly."

"Forgive me, Admiral, but he won't talk," the captain replied coolly. "Interrogation methods like these are necessary."

Brianna regained her wits and slowly drew in a breath, relieving her screaming lungs. Neither man, nor the two soldiers, seemed to notice. She kept her eyes closed and her body limp.

"He was our only lead on Buck, and you drowned him. We are in His Majesty's service. We do not drown boys like rats. We maintain our honor."

"Forgive me, Admiral Harcourt," Captain Waverly said far more sarcastically this time. "But pirates do not deserve *honorable* treatment. They slaughter our men and rape women and enslave children. How could you treat this man with honor when he himself has none?"

His words made Brianna bristle inside, because it had the sting of truth to it. Most pirates were lawless creatures who acted on baser instincts, but not her father and not her father's crew. They only took lives when they had to, kept no prisoners or slaves, and women were respected. She'd chosen men for her own crew that she could trust and felt would be as honorable as pirates could be.

Other pirates, of course, were not like this. Brianna was anything but naïve. But for this man to throw all pirates in the category of such villainous dogs . . .

"Honey draws far more bees than vinegar," Admiral

Harcourt said. "If you had let me try with the boy . . . But now it's too late."

"Take his body and hang it in the iron cage by the docks," Waverly ordered. "The birds can pick off his flesh. He'll be a lesson to other pirates who dare to come into Port Royal."

Brianna almost tensed at the chance for freedom and had to keep herself relaxed. The soldiers cut her wrists free so they could hoist her up by her arms and legs to carry her away.

She kept her eyes closed as they walked, but just before they reached the gates, Captain Waverly called out, "Hold on! I want to be sure he's dead." The sound of a blade being drawn out of a scabbard was Brianna's undoing. She was not going to let this man stab her just to satisfy his curiosity.

She jerked fast, and the two soldiers holding her shouted in alarm and dropped her. She landed with a thud and grunted as the air whooshed out of her lungs.

"Ha!" Waverly snarled as he held the sword tip at her throat, pressing down just enough to draw a drop of blood from her skin.

"Captain!" the admiral shouted with such sharp natural command that the captain flinched. It was so small a reaction that Brianna would have missed it if she hadn't been looking directly into Waverly's eyes.

"It is *my* turn to question the boy," Harcourt said. "Please take him into my office."

Waverly stepped back as the soldiers hoisted Brianna back onto her feet. She gave Waverly a smug grin as she was escorted past him to the spacious office of the admiral. The office was full of expensive-looking furniture, a fine oak desk and silk brocade chairs. There was a large globe on a stand, and the sunlight from the windows illuminated the colorful continents and oceans upon its surface. It looked like a room one would find in a tea planter's estate, not in a naval fortress.

"Please, sit." The admiral nodded at a leather chair with gilded arms.

She glanced down at her wet body uncertainly. "I'd better not, sir," she replied respectfully. This man would not be amused or riled by her clever or sarcastic replies. But respect —that he would appreciate. She gestured to her dripping shirtsleeves and to her back where the water from the trough had sluiced down her body.

"It's only a bit of water, lad." His tone was calm, almost gentle. Brianna sank into the chair gratefully. It was infinitely softer than the cot in her cell.

"Now, what's your name, lad?" the admiral asked.

It was smart to play along..

"Bryan Holland, sir," she said. It was foolish to allow hope in, but she wondered if this man might not hang her if she could give him enough false information to get him to trust her.

"I assume you're hungry and thirsty?" he asked as he waved at someone behind her.

She nearly leapt to her feet as a man she hadn't seen walked around from behind her to place a tray of sliced meat, bread and a few bits of fruit on the desk between her and the admiral. He also set down a pitcher of water and a glass. The admiral had guessed she was hungry and thirsty. It didn't escape her notice that he was a smart man, perhaps even smarter than Waverly, because with food like this, she could see how many a prisoner would loosen their lips and spill secrets they shouldn't.

"Please, eat what you wish and drink your fill. Captain Waverly may control prisoners in the cells of the garrison, but here I can restore some semblance of fair treatment. This is a naval fortress after all and I have the final say in your fate."

Brianna's stomach grumbled loudly, and she knew lying about her hunger would be foolish. She reached for a slice of cold ham, and she barely stopped herself from moaning at the sweet taste. She consumed several more pieces of meat before washing it all down with a glass of water.

"Take your time," the admiral said. "There's no rush."

When she'd eaten and drunk to the point that her belly was bursting, the admiral leaned back in his chair.

"Mr. Holland, unfortunately we find ourselves in a difficult position. You assaulted Captain Waverly in the market—"

"With a *deadly* tomato," she cut in. "Didn't know they hanged people for that."

The admiral's lips twitched. "Yes. Harmless as it was, it was still a sign of aggression upon an officer of His Majesty's forces. When we searched the marketplace for you, several witnesses came forward to say you were seen talking with Joseph McBride. Do you deny that?"

Brianna had to think quickly.

"I met him that morning. He walked into the market and was asking my advice on a few places to purchase supplies. He was a nice bloke, sir, but I'd never seen him before that morning."

"And you? It is clear you are not a native of Port Royal,"

the admiral guessed shrewdly. "You speak well, and you care for yourself properly. Where do you hail from?"

"I come from Cornwall. My father has a merchant ship, the *Dutch Lady*. She dropped me off that morning." Brianna remembered spotting the ship leaving the harbor as she and Joe had rowed their jolly boat into the bay.

"That ship is not due to return here for several months."

"Yes, sir. My father wanted me to stay behind to try to build some connections here. He was hoping to hire men to protect us from pirates. Had I known, sir, that the man I was helping was a pirate, I would've turned him in."

"Then why didn't you tell Captain Waverly this when he first asked you?"

Brianna feigned a wince. "I'll be honest with you, sir, since you've been treating me so fairly. When I first arrived here, a couple of your soldiers were rough with me inside a tavern down by the docks. Drinking was involved, tempers flared, and I was more than a little sore about the whole affair." She had seen some soldiers scuffle with a patron of a tavern when she'd arrived, but even if she hadn't, such events were commonplace.

"So when I saw the captain marching down the street all pretty as can be, I admit I let my temper get the better of me. I know it was wrong, and I'm sorry for it, but once the captain had his sights set on me, he didn't want to hear nothing other than what he wanted to hear, if you take my meaning, sir. He was already certain of my guilt, and anything I told him would only have been twisted against me as proof of it. There's no convincing that man that the sky is blue if he has his heart set otherwise."

"I see." The admiral's expression looked troubled.

"Well . . . I would like to believe you, Mr. Holland, but it's not that easy. You struck an officer, albeit with a tomato, but it is still an assault. I will endeavor to determine if what you told me is true, but if I can find no evidence, then we must have another difficult discussion as to your fate."

Brianna swallowed hard. Her story was sound, but there would be no one to corroborate it.

"I understand, sir."

"Now . . ."

The door to the admiral's office burst open, and a stunningly beautiful woman swirled in on a rainbow of color.

"Papa, what are you—?" The woman stopped right beside Brianna. Her auburn hair was piled atop her head, and the elaborate green-and-pale-pink striped gown she wore whispered on the carpet as she turned to face Brianna. She looked as pretty as a confection in a baker's shop. Her eyes held no fear, though, only curiosity.

"Roberta darling, how did you get in here? I had men stationed at the door. This man has possible pirate connections. You shouldn't be here."

Roberta's eyes swept over Brianna with pity. "Oh?"

"Yes, please go back to Dominic, my dear. You need to be more careful. You can't run about the fort without protection."

"Very well." She let out a long-suffering sigh as she bent to kiss the admiral's cheek, and then she faced Brianna as she passed her.

"Good luck," she murmured so softly only Brianna could hear. For a split second she saw something in the young woman's eyes that was, well . . . she wasn't quite sure.

Good luck? What the devil did the woman mean by that?

"Well, think of what we've spoken of, Mr. Holland, and I will do what I can to verify your story." The admiral called out for a pair of soldiers to escort Brianna back to her cell, where she was tossed unceremoniously to the floor. No doubt *these* men listened more to their captain than the admiral since they wore red uniforms and not the naval blue. The door slammed shut and the lock twisted into place.

Brianna fell to her knees, exhausted from the water torture by Captain Waverly and her full stomach of food. It was going to be a long day, and she needed to think. There had to be a way to escape. There were holes in every system —she simply had to find the holes in this one. But first, she ought to rest. Then she would plan.

ADMIRAL HARCOURT STARED AT THE DOOR TO HIS OFFICE, a wave of guilt sweeping over him. The Holland boy was young, so *very* young, a mere lad, yet he was facing a death sentence because he'd been seen in the company of Joseph McBride. If the lad's story about the *Dutch Lady* was true, he might save his neck from the noose, but if not . . .

The door to his office opened again, and a soldier stuck his head in.

"Er . . . there's a prisoner who says he has information on the Holland boy."

"What? What sort of information?"

"He says he will only speak to you," the soldier replied.

"Is that so?" Admiral Harcourt sighed. "Very well. Bring the man to me. What's his name?"

"Joshua Gibbons, sir." The soldier bowed and left to

retrieve the prisoner. Harcourt soon found himself gazing at a wizened old man with cunning eyes and a few missing teeth. By the looks of his weathered skin and ragged clothes, he'd seen a rough life on the sea for many years.

"Mr. Gibbons?"

Gibbons smiled. "Aye, that'd be me."

"You may wait outside," Harcourt said to the soldier. Once they were alone, Harcourt spoke to the man again. "You said you have information about Bryan Holland?"

"That I do, that I do. But I willna be telling ye for free."

"I see." Harcourt tapped his fingers impatiently on his desk. "And what do you want for this information?"

"To go free and not hang."

"Of course," Harcourt murmured softly. "Because your information is *that* valuable?"

The pirate flashed him a toothy grin. "Exactly."

"Very well. If and *only* if your information proves credible, you will be freed." Harcourt wrote up an order and let the man read it.

The pirate stared at it. "I can't read, but I trust ye, Admiral."

"Very well. Now tell me what you know."

The pirate glanced about as if afraid to be overheard.

"That man Holland . . . he is Buck's right-hand man, even more than old Joe McBride is. Not a member of his crew mind you, but quite a favorite of Buck's, he is."

That was certainly not what Harcourt expected to hear.

The man grinned at his reaction. "Rumor is, he and Buck are close."

"But . . . Buck is forty-five and the lad can't even be

twenty. We've never even heard of Holland until today. He's not a member of the crew of Buck's ship, the *Sea Hawk*."

The pirate tapped the tip of his nose with one finger and winked. "Aye, and wouldn't it be a smart captain like Buck who would hide and protect, oh . . . say, a child?"

"You mean to tell me that Holland is Buck's son?" Harcourt was at a loss. Surely they hadn't caught so valuable a prisoner on accident?

"Whether he is or not, 'tis only a rumor, but it's no rumor at all that Holland is Buck's man through and through. I saw it myself last year in Cádiz. Thick as thieves they were." The pirate paused. "Will ye set me free now?"

"Once we prove the truth of your statements," Harcourt said before he had the man escorted back to his cell.

If Buck had a son, he'd clearly guarded his existence well. And if Holland was that son, he would not willingly betray his father, which meant they would need to gain the lad's trust. No man in uniform would achieve that.

Harcourt hastily wrote a note to Lieutenant Nicholas Flynn, a man he trusted with his life. Flynn was a man of honor and wouldn't like the task, but he would do it if Harcourt asked him to. He sealed the letter with his family's signet ring and passed it to one of his personal naval officers who he trusted.

"Deliver this to Lieutenant Nicholas Flynn. He is staying at King's Landing."

"Yes, sir."

The officer left, and Harcourt began to plan his next move. Flynn was the best friend of Harcourt's son-in-law, Dominic, who was a former pirate but also the future Earl of Camden. Dominic and Nicholas were fast friends. If anyone could gain the trust of a pirate, it was Flynn. He knew pirates.

In no time at all, Flynn would have Holland's confidence, and Buck's days as the Shadow King of the West Indies would be over.

CHAPTER 3

A whole day passed before Brianna heard the ominous sound of booted steps coming toward her cell. She straightened her shoulders and prepared to face another round of interrogation.

The cells in the garrison were enclosed entirely in stone, except for the barred window facing the yard and the small window on the door of her cell. It afforded her privacy, a privacy she desperately needed to maintain her masculine ruse. The lack of natural light also kept her hidden from the soldiers. Out of sight, out of mind, was Brianna's strategy until she came up with a real plan.

Scuffling outside her cell forced her flat against the wall.

"Let go of me, you bloody bastards!" a man shouted. Keys jangled in the lock on her door, and it swung open.

"Shut up and get inside!" A soldier shoved someone into her cell and kicked him square in the back. The man went down hard, crashing to his knees on the floor. He uttered a curse as the cell door clanged shut behind him.

The man squinted in the semidarkness; his eyes fixed on the window in front of him, the only source of natural light. He hadn't noticed her yet, but he would soon. From her corner of the cell, she had a decent view of him, thanks to the sparse light from the window. Brianna looked him over, trying to assess the level of threat he posed.

He was in his midtwenties, perhaps older, with sandy-blond hair and blue eyes. He was tall and muscled, and his buckskin breeches molded to his large thighs as he straightened on his knees and stared at the window.

As he moved, Brianna's throat ran dry. She stared at the way his white shirt gaped open at his throat, revealing tanned skin and a faint dusting of golden chest hair. His waistcoat was like a second skin across his broad chest and tapered down to his lean hips. He looked like a gentleman, but a truly masculine one who could charm the skirts off any woman he pleased, including her. Brianna's thighs clenched at the sudden blossoming of desire she felt for this complete stranger. What the devil was he doing in here in a jail cell?

Brianna swallowed hard. She had to hang on to her masculine illusion as long as she could. If she showed him any hint of the desire that he created in her, he might soon guess that she was a woman.

She squared her shoulders and spoke in a deeper voice. "Who the devil are you?" She kept her tone quiet, concerned but not openly threatening.

The man shot her a glance, appearing only somewhat surprised to find he wasn't alone.

He got up and brushed the dust off his breeches and stared at the two cots on either side of their cell. "Me? Who

I am is of no importance to you." Seeing her already sitting on one cot, he smartly chose the other and sat down.

"It damned well is if we are to share a cell." She spoke more boldly now and leaned into the light. Perhaps friendship was the way to approach a man like this rather than antagonism. "Holland." She held out her hand.

The man stared at her a long moment, his blue eyes piercing, and Brianna was glad he was staring at her hand and not the rest of her. Those eyes were both beautiful and dangerous, like a freshly forged rapier. They shimmered and yet would cut straight through to her core if she wasn't careful.

He finally clasped her hand in his and shook it. Her heart gave a violent leap within her as a wild pulse of something shot between them. His eyes held her in place, mesmerizing her like the trained cobras she'd seen in the exotic markets of Cádiz. Her focus dropped from his eyes to his mouth. A man shouldn't have a mouth like that, one that made a woman obsess over imagining how he kissed. Lord, she'd gone without the touch of a man for at least six months, and she was all too aware of how much she'd missed that sort of intimacy.

"Flynn. Nicholas Flynn."

This time, those dangerous eyes of his melted her inside, making her forget who she was. For a moment, she was simply a woman desperate for the touch of a man. She started to lean in toward him before her mind shouted a warning that she couldn't betray herself. She hardened her features in the way she'd done a thousand times before.

Please see a man . . . a mere man, she prayed. If he learned of her gender, he might use that to bargain for his own release. She had to find a way to distract him.

"What are you in for, Flynn?"

"Piracy. Got a bit drunk when my ship docked in port, flapped my mouth to the wrong people. Damned redcoats were on me before I knew what happened. Bastards," he muttered.

"Bastards," Brianna agreed. "They caught me stealing from the marketplace." Brianna lied automatically. She wasn't about to mention Joe or her father. Information in a place like this was currency to barter for one's freedom. "Threw me in here and left me to rot, I suppose," she added.

She stood up and approached the raised barred window facing the yard, trying to avoid looking at Flynn. The prison cells were in a sort of basement, and the windows were just level with the yard where the prisoners could walk when permitted to. It was also where the erected scaffolding was, which served as an ever-present reminder to the cells' occupants who were fated to hang.

Flynn was staring at her again, she knew it, and heat flooded all sorts of places it shouldn't, making it hard to think.

Sing . . . she ought to sing. That would distract her well enough, she hoped. She started to hum a tune that her father used to sing to her as a little child. Then she let the words flow, singing in a soft but deeper voice as she'd often done for years.

"To the execution dock I must go, I must go,
To the execution dock I must go.
To the execution dock, while many thousands flock,
But I must bear the shock, and I must die.

Take a warning now by me, I must die, I must die,
Take a warning now by me, for I must die.
Take a warning now by me, and shun bad company,
Lest you come to hell with me, for I must die."

She felt Flynn's gaze on her long after the song ended.

"What did you steal?" he asked.

"Hmm?" She pretended not to hear him.

"You said you stole from the marketplace. What did you take?"

"A tomato," she replied with a casual shrug of boyish defiance, then sank back down on her cot. She stretched out on her back, ignoring the bits of straw that poked through the cloth of the mattress, throwing herself into a pose of relaxation that she'd seen many men do over the years.

"They tossed you into a cell over a tomato?"

"It may have been what I *did* with the tomato." She could see from his puzzled reaction that he would need a full explanation, and she was rather going to enjoy telling the story.

She folded her hands behind her head and looked up at the ceiling, ignoring his pointed focus on her. "I threw it at that oaf they call a captain. Got him good too. The tomato splattered all over his face and that pretty uniform." She chuckled at the memory. Maybe that would be her last thought on the gallows, picturing that buffoon covered in red juice. She'd die laughing, which wouldn't be a bad way to go.

"You didn't," Flynn said, clearly disbelieving.

She sat up a little, propping one arm on her cot as she looked at him. "I did. He was furious. I thought his eyes might pop out of his skull."

"Why would you do that?"

"I was having a bad day, and some soldiers had roughed

me up down by the tavern earlier. I wasn't exactly thinking with my head, but it was worth it." She told him the same lie she'd told the admiral. It was always better to keep one's story the same when one had to lie.

Flynn's solemn face broke into a grin. "I would have loved to see that."

Brianna chuckled. "It was perfection. Simple perfection."

They fell into a silence that lasted an hour. Every now and then he would shift restlessly, and even though he was five feet away she'd feel that movement as if he'd touched her. She didn't look, except out of the corner of her eye when she was certain he wouldn't notice.

He rolled up the sleeves of his shirt, which exposed forearms that were thick with muscle. Seafarer's arms for certain. They shifted and corded out against his skin as he adjusted his cot, and she had to close her eyes, trying not to imagine too much how it might feel to have those arms pin her down, or wrap around her waist, or . . .

Lord, the waves of heat just kept coming, the more she thought about him. He was impossible to ignore..

"Up on your feet, you two." She had been so distracted she hadn't even heard the guard approach. "Admiral's orders that the prisoners get time to walk in the yard."

There was only one soldier there, and Brianna weighed her chances of rendering him unconscious and escaping. But with the garrison full of troops, she needed more information about their positions before she could attempt a proper escape.

She got to her feet, and Flynn waved for her to go ahead of him. They walked down the corridor and through the door into the prison yard. Several other men were walking about beneath the bright sun. Flynn studied the yard and didn't move away from her.

"Are all of these men here for piracy?" he asked.

"I suppose so. See anyone you know?" Brianna's question was half teasing, but he took her seriously.

"Thankfully, no," he said. "My crew was smarter than I was, it seems."

"What ship did you sail with?" She had to admit she was curious about him. He was as tall as she had guessed, at least a good six or seven inches above her in height, and even posing as a man, she wasn't considered short at five feet and seven inches.

He cut her a sharp look. "Looking to trade information on me, lad?"

"No, no." Brianna held up her hands in surrender. "It's only that, well . . . I might have a few, let's say, *friends* in common with your friends." She was beginning to sense he might be a real pirate like her, not like some of these poor souls who'd been captured who had no real ties to pirates.

His blue eyes seemed a bit harder in the bright sun. He once more watched the other prisoners stretching their legs before he spoke. This time, his voice was a whisper.

"I recently sailed with the *Emerald Dragon*. I sailed with Dominic Grey before he left his ship to a man by the name of Reese Belishaw. Good man, Belishaw, and I've put him at risk." His gaze dropped to his feet, and she recognized guilt and shame all too well. She'd been doing a fantastic job of ignoring her own fate, and that of her father, but now she couldn't escape her own guilt at being caught in the first place.

"Chin up," she said. "Maybe they'll hang you, make it quick like, and you won't say anything."

Flynn sighed and rolled his shoulders restlessly. Brianna found her eyes drawn to the leonine movements he made. She had grown up around bearded, shaggy, and sea-hardened men all her life. Flynn was nothing like them. He was more like her father and Joe. There was a rakish and courtly grandness to him that made the feminine part of her sit up and take notice.

Out in the light, he looked like those fancy gentlemen who sometimes came into the taverns late at night looking to tumble a wench into bed, though he wasn't as polished as those men. There was a hardness to him, a grim set to his jaw, and his forearms were tanned, with faint scars beneath his rippling muscles as he clenched his fists. The man looked ready for a fight, but with whom?

"So, Reese Belishaw," she said. "What's he like? I've never met anyone from the *Dragon*'s crew. They keep to themselves." That was a lie, she'd known both Dominic and Reese through her father, but she wanted to hear this man speak of them. Thomas Buck orchestrated a lot of pirate activity in the West Indies, but many ships were not under his direct command. More often than not, other captains and crews coordinated attacks with Buck's ships.

"Belishaw's a sound man. He can sense storms hours before anyone else has an idea they are coming. He knows the sea too, like he created every wave. He's a masterful captain." Flynn's lips softened in a hint of a smile. "Thank God he and the others left."

"They left you behind," she guessed. It was what her crew was supposed to do.

"Yes, they had to. It's our code. If one is caught, the others leave. One life for all lives."

"Hmm . . ." Brianna hoped that Joe had done the same. For any other man beside Buck, he would have left, but for Buck's daughter? He might risk staying. Or he would go straight to her father, and then they would both come here, risking their lives. She had to find a way out before they tried anything foolish.

"I may be on the lookout for opportunities." She shouldn't trust him, but she wanted to. Perhaps it was the pained look in his eyes as he spoke of his ship and his mates, or perhaps he was simply too beautiful for her to resist. She had taken a liking to fancy men before, but she didn't let them get close, at least emotionally. Physical pleasure was an entirely separate matter. *Bryan* was her identity as far as most of the world was concerned, and only her father's crew and her own crew on her ship knew she was a woman.

Flynn gave a subtle jerk of his head to indicate they should move about the yard. "Opportunities?"

"Yes, I was thinking of—"

Before she could speak further, Captain Waverly stormed across the yard. Brianna braced herself. She had been expecting him to come after her again.

"You there, boy! 'Tis *my* turn again." He sneered in evil delight.

"What does he mean by that?" Flynn asked in a low voice.

"That's the man I hit with the tomato," Brianna replied breezily, even though her heart was beating like a frantic caged songbird. Normally she would have handled this situation with easy bravado, but this wasn't a tavern. This was a place where she'd be flogged to within an inch of her life, possibly tortured and eventually hung.

"I see." Flynn moved to block Brianna from view and crossed his arms over his chest. "Stay behind me. Whatever that man will do, you might not survive." His caution was whispered, and rather than upset her, she felt glad someone here was protecting her, even though she also hated herself for such a moment of weakness. She was out of her depth in this sea of Waverly's fury. Flynn was right. She could see almost a madness shrouding the officer's face. Waverly *would* kill her if given the chance.

"Out of my way," Waverly barked as he came toe to toe with Flynn. Flynn was an inch taller and slightly broader in the shoulders, but Waverly was thick with muscle, almost brutish in build compared to Flynn's leaner form. If it came to blows, it would be a fairer fight than Brianna wished it to be. She would much prefer for Waverly to be a fat little toad who couldn't throw a punch.

"Flynn," she warned softly.

"What is there to question the boy about? He stole a tomato and ruined a uniform. What real harm has been done?" Flynn challenged.

Waverly's eyes narrowed as he leaned to the left to peer at her around Flynn's shoulders.

"That boy is also charged with piracy. He's one of Thomas Buck's men."

"Can you prove it?" Flynn demanded.

Waverly's rage transferred to Flynn in an instant. "And who are you to question me, *pirate*?"

"Challenge me and find out," Flynn warned. There was such danger in his voice that Brianna flinched back a step instinctively. She wondered how this man had ever been drunk or foolish enough to get caught by a patrol. She couldn't picture him doing anything so reckless.

Waverly whistled sharply, and the two soldiers standing nearby grabbed Flynn roughly. "Take him to the post. Bring me my cat. This man needs to be reminded of his place here."

Flynn pulled free of one man and landed a blow on him, knocking the soldier onto his back. Flynn spun on the other man and kicked him back with a blow to his chest. The man clutched at his ribs, wheezing as he bent double.

The joy Brianna felt was silenced as Waverly grabbed her from behind and the cold metal of a pistol was pressed against her temple. Flynn whirled on them, fists raised, but he froze as he saw Brianna.

"Stand down! Or I shall put a bullet through the boy's head."

Flynn lowered his fists and glared at Waverly. The men he had knocked down struggled to their feet and grabbed him once again.

"Lash him to the post," Waverly said.

Flynn didn't fight this time. They hauled him to a thick wooden post near the gallows. The wood was stained with dried blood, blackened by the sun. Waverly shoved Brianna away from him once Flynn was taken to the post.

Flynn's waistcoat was removed and his shirt pulled over his head before his wrists were wrapped in thick cords and tied to a brass ring on the top of the post, forcing his hands above his head. He was stripped bare to the waist, his broad back completely exposed. Brianna's heart stopped as she noticed faint scars covering him. He had been whipped before. He knew the agony that he was about to face, and it was because of *her*.

"Stop it! Your quarrel is with me, not him!" she shouted. Two guards grabbed her arms, holding her back.

Waverly shot her a dark smile. "Oh, you shall have your turn in due course, I assure you."

"You bastard!" she snapped.

He whirled and struck her across the face. Pain knocked her off her feet, and the men holding her nearly dropped her as she sagged with a groan.

Waverly shrugged off his uniform coat and rolled up his shirtsleeves. He caught the whip when one of the soldiers tossed it to him.

"Stop! Don't do this." Brianna pulled free of the two soldiers, who clearly thought she'd passed out. She ran toward Waverly and grabbed his arm as he uncoiled the cat-o'-nine-tails.

When her hand met his arm, he spun on her, the back of his other hand connecting with her face so hard that she fell, briefly blacking out. She came around to the sound of a whip biting into flesh.

Flynn's cry of pain shot through her as she struggled to her knees. Her face ached like the devil, but she didn't care.

Flynn hung weakly against the post. Blood trailed down his back, and his flesh was striped with deep cuts from the whip. Rage filled Brianna, a rage as mighty as the earthquake that had once swallowed Port Royal. Waverly glanced her way, saw her face, and his cold, dark smile only deepened. He tossed the whip to the ground and pulled a pistol out of his belt and aimed it at Flynn's back.

"Better to put a rabid dog down," Waverly said to her.

"He has no information worth hearing. It's *you* I'm interested in." He turned back toward Flynn to aim at his head. Brianna surged to her feet, flying across the sandy ground of the prison yard straight at Waverly.

Years of breaking up fights between her crewmen had taught her a thing or two. The bastard didn't see her coming. She leaned forward, her shoulders tense as she aimed for his waist. Then she tackled him from the side just before he could fire. Waverly grunted as he fell, his pistol sliding out of reach when Brianna landed on top of him, her balled fists coming down on his face over and over.

A half dozen hands grabbed her, dragging her off the captain and throwing her to the ground. A boot kicked her in the ribs, and she felt something break. She tried to angle herself away from the next kick, which landed on a softer part of her body, but she was surrounded on all sides now and there was nowhere to run.

This was it—she was going to die here. She'd never see her father again, or Joe. Pain rained down on her as everything around her grew dim . . .

The crack of a pistol froze everyone in place.

"Stop!" a voice bellowed across the yard. "Stop, I say!"

Brianna shuddered. Each breath she managed to take felt like it was shattering her rib cage. She tried to lift her head and look about. The rest of the prisoners in the yard were huddled in a few spots of shade, their faces grim as they stayed out of the fight. Several guards stood all around her. And Flynn sagged bloody and broken against the post, with Waverly standing far too close to him.

Admiral Harcourt still held his pistol aloft, though its shot had already been spent.

"Take the boy back to his cell. And fetch a surgeon for that man." He pointed at Flynn. "Captain, you will see me in my office once things have settled down, understood?"

Waverly wiped blood from his mouth, his eyes black with hate. His nose was broken, and Brianna smirked in open defiance, even though her body now screamed in pain.

"You are *dead*, boy, *dead*," Waverly hissed as he retrieved his coat from the ground and stalked past her.

Brianna looked back at Flynn, who was slumped against the post. Her heart lodged in her throat. His eyes were closed, and blood poured down his back, his flayed skin bright scarlet. The sweat that dampened his hair had turned it a dark bronze, like a halo.

The admiral approached Flynn and spoke softly to him, his eyes full of pain. Not for the first time, Brianna thought the admiral had too much heart to be a Royal Navy man.

"Come on, you. You've caused enough trouble," a soldier growled and started to drag Brianna away from where she lay on the ground. She dug her fingers into the soldier's arms, clawing to get free, to get to Flynn. She had a sudden fear that she might not see him again.

"Flynn!" she shouted, and then again twice more before the soldiers forced her from the prison yard. Flynn struggled to his feet at her cry. Before she lost sight of him, she saw his strength fail and his legs give out beneath him again.

A hollow pit formed in her stomach as she fell back onto her cot and the cell door slammed, closing her in. She'd cast her lot in with Flynn now. Whatever came of it, she would be loyal to him for saving her life, even if he had only given her a few more days. She wanted to tear into Waverly, let out the fierce rage that had built inside her when he'd whipped Flynn. It was all her damned fault. If Flynn didn't make it . . .

No, she wouldn't even think that. He was strong. He wouldn't let Waverly end him.

She prayed that whatever god of the sea cared for pirates might hear her. *Be strong, Flynn. I'll find a way to get us out of here.*

CHAPTER 4

"*Flynn!*" The shout was still buried in Nicholas's skull. The terror in Holland's voice had only made the agony of his injuries greater.

"This is not what I agreed to, Admiral." The words escaped Nicholas's lips as his strength gave out and his legs buckled beneath him. "I should have stayed at King's Landing with Dom and enjoyed the rest of my leave." That's what he'd been doing before all this had started. Taking a few weeks of much-deserved rest and contemplating his future with the navy. "Instead, that bloody madman nearly shot me."

"I know, my boy. This is my fault. I didn't want that man here in my fort, but I didn't have much say in the matter. His family is well connected and, unfortunately, as aware of his . . . madness as I am because they've sent him far away from England. What better way to rid themselves of a man like that? They sent him here, where the harm he does would rarely reach the ears of anyone back in London."

Nicholas tried to process that, but he still didn't understand why Waverly had attacked him. "Did you tell him about me?"

At this, Harcourt shook his head. "I didn't have a chance to tell him you are an officer or that we have a plan. He was supposed to be busy with patrols on the island today, not here going after that boy."

That boy. Nicholas was too weak to laugh. "That boy is no *boy*, Admiral."

The admiral waved away a pair of soldiers coming toward them and freed Nicholas's bound hands.

"What the devil do you mean?" he asked.

"Bryan Holland is not a boy. He is a *she*." Nicholas trusted the admiral with such information. He had a daughter, a beloved one at that, one who was close to this girl in age. He had faith that Harcourt would do all he could to protect this young woman from the indignities of less scrupulous men and prove she was innocent of any crime. Of course, if she was found guilty, she'd be hung—a pirate was still a pirate, after all. Being a female wouldn't save her from the gallows, unless she got herself with child, and even then it would only delay her fate until after the babe was born.

"You're telling me the truth? Holland really is a . . ."

"Woman, yes." Nicholas's vision spiraled and his head grew heavy.

"Good God, someone get that bloody surgeon here." Harcourt's bellow made Nicholas's ears ring for a moment before he collapsed and blacked out.

He woke on a bed in the garrison's infirmary. He was stretched out on his stomach, and every muscle screamed with pain as he tried to move.

"Lie still, Lieutenant." Harcourt's voice was nearby, his tone soft.

The events that had led to this moment of physical agony came rushing back to him. "Holland . . ."

"She's fine, back in her cell. I've sent a soldier I trust to watch her. He won't let anyone near her, not without my consent. I still outrank Waverly—I doubt he would openly defy me."

Nicholas kept his eyes shut as he drew a painful breath. Every time his lungs filled with air, the flesh of his back stretched and ripped open again. A pained groan escaped his lips.

"Take it easy, Flynn. You took a bad whipping. It will be a while before the wounds heal. The surgeon will need to apply salve frequently to keep them from opening up and becoming inflamed."

Nicholas fell asleep while Harcourt continued to speak, and it was a long while later when he became aware of himself again. He was alone in the infirmary. His body ached so fiercely that it was hard to take air into his lungs. The door opened, and the surgeon came toward him.

"How do you feel, Lieutenant?"

"Like the devil himself tried to flay me alive," Nicholas muttered.

The surgeon smiled. "That is a good sign. Feeling nothing would indicate severe damage."

Nicholas didn't reply. He stared at the surgeon while the man bustled about near his cot.

"Oh, right, drink this. It will dull the pain."

He gulped down the liquid, and the pain began to fade within a few minutes.

He was only half-awake when Admiral Harcourt returned.

"How is he?"

"Lucky for the man, he's young and fit. The wounds aren't shallow, but thankfully Captain Waverly didn't have enough time to do lasting damage, at least not worse than what some other man already did to him. He has quite a few scars from older lashings. Waverly's blows were just starting to go deeper through those old healed wounds. That boy intervened at the right time, and the lieutenant owes him a great debt for it."

Despite Nicholas's pain, he was clearheaded enough to realize something.

"Admiral," he said, interrupting the surgeon and Harcourt's discussion.

"Yes?"

"Put me back in the cell with Holland."

"What? No, you need to heal under a surgeon's supervision," Harcourt argued.

"The surgeon said I'll be fine—let Holland tend to me. He owes me a debt now. That sort of thing builds trust, if you understand my meaning."

He needed to get back into that cell. She needed protection—*his* protection. The girl was wild and impulsive and would get herself killed if left alone for too long. Even if he was currently rather useless with his injuries, he was certain he'd be more able-bodied in a few days if he could rest and see that she was safe with his own eyes. Hopefully, he could convince the admiral that being tended to by the girl would be a good idea so he could protect her .

Harcourt was silent a long moment. "You still wish to

continue this mission?"

The lashing today had somehow deepened Nicholas's resolve to find a way to protect the female pirate. She had trusted him—or was starting to—and had attacked Waverly to save him. To take on a man twice her size, a man clearly bent on hurting her, she had put her secret at risk and thereby her safety . . . *for him*. He owed her a debt now too, and if he could, he'd find a way to make her disappear when all this was over. If she had a chance to start a new life, one far away from here, she'd avoid a doomed fate on the gallows.

"Yes, I do," Nicholas said. "Have the surgeon instruct Holland on how to tend to me."

Harcourt's eyes sharpened in understanding. "Yes, you could be right. Very well. Doctor, you will give prisoner Holland instructions on caring for the lieutenant. Holland is not to know this man is an officer, you understand? We need the lieutenant to gain this prisoner's trust by any means necessary."

The surgeon nodded. "Yes, Admiral."

Nicholas was given a few more hours rest, and at nightfall he was carefully walked back to Holland's cell by two soldiers. The surgeon followed them. When the door opened, the girl bolted upright and rushed toward Nicholas. She seemed to quiver with concern as she reached out to help him.

"Move back, boy," one of the soldiers barked. She obeyed, but her anxious gaze didn't leave Nicholas's face.

When the soldiers released Nicholas, he didn't have to fake a stumble. He was still weak from whatever the surgeon had given him to dull the pain. He knelt on his cot and slowly lay down on his stomach.

"You," the surgeon said as he stepped into the cell.

The girl stepped forward. "Yes?"

"I don't have time to play nursemaid. You will clean his wounds twice a day and apply this before bandaging them." He gave the girl a brown glass pot of salve and several clean bandages. "You will have fresh water and rations to tend to him." This was said more to the soldiers than the girl.

"Why?" the girl asked, suspicion layering her words.

"Because this man needs to be questioned by the admiral, and I would rather not be held responsible for his death. If you value your life, you'll keep him alive."

The surgeon nodded to the soldiers, who placed a bucket of fresh water in the cell before slamming the door shut. Nicholas let out a sigh and closed his eyes. He missed the comfort of the infirmary bed already.

"Are you all right, Flynn?" The girl's soft voice tempted him to smile, but he resisted. Even in male togs and with short, cropped hair, he could tell she was beautiful. It astounded him that no one else had figured out the truth, but no doubt the way she normally carried herself dispelled suspicion. It was only at times like this that she dropped her guard.

"Aye, lad."

The girl cleared her throat and deepened her voice. "What you did for me—thank you."

"You're welcome." Nicholas opened his eyes to find her hovering near him. "Fetch me some water, lad?" He glanced at the fresh pail of water, and she used the wooden cup floating inside to retrieve a full serving for him. She held the cup to his lips, and he drank it until it was drained.

"More?" she offered.

"A little more, then have some yourself." He knew the kind of food and water she had been getting up till now. He closed his eyes, pretending to sleep.

"Don't worry, Flynn. I'll take care of you. I owe you." The girl's voice betrayed her tenderness. She shouldn't be in a life like this.

What was her connection to the infamous Shadow King of the West Indies? A child of his? A friend? A lover, perhaps? She had to be valuable to him somehow, and no one would think this girl worthless. A pirate like Buck would have some affection and likely some use for a girl like Holland. Regardless, Flynn would do what he could to help her escape this life once he learned what he could of Thomas Buck.

As the girl started to hum, he fell under the spell of her voice.

BRIANNA WAS CONCERNED ABOUT HOW MUCH SHE WORRIED about Flynn. She was a carefree, wild pirate, yet here she was fretting over every little thing Flynn did in his sleep as she acted like his nursemaid.

It's only because he took a whipping intended for me.

She had never caused another person pain like *this*. Sure, she had coshed a few merchants and their crewmen over the head with the butt of a pistol in the midst of boarding a ship, and she'd fought in fistfights and knife fights in taverns with drunken men.

But this was different. Waverly'd had death in his eyes. If Nicholas hadn't stepped between them, she would no longer be among the living. Instead, she would be hanging from one of the metal cages until carrion birds pecked off her flesh.

And all over a tomato. I've seen volcanoes with better temperaments.

Flynn groaned and shifted on the cot, jarring Brianna out of her thoughts. She let out a breath she hadn't realized she'd been holding.

"I need some assistance," he grumbled.

She moved to his side. "What do you need?"

"Help me over to that bucket." He nodded at the bucket in the corner that didn't contain water.

"You need to—?"

"Relieve myself," he finished with a pain-roughened chuckle.

"Oh, right." She helped him up. He put one arm on the cell wall as he walked toward the bucket, his back covered with bandages. He hissed in pain as he moved to undo his breeches, and she turned away, trying to give him some semblance of privacy. A flash of panic hit as she realized *she* would need to use that same bucket very soon in front of him. And she wouldn't be standing up like he did.

"Thank you," Flynn muttered as he came back toward the cot. She gripped his waist as she helped him back down. His body was hard and warm in her arms, and being this close, embracing him, sent a dizzy current of excitement through her.

Flynn lay back down on his stomach and angled his face toward her. He closed his eyes. "Sing to me, lad. It will help me sleep."

"I'm all sung out, I'm afraid," she said.

"Then tell me a tale."

"A tale?" She thought back to all the stories her father had told her when she'd been younger. "Do you know of the pirate queen Artemisia of Halicarnassus?"

"A pirate queen, you say?" Flynn chuckled. "Can't say I've heard of her."

She settled down on her cot and looked up at the ceiling. "Well, according to Herodotus's *Histories* and Polyaenus's *Stratagems of War*—"

"You've read Herodotus and Polyaenus?"

Flynn's dubious tone made her frown, and she shot him a glare. "Do you want to hear the story or not?" His blue eyes were open and fixed on her so intensely that she shivered.

"First, answer me this. How does a pirate lad end up reading Herodotus?"

"I never said I was *a pirate*," Brianna reminded him.

"You're in here. You're either a pirate or friends with one."

It was a fair point, she had to admit. "Or I threw a tomato at an overzealous officer who likes whipping people for fun."

"Touché," he chuckled. "So how did you end up reading such scholarly works?"

"My father read them to me when I was young, and then I read them again on my own when I was older. He wanted me to have a classical education. He is a gentleman, and he wanted me to be a gentleman too."

Nicholas nodded in understanding. "I had a similar education, but I ran away at a fairly young age. I never got around to finishing Herodotus." He winked at her, and she let a laugh slip before she could stop herself. She cleared her throat.

"Right, well, what's known of Queen Artemisia is limited, but here is what I remember. She was the daughter of a government official in Halicarnassus, a coastal city in Caria."

"Caria?" Nicholas shifted on his cot as though settling in.

"What we call the Ottoman Empire. She married the king of Halicarnassus, and they had one son before the king died. She ruled in her dead husband's stead. She often went to war and sailed on her own ship as a captain. She was always at war with nearby rival city-states and often took the helm of her own ship. Can you imagine?" Brianna smiled wistfully.

"And what happened to her?"

"Well, women in Halicarnassus were allowed to live in society rather than be hidden away, so she was able to rule and roam with a freedom unimaginable. Her first piracy adventure must have given her a taste of glory."

"A taste of glory?" Nicholas snorted.

"Hush. I'm telling the story," she reminded him. "Artemisia decided to sack the rival city of Latmus. She and her men camped outside the city walls and staged a full-blown festival, complete with dancing and music. Naturally, the people of Latmus came outside to see the festival. When they opened the city gates, Artemisia and her crew stormed in and took the city."

"And what did this clever queen do then?" Flynn's entertained and bemused tone stirred something inside her that she'd rarely felt before. He was actually listening to her. Only her father really listened when she talked about something in the realms of academia. Joe sometimes did, but he was often distracted with ship matters.

"Well, she vanished from history after the great sea battle

of Salamis when the Greeks defeated the Persians. Some say the ruler of the Persians sent her to Ephesus to raise his sons as a surrogate mother and that she lived out her days raising his children. But I don't believe it."

"Oh? Why not?"

She briefly hesitated about speaking her true feelings. What man, after all, would think the thoughts she did about a woman's place? Still, there was some part of her that wanted to be honest with Flynn, to show him who she was inside and out . . . and to see what he thought of her then. Would he run away? Would he laugh? Would he sneer in disgust? Or would he *listen*? So she took a chance and spoke truthfully.

"Because all stories written by men about women are the same. They always end with the woman returning to her *true* place in society, her place according to men." She couldn't keep the bitterness out of her voice, but she realized she might have said too much about the only secret she truly had to hide aside from her gender, so she lied. "My mother was unhappy with her lot in life, or so I'm told. She died when I was young, but my father said she was always upset that she wasn't allowed to travel with him. Why should men be the only ones allowed to explore the wild islands or feel the sea breeze on their faces as they chase new horizons? Isn't the sea female? Aren't ships female? Everything about the ocean is feminine, from her peace and beauty to her wrath. It is only right that women be explorers of the sea. I guess I've always been a bit angry she was denied the things she wanted for no good reason."

Flynn chuckled. "A pirate queen . . . I like that. The very idea is . . . exciting, don't you think?"

There was a look in his eyes that made Brianna turn her head so he wouldn't see her blush.

"So, no home or hearth for you? For any wife you might have, I mean?" Flynn watched her with that intense gaze that made her uncomfortable. It wasn't unwelcome, but it did make her wonder if he suspected more than he let on about her.

Brianna was quiet a long moment. "I want to be free. I would want anyone I loved to be free too. But that's not the sort of world we live in, is it?" She turned to face him. "What about you? Do you have a wife tucked away by some hearth somewhere?"

Flynn's eyes darkened. "No. I lost a friend when I was very young, and I went to sea to find him. I spent so long searching for him that . . ." Flynn paused, and his next words were filled with pain. "I lost myself."

Something about the pain in his voice burrowed into her heart. To be lost, to have no sense of direction—it wasn't a fate she'd wish on anyone. Except perhaps that damned Captain Waverly. She wished him straight to the devil.

"My father says that you either find yourself or lose yourself upon the sea, but to me, lost and found feel the same. Both are freeing."

"Your father sounds like an intelligent man. Does he live here on the island?" Flynn closed his eyes again, and the question was softer, sleepier, as though he was on the verge of drifting off.

"My father lives . . ." She stopped herself from saying anything further, and after a moment she heard Flynn's breath deepen in sleep. A smile curved her lips as she listened to him breathe.

❦

THREE DAYS PASSED, AND NICHOLAS'S CONDITION SEEMED to slowly worsen. His wounds had scabbed over and he was able to lie on his back now, but he was pale and his skin was warm, and he fell asleep to fevered dreams. Brianna kept watch, applying clean bandages from the surgeon and placing a soaked cloth upon his brow, telling him stories of female pirates like Mary Read and Anne Bonny, which seemed to amuse him.

On the third night, his body was so hot to the touch that she feared he would die. She called for the guards to bring the surgeon. When the surgeon came and examined Flynn, he pressed his ear to Nicholas's lips as he pushed lightly on his chest to feel for breath.

"'Tis fever."

"Can you help him?" she asked.

He shot her a sharp look. "If it is a fever, there's nothing I can do. Best to keep him here and hope for it to break. You are doing the best for him, lad. Keep it up."

Brianna moved her cot next to Nicholas's. Tending to him through the night, she eventually collapsed in exhaustion.

"Come on, Flynn, you must get better." She placed her fingers on his forearm and stroked his skin. He was too sick to feel her touch.

Or so she thought.

"Don't stop."

She withdrew her fingers from his arm as if it had burned her. "Don't stop what?"

"Touching me. It's been too long since a woman touched me like that."

Her heart stopped when he said the word *woman*. "It truly is a fever."

"Please," Flynn said again.

She stared at him. "I'm *not* a woman."

Flynn's eyelids fluttered and finally opened. He turned his face toward her. "You can stop playing. I knew it when I first saw you, that you were a woman and not some boy." He let out a breath, and his eyelids fluttered closed again. "All that talk of pirate queens and anger at a woman's place in society . . ."

She wanted to protest, but realized she'd only dig her hole deeper.

"I could see through all that, and all I could think was, *How am I the only one who sees this beautiful woman under a boy's disguise?*"

Flynn thought she was beautiful?

He moved his hand to grasp hers and laced his fingers through her own. His breathing turned shallow.

"Give a dying man one wish."

Brianna leaned over him, putting a fresh new cloth soaked in cool water over his skin, wiping at his face and then his neck. "What wish?"

"A kiss . . ." He moved their joined hands to rest on his chest, and his lips parted. "Please." His lashes flew open and his blue eyes glowed in the faint light.

She stared at him. "*What?*"

"You heard me. One kiss. Let me die knowing how you taste."

How could she deny him? The sinful picture his words

painted shouldn't have affected her. He'd risked his life for her when he had taken that lashing. If he was dying, one kiss wouldn't hurt.

She squeezed his hand that held hers tight and leaned down toward him.

"One kiss, then."

The second her lips touched his, she knew this was a mistake. She had kissed her share of handsome men, but Flynn was different. For a moment, she thought her body burned with a fever all its own as his free hand came up to touch her hair. When she felt his fingers start to latch into her wig, she pulled away from him with a frightened gasp.

He let out a soft sigh. "Even better than my dreams."

"Wh—what is?"

"*You*. The sweet kiss of a pirate queen."

"I'm *not* a pirate," she hissed, afraid the guards might overhear them.

"Aye, you are. The prettiest pirate queen I've ever seen . . ."

His words sent a rush of joy and fear through her. They were both doomed to die, and even then, she was afraid that one small mistake could betray her connection to her father. She would die before letting that happen, but now . . . Now she knew with growing dread that letting Flynn kiss her had put not only her secret at risk but also her father's life. She stared at his face as he fell asleep, still under the influence of a fever. Would he remember that kiss when he woke? Would he remember anything they'd shared tonight? The frightening part was that she wanted what had happened between them tonight to matter.

CHAPTER 5

The kiss had been a mistake.

Nicholas had known it the moment he'd asked her for it, but he couldn't help himself. The fever he'd had the last few days was not nearly so bad as he'd let her believe, and he'd spent the time she cared for him observing the little pirate queen. And his observations had given him the need to touch her—as more than her impromptu patient, but as a man. And so he'd given in to the temptation and tasted her, and he would never be the same as a result.

Worse still, it had changed their dynamic. Gone was the camaraderie she'd allowed him when she'd felt secure that her disguise fooled him. The trust he'd gained when she presented as a boy would have to be rethought now that she knew he recognized her as a woman. And a woman's trust was such a very different, and more delicate, thing than a boy's. As evidenced by the way she'd pulled away from him, wrapping herself in that cloak of mystery all women possessed, shielding her thoughts and emotions from him.

"I won't tell anyone," he said, his tone quiet. "I would never expose your secret, not to the guards or anyone else."

"Tell anyone what?" Her reply didn't come quickly. Each word seemed to be dragged out of her with great reluctance.

He eased down upon his cot, wincing as his back screamed in protest at the movement. "That you aren't a man." One never knew how much one's body used back muscles until those muscles were injured.

She didn't look his way. She lay on her back, staring at the ceiling. She'd dragged her own cot back to where it had been while he was asleep. He'd liked it before when she'd slept close to him and he could feel her heat, her hand touching his skin. The surprising comfort of her touch had gotten him through the worst of his fever.

"I think your fever must have been particularly bad. Me, a girl?" she laughed.

"Come now, Holland, I didn't imagine how sweet you tasted, how it felt when your lips softened under mine. A man can't imagine a heaven like that."

He'd expected his words to affect her, and perhaps they did, but she didn't show it. She remained quiet.

"Do you plan on ignoring me forever?" he asked her.

"Yes."

"At least tell me your true name. I assume Holland is either your surname or a false name. Won't you tell me who you really are?"

"No."

He chuckled. He'd always had an easy way with women. His handsome looks and quiet reserve often drew the fairer sex to him, but this prickly little rogue didn't like him at all. Or perhaps she didn't want to admit that she did.

She was certainly brave to live in a man's world the way she did, he had to give her that. It was clear that she'd modeled herself on the famous female pirates from her stories, possibly even more than she realized, and exposing her true self had only driven a more rebellious streak into her. That was not good. He needed her to trust him if he was going to save her life.

"Well, it's a pity you continue to ignore me, because I plan on escaping, and I rather thought I might take you with me."

For a scant second, her breathing stilled. Then she puffed her chest out dramatically. "And what if I was the one who planned to escape? Mayhap I'll bring you with me?" she challenged.

Lord, he found her bravado delightful. She was a rare specimen, for certain.

She reminded him a little of Roberta, his best friend's wife. Roberta was strong-willed and brave, but more feminine than this creature, of course. Not that it bothered him. He would like his little pirate lass in breeches or fine gowns. She was fascinating, regardless of how she dressed. Quoting Herodotus like a scholar, then singing a bawdy sea shanty. Quite the combination.

"Very well, I will *allow* you to rescue me." Flynn climbed to his feet and leaned his forearms on the window overlooking the yard. "What's your cunning plan to get us out of here?"

"Why should I tell you?" she hissed.

Nicholas simply smiled at her. "If I am to help, I need to know your plan. Or do you plan on doing all the work?"

She glared at him, her eyes bright. He wanted to kiss her again, wanted to peel off those clothes and see her womanly curves. He wanted to fist his hands in her real hair. She wore some mop of a wig, which puzzled him. He'd figured out about the wig when he'd tried to touch her hair during that kiss. She'd jerked back the second he'd started to touch it, no doubt frightened that she would be discovered.

Holland's lips parted and she huffed. "My plan is—"

Footsteps coming down the hall silenced her.

"Guards," he muttered, and she nodded in agreement.

Nicholas moved in front of her, unsure what was about to happen. The cell door opened and Captain Waverly stood there, his red-and-white uniform perfectly pressed and his hair pulled back in a queue at the nape of his neck, tied with a black ribbon.

"I'm here for Holland, not you. Stand aside," the captain ordered.

Nicholas clenched his fists. The man knew now that he was an officer working to gain Holland's trust. Torturing her for information would be counterproductive.

"And if I don't?"

"Then you will be reminded of the outcome of our last encounter." The cold smile on Waverly's face nearly broke Nicholas's self-restraint.

"I'd wager that in a fair fight, the outcome would not be to your liking. Tell me, does the admiral know you're here?"

Waverly's nostrils flared. "You're on dangerous ground, Flynn."

"As are you." Nicholas felt the energy of Waverly's attack

a split second before it happened. He shoved Holland into the corner safely out of the way an instant before the captain moved.

Waverly lunged, and Nicholas dodged him. The captain stumbled into the cell, and Nicholas kicked him in the back as he passed. Waverly caught himself in the whirling motion, his fists raised. He swung a punch, landing a blow to Nicholas's jaw, but Nicholas came back swinging. They bloodied their knuckles on each other's faces for the next minute, each one trying to wear the other down.

"Yield!" Waverly snarled.

"No," Nicholas growled. Blood from his split lip filled his mouth with a salty taste. He spat on the ground. His back hurt like the devil had raked claws over his flesh, but he wouldn't yield.

"Damn you, Flynn!" Waverly lunged at him, but a shout halted them both.

"What are you doing?" The admiral's sharp voice cut across the narrow room.

"Admiral Harcourt, he—"

"My office, Captain. Now." The admiral's face was stony and somehow far more frightening than Waverly's usually cruel expression.

"Sir, I—"

"*Now.*"

Waverly shot Flynn a venomous look as he left.

"And you, Mr. Flynn, will come with me as well. If you are able-bodied enough to fight, you can damned well answer some questions about your activities aboard the *Emerald Dragon.*"

Nicholas gave the Holland girl a reassuring glance before

he followed the admiral into the corridor. She gave him a nod as if to reassure him that she was okay before the cell door shut behind them.

No one spoke until they were in the admiral's office with the door firmly closed. The admiral glared at Waverly with all the power he could muster.

"Does the chain of command mean nothing to you, Captain? I told you that Holland was my responsibility."

"And I told you that force is necessary with that boy," Waverly shot back. "And he"—Waverly stabbed a finger in the air at Nicholas—"*interfered*."

Nicholas ignored Waverly's attempt to draw him into another fight, and spoke to the admiral as if Waverly wasn't there.

"Sir, I've come up with a new plan, but it will require trust from you."

"I'm listening," Harcourt said.

"I believe your information is correct. Holland is connected in some way to Thomas Buck, perhaps some sort of family relation. I think if we let Holland escape, he will lead us back to Buck."

"Just let him escape? How the devil would you know where he goes?" Waverly argued.

"I shall escape with him, try to join his crew, and send a report back of Buck's location. We can set up a trap and nab the entire crew at once. Better still, we might learn what activities Buck has orchestrated and disrupt his entire fleet."

The admiral tapped his fingers on his desk as he considered it. "High risk," he said, half to himself.

"High reward," Flynn countered.

Waverly scoffed. "Rubbish. If we break the boy, we'll have all the information we need."

But the admiral was ignoring him. "If you think this will work, Lieutenant, we can arrange to let one of the gates go unguarded at an opportune time. That fellow, Black Barney, is scheduled to be hanged tomorrow, and I am sure he will put up a fight. I will have only one guard there to walk him to the gallows. When he does resist, you and Holland can make your escape in the chaos that I am sure will follow."

"Madness. This is a terrible idea," Waverly said.

"Despite what you may believe, I still control this fort. Flynn, you'll have your chance tomorrow. Waverly's troops will be sent on patrol. That's what you'll tell Holland to reassure the boy escape is possible."

"Thank you, Admiral." Flynn turned to follow the soldier outside back to his cell. He hid his sense of relief as he passed by a scowling Waverly.

This wasn't just the best way to track down Buck—it was the only way he could do so and still have young Holland escape the noose.

The only problem was, he would have to trick her into betraying Buck.

❧

"FLYNN!" BRIANNA NEARLY POUNCED ON FLYNN WHEN HE was put back in their cell, but she held herself back.

"I'm all right, lass." His lips were quirked in a rakish smile. "I rather like that you were worried about me."

Brianna scowled. "I *wasn't* worried, you daft fool." She

wasn't. Truly. It was just . . . well, damnation, she had been worried. What if he'd been whipped again, or worse?

He grimaced as he moved, and she wondered if he had reopened any of his wounds. Some small part of her wanted to wrap her arms around his neck and whisper soothing things into his ear as she checked his wounds. But that was ridiculous. She wasn't some nurse.

"Are you . . . ? Did you . . . ?" She pointed at his back, and he shrugged.

"Nothing that won't heal again," he said with a wry chuckle that turned into a wince.

"Waverly?"

"Who else?" Flynn muttered, then sat down on his cot. "Have you heard the news?" He wiped his face of dried blood with one sleeve of his shirt and then drank a cup of water. Brianna watched him, a pit of dread forming in her stomach.

"What news?" She tried to sound as though she didn't care. What if they'd found Joe? What if her father had somehow been captured?

"Black Barney is to be hanged tomorrow."

"Oh?" Brianna felt the weight of guilt at being relieved. Barney was a bastard, but he was still one of the Brethren. Not a particularly good one, but a pirate nonetheless.

"I imagine they'll force us to watch." Flynn's grim tone only made her stomach turn.

"They will," she replied in a whisper. She had seen a hanging the day before Flynn had been put in her cell. All of the prisoners had been escorted into the yard to watch.

She'd seen men die before, bravely in the heat of battle or stupidly during a fight in a tavern, but a hanging was different. You were no longer the master of your fate, and everything about the ceremony was meant to reinforce that fact. It made you feel small. Powerless.

And this hanging hadn't gone well. There hadn't been enough slack on the rope for the drop to break his neck. There was something truly terrifying about watching a man dangle in the air, his face turning purple as he struggled for breath.

"They fixed the gallows, I heard. It will be over quickly," Flynn said. But Brianna still couldn't get the last man's hanging out of her mind.

Flynn cleared his throat, drawing her attention away from thoughts of Barney swinging from the noose. "I was thinking, if you want to plan our escape, we might have a chance during the execution."

At this, she tilted her head. "You think so? I thought they would have more guards present for the hanging."

He shook his head, and his dark-blond hair fell into his eyes. "I heard they'll be patrolling the south side of the island looking for Thomas Buck. Most of the men will be out during the execution. It might give us time to escape. We could overwhelm a guard or two if needed."

"Sounds riskier than what I had in mind." Truth was, she didn't really have a plan, but she'd imagined sneaking out at night if she could only get out of their cell. "But my plan was really more of a one-person job. I suppose if you're going to tag along, that would be as good a time as any. Still, why would you want to risk an escape with me?" It was in her nature both as a woman and a pirate not to trust anyone.

Flynn came over to her, and she almost stepped back when he invaded her space. Lord, not many men were taller than her, and fewer still were built like Flynn. Strength and raw masculine power radiated off him in a way that made parts of her shiver, though not from fear. She couldn't help but wonder what it might feel like to give herself to this man, to let him sweep her away with passion, take control and let her feel safe beneath his hold. She shook herself free of the foolish daydream. She could never let a man have control—it was too dangerous to her freedom.

Flynn reached up to touch her and brushed the backs of his knuckles over her cheek.

"I *like* you, Holland, and I more than like kissing you. It seems I need a crew to sail with until I can find my way back to the *Emerald Dragon*. Besides, I don't fancy either of us staying here until it's our turn to hang, do you?"

His words made sense, but the part about him kissing her . . . that alone repeated over and over in her head. She *more than liked* kissing him too. And it had only been one bloody kiss. How would she like it if he did far more than kiss her?

"So what say you? I help you escape, and you convince your captain of whatever crew you sail with to let me join?"

She drew her bottom lip between her teeth, too distracted by how his hand had moved from her cheek down to her neck, still stroking her skin in a way that clouded her thoughts. She pulled away, feeling manipulated. "So you're just looking for someone to share lonely nights on the high seas?"

Flynn chuckled. "I admit I've thought of the advantages of such a partnership, but nothing will happen without your leave, I assure you."

"Of course it wouldn't. Because if you tried, you'd find yourself hanging from something *other* than your neck." She countered his gentle caress with a quick grip and a squeeze that made her point all too clear. "Understood?"

Flynn winced, his voice higher pitched as he replied. "*Perfectly*."

She relaxed her grip. "Well . . . I suppose you can come along. But don't be getting any ideas about taking over the ship for yourself."

"I swear to obey your captain, whoever he is. Besides, I'm hardly likely to take over a ship all by myself, am I?"

She almost chuckled. He was in for a surprise when he found out *she* was the captain.

She pulled away and returned to sit on her cot. "I'll hold you to that. Now, why don't you tell me a story?" They had a long night to wait before the hanging at dawn.

"Me tell a story?" He laughed softly, the sound deep and decadent. Sinful, even. And she knew a thing or two about sin.

"Yes, tell me something amusing. It's your turn."

"I regrettably do not know tales of wild pirate queens as you do."

She smiled and bit her lip. "That's all right. I know every story of every pirate queen already."

"How about stories of Cornwall treasure smugglers descended from the Vikings themselves?"

She lay on her side and propped her chin in her hand as she watched Flynn. "Now that sounds like it might amuse me."

"They say there is a family living off the coast of Cornwall who have pure Viking blood in their veins. Tall, fierce, and cunning, they wait like wraiths in the dark for ships to crash upon the rocks during storms. And then they begin their hunt . . ."

❧

BEFORE DAWN THE FOLLOWING MORNING, THE PRISONERS in Port Royal's garrison were escorted from their cells. Each man was shackled together with his cell mate. Brianna's left hand and Flynn's right hand were chained together, only a foot separating the two manacles. That was not what they had done to the prisoners at the last hanging.

"Must be to make up for the lack of guards," Flynn mused.

But by the look on Captain Waverly's face, Brianna guessed this was *his* idea. His men were patrolling the island, but he'd stayed behind to watch a man hang.

"Still with me, Holland?" Flynn leaned in to whisper as they joined the ranks of their fellow prisoners.

"The question is, are *you* with *me*?" The manacles would make it more difficult to escape, but if Flynn knew what he was doing, they could manage it.

A naval officer in his dark-blue uniform and powdered wig stood beside the gallows and unrolled a bit of parchment.

"You are gathered here to witness the execution of Barnabas Black. He has been convicted of two counts of piracy and one count of theft. He has been sentenced to hang by the neck until dead."

Four soldiers in red uniforms stepped forward, snare drums hanging around their waists. They began to tap out a steady, ominous rhythm, heralding the doomed man.

Black Barney was the final prisoner to be escorted from the cellblock. He marched past Brianna, Flynn, and the others on his way to the gallows.

The pirate's eyes were red and wild as he threw his head back and forth like a mad dog looking for his next victim. Brianna tensed.

"Steady," Flynn murmured. Any moment now, Barney would put up a fight. They just had to wait for the right moment.

Brianna glanced at each of the garrison's entry and exit points. She counted only seven guards. There were two talking at the gate behind them, which was closest. Neither man looked interested in the hanging of the prisoner in the yard. The south gate was the only one that led toward the dense cover of the island's vegetation. That was the garrison's weakest spot.

"The south gate," Brianna whispered to Flynn.

"I see it." His eyes darted to the gate and back to Black Barney, who had reached the base of the gallows.

Without warning, the man whirled on the soldier escorting him, hitting him with such force that he barreled into the nearby wall. In that moment, peace and order turned to bloody chaos.

"Fight for Barney!" a cry sounded, and the prisoners around Brianna and Flynn launched themselves at the guards closest to them. Brianna couldn't believe their luck.

She pulled hard on her wrist and bolted for the south gate. "Come on!"

Flynn rushed along with her, having little choice but to keep pace. The two soldiers were raising their rifles, but they had been focused on Barney instead of her and turned too late to face her. She knocked the first man flat on his back and punched him hard with her free hand. His eyes rolled back as the second guard landed in a heap beside the first, knocked out by Flynn.

Flynn crouched beside her as she searched the guards for the gate key. When she found it, she tossed it to Flynn. He unlocked the gate, and they rushed through it toward freedom as they dove into the dense vegetation that would shield part of their escape.

"So what's the next part of the plan?" Flynn asked as he followed her. The blend of palm and mahogany trees provided decent cover as they fled from the naval garrison.

"Oi, Holland?" Flynn demanded as they slowed in their running. The fort wasn't visible any longer, except as a distant stony peak over the tops of the trees.

"I should have a jolly boat waiting for me up ahead. I *hope* . . ." She added the last bit in a whisper to herself. If Joe had done the smart thing, he would have left her. But Joe often didn't do the smart thing when it came to her. Now she found herself damn well hoping he had waited for her rather than sailing back to their ship.

They ran down an animal trail until she found the familiar path that would take them to the secret boat landing. It was a path her father had taken for many years, and she had learned it well as a child. It was well worn, but narrow, used only by Buck's men and now her.

"Tell me you're joking. We can't outrun the navy in a jolly boat."

Please be there, please, she silently prayed.

"I thought you trusted me," she said aloud.

"Not if you sail on a damned jolly boat."

"Of course not," she scoffed. She didn't have time to explain. She needed to focus. Joe, if he was still here, would be hiding well covered.

The trail thinned as the little cove came into view. It wasn't visited often, as there was no place to bring in larger ships. Jolly boats and lifeboats were the only vessels able to glide over the reefs in the shallow water, but it was too far a hike to be convenient as a landing point for anyone but pirates.

Brianna halted at the edge of the vegetation and studied the empty beach. There was no sign of the boat or Joe. Fresh panic set in. She'd been desperately hoping he'd waited.

"Damn. I thought he might have waited for me."

"Who would wait for you?" Flynn asked in frustration.

"Me," a deep voice rumbled behind them.

Flynn whirled around, fists raised in defense. Brianna, jerked along by the chains, shouted for him to stop, but it was too late.

CHAPTER 6

"Who would wait for you?" Nicholas asked as he scanned the empty beach.

He saw Holland's face turn pale as she searched for whoever she had hoped to meet. It seemed this little escape was going to end far too soon. Right now, they were exposed on the beach, with the dense foliage of the island behind them, where Waverly's men could easily hide. He didn't like this one bit.

"Me," a voice rumbled.

Every instinct and reflex sent Flynn flying at the man who'd snuck up behind them, jerking Holland along with him. The man attacked at the same time, but Flynn was a split second faster. He hit the man square in the jaw, while the other man's blow glanced off Flynn's cheek.

"Stop, you fools! Stop this!"

Flynn found himself being shoved away before he could get his hands properly on the other man.

"Joe, stop!" Holland bellowed in a commanding tone.

The man called Joe stepped back.

"Who is he?" Nicholas growled at the same time Joe said, "Who's this, eh?"

"Joseph McBride, this is Nicholas Flynn. Shake hands. We are all friends here, aren't we?" Holland's tone brooked no argument from either of them.

Joe grunted and with great reluctance held out a hand to Nicholas. Nicholas had a moment to take the measure of the man as he accepted it. Joe was built like a frigate, armed with thick muscle and a steely demeanor to match. He appeared to be in his late forties, and his skin had been bronzed by years in the sun. No doubt another pirate.

"Flynn," Joe said.

"McBride," Nicholas replied. They let go of each other's hands, still staring at one another.

"Wonderful. Now that we're all friends, let's get the bloody hell out of here before the redcoats find us."

"Redcoats? How far are they behind ye?"

"I'm not sure—we don't have time."

"We're taking him with us?" Joe jerked his thumb at Nicholas.

She gave Joe a look that Nicholas didn't miss. "Yes." She waved their manacled hands in the air. "I'll explain later." She was censoring her information in front of him.

"Right. This way, then." Joe started down the beach and paused at a spot on the ground where dozens of palm fronds had fallen to cover the sand.

Nicholas had to keep up with Holland's pace since they were still manacled together. Joe kicked away several of the palm fronds and reached down into a crevice that he'd exposed. Sand shifted and more palm fronds fell away to reveal a large pit dug into the wet sand. It went deep toward the trees and away from the water. A jolly boat was hidden in the massive space. Nicholas stared at it in wonder. The cavern was a marvel that left him almost speechless.

"How in the blazes . . . ?"

"It was built years ago," Joe said as he dragged the boat out of the cavern and up onto the sand. "The walls are fortified and nailed to the underground roots of the trees, far enough inland that high tides canna touch it."

The three of them hauled the boat out into the shallows, and then Holland and Joe covered the cavern with fronds and sand again.

Once they were done and in the boat, Joe dropped a pair of oars in the water and started rowing as they navigated their way out of the cove. Once they got beyond the cove, they'd set the small sail and Joe could pull in his oars. Nicholas prayed they would go unnoticed by any vessels prowling in the nearby waters.

"Where's the *Serpent*?" Holland asked.

Joe nodded in a vague direction. "The usual place. She's waiting for us."

"Thank God." Holland focused on working the rudder, seemingly lost in steering the small ship. Nicholas stayed close to her, the chain joining their manacled hands allowing very little distance between them.

"So . . . Flynn, is it? How is it ye both escaped the garrison?"

Nicholas knew the man was testing him, wanting to see what he'd say.

He waved their bound hands. "We were rounded up and

forced to watch them hang a man in the yard. All the prisoners were bound in pairs."

"Who did they hang?"

"Black Barney," Holland said. "I didn't like him, but he was no villain, not one worthy of that sort of death."

"Aye. May he rest in peace," Joe said. "But I don't expect ye just walked out the front gate while no one was looking, am I right?" He looked at Nicholas again.

"Barney fought the guards and caused a small riot. We took advantage of that to escape through the south gate. Holland led me straight to you."

Joe looked to Holland, uncertain. "Does he know . . . ?"

"Apparently, he guessed it right away. He's not like the others." Her voice was softer as she said this last part. Nicholas wasn't sure why, but it seemed to make the stony look in Joe's eyes harden further.

"Oh, aye, he isna like the others at all." Joe narrowed his eyes at Nicholas. "I'll tell ye what I tell the crew. Ye touch her, ye lose a hand. Ye hurt her, ye lose your life. Ye ken?"

After a pause, Joe spoke again. "So, Flynn, who do ye sail with?"

"The *Emerald Dragon*. I'm one of Belishaw's men."

Recognition flashed in the pirate's eyes. "Belishaw? Did ye sail with Captain Grey, then? The captain before Belishaw?"

"Yes, Dominic is one of my oldest friends."

"Sad thing, to see him join those fancy-coated fools."

"He did what he had to do for love," Nicholas said. It was the truth. Grey couldn't have remained a pirate. Only a pardon from the king had saved his life.

Joseph gave a sharp smile. "What a damned fool,

marrying an admiral's daughter like that. I still admire the man, but I dinna trust him. Not when he beds the enemy."

Nicholas gritted his teeth at Roberta being talked about as the enemy. She was a wonderful woman. She'd saved Dominic's life, and his too. The three of them were bound in a way he'd never be able to explain to anyone. He'd even made a promise to Dominic that he would marry Roberta and take care of her if they couldn't save Dominic from the gallows. Thankfully, that hadn't happened. Dominic's father, the Earl of Camden, had ridden quite literally right up to the gallows with a pardon for Dominic's crimes of piracy from the king himself. Then Dominic had been free to marry Roberta and live a life of leisure befitting his station.

"It was actually rather clever, marrying an admiral's daughter," Nicholas argued. "It bought him protection and access to naval fleet information. He can warn Belishaw and the *Dragon*'s crew whenever he needs to."

Though Nicholas was aware of this, Admiral Harcourt appeared not to have considered the possibility, convinced of his son-in-law's transformation from pirate to gentleman.

"I hadn't thought of that," Joe admitted. "Still, better to avoid the man, lest he have a change of heart and betray the Brethren."

Holland was perched at the front of the jolly boat, her eyes fixed on the horizon and the growing shape of a ship's mast in the distance. It looked like it was hiding at the edge of a cove just a bit farther up the coast. The manacles they wore kept them close, and Nicholas couldn't help but smile at Joe's disapproval whenever he saw their bodies bound so close together.

He wasn't sure why he liked rankling the other man

about his proximity to Holland. He usually wasn't the sort of man who enjoyed a situation like this, but Holland brought out a different side to him. She made him feel . . . wild. Every hunger and every desire he'd ever repressed as he was raised to be an upstanding English gentleman became almost overpowering. He wanted to toss the girl over his shoulder and carry her off like his Viking ancestors would have. Instead, he took the time to admire the sunlight upon her face as she closed her eyes and breathed in the sea air as they approached the pirate ship she'd been sailing them toward.

Soon the jolly boat came alongside the *Sea Serpent*, and Nicholas was impressed by what he saw. It was a beautiful ship, one that made him think of the sketches he'd seen of Captain Kidd's vessel, the *Adventure Galley*, that had sailed almost fifty years before.

Its lower hull was painted black and the upper hull green, giving the impression of a sea monster slithering across the water. Push oars could be used for more speed or dexterity, and her three masts gave the *Sea Serpent* an edge. The eighteen guns he counted made that edge sharp. Faces appeared over the railings, and given the size of the ship, he estimated the crew to be between sixty and eighty, though they no doubt could operate with far fewer if need be.

A rope ladder was dropped over the side, and Holland tugged at the chain that bound them to get his attention.

"You'll have to follow me up," she said.

They moved up the ladder rungs, but it was an awkward venture. There wasn't much slack between their wrists, and more than once he had to hold on to the ladder with her body between him and the ship. She was warm, and the scent of the sea clung to her skin. As he leaned in and adjusted his grip on the ladder, he couldn't help but inhale and close his eyes. Their bodies would often bump into each other, and it was, to say the least, distracting.

Back in the dank prison cell, it had been easier to keep his distance from her, so to speak. But now, feeling her, smelling her natural scent mixed with the ocean breeze, everything felt different. The world was alive with possibilities, and most of them included her.

"I think you're enjoying this," Holland muttered and wriggled beneath him. It only made the temptation she presented far worse.

Unable to resist, he pressed his hips into her bottom more firmly. "Aren't *you*?"

"Ach, men, you're all the same." She grunted and rammed her elbow into his stomach in reply, but he might have caught a hint of a smile on her lips. His loose grip on the ladder nearly sent them both toppling into the waves below, but he fumbled and caught hold just in time to save the both of them. It was worth quite a bit of physical hell to be this close to a fascinating woman like Holland.

They reached the top of the side of the ship and slipped down onto the waist of the ship, where a cluster of men surrounded them, talking all at once like young boys.

"Well now, seems like she's gone and gotten herself leg-shackled . . . er . . . or is it hand-shackled?" A portly fellow laughed, his black-and-red striped pantaloons billowing in the wind.

"Yer thinking of a handfasting. Ain't that right, Joe?" another pirate asked as Joe climbed over the edge of the rail and dropped down onto the deck.

"Aye, 'tis handfasting when ye marry in Scotland."

"So she's married, then?" another man piped up, confused. Most of the other pirates groaned or rolled their eyes.

Nicholas tried to keep from laughing at the blush that now covered Holland's face and neck. Her reputation on board had just taken a hit to the broadside.

"Enough of that, lads. The only thing I'm married to is the sea. Now stow your gossiping and make ready to sail," Holland barked in natural command.

"Aye, aye, Captain," came several calls, and then the men scattered to their stations. Half a dozen men shot up the rigging like monkeys to adjust the sails.

"*Captain?*" Nicholas spoke the word in shock.

Holland, now recovered from her embarrassment, laughed. "Did I fail to mention that?" She tugged on their bound hands, pulling him a step closer to her. Their eyes met, and her lips twitched in a ghost of a smile. "Just remember your promise to obey the captain."

Lord, she was a beautiful creature, powerful, brave, and right now he was completely at her command.

"Once we're properly separated, I want you to mend the ropes and the cables for the rest of the day."

Nicholas closed his mouth, swallowing any disagreement.

"Where's O'Malley?" Holland shouted.

"In the middle deck, checking the guns," one of the crew volunteered. "I just saw him go down."

"Come on, Flynn." Holland had him follow her belowdecks, where a man was checking the port-side guns on the middle deck. Flynn ignored the stares of the crew as he passed them. They were all busy about their various duties, but he could feel their eyes boring into the back of his head.

They didn't know him, and he would have to work hard to earn their trust.

"Captain." The Irishman nodded at her. "'Bout time you got back."

"I need your assistance, O'Malley." She held up their bound hands. "As charming as this man is, I believe we will both be much happier with these irons removed. Wouldn't you agree?"

The man chuckled and retrieved a hammer and a large nail.

He pointed to the rounded surface of one of the cannons. "Lay your hands down here." Nicholas did so, and the Irishman used the nail to drive the metal links of their chains apart. After the links separated and they broke away from each other, the two breathed a sigh of relief.

Next, O'Malley used his hammer to drive out the nail that kept her shackle around her wrist secure. When that fell free, Holland slipped her wrist out of the metal band. Holland shouted a few orders at the men nearby who had been watching the show.

"Glad to see you back, Captain. We weren't sure how long to keep checking for you at the cove. We only just got back from three days at sea to avoid island patrols spotting us."

"I was kicking my heels up in the Port Royal prison, as you do." Holland chuckled, sounding relaxed. "I was due a holiday, but it's back to work now."

It amazed Nicholas that she could act so carefree after such an experience. But how much of that was for her crew's benefit, and how much was who she really was? The closer he looked, the more he saw her smile was tight and her eyes shadowed. So it had left a mark on her after all . . . It was damned good they were free at sea. He'd just have to find a way to keep her free, even after Buck was captured.

O'Malley nodded to Nicholas. "All right now, your turn." Once he was freed, he rubbed his wrist and glanced at Holland again.

"Now, I believe you have a job to do, don't you?" She fixed him with a coy smile.

Nicholas considered the best way to answer and settled for, "Aye, captain."

"Well then, get to work." She then marched off, her chin held high, leaving him alone with O'Malley.

"One of the topmen ran by me before you came down here, and he said you married the captain. Is that true?" O'Malley asked.

"What? No, of course not," Nicholas stammered. He headed for the upper decks, trying to ignore the Irishman's laughter as it followed him up the stairs.

BRIANNA ENTERED THE CAPTAIN'S QUARTERS AT THE STERN of the ship and closed the door, leaning against it a long moment while she drew in a shaky breath.

Of all the situations to find herself in. Prison was one of those risks one ran as a pirate, and she'd had a few close calls in the past, but this was the first time she'd actually feared a hanging might be in her future. It had shaken her usual bravado and made everything in life feel that much more uncertain.

And then there was Flynn. There was no denying the

attraction she felt for him, but bringing him onto her crew was going to be a mistake, she could feel it. But she owed him, and had to do right by him until she could get him to his old ship.

She pushed away from the door and stared around her cabin, feeling restless and weary at the same time. At least she was home now, and the comforts of her cabin were a welcome sight.

Her bed sat in one corner, and a table and a desk were nailed down in the center of the room. A small storage area full of trunks of clothing and weapons was near her bed. There was also a large copper tub in the corner near the glass windows that overlooked the sea. She stood in front of those windows now, glad to be alone for a moment. Glad things had mostly returned to normal. Mostly. She examined the reddened skin on her wrist where the iron manacle had rubbed her raw.

The door to her cabin opened. She knew it was either Joe or her cabin boy.

"Are ye all right, lass?" Joe asked from behind her.

"Yes." It wasn't a lie. Not exactly.

"So, what happened after we split ways in the market?"

Brianna sat down at her table, where several charts were laid out, weighted down with heavy stones. She traced a trade route on the nearest map with her fingertip as she told Joe everything that had happened. Well, almost everything. She left out her kiss with Flynn. Joe would not react well to that.

Joe nodded once she had finished. "Yer father willna be pleased. He didna want ye to make that supply run."

"We needed those supplies."

"Aye, but we could have sent some of our men instead of going ourselves."

"Our men don't know our contacts in the market like we do."

"That's the problem. Too many people know us."

He had a point there. After all, it was Joe's picture on a wanted poster that had started this whole affair. "Fair enough. Next time, we'll bring a couple of men with us, introduce them as our representatives on future visits."

That had Joe raising an eyebrow. "Yer not joking, are ye?"

"Why would I be?"

Joe chuckled. "That prison must have shaken ye up something fierce if yer actually listening to reason and are willing to delegate work to others like that."

Brianna felt her face go red. She did have a habit of putting herself on the front lines, as it were, even when it made more sense to let others handle it. Joe didn't press the matter further. "We'll try Kingston next time," he said. "Fewer English soldiers running about."

"Sounds good, once we let some time pass. Those men at the garrison are searching for my father. We can't lead them back to him."

"True enough. What's our heading, then?"

She considered for a moment. There was really only one place safe enough to go that was a pirate refuge, even though piracy had been banned long ago. It was a place that the redcoats didn't bother since the cove where the port was located made it hard for bigger frigates to make berth.

She studied the maps and tapped a place for Joe to see. "Sugar Cove. If we are followed, the navy will have to ferret us out amongst all the other pirates there. The supplies aren't the best, but we'll be able to get something."

"I'll have the crew make for our new heading." Joe moved to leave, but paused at the door. Brianna didn't look at him. She pretended to focus on her charts because she knew what he was going to ask and she didn't want to talk about it. "That man, Flynn—he didn't hurt ye, or . . . ?

"Flynn? No, he didn't," Brianna reassured him. "He's a good man, just a flirt." She was lucky. She'd never been hurt by a man, not in the way Joe feared. Not that some men hadn't tried, but no one bested Buck's daughter.

"There isna a good thing about the way he looks at ye, lass."

Brianna sat up a little, her body tensing. "What do you mean?"

"He looks at ye like a man out of rum and who's just stumbled upon an entire cargo of rum-filled casks."

For some reason, this made her fight off a smile. "I've had my share of rum, Joe."

That made Joe blanch. He'd probably scrub the comment from his memory as soon as he could. Part of him would always see her as a girl, not a woman. "I'm jest sayin', ye'd better watch out for him. A man can be foolish when he's thirsty, ye ken."

"I know," Brianna sighed. "Oh, Joe, have Patrick heat some water from my bath? I smell like a prison cell."

Joe nodded respectfully. "Yes, Cap'n."

Half an hour later, Patrick, a cabin boy of sixteen, hauled bucket after bucket of hot water into her quarters, pouring them all into the copper tub.

Once she was alone, she removed her clothes and

dropped them in a heap at the foot of the tub. Then she dipped a toe in the hot water. It felt so good. She stepped in and eased herself down into the water. Sleeping on that thin cot for a week, her encounters with Waverly, then her escape —all of it had taken a toll on her.

She reached up and carefully unpinned the auburn-haired wig she wore and then dropped it to the floor beside her clothes. Then she pulled the pins that held her long blonde hair coiled up against her scalp and freed her tresses. Her head felt lighter. She sank beneath the water, holding her breath as she kept herself fully submerged.

She let the seconds pass. At first she simply enjoyed the moment, but soon unwelcome thoughts intruded on her peace. Her mind replayed those moments when Waverly had had her bent over the water trough, her body struggling for air while she tried not to let herself breathe. She'd never feared death at sea, but to be drowned in a watering hole for beasts by a cowardly brute? That wasn't something she'd been prepared for. He'd attacked her, and she'd been completely at his mercy, unable to fight. That sort of powerlessness had been terrifying. She never wanted to feel that way again.

Brianna burst up from the water with a gasp and wiped it clear from her eyes. She drew in breath after shaky breath.

"I was wondering if you would surface," a deep voice said.

Brianna froze, hands on the rim of the tub. That wasn't Patrick—it was Flynn. She'd been in such a hurry to relax that she'd forgotten to lock the door.

The thought of him standing there, seeing her naked as she bathed, sent flashes of heat racing across her skin like dolphins chasing the wake of her ship. She tried not to wriggle farther down in the tub to hide. She wished she could reach for her sword, if only to make a point about respecting personal privacy, but it was over on the desk with the maps.

"I thought I told you to mend the ropes and cables," she growled.

"All done. I saw that boy fetching water, and I thought you might need one more bucket." His voice drifted closer, and suddenly warm water poured down over her shoulders in the most wonderful way. She forgave his intrusion, just a little.

"I don't know how things are run on board your ship, but on the *Sea Serpent* we respect the captain's privacy." She slowly moved to shield her breasts from his view, even though they were beneath the water. Better to act as if his presence didn't matter rather than shriek at him like a girl to leave her cabin at once. "If Joe were here, he'd be throwing you overboard."

"Of that I have no doubt," Flynn said.

Right now, she had a choice. She could order him to leave, and he likely would. His presumption of being welcome here due to their shared personal moments in the prison was understandable, but still out of line.

And yet, part of her remembered that while he was one of her crew now, he wouldn't always be. In time, they'd return him to his ship. Who knew if their paths would cross again after that? Perhaps it wouldn't be so bad to enjoy his company while she had the chance?

"Since you seem to have nothing else to do, fetch me my rose oil." She nodded her head at an intricately carved box on her desk. She felt safer when she was commanding him to do things. Flynn went to the desk and flipped the lid open. He pulled one of the bottles up, removing stoppers and sniffing each one until he found the rose oil.

Brianna stared at his back, her eyes trailing down over his body. A fine specimen indeed. He returned with the bottle, eyes fixed on her face, but she still felt exposed. Of course, she could see how hard it was for him *not* to look farther down than her eyes. It was thrilling, this tension between them. She was naked, weaponless, and he was able to do whatever he might like with her if he wished to. It terrified her—it terrified her because it *thrilled* her.

"Why didn't you tell me you were the captain?" he asked, holding the rose oil loosely in strong, elegant fingers of his. She wondered what magic those fingers could work upon her skin, and it made her shiver with a longing to find out.

"Does it make a difference? Would you not have listened to me or taken orders from me had I told you?"

He didn't hesitate. "It makes no difference. I was merely surprised."

"That's the right answer." It was also one she hadn't expected. Most men did not take kindly to taking orders from a woman, but most of her crew had known her back in the days when she'd sailed alongside Buck, and as far as they were concerned, she was one of the lads.

He crouched by the tub, lifting up the wig. "Why wear this? Why not just cut your real hair?" His tone was curious rather than judgmental. With his free hand, he dipped his fingers into the hot water, trailing them close to her body, but not quite touching, before he flicked droplets playfully at her shoulder. She found his impertinence both infuriating and arousing. She'd never thought she'd like it when a man didn't obey her commands, but there was something exciting about a man who simply did what he wanted when it came to her.

"I only wear it when I'm in foreign ports. It's silly, and I doubt you would understand."

Flynn chuckled, and the sound warmed her more than the water in her tub.

"I doubt much of anything you do is silly. Impulsive, perhaps—even reckless. But not silly." He let the wig drop and lifted his hand toward her golden hair that lay in damp locks around her shoulders. She could've ordered him to leave. She should have. But she didn't. He coiled a wet tendril around his finger, and she grew still. Her breath turned shallow as she waited for him to dare to do more than touch her hair. His eyes lifted from her hair, and he raised his brows, still waiting for her answer.

"It's not easy captaining an all-male crew, or having to pretend you're someone you're not when you go ashore. I wanted the freedom to feel feminine whenever I wished to," she finally admitted.

"See, not a silly reason at all." His voice had turned wonderfully husky. "It would've been a shame to cut all this." He lightly pulled on the strand, bringing her closer to him.

"A shame?" she echoed, her gaze drawn to his lips as he spoke.

"Yes. You see, I like to fist my hand in a woman's hair and hold her captive to me while I kiss her. To feel all that silk in my hand and her warm body against mine . . ." He leaned in, his hand sliding into her hair at the nape of her neck just as he'd said. Brianna's skin burned as though she were on fire. One more kiss couldn't hurt. She could go back to being captain in a moment. But for now, she could just—

Flynn's lips brushed hers, but it was a ghost of a kiss.

"You know where to find me, should you want anything, Captain."

He stood and left the cabin without another word.

Brianna cursed and ducked back beneath the hot water. She needed to take a lover, *any* lover but Flynn. What madness to let him toy with her this way. To let him tease her with thoughts of *him* mastering *her*. The nerve.

As soon as they got to Sugar Cove, she would find someone to take to bed. Satisfying that itch would keep her from making the biggest mistake possible with someone like Flynn. Even though his eyes promised her sinful delights, she was afraid of what would happen if she let herself go with him. He wasn't like the other men she'd been with. He was different in this case, different was dangerous. Perhaps they would even find Flynn's ship docked at Sugar Cove and she could return him to it, all debts paid. If luck was with her, she would be away from the temptation of Flynn soon.

CHAPTER 7

Nicolas spent a restless few hours in his hammock with the rest of the crew in the belly of the ship. All around him men snored, and occasionally one would scratch his belly, roll over, and mutter in his sleep. Nicholas tried closing his eyes but couldn't fall asleep. Sleeping among the enemy left him feeling edgy.

None of the men on the ship were bad, not in the way many pirates could be. They were ordinary men, simply working for their livelihoods like any common sailor with just one catch—they raided merchant ships. He wasn't supposed to like these men, let alone bond with them.

And he certainly wasn't supposed to become obsessed with a pirate queen like Holland. What had possessed him to go to her cabin and flirt with her while she bathed like a damned scoundrel? That was something Dominic would do, not him.

With a curse, he slipped off his bunk and padded quietly

between the swaying hammocks until he reached the companion ladder to the upper decks.

He scanned the decks, then up to the three masts of the ship. On the foretop of the foremast was a lone figure, legs draped over the side of a flat platform halfway up. Nicholas grinned as he recognized the dainty ankles of his little pirate queen. What was she doing all the way up there at this time of night?

He watched her a long while, wanting to go up and join her. He doubted she would welcome the intrusion after his visit to her cabin. She was, after all, the captain of the ship, and he was playing a dangerous game with her. He didn't want to upset whatever balance she had created amongst the men.

Something was different about this woman, though he had trouble pinning down what it was. She was as alluring as a pile of Spanish galleon treasure and as beautiful as rare jewels, and she made him want to toss all of his polite, gentlemanly manners overboard. She had made him more of a pirate at heart than he ever could have imagined. He was hungry for her now in a way that was hard for a man to control. Though she was no dainty creature festooned in fine silks and wearing feathers in her hair, she was just as captivating. She was fierce, she was clever, she was brave.

This was the sort of woman who would put a dagger between her teeth and scale the riggings in the midst of a dangerous storm to cut a snagged rope. Yet as he'd knelt beside the copper tub and touched her skin with the backs of his fingers and wound a tendril of her golden hair around his finger, he had seen her heart in her eyes.

Those lovely green eyes had held him prisoner, conveying

her attraction and her hesitation about what to do with him. He had nearly confessed his wish to be her devoted servant then and there. The spell she cast was far more powerful than any witch. Holland needed no spells or potions. She had only to look at him with those eyes and he became enchanted.

The ship rolled smoothly over the sea, and he felt his body relax as it always did on the water. It was land that felt unstable after all these years at sea, which was such a strange thing to him, given that he'd planned for a different destiny than a sailor's life at sea. He had never wanted to be a sailor, nor desired to be a navy man. Yet when Dominic had gone missing when they were boys, Nicholas had guessed he'd run off to sea. So Nicholas had followed, joining the Royal Navy at an early age.

He had searched for years for his friend, but he'd only found Dominic a few months ago. When he had, he'd been anguished to find they were on opposite sides of the law. Dominic a notorious pirate, and he a naval officer. But no amount of years could change how he felt about his dear friend. They were as close as blood brothers, and for Nicholas, the years lost between them ceased to matter in an instant.

Now, he was as much a sailor as his friend was, which amused him even as it saddened him. Their lives had become so different from what they had planned as boys. Dominic was the future Earl of Camden, but he had spent more than a decade pirating in the West Indies, while Nicholas had bound his life in service defending the Crown.

With a sigh, Nicholas leaned back against the railing of

the quarterdeck and braced his arms on the wood as he kept his gaze on the foretop.

"Nice night," a voice said. Nicholas's heart jumped, but he didn't let his body betray the fact that he'd been startled.

Joe McBride came the rest of the way up the companion ladder to the quarterdeck.

"It is," Nicolas agreed.

Joe's eyes rose to the foretop where Holland was. "Lovely view too."

"On that we agree as well." Nicolas knew he was treading water above a shark, and it would be best not to give Joe a reason to toss him overboard. He doubted Joe had any romantic interest in Holland, but he was damned protective of her, and that made him a very dangerous man.

"She says nothing happened between ye in the prison. I want *yer* word on that."

Nicholas chuckled before he could stop himself. "You want the word of a *pirate*?"

Joe didn't break his stare. "Aye. We're all pirates here, but we still have a code between us."

Nicolas met the man's eyes. "Very well. She kissed me, but that was her choice, and I was half-dead at the time. Other than that, nothing has happened between us."

Joe's brow arched in suspicion. "Half-dead, were ye? How'd that happen?"

Nicholas pulled his shirt out of his trousers and up over his head to expose his still-healing back.

"God's blood," the other man hissed through his teeth.

Nicholas turned to Joe as he tucked his shirt back in. "I paid for her loyalty in lashes, and she earned mine when she stopped Waverly from murdering me. You have my word, Joe. The girl is safe with me." *Safe from harm but not seduction,* Nicholas thought. He was a gentleman, after all—a gentleman who had very *piratical* thoughts when it came to her.

"But is her heart safe?" Joe countered. "She isna acting like herself. She's changed, and I blame ye for it."

"Blame? What have I done?" Nicholas asked.

"Y'arna the first handsome lad she's taken a shine to, but yer the first she canna control. Call it an old sea dog's intuition. I dinna think she kens what to do about ye. And a captain that is unsure of themselves is a captain who ends up marooned while the crew sails away with their ship."

"Are you planning to maroon me, then, to protect her?"

"It shouldna come to that, if'n you behave. But no looking at her like ye were today on the jolly."

Nicholas couldn't resist asking, "And how was I looking at her?"

"Like ye wanted to bed the lass for a week straight. Ye arna the first man to want her, and ye will not be the last, but if ye so much as upset her or this ship, ye'll have *me* to deal with."

"I won't upset her, Joe." Of course, it was a lie. Everything about his mission would upset her and doom her crew. And if her father was indeed Thomas Buck, it would destroy her.

If her father was like her—brilliant and fascinating and brave and good at heart—Nicholas was worried he might not be able to complete his mission. But if he didn't, what could he do? He couldn't return to the admiral empty-handed, or refuse to provide whatever information he had. Waverly, that bastard, would no doubt argue that Nicolas had turned to piracy and would try to have him hanged.

"By the way . . . I assume Holland isn't her given name?" he asked.

Joe narrowed his eyes. "Holland is her family name."

"So what is she called, then?"

"*Captain* Holland to you," Joe said with rather too much glee.

"And to you?"

"To me? She's just *lass*," Joe replied before he walked back down belowdecks, leaving Nicolas to frown after him.

Nicolas shook off the first mate's warning and his own better judgment and went up to the poop deck. He gripped the ropes of the shrouds and started to climb toward the foretop where Holland was sitting. Why was he doing this? She'd only tell him to leave. He wanted to . . . well, he wanted to just be near her. He wanted to talk. It was late at night, and only a handful of crewmen would be up and about on watch to see him if they were looking.

"Who's there?" she called out a moment before he reached her feet.

"Just me." Nicholas lifted himself up past the foretop so she could see him.

"You," Holland sighed dramatically, and he grinned at her exasperation.

"I thought you looked lonely up here, *Captain*." He inclined his head respectfully, even though his tone was teasing. As he pulled himself up beside her to sit, she scowled at his cheeky tone.

"You promised to take orders from me," she reminded him.

"And I shall." Nicolas sensed there were something more to reminding him of that promise, like she needed reassurance he wouldn't try to take her ship away from her. Had another man tried that? No honor among thieves, he supposed.

"What's your name? Your given name, I mean. You aren't actually Bryan, and I cannot simply call you Holland."

"Why not? The rest of the crew does, and I call you Flynn."

His gaze lingered on the sea a moment before he answered. "I'd rather you call me Nicholas." It was a strange thing to say, but right now he craved even the smallest intimacy from her.

Her mouth parted, and he fought the urge to lean over and kiss her. She was so damned tempting. He suspected if he tried to kiss her, that was a sure way to get tossed off the foretop.

She remained quiet a long while. "What do you want from me, really? A night in my bed?"

"I won't deny the appeal of that offer, but I don't *want* anything from you. I *like* you. I desire to call you by your given name because we are friends." He felt a tug of guilt at saying that, not just because he was trying to gain her trust for his mission but because it was also true.

She seemed to look right through him. "Are we?"

"I'd like to think so. We faced quite a bit together in Port Royal. Even if you don't consider me one of your friends, I consider you one of mine."

She was quiet again, much longer this time, before she finally gave him what he wanted.

"Brianna . . . My name is Brianna. But you must address me properly in front of my crew."

"Of course. Captain Holland it is, then, unless we are alone." He leaned back against the mast, and she did the same, their shoulders touching. It felt nice to be this close to a woman in companionable silence. He hadn't been alone with a woman in some time, not like this. He'd tumbled into and out of beds often enough. Most sailors did. But to sail with a woman like her, to talk with her and spend time with her like this, was something he'd never experienced before. Most of his interactions with women were either in ballrooms or bedrooms.

"I used to be afraid of heights," he said idly.

"Oh?" She swung her legs over the side. "How did you manage to get over that?"

"Let's just say my first few years at sea weren't easy. I was punished quite a bit by the first captain I served with." He didn't say more for a long moment and neither did she. They both knew the kind of punishments he'd suffered.

"Why did you go to sea at all, then? Did your family need the money?"

"No, my father is a country gentleman, and my mother is a lady. We had no need for money." He had decided to tell her the truth, or as close to it as he could manage.

"Why, then?"

"A man named Dominic Grey. My best friend. He was kidnapped as a boy, and we never knew what became of him for many years. I knew he loved the sea, and I believed he might have wandered down to the docks and been taken. It was a long time before I learned that he was taken by pirates. His father had searched everywhere for him, but to no avail.

I waited a year after his disappearance, then begged my father to let me go to sea and start my own search. It was only a short time ago that I found him again."

Nicolas watched the moonlight pour over the open water and tried not to think of the years lost between him and his friend.

"I've met Captain Grey," Brianna said. "He had an intensity to him that was almost frightening. I heard he suffered much as a lad, though I didn't know how."

Nicolas stared down at his feet. "Bad people in positions of power often take advantage of young children." He had shared a similar fate.

"Did something happen to you?" she asked quietly.

He nodded. His throat unexpectedly tight, he spoke haltingly at first, telling her all that he'd gone through. Nicholas had never imagined he would tell anyone this, but with Brianna it felt as easy as breathing.

"In those early days at sea. . . A few men tried to hurt me, to *use* me, and I received my first beating after I broke a man's hand when the man tried to harm me. I was too afraid to tell the captain why I'd attacked a topman who was valuable with the sail work, so I was whipped with a leather strap as punishment.

"Then I refused the advances of the first mate and was keelhauled. My first captain had a draconian vigor to him. So I was tied to a line and tossed overboard and dragged behind the vessel for a full two minutes. It should have killed me—but I kept a small dagger tucked in the waist of my trousers, and I cut myself free beneath the water and surfaced near the back of the ship. I waited for them to attempt to drag up the cut line, and then I swam into view, pretending to cough and gag as though I'd been underwater the entire time."

Surviving that had bought him the respect of the crew, who counted him among their number even though he was technically an officer. From that day on, he had silent protection from them. Anyone who threatened him always seemed to leave the ship sooner than planned or was hastily reassigned for personal reasons.

Brianna reached out and put her palm on his knee. "I'm sorry that happened to you, Flynn." She was about to pull her hand away, but he stopped her by covering her hand with his. She tensed as though expecting him to do something crass like push her hand toward his lap, but that wasn't what he wanted. This wasn't a touch related to passion. It was something far different. After a moment, she turned her hand over beneath his, and he curled his fingers around hers.

"I owe you my life, Brianna. I might have promised to obey you as my captain, but I made a stronger vow to myself to watch your back."

He didn't want to hurt her, but he had a job to do. As honorable as this crew seemed, they did not reflect all pirates, and it was possible many of them had a connection to Thomas Buck like their captain did. He didn't know much about Buck as a man, only knew of his reputation as a successful pirate. They said dead men tell no tales, and it was impossible to know how many of the lost ships and crews that had vanished in the West Indies weren't from storms but from pirate attacks under Buck's command.

The first threads of a plan were beginning to form, but it was his intention to bargain for Thomas Buck's location in exchange for Brianna's safety. He might not be able to save her crew, but he could save her.

Brianna stared at their joined hands a long while before she cleared her throat.

"Do you remember me telling you about the pirate queen Grace O'Malley?"

Nicholas smiled. "You spoke of so many female pirates while I was suffering fever. Remind me." Nicolas had a feeling that she was using these stories to distract herself from her worries, but he let her.

"Grace was born more than a hundred years ago in a land of warring chieftains and feuding clans in Ireland." Brianna's expression softened into a smile. She loved the stories, and he was beginning to love her telling them to him.

"Henry VIII wanted to make Ireland an English colony, and his daughter, Elizabeth, wanted to make her father's dream a reality. She sent Richard Bingham to be Ireland's governor for the area of Connaught, and Grace ran pirate raids right under his nose. Bingham despised Grace for her free spirit, and she conducted three rebellions against Bingham."

"Successfully?" Nicholas was fascinated. The stuffy old tutor he'd had as a boy never told stories of women in history. Far too often, historians pretended as if they didn't exist except as the shadows to men.

"Almost, but Bingham finally captured her. He was going to hang her, but she was spared when a chieftain exchanged prisoners for her life and she was freed. Bingham then captured Grace's two sons and killed one of them. She was so furious that she went to the queen herself to demand her other son's release."

"She went to the *queen*?" Nicholas could only imagine the bravado that had taken. He smiled, imagining Brianna capable of doing the same if she had to.

"They met in the fall of 1593 and spoke only in Latin, since Grace spoke little English. Whatever was said is lost to history, but Grace's boldness and Elizabeth's unique sense of humor most likely made it a lively encounter. In the end, Grace was sent home and her surviving son was set free on Elizabeth's orders. Grace vowed not to attack any more English ships and was to defend Elizabeth on land and sea, which allowed Grace to resume her piracy, this time with the queen's blessing, against England's enemies."

"She sounds like a formidable woman." Nicolas took a deep breath of the sea air and stared into the distance. Then his eyes widened.

Brianna saw what he did. Rain and wind were sweeping across the horizon toward them, whipping what were once gentle, rolling waves into a wild frenzy of white-capped water.

"Blast!" She pulled her hand free of his and with surprising agility dropped over the edge of the foretop, grasping the rigging. She beat him down to the deck, though he was fortunately able to keep up with her.

"What are your orders?" he asked without hesitation.

"Find Joe. I have a bad feeling about that storm." She stared at the turbulent clouds and the way the wind was digging into the water, creating deadly troughs.

"Aye, aye, Captain," Nicolas promised. He was no stranger to storms like these, and one never took them lightly. Sometimes a storm could sweep through and capsize a ship in seconds.

He found Joe in the first mate's cabin, reviewing maps, moving a sextant over the charts with the ease of a seasoned commodore.

"Joe, Captain sent for you. There's a storm coming."

Joe's head snapped up. "Must be a bad one if the lass is worried enough to send for me."

"It's moving fast," Nicholas said. "We need all hands."

"Aye, head back up on deck, make sure she's all right. I'll rouse the crew."

Nicolas rushed back to the deck just as the storm reached them, and the ship pitched and dove into the hollow base of a cresting wave. A flash of lightning lit up the sky, and Nicholas's breath caught as sheer terror pinned him in place. A wall of water arched over the decks, ready to sweep Brianna clear from the ship's helm.

"Brianna! Hold fast!" He couldn't reach her in time. He dove for the nearest bit of rigging and wrapped his wrist and one ankle in the straps. The water slammed into him a moment after it hit Brianna. His last glimpse of her was her vanishing beneath a black, angry sea.

CHAPTER 8

Brianna had barely reached the helm in time to strap herself to it with a bit of rope when the wave surged over the side of the ship. There was a terrifying moment of suspension as the *Sea Serpent* nearly capsized, and then the water burst across the deck and straight into her.

The impact knocked the breath out of her. Black water enveloped her, trying with all of its might to rip her free of the sturdy wooden helm.

Chest burning, she fought off the urge to breathe. She loved the sea, but at times like this it frightened her. Storms were always dangerous, but ones like this were made to destroy ships like hers.

The wave passed, and not a moment too soon. She sagged against the spindles of the helm and breathed sweet, glorious, salt-filled air. She lifted her face to search for new waves and spotted a man at the base of the rigging by the mainmast. *Nicholas*. The relief she felt at seeing him alive surprised her. She'd been so terrified about her ship capsizing that she hadn't been aware of much else. When she was focused on a storm like this, the men around her normally faded and all she saw was sea, masts, and decks until the crisis was over.

Nicholas struggled to free himself from the tangle of rigging. "Brianna!"

"Stay there!" she shouted back, but the roar of the next wave swallowed her words. She braced for the impact and held her breath as she was pulled tight against the ropes. They bit into her skin and cut deep, but the ropes held fast, keeping her at the helm.

When the wave cleared the deck and she was once more breathing, Nicholas was gone.

"No . . ." The word cut her lips as it escaped. She blinked away the rain and stared at the furious waves over the side of the ship.

Just then, a hand slapped onto the top rung of the stairs leading to where she stood. A head and then shoulders followed as Nicholas clawed his way up to a standing position before he leaned heavily on the railing at the top. His broad chest heaved, and his white shirt was plastered to his body, showing the outline of every taut muscle that had just helped to save his life.

"You daft fool! Get below!" she bellowed at him.

He pointed at the full-blown canvas pulled tight in the wind. "We have to release the sails!" He moved to the helm and held on to the spindles with her, his hands covering hers.

He was right. But even with the two of them, they couldn't manage it. She shook her head.

"We can't. No one can get up the rigging and stay there in these swells."

"Watch me." Nicholas flashed a grin, and suddenly he was leaning in and gripping her shirt to hold her close as he kissed her soundly, roughly, wildly.

"For luck," he said, then raced down to the quarterdeck. Another wave rose above them, and he made a running leap, catching the ropes of the mainmast a mere instant before the wave could wash him overboard.

Wave after wave crashed into the ship, but he worked his way up rung by rung, and she stared in amazement as he reached the main yard. He cut the sail free, and the white cloth rippled loosely. Then he continued up the mast to the main topmast yard in the main topgallant yard after that.

Joe and a few other expert topmen came out on deck and joined her at the helm. "Bloody hell, the man is mad," Joe said. The other seamen braced themselves and then started the deadly climb up toward Nicholas.

"He may be mad, but he might save our lives." The ship was fighting the wind and the sea less. Despite the large swells, the *Serpent* was coasting smoothly now that she wasn't being pulled directly against the waves parallel to them. With Brianna gripping the helm and not fighting against the might of the wind, she could move the ship safely into the waves at a slight angle.

"Where do you want the crew?" Joe asked.

"Have them tend to the mizzenmast and foremast," Brianna ordered.

"Aye, aye, lass." Joe winked and then bounded down the steps and vanished belowdecks. A moment later, the crew swarmed the deck, rushing to the remaining masts to free the sails.

For the next half hour, the ship was tossed through the

worst of the storm until it finally pushed its way into calmer seas. Brianna manned the helm, watching soft gray skies above until she was certain the storm had blown in the opposite direction. Then she called for Joe, who reached her the same moment Nicholas did.

"Someone cut me loose," she said. She'd gotten herself into the ropes, but they had swelled and tightened with seawater to the point where she couldn't get herself free.

"I'll free her, Joe," Nicholas said. "You should have the helm."

Joe looked to Brianna for confirmation. Brianna was too exhausted to care that Nicholas had ordered her first mate about. That was not a fight she could handle right now. She was dead on her feet.

She nodded to her first mate. "The helm is yours."

Nicholas studied the ropes binding her. Then, with extra care, he sawed his short dagger through the bonds at just the right spot. She sagged against him the moment she was free. Her legs had grown as wobbly as a landlubber taking his first steps on a rolling deck.

"Easy there, Captain." Nicholas slid an arm around her waist and lifted her up with ease. "Where to?"

"My cabin . . . no, wait, the sick bay."

"You have to direct me there." He pulled her to a stop just at the base of the companion ladder and pressed his lips softly on hers. She was so startled she didn't move; instead, she just embraced the moment, the tenderness of the action and how it made her feel all quiet and still inside. *Peaceful.* Yes, it made her feel peaceful. Was a man's kiss supposed to make her feel that way? Then he stepped back, a relieved look on his face.

She guided him two decks below to the middle of the ship and, feeling a little stronger, gave him a glare. “Was that for luck?”

“It worked, didn’t it? I thought a second one was in order, given that the first one worked out so well.”

She had to chuckle at that, and so did Flynn. But when they entered the sick bay, he frowned.

“Where’s the surgeon?”

“Drunk off his ass in a brothel in Cádiz, last I remember.” She limped to the cabinets and opened the nearest one. There were dozens of bottles and jars made of blue, brown, and green glass. None of them were labeled, though. She needed a salve or an ointment, something that could ease the pain a little.

“You don’t have a surgeon?”

She shot him a withering look.

“Every ship needs a good surgeon,” he added, a bit more cautiously.

“And it’s damn hard to keep one. The ones we find are often drunken louts. Try having one of them treat an arm wound, you might lose a leg instead. The best surgeons are all on Royal Navy ships or living on land. You’d have to kidnap those men to get them to work on a pirate ship. The *Serpent* may fly the Jolly Roger, but we don’t kidnap people.”

Nicholas gently pushed her away from the cabinets. “Let me see.” He dug around through the various bottles and jars of ointments. He unplugged the cork stoppers and sniffed each until he found one he seemed to recognize.

“This will do well enough,” he said.

She held out a hand, but he caught her arm and turned it over. She cried out.

"Blast, it's worse than I thought." He peeled back her sleeve. Raw, bloody stripes marred her wrists and forearms. It looked worse than she had imagined, but it hurt as bad as it looked.

"You need extra care," Nicholas said. "Let's get you into bed so that I can—"

She jerked away when he tried to put his hand on the small of her back. "This is not the time to take me to bed, you oaf."

He sighed and looked heavenward. "It's not to bed you, stubborn wench. It's so that I can tend to your injuries and you can *rest*."

"Oh." She was relieved, but also a bit disappointed.

Nicholas smirked, and the smug look was far too appealing on him.

"I won't refuse, should you offer, but you are my captain first and foremost, and right now your health and well-being are more important to me than the pleasures of your bed. Now, listen to your temporary surgeon and come with me."

Flynn escorted her to the captain's quarters at the stern of the ship and helped ease her down onto the bed, her legs still shaking. Nicholas knelt in front of her and removed her waterlogged boots, tossing them a few feet away to dry.

"You had better remove everything," he said, gesturing at her wet clothes.

"It's just my wrists," she protested.

"You were tossed around quite a bit. Best I check everywhere for injuries."

She stared at him until he turned his back to afford her some privacy. She stripped out of her clothes and then rummaged in her sea chest at the foot of her bed for a spare white shirt. It only covered her body halfway down her thighs, but it would have to do. She didn't have any proper nightgowns like a lady would.

She perched on the edge of her bed. "Very well, *Doctor*."

When Nicholas faced her again, his eyes widened at the sight of her bare legs crossed in front of her. She saw the heat in his striking blue eyes, but he said nothing as he sat on the bed beside her and began to check her for injuries. First along the legs, then her arms, followed by her back and then her midriff. When he attempted to open her shirt a little *too* wide, she tugged the two sides shut.

"*Those* are fine, I assure you."

Nicholas smirked again. "Of that I have no doubt. Very well." He rolled up her sleeves to expose her forearms and wrists.

"This will hurt," he warned as he dabbed a finger into the gooey salve and applied it to her skin. She flinched and hissed but didn't pull away. She didn't like being injured. A captain should *never* be vulnerable. Still, she'd suffered worse, but anyone who claimed they didn't mind pain was a damned liar.

"There now, 'tis not so bad," he soothed in a gentle tone like one would to an injured animal. He blew softly on her skin, which felt rather good against the raw and heated wounds.

"You've done this before."

"Unfortunately, yes." He didn't elaborate, but it wasn't hard to imagine some harsh punishment he may have suffered at the hands of a cruel captain.

She studied his face as he worked, noting with a strange pleasure the way dark golden stubble showed on his jawline.

It made the gentlemanly Flynn far more the pirate that he'd first appeared to be in the jail cell in Port Royal.

Her heart skipped about as he massaged her wrists and then raised his gaze to hers. Outside, the retreating storm clouds created a rippling shadow over the water as the *Sea Serpent* sailed into safer waters.

Brianna was all too aware of the sensual charge in the air, like the static pulse before a storm rose up, but this was a storm of passion. That didn't make it any less dangerous.

Nicholas reached up to cup her cheek in his palm and traced her lips with his thumb.

"Permission to kiss you, *Captain*?" he asked, his voice slightly rough.

A shiver rippled through her. "You forget your place, Flynn."

"Perhaps. But wouldn't you like to forget your place, just for a little while?"

It was too much. She bounced back and forth in her head between desire and rejection and finally decided to choose between the two. She nodded and leaned in before she could change her mind.

The kiss was soft, but there was *nothing* innocent about it. She parted her lips beneath his as his tongue teased the seam of her mouth. He tasted like a fine glass of scotch at an upscale tavern in Port Royal. Fine, rich, hard, and *intoxicating*.

His hand slid around to cup the back of her neck and cradle her head. She moaned at the way he kissed, as though he needed all of her to draw his breath. Even someone like her, who knew the wooing ways of men, couldn't resist the addictive feeling of a kiss like this.

Somewhere in the back of her mind, a little voice reminded her that it was dangerous to get too close to this man. Was she getting too close, though? There was nothing stopping her from leaving him at Sugar Cove and wishing him well, but part of her didn't want to. Part of her wanted to keep him. She was becoming attached, and the feeling was bloody wonderful. It thrilled her and terrified her all the same.

Their lips broke apart, and they both struggled for breath. She leaned her head against his, and he smiled faintly as he closed his eyes.

"Who *are* you, Brianna? I want to know everything." He opened his eyes again and simply held her face in his hands.

She smiled enigmatically. "Does it matter?"

"It does to me. I want to know *you*." He moved to embrace her, but pain sliced across her back and she hissed.

"Christ, I'm sorry. Did I miss something back there?"

She shook her head. "No, I think it's merely bruising. I was thrashed about quite a bit while at the helm."

Flynn pulled back and smiled. "Another time, perhaps. For now, tuck yourself under the covers and rest. I'll ask Joe what still needs to be done above deck, if that's acceptable to you?"

She crawled beneath her blankets, wincing only a little as her back touched the feather tick mattress. Nicholas brought the covers up to her chin, tucking her in.

"Only my father ever did that." She chuckled drowsily. It was so nice to be in a warm bed after that storm.

"Your father? Is he still alive?" Nicholas asked.

"Yes, of course . . . he's . . ." She yawned and forgot utterly what they were talking about before she fell asleep.

NICHOLAS STARED DOWN AT HIS LITTLE PIRATE QUEEN, both amused and a bit frustrated. He had come so close to confirming her connection to Thomas Buck. He had also come close to claiming her in bed. His hunger for her was growing, and it was more than worrisome. His affection had begun as a means to get close to her, but now it was becoming a liability. Things could end only one way for her father and those who followed him, and there would be no place for him in her life after that. But he would protect her, even if she hated him for it. He owed her that much, and he would rather suffer her undying hatred than let her swing from the gallows.

After ensuring she was warm enough by adding a second blanket to her bed, he left the cabin and found Joe on the waist deck issuing orders to the rest of the men.

"Is the lass all right?" He jerked his head to indicate Nicholas should come over to him.

"A bit bloody from the ropes and bruised from the storm, but she'll be fine. I found a pot of salve in the sick bay. She said something about your last surgeon being drunk in a brothel in Cádiz?"

Joe chuckled. "Aye. We left Dr. Simmons with a bottle of gin in his hand and his face buried in the bosom of a plump lady. Sad to say, we've been better off without the man."

"When we reach Sugar Cove, I will help you find a surgeon."

"Oh, aye? And how do ye be intending to do that? Kidnappin'?" Joe chuckled. "That isna our way, lad."

"I'm aware." Nicholas smiled a little. "She lectured me on that point."

They watched the crew working now to catch the loose sails and resecure them.

"Joe, is she truly Thomas Buck's daughter?" he asked. He acted calm, as if he wasn't secretly interrogating Joe.

"Where did ye hear that?" Joe asked in a low growl.

He shrugged. "Men in prison talk. There's not much else for them to do. They all thought her to be a man, but they still believed she was connected to Buck somehow, and I think our captors suspected it as well. It's why I encouraged her to take our chance at escaping. She had hoped to bluff her way out of the gallows, but they weren't going to believe her. One army captain in particular wanted her dead." Nicholas kept his tone as cool and casual as possible.

"And what interest do ye have in Buck?" Joe asked him.

"Buck is a legend. I admire that. He commands most of the Caribbean, and those who serve under him are the most successful pirates around. But the truth is, I just wish to know who Brianna truly is. What sort of world she comes from."

Joe frowned at him. "So she told ye her name, eh?"

"She told me."

"I suppose she trusts ye, then."

"Perhaps with her name, but not with her past. Won't you tell me anything about her?"

"Ye'd be a rare one to want to know more about the lass. Most only want to share her bed. Our lives dinna usually mix well with attachments."

Nicholas's face reddened, and he glanced away. Attachments. It was almost like Joe was reminding him of what a mistake that would be.

"I know, but my interest in her goes beyond appeasing appetites of the flesh." He kept his answers to Joe honest. The less he lied, the more believable he would be. Being obsessed with Brianna as a man was far less suspicious than being a naval officer asking questions about a notorious pirate's daughter.

"Well, ye might not be the worst sort for her to get involved with, but I willna share her secrets. That choice is for her and her alone."

"So there *are* secrets?" Nicholas asked the first mate with a grin.

"We *all* have secrets, lad. Now, stop worrying about moony nonsense and go help the other lads fix the sails ye cut."

"Aye, aye." Nicholas held back a laugh and headed for the rope shrouds at the base of the foremast.

As he climbed the rigging, he looked in the direction they'd come from. The storm was still raging, but they were out of its reach . . . for now.

CHAPTER 9

"Ye have to stop looking at the man like ye are, lass."

Brianna was pulled out of her daydreams. She was leaning forward on the railing of the deck, watching Nicholas wind up ropes with two other crewmen. He laughed at something one of the men said, and she couldn't help but smile too. His good mood was infectious.

"I'm not looking at him any different than any other man," she argued.

"Oh? I dare ye to make a nice face like that at Three-Toed Jim." Joe pointed at one of the sailors who was sitting in the sunshine on the quarterdeck, resting and wriggling his three remaining toes on his left foot. He'd lost the other two to a cannonball years ago. The scraggly bearded man had no teeth, and his skin was a leathery brown from decades in the sun. He was also about as charming as a barnacle unless he had two pints in him.

"Point taken."

"Aye, I can see ye are getting calf-eyed over Flynn, but the rest of the crew willna like it. It isna wise to show favoritism like that."

Joe's words fired up her temper. "Would a male captain have a problem like this?"

"No, because most captains have the good sense to leave their bed partners in port, and up until now, so did ye."

"You'd think being captain would come with certain privileges."

"Aye, but how would ye like it if ye were in their place? If anything, ye'd be putting Flynn in a dangerous position. It will always be different for ye, because yera woman, lass."

"Well, that's hardly fair. And if you dare say life isn't fair—"

Joe held up a hand in surrender. "Well, life isna fair, lass. There are some truths that ye can't ignore."

Brianna looked away from the enticing Flynn and back to her own duties. But by the evening, she'd noticed that some of the men looked at Flynn out of the corner of their eye. Most didn't seem to mind Flynn's presence, but among her crew of sixty-five, at least a third of them appeared to distrust him. But perhaps that was only because he was new on board.

Or perhaps Joe was right and it was because they knew he'd caught her eye.

She went below to her cabin, where Joe was already waiting for her. He had his charts as the pair of them often went over the next day's sailing course together. Joe leaned over the table, rolling out the worn charts and pinning them down with weights. One of those weights was a large brass compass, while the rest were beautiful rocks or shells she had collected during her years at sea.

"Well, how do things look?" she asked as she closed the door.

"We were blown off course, but only by a day or so. We should reach Sugar Cove soon enough."

"Thank God for that. I think you're right, Joe."

Joe's eyes opened wide. "Say that again, lass?" he asked in a mock shocked voice.

"About the men. Flynn may well have a target on his back. We need to get to shore and let the men forget him while they celebrate in the taverns."

"What do you mean to do about him, then?" her first mate asked.

"I . . ." What she wanted to do was not what she should do. "I suppose I will help him find the *Emerald Dragon*. They make berth in Sugar Cove as frequently as we do. Perhaps we'll find his crew and he can rejoin them."

Joe's eyes squinted, as if trying to see something about her that wasn't quite right more clearly. "There's something different about this one, isn't there?"

"What do you mean?"

"I don' pry into yer private affairs on shore, as ye well know, an' up till now ye've had no cause to bring them aboard this ship. If he was just a good time to ye"—Joe stopped a moment as if discussing this part of her life made him seasick—"I doubt ye would have such a forlorn look on yer face."

Brianna had to admit there was some truth to his words, but she dared not say so aloud. Joe's eyes softened in a way that warned her what he was going to say next would upset her.

"If ye like the man, lass, why not make yer father proud and take a husband? Ye could have a real life, one with a home that wouldna sink, and fill it with wee bonnie bairns."

She had always fought against the expectations pressed upon her as a woman, fought against the idea that marriage and children were all she could offer the world.

For a moment she had an image of herself cradling a small infant in her arms, Nicholas behind her, eyes fixed upon the child as he wrapped his arms around her. A strange flutter within her chest grew. But that would mean losing the sea, losing her ship—losing her freedom. It choked her.

"I can't, Joe, even if I am tempted. The moment I let go of all this, it's gone forever." If she lost the *Serpent*, she'd lose a part of herself.

She sagged into a chair at her table and dug her hands into her hair, tugging on the strands a little. The pinch of pain brought her back to herself again. She couldn't indulge in sentimentality like this.

Joe cleared his throat. "Well, as I said, one or two days before we reach Sugar Cove on favorable winds. Perhaps we should let the crew have an extra ration of rum to brighten their spirits?"

"Yes, let's do that. Rum usually makes for smoother sailing with this lot."

Joe chuckled. This crew was a sight better than Brianna's first. Those men had abused their rum rations and had been too drunk to stand half the time. It had taken her three years to weed out the bad eggs to get her current crew. She might not trust her life with them, but she trusted her ship with them. And that, in many ways, was more important.

Joe placed a fatherly hand on her shoulder and gave it a gentle squeeze. "I'll inform the men."

"Send Patrick in when you have a chance." She waited until Joe was gone before she knelt at the sea chest at the foot of her bed and rummaged around through the various bits of clothing until she found what she was looking for—a deep burgundy dress with an embroidered stomacher and full skirts.

It was her finest dress, but it couldn't hold a candle to the gowns she had seen the ladies wearing in Port Royal. But it was all she had, and if she and Flynn were to part ways in Sugar Cove, she wanted to know what she would be giving up. And tonight she wanted to feel feminine, to let him see her as he would other women, to have him desire her.

It was foolish to torture herself like this, but she would regret it if she didn't. Just one night—that would have to be enough to let her dream the rest of her life about what might have been.

Brianna held the dress up to her body, then took it over to the small mirror that hung on the cabin wall. She stared at her reflection and winced. Her blonde hair was frazzled and windblown. It had lost its silkiness from the briny sea breeze. She would have to brush it until it shone again, but no amount of brushing would make it completely perfect. Draping the dress across her bed, she stripped out of her breeches, waistcoat, and shirt before she changed into the gown.

The laces up the front of the bodice made it easy to cinch up and unfasten herself. Then she knelt again by her chest and dug around until she found the silver-handled hairbrush her father had given her so long ago. He said it had been her mother's. She traced her fingers over the carved scrollwork on the handle. It was pure silver; she had to polish it frequently due to the humid sea air tarnishing it, but it was worth it.

Brianna smiled as she pictured her mother using this brush and how captivating she must have been to her father. He had never remarried after she died. He rarely spoke of her except to say she had been so very brave the night she had brought Brianna into the world. When Brianna was little, she had once asked her father if he blamed her for her mother dying. Her father had picked her up and settled her on his lap, holding her close.

"Brianna, I would never blame you. 'Tis no child's fault when a parent dies. Your mother fought like a lioness to bring you into this world, and you fought to stay here after she was gone. You're both warriors to me. I only wish that . . ."

But he had never finished that sentence, and she'd never dared to ask him to.

Her father always reminded her he was no saint, but he was still the best man she'd ever known. She'd have gone to the gallows in Port Royal before betraying him. He had loved her and given her what no other man would have—the freedom to be whoever she wanted to be. He had given her command of the *Sea Serpent* at seventeen years old. With Joe at her side, she'd learned to lead her crew and take what she wanted from life. Tonight was the first night she'd dared to dream of something *different*.

Brianna brushed her hair in long, gentle strokes until it was soft and loose about her shoulders. She was just checking her appearance once more when she heard the frantic thud of boots in the passageway outside her cabin.

"Captain!" Patrick gasped as he burst into her cabin. His lip was bleeding, and one of his eyes was swollen.

She reached for her pistol and cutlass on the bed. "What's happened?"

The boy blinked as he took in her feminine appearance before he spoke in a quick rush.

"They're going to keelhaul Flynn!"

Brianna snarled and raced after Patrick toward the distant shouts of her crew. "Over my dead body."

"YOU IN, FLYNN?" SOMEONE ASKED AS FLYNN ENTERED one of the spare rooms. The crew were playing dice, and the man who'd asked was Javier Esperanza, a pleasant Spaniard he'd formed a friendship with in the last few days while they'd worked as topmen with the sails.

Javier leaned back against the wall, watching the game play out with mild interest.

"Me? No, I don't play anything that's left to chance. I prefer games of skill." He joined his friend to watch the men scoop up their dice in a wooden cup and wager on the numbers that would show before rolling the dice across the tabletop. When one of the men won, the others barked good-natured insults at the winner.

"I heard our rum rations were increased," Flynn told Javier. He rather liked that Brianna gave them real rum. Most ships only passed out grog, which was watered down.

The Spaniard grinned. "Oh, that is good news." He was

close to Flynn in age and one of the more physically fit members of the crew. He'd managed to keep pace with Flynn when they were fixing the sails earlier that day, and he admired the man's skillful seamanship. Nicholas missed the collegiality of his fellow officers in the Royal Navy, but there was a certain egalitarianism among a pirate crew that had its own appeal.

"More rum, you say?" one of the men seated at the table called out, clearly having overheard them.

"Aye," Javier called back. "Best to get it now, eh, before the rest of the crew hears?"

The men abandoned their dice game and headed to the hold, where the cook guarded a recently opened cask. A line had formed, and when they got to the front they passed their cups to the cook, who filled them before calling the next man forward.

Nicholas didn't drink rum often, but tonight he was in the mood. It might take his mind off Brianna for a while.

"So, Flynn, rumor has it you'll jump ship in Sugar Cove?" Javier asked as they waited in line.

"Probably. My crew may be in port, but I admit, I am tempted to stay on the *Serpent*. I rather like it here."

At this, Javier chuckled. "You like *her*, you mean."

Nicholas didn't pretend to misunderstand him. "I'm a man and I have eyes. You can't fail to appreciate the captain."

"Oh, aye," Javier agreed. "But she's never looked at any of the crew the way she looks at you. You'd best be careful. Many on this crew would give anything to have the captain favor them. Jealousy is a dangerous thing on any ship, but it's far worse on a pirate one."

Nicholas doubted that. Men were men, no matter what flag they flew under, and where men vied for power or treasure of any kind, there would always be trouble.

"She doesn't favor me."

"You have been to her quarters more than any man on the ship aside from her cabin boy or her first mate. No one is jealous of a young pup like Patrick, and no one worries about Joe—the man is like an uncle to her. But *you* . . ." Javier grinned mischievously. "You get the looks she gives no one else."

"What looks?"

Javier placed his hands under his chin and batted his eyelashes and smiled dreamily. "Like *this*." He puckered his lips as though waiting for a kiss.

"Don't be daft. She doesn't look at me like that." Nicholas would have remembered that look. Sure, when they were alone she looked at him with heat in her eyes, but never among the crew. If she'd given him one of those looks around her men, he would have noticed.

"She does, mate, she does, and it's not making you many friends here. You might want to go back to the *Dragon* when we reach Sugar Cove."

Nicholas frowned. He couldn't leave Brianna, not unless he found another way to find Thomas Buck.

He nodded his appreciation. "Thanks for the warning."

Javier nodded in return.

"Watch it, you little bastard," a man snapped at the cabin boy as he rushed past them with an armful of clothes. The man raised a hand against the young lad.

"Stow it, Billy," Javier shouted.

Billy, the lout who had threatened to hit the boy, cursed

and stomped off. The lad rushed away to return to his duties. Javier and Nicholas finally retrieved their rum rations and returned to the dice room.

"Come on, one toss, Flynn," one of the men at the dice table challenged.

"Fine. One roll." He set his mug down and came toward the table before taking a seat and rattling the cup of dice.

"Your wagers?" another sailor asked the men at the table. Numbers were tossed out. "Flynn?"

"Three sixes," Flynn said. "Two shillings on it."

Another laughed. "Two shillings? On *three* sixes?"

"What's life without a little risk?" Flynn countered, even though he'd told the men minutes ago he wasn't interested in games of risk. He decided he needed the distraction.

"Your loss. Roll it, man!"

Flynn shook the dice and tossed them across the table. Three sixes stood up, and a mix of groans and awe filled the room.

"On his first throw!" one gasped.

"I don't bloody believe it!"

"Damn it all!" another groaned. The bettors reached out to pay their shares.

"Keep it, lads." Flynn had no need to line his pockets with pirate treasure, and it might just earn him the respect of the crew for his generosity.

Flynn stood and collected his rum as Javier took his seat at the table and took his place. Flynn stepped out of the room into the passageway. The creaks and groans of the ship mixed with the whooshing pattern of waves lapping at the sides of the ship comforted him like a gentle lullaby.

He took a small sip of his rum and started for his

hammock but halted abruptly when he heard a whimper coming from the darkened companion ladder leading down to the deck below. The hairs on the back of Nicholas's neck rose. He backtracked toward the companion ladder with light steps and descended deeper into the hull in the bow of the ship.

Someone gasped in pain. Nicholas's eyes soon adjusted, and he saw Patrick cowering in a corner between the bulkheads while Billy raised a hand to him, clearly intent on striking the lad again.

"What's going on here?" Nicholas asked. He'd thought Patrick had made an escape from Billy but it seemed the man had found him again.

Billy whirled, snarling. "None of your business, lubber. Just a little discipline in action."

"What has the boy done?"

"The little bastard is always in my bloody way. Is that reason enough for ye?"

Flynn stood his ground. "I believe that Mr. McBride is responsible for meting out punishments at the orders of the captain."

Billy's eyes bulged at that. "You have no right to talk about the captain. Me and the others, we see what you're doing. You're playing her so you can take the ship."

"That's nonsense. I don't want her ship."

"Ah, but you want *her*, don't you? She won't spread her legs for the rest of us, but for you, she just might." He clenched his fists. "And for that, we have to deal with you, don't we?"

Nicholas was prepared for an attack, but he didn't let Billy see. He had to get Patrick out of the man's reach first, and then he could deal with this. Nicholas downed the rest of his rum nonchalantly and then, with what could have been mistaken for a casual toss of his arm, threw the cup, nailing Billy between the eyes.

Billy roared and lunged at Nicholas.

"Run, lad! Fetch the—!" His words were cut short as Billy collided with him. Patrick tried to get past them up the companion ladder, but Billy grabbed the boy's leg and yanked. Patrick's head crashed into one of the steps, and he slumped to the floor, unconscious. Nicholas threw a punch at Billy, but his hand didn't seem to move as fast as before. Billy knocked his intended punch aside and hit Nicholas's jaw hard.

"Feeling slow, Flynn?" Billy laughed darkly.

Nicholas landed a blow, but the strength in his fists was fading fast. *What the devil?*

"I didn't think you'd finish your rum." Billy hit Nicholas hard in the stomach, and Nicholas grunted in pain and fell back against the steps.

"The lads have been talking, and we agree that it's time for you to leave." He put two fingers into his mouth and whistled sharply. Nicholas blinked as he heard steps thunder above them. Then men surrounded him at the foot of the companion ladder. They hauled him up roughly and half dragged him to the waist deck topside.

"Bind him good, lads. The rum may not keep him down for long."

They drugged the rum . . . Nicholas groaned as the pitching of the ship made his stomach turn.

He was thrown down onto the deck, his ankles bound and his wrists tied behind his back.

"What are we gonna tell the captain?" one man asked the group.

"That it was a bit of fun, that's all."

"But keelhauling?" another man asked. "Billy, are you sure?"

"On some ships, it's a tradition to dunk a man in a line-crossing ceremony," Billy said.

"But this ain't a dunking, and we ain't crossing the equator," someone argued. "And the captain—"

"We're doing this *for* the captain!" Billy reminded him. "Now haul him up."

Nicholas was brought to his feet and teetered at the edge of a spot where the railing wasn't there to stop him from falling overboard.

Someone shouted, and he glimpsed Brianna behind him on deck in a red gown, her blonde hair flowing in the moonlight. She raised a pistol, its barrel aimed in his general direction, her face full of radiant ferocity like an avenging angel.

A shot fired, and a moment later both Nicholas and Billy were falling into the ocean. Cold, dark water sucked them down into the silent black depths.

His last thought was one of regret that he hadn't had one more kiss from Brianna before he died.

CHAPTER 10

The water above Flynn shimmered with the wavering rays of dying moonlight as he sank deeper and deeper into the sea. Nearby, Billy struggled, kicking his legs, but a cloud of dark-red blood muddied the water around him, until he struggled no more.

She had shot Billy to save him. The realization drifted through his mind, muffled beneath the silent screams he held back so he wouldn't suck water into his lungs. He pulled at his wrists and ankles, but the rope was tight. Bloody sailors and their knot-tying skills. There was no hope of escape, not this time. He ought to face his death calmly, but it was bloody hard when he had so much to live for.

The light above him rippled and darkened as a shadow suddenly plunged into the water and sank toward him. The figure swam down into the crushing depths. He saw blonde hair cascade out, and he knew it had to be his pirate queen coming to save him. By God, the woman was truly magnificent, but he feared he wouldn't live long enough to tell her.

Brianna moved her arms and legs in sure, strong strokes as she swam toward him, a dagger between her clenched teeth. When she reached him, she began to use the dagger to free his wrists. Nicholas wasn't going to make it if he didn't get air soon. He fought to remain calm while she sawed at his bindings. The second the rope loosened around his wrists, he started clawing his way frantically toward the surface. She grabbed his arm and kicked hard, propelling them both toward the surface.

Just a bit farther. He prayed his body would hold on a second longer. His head burst through the surface, and he sucked in a glorious breath before gasping and coughing, Brianna right behind him.

She pulled him toward the side of her ship.

"Throw a line down!" Joe bellowed from above. A rope ladder flew over the side of the ship and unraveled toward them.

"Lift your feet and hold on to the bottom of the ladder," Brianna ordered. Flynn grasped the rope and lifted his legs up to the surface, where she had an easier time sawing through the rope binding his ankles.

"You go up first, Captain," he said the second his legs were free. He didn't want her to have her back unprotected, even to the sea.

She climbed up ahead of him, her skirts heavy and almost black with water. It amazed him she'd been able to swim and not drown wearing such clothes. The moonlight shone on her hair that hung in wet tendrils down her back and shoulders.

When he reached the top of the ladder, Joe pulled him to

safety. His head ached and his thoughts were still muddled, thanks to whatever had been in his rum. His body was cold, so bloody cold his teeth started rattling. Brianna accepted the blanket Joe placed around her shoulders.

Several men, the ones he recognized as Billy's coconspirators, had been rounded up, pistols aimed at their chests by other members of the crew.

"Lass?" Joe spoke the word softly, a question: What did she want to do with them?

Brianna shivered as a cold wind kissed the occupants of the deck, and she stared with rage at the members of her crew who had tried to kill Nicholas.

"Billy got what he deserved. As for the rest, you know the code. If you attempt to murder a member of this crew, you are to be marooned."

Whispers rippled across the deck as the accused shared terrified glances. No man wanted to be left on a small uninhabited island with enough water for one day and a pistol, shot, and powder. When someone was marooned, they would be abandoned on a spot of land that flooded when high tide came. The pistol they were given was so they could kill themselves rather than die from drowning, starvation, or sharks.

"But, Captain . . . ," one man began uncertainly.

"You agreed to Buck's code when you came aboard. There is no more to be said."

The man who had hoped to plead their case let his shoulders drop. Brianna's head was held high, her chin defiant, even though she was cold and wet. Nicholas stared at the men who had tried to murder him. Some of them looked remorseful, the rest full of terror. Nicholas had learned one thing above all others serving in the Royal Navy. By helping another man, you offered him friendship. Here was a chance to win over the rest of the crew.

"Wait," Nicholas called out. He approached Brianna, careful to stand between her and the accused men. He wanted them to see his exposed back as a sign of trust. "Permission to speak, Captain?" He prayed Brianna would understand that he wasn't challenging her authority, merely trying to win the trust of her crew.

Brianna looked weary, so weary that he wanted to scoop her up and carry her to bed. But he didn't dare. She was strong, she was the commander of a ship, and he would not do anything to make her appear weak in front of her crew, no matter how badly he wanted to care for her. Though she was a strong woman, she roused every protective instinct in him. That primal voice in his head he tried to ignore growled that she was *his* whenever he looked at her.

"Permission granted," Brianna said.

"These men were doing what they believed to be best for the ship and for you. They saw me as a threat. But"—he turned to the men—"know this, I would do anything for the captain, same as you. Does she like me? Perhaps. But I ask you, can you blame her?" He chuckled roguishly and gestured to his physique, playing up the part of a Lothario pirate. It seemed to work.

"I won't do anything to betray the captain, I swear it." Then he faced Brianna. "I beg you to show mercy to these men. Billy paid with his life, but give the others a chance to prove themselves. Let them stay on board and do not maroon them."

He met Brianna's gaze, and for a brief moment the world melted away, leaving only her. He shook himself out of it, returning to the matter at hand. He could feel the tension of the accused men behind him building as she silently came to her decision.

"Like my father, I believe in second chances. You will not be marooned for your crimes, but you will have extra duties assigned, and you will treat every member of this crew with respect, including Flynn. You will leave this ship and my crew when we reach Sugar Cove. You're lucky I'm feeling merciful, or I'd toss you all overboard right now."

Brianna glanced at Joe, then back at the men standing behind Flynn. She stared at each man in turn before she added in a quiet but deadly voice, "And who I choose to take to my bed is no one's business but my own. The next man who thinks he has a right to say otherwise will endure a fate far worse than keelhauling."

With those words, she turned with quiet dignity and returned to her cabin.

"Back to yer duties, lads, all of ye lazy louts!" Joe roared. The men scattered, and only a few dared to make eye contact with Flynn as they passed.

Flynn let out a long sigh. Between the drugged rum, the struggle with Billy, and nearly drowning, he wasn't sure how he was still standing. But in some ways, Brianna had looked worse. This betrayal by her crew had shaken her, and someone should check on her.

"You should see if she's all right. She looked ill," he said to Joe.

The first mate shook his head. "I believe the lass would be better if *ye* were the one to see her."

"That might not be the best idea, given what just happened," Flynn said, then realized that Joe had actually suggested he go see Brianna. "So now you approve of me? Don't tell me you've grown soft."

Joe snorted. "No, but what ye did for those men . . ."

"I did it for *her*," Nicholas corrected. "I don't think she wanted to live with the burden she was about to place on her own soul. It would haunt her."

"Aye, it would. And that's why I'm telling ye to go after her while ye can."

While he could? "Joe—"

"Show the lass how much ye care, then find yer crew in Sugar Cove and move on."

Ah. So he was to have a night of bliss and then take his cue and leave.

"'Tis for the good of everyone," Joe said, as if reading his thoughts.

"Very well, I'll see to her." Nicholas went below in search of his pirate queen. Joe might expect him to leave in Sugar Cove, but Flynn had other plans. He'd been at sea so long that he'd forgotten what mattered outside of his duty to the Crown and to his crew when he sailed with the navy.

Even if he wanted to let this ragtag band of pirates and their captain worm their way under his skin, he had to resist. He could almost hear Dominic's laughing voice in his head, telling him that there was more to life than duty, but Nicholas was afraid to ever let anything in his heart matter more than his duty, especially if the thing that mattered was a beautiful green-eyed pirate queen.

BRIANNA PACED THE LENGTH OF HER CABIN, CURSING herself. In less than a week, Flynn had nearly caused a mutiny on her ship. There was a soft knock on her door.

"Who is it?" She wasn't in the mood to see anyone.

"Patrick."

Brianna stopped pacing and stood by the tall windows overlooking the moonlit sea. "Enter."

The door creaked, and she heard the boy clear his throat. "Captain, I wanted to . . ."

Brianna turned to him. "Yes?" She waited for Patrick to regain his courage.

"It was my fault. I made Billy mad, and Flynn stepped in to save me. He didn't have to, but he did. I didn't know they had drugged his rum. I—"

"It's all right, Patrick. You did the right thing coming to me."

The cabin boy didn't seem to believe her.

"Go to bed, Patrick. I'll see you on deck in the morning." She turned back to the windows, indicating he was dismissed for the night.

She wasn't sure how long she stood there at her windows, but eventually she heard another creak by the door.

"I said to bed with you, Patrick—" She turned, and her throat tightened as she saw Nicholas standing there in the doorway to her cabin.

"Flynn." The name was both a warning for him to leave and a plea for him to stay. He closed the door behind him but did not approach, waiting for some sign of approval from her.

"Lock the door," she said.

He slid the bolt into place. No one would interrupt them.

He moved toward her, his measured steps both comforting and frightening. One night. It was what she wanted. But her plans of looking her best had been ruined, thanks to that bastard Billy.

"That was quite the gown," Nicholas said. "Hope it's not ruined."

"I had planned on a special night before we reached Sugar Cove," she said.

Flynn allowed himself a smile. "Did I feature in those plans?"

"You did, but now . . ." She found herself stupidly wanting to apologize to him. Her hair was a mess of tangles, her gown was soaked, and she looked like a drowned rat. Not exactly how she'd imagined this moment. So much for acting like a pretty, genteel lady. Not that anyone would ever believe her if she tried, but still, she'd wanted to look her best.

When he reached her, he brushed the backs of his knuckles over her cheek.

"I rescued a kitten from a rainstorm once," he said. "The creature was half-drowned, but it was a fierce little thing, strong as hell." He smiled as if at some old memory. "That cat grew up to be an excellent mouser and a wonderful companion for a small boy who had lost his friend." He trailed his fingers down her neck. "I think that cat saved me, rather than the other way around." His lips parted a little as he trailed his fingertip along the tops of her breasts, which were pushed up tight against her wet bodice. Heat blossomed in the wake of that touch.

"What does that have to do with—?"

He silenced her with a kiss. She gasped as he wrapped his

arms around her and pulled her flush against him. He was soaking wet but not nearly as cold as she was, and she basked in the heat of his body.

The kiss ended too quickly, but he didn't let go of her.

"You're cold from the sea. Let me warm you up, Captain," he murmured.

"Brianna," she whispered. "Tonight, I am Brianna."

"As you wish."

She smiled at that. He made it sound like he was taking an order from her, but there was an undeniable tenderness in those three words, *"As you wish,"* that made her tremble with longing.

Flynn nuzzled her cheek. "You take care of this crew every day, Brianna. Tonight, let me take care of you." He nuzzled her throat next as his hands roamed her back, soothing and enticing.

"Yes, Lord, yes," she whispered. His teeth teased along her throat, and she felt her whole body surge to life.

He backed them up to the nearest wall of her cabin and with an aching slowness began to tug at the laces of her corset.

She didn't have a chemise on under the gown, and so with each lace he loosened, a sliver of her flesh peeked out from the wet fabric. He was quick but sure, and in no time at all her bodice fell to the floor and her breasts were bared between them.

Nicholas cupped one breast in his palm and traced a circle around her nipple with his thumb. The touch made her feel such a violent hunger that she closed her eyes and tried to tamp down the flood of desire that wrapped around her like fog.

"You have a sure hand, Flynn. Have you been with many women?" she asked. Though she sounded confident enough, part of her worried that she might not measure up to his expectations.

"A few," he admitted. "Have you been with many men?" He still stroked her breasts, and her eyes opened.

"A few," she said, being equally vague. "Does that bother you?" She had never worried about being a virgin before, but she knew that most gentlemen preferred it, expected it. Yet another case where a man was held to a different standard than a woman.

"No, not so long as you wanted to be with those men." Nicholas smiled softly. "You have a right to live and love, same as anyone else. And tonight there will be only pleasure between us," he promised.

Though she wasn't a virgin, at least in the physical sense, part of her felt like one all the same as he turned her away from him and his hands began to unfasten the hooks on the back of her dress. The skirts soon pooled at her feet, and she shimmied out of the single petticoat she wore. Brianna glanced over her shoulder at him and was relieved to see that his desire for her matched hers for him.

"My God, you're breathtaking," he said, his voice hoarse.

He raised her up in his arms, and she squealed in surprise as he carried her to the bed. He laid her down tenderly, then tugged off his boots before removing his clothes. She saw the still-healing scars on his back, wounds he'd suffered protecting her from that madman Waverly. She'd saved his life twice since then, and yet it still didn't feel like they were even.

He was beautiful, even with the scars from his injuries.

She had her own scars too, faint white lines etched into her skin that proved she had lived a pirate's life of risk and reward.

Nicholas sat on the bed beside her. "Pull back the covers, love."

She did as he asked, and he slipped beneath the sheets with her. They lay beside each other a long while, and as he leaned over her and placed coaxing kisses on her cheeks, her eyes closed. He kissed her chin, her forehead, her eyelids. She was unused to this, this lovemaking.

The other men she'd been with in the past had been eager to have their pleasure and she'd been eager for hers. They had coupled quickly and with excitement, each seeking and finding their own gratification. But there had never been *this*. Every single touch, every single kiss held the promise of something deeper, things she'd never wanted with any man before. It was a promise of more. Nicholas's body pressed to hers, and a quiver of longing that went beyond her flesh made her push tighter to him. He nuzzled her ear and pressed a kiss to the shell, sending a spike of desire through her.

"Flynn," she whispered. "Please. I need you."

"Nicholas," he corrected with a teasing chuckle. "Tonight, I am Nicholas."

She smiled. "As you wish."

The nuzzling continued until at last she became frustrated by it. She pushed at his chest so he had to lift his lips from her throat. "Nicholas?"

"Yes, my pirate queen?" His lips twitched with a wicked smile.

"You're going too damn slow. It's maddening." She almost groaned in frustration.

"Am I? Well, we can't have that, can we?" He slid down her body, then placed his hands on her knees and pushed her legs apart.

Though she was experienced in the bedchamber, what he meant to do was completely new to her. "Wait, what are you—?"

"Silence, wench," he growled. His forceful tone made her wriggle and laugh.

"Wench, am I? I'll have you hung from the—oh my *God*." She shrieked as he grasped her buttocks and bent his mouth to kiss her mound with a ferocity she'd never felt before. There were no words for how it felt for him to torture her with his tongue like this, the riot of sensations she felt. Next he pushed a finger into her, gently penetrating her with it while he suckled the tender bud at the top of her mound. She dug her fingers into his shoulders, desperate to find relief from his mouth, and yet he only took more of her into him.

Her climax was so close, so wonderfully close. She wriggled in encouragement, and he gave her bottom a light smack as if to remind her he was in charge right now. That was all it took. The climax that followed burst apart inside her like a tender flame dropped into a barrel of gunpowder. She screamed, and the sound echoed off the walls, but she didn't care.

"Are you all right?" Nicholas slid back up her body, his slender, muscled hips nestled into the cradle of her thighs.

"Y-yes." Oh, she was *more* than all right. "But you didn't . . ." She rocked her hips up, encouraging him to enter her.

"Soon." He feathered his lips over hers and then flicked his tongue against hers while he adjusted his body and the hard length of him nudged at her entrance. "You feel so tight," he said. "I don't want to hurt—"

"Take me, Flynn." She dug her fingertips into the hard muscles of his buttocks, and he surged deep into her.

They shared a moan as he sank in. Her body almost hurt from the pressure she felt with him filling every inch of her until there was no ending or beginning between them.

It was wonderful—and then he moved inside her and it became rapturous. His warm breath mixed with hers as he claimed her fully, completely. Nicholas's lips captured hers in slow, drugging kisses as he thrust deep over and over, the intensity rising until neither of them could do more than simply gasp for breath.

They moved together, lost in each other and the spell of the moment. She surrendered to another earth-shattering orgasm, and then he joined her and shouted her name as he released. Warmth filled her, and she burrowed her face against his neck, kissing him and tasting the sea salt on his skin, completely and utterly spent. A peace she had never imagined possible wrapped her up, and she sighed in bliss. He shifted as if to leave, and she protested with a soft sound and held on to him.

"I'm not going anywhere, love. I just need to get my weight off you." He kissed her brow and withdrew from her body, but thankfully not her bed. He pulled her to lie against his side, and she snuggled into his arms.

They lay there a long while before she dared to speak. "Tomorrow, we must not—"

"I know," he replied. "One night. I understand."

As she felt sleep tiptoe toward her, she wondered . . . Did either of them believe one night would ever be enough? What would happen once they reached Sugar Cove? The thought of never seeing him again dug into her heart like a sharp dagger, and she closed her eyes, wishing for just this moment that there was no tomorrow.

CHAPTER 11

The port of Sugar Cove teemed with a mix of pirate vessels and merchant ships of questionable reputation. The docks had sailors from more than a dozen crews handling cargo and fraternizing.

Brianna stood atop the gangplank, watching her crew depart with their pockets lined with coin. They had a few days to run amok between the taverns and brothels before they would need to return to the ship. It would rally their spirits after the harsh storm, Billy's death, the dismissal of the crew members involved in the attempted murder, and the unexpected delays her time in Port Royal's prison had caused them.

The final crewman rushed down the gangplank, jangling his coins in excitement.

"That's the last of them," Joe said.

"We had better see to the supplies first since we lost our chance in Port Royal."

Brianna stared at the chaos ahead of her, never more glad

to be in her breeches, blouse, and waistcoat. Her wig was in her cabin; that was something she wore only in the more "civilized" ports where she needed to pass as a man. Besides, women in Sugar Cove who wore skirts were usually prostitutes or the wives of wayward pirates, and she didn't want to be mistaken for either of those. Better to wear her breeches and be left more or less alone by the men here. Most already knew better than to make a pass at her.

"Have you and Flynn parted ways for good?" Joe asked.

Brianna nodded. "He left early. We agreed he should find his crew if they were here."

The truth was she hadn't wanted to say goodbye. She'd let him pull back the covers and step out of bed. Her gaze had lingered on his gloriously naked ass as he collected his clothes from the floor and dressed. Once he'd left, she'd pressed her face into the warmth left on his pillow. She'd closed her eyes, imagining for a moment he hadn't left.

It was better this way. She had to keep the peace with her crew, and the other day's events were proof that his presence would only make trouble. Pirate crews thrived on a sense of equality, of a sort, with their captain. Anything that bred jealousy could lead to mutiny.

Joe patted her shoulder. "I'll see to the supplies. Why don't you go send word to your father?"

Her father had a small but profitable plantation on the island of Saint Kitts, where his crews worked in land-based occupations during times of bad weather. It was particularly useful during hurricane season and in the winter. Her father had sailed less and less these past few years. In private company with her and Joe, he had made talk of retiring, leaving behind his title as Shadow King of the West Indies.

More than once, she and her father had quarreled over this. Brianna didn't want to hear him talk of letting go of what in her eyes defined him, and he had dared to tell her she would understand when she was older—understand what it meant to find peace in a new way of life.

Peace . . . she didn't want peace. She wanted *life*.

"I'll send word to him," she said and left Joe to manage their supplies. She leapt off the gangplank and strolled down the wooden walkways toward the village, where she could already hear the exciting cacophony of sounds that made up pirate life.

There was never a dull moment in the pirate haven. Sugar Cove was full of men fighting, gambling, wenching, and sometimes all three at the same time. Someone was playing a hornpipe as drunken revelers danced in the streets. Careful to dodge brawling men and prostitutes offering their services, Brianna made her way to a small apothecary on the outskirts of the village.

A little wooden sign that read *Dr. Melody's Medicines* hung over the door. The interior of the shop was dim and even more unwelcoming than the chaos outside in the streets. The paint was cracked and peeling, dusty jars filled the shelves lining the walls, and pots of various ointments and salves were nestled in between.

"Brianna!" an old man with a whiskered jaw greeted her from behind the grimy counter. He wore a pair of thick spectacles that enlarged his eyes in a disturbing way that reminded Brianna of an owl. But this was one of the few men she trusted with her life—and her father's. He'd once sailed under Buck before he'd gotten too old to weather the sea.

"Dr. Melody," she said in a soft voice. Though the shop

was empty, she didn't want anyone outside to hear their conversation. Sugar Cove was full of eyes and ears that could be bought by anyone for the right price.

"What can I be making for you today? More salves for sunburns—"

She leaned over the counter. "I need you to send a message." At this, he cleared his throat and removed his spectacles as he peered at her closely.

"And what message should I be relaying?"

"Lions prowl the harbors and hills. We will come to you." Her father would know what she meant, that the navy was searching for him on land and sea. There was no sense in him leaving his plantation until she came up with a clever way to send the navy off on a wild chase.

"I can do that. My man will be here any minute. He'll know what to do."

"Thank you." Brianna collected a pair of jars of salve and tossed a few shiny coins his way, which made his eyes glitter at the sight. She left Dr. Melody's shop and carried her purchases in a leather satchel. If anyone was following her, she'd appear to have bought goods from the apothecary and nothing more.

She returned to the town square and spotted several familiar faces, men who had sailed with Dominic Grey in the past. They lounged about near the opening of a tavern, each of them drinking mugs of ale and talking. Luck was with her, it seemed. The *Emerald Dragon*'s crew was here, which meant Nicholas could join them, assuming he hadn't already found them.

She started toward the group but halted when she saw Nicholas round the corner. He stumbled into the midst of his own crew, who all stopped drinking to look at him. There was an uneasy moment where the other sailors stared at him, tense, wary, as if ready for a fight.

What was this all about?

Brianna watched from the hidden vantage point of a boardinghouse across the square. Flynn spoke to a man in the group who might have been the *Dragon*'s newest captain, but she was too far away to hear what was being said. After a moment, the rest of the men relaxed, and one man even offered Nicholas a mug of ale. So some bad blood, perhaps on account of him being caught, but all was forgiven.

Nicholas glanced around the square, and Brianna sank deeper into the shadows. He was with his crew, and that was all that mattered now. It was best if she no longer looked back at what might've been. It wouldn't be the first time.

"WELL BLAST ME, IF IT AIN'T NICHOLAS FLYNN!"

Someone hollered a laugh of recognition, and Flynn relaxed. He had stumbled quite unexpectedly straight into Dominic's old crew from the *Emerald Dragon*. For a moment, he had feared the worst, that the crew members would decry him as a spy for the Royal Navy. But then he saw the new captain among them, Reese Belishaw. If Reese welcomed him, the others would follow.

"Well met, Flynn." Reese gripped his hand, and the *Dragon*'s first mate, a man named Chibbs, thrust a mug of ale at Flynn.

"What the devil are you doing here?" Reese asked. "Is Dom with you?"

"No, he's still in Port Royal with Robbie." Nicholas hesitated. "Reese, may I beg a favor of you?"

"Of course." In another life, he and Reese would have been fighting sword to sword, pirate against naval officer, but Dominic had united the two in trust and friendship. Nicholas didn't want to lie to Reese, so he would do his best to win the man's cooperation with a few stretched stories.

"I came to port on the *Sea Serpent*."

"Did you now?" Reese drawled out slowly, and his gaze intensified. "How did you manage that? The captain of the *Serpent* runs a tight ship."

"He certainly does." Nicholas jerked his head to the side to indicate they should step away from the others for a moment.

At the subtle emphasis of the word *he*, Reese moved away from his men and moved into a more secluded part of the tavern.

"So you've met her, then," Reese said, keeping his voice low.

"Yes, and she's rather magnificent." Nicholas probably should have described her some other way, such as *impressive* or *remarkable*, but such words felt inadequate. He smiled at the memory of his pirate queen lashed to the helm in the midst of a storm and how she'd risked her life to save his. But more than that, he remembered how she'd felt in his arms, how she'd made him feel more alive than anything else had in his entire life.

Reese chuckled. "Ah, so you are in love with her."

"I don't love—" Nicholas stammered, but Reese waved a hand.

"It is a lucky man to *love* her. Few men have known her well enough to say that."

For a moment, Nicholas suffered a small flare of green-eyed jealousy. Reese was an attractive fellow, tall with stormy grey eyes and built like a warrior of old. Had he known pleasure in Brianna's arms? "Are you one of them?" he asked quietly.

"No, I cannot tame such a wild woman, not when I am also wild. We would burn down the world together," Reese said. There was something sad in the way he said that, as though he might never find someone who would suit his nature, or perhaps tame it a little.

"She is wild," Nicholas admitted, but he didn't want to think of Brianna as a tamed, docile creature. She was as free as the stormy petrels that took flight over the shores of Cornwall. He'd often sat upon the rocks and watched them catch and ride the wind with their wings. Men harnessed the wind with canvas sails, but petrels rode it like no other beast on earth could.

"So what is this favor you need of me?" Reese asked, getting back to their discussion.

"I told Brianna that I have been sailing on your ship. She and I were supposed to part ways, but I don't want to walk away, not yet. Could you convince her to partner with your crew and chase a few merchant ships on the way to Cádiz?"

Reese sipped his ale again. "And are there such prizes to be chased? Or is this simply a way for you to spend more time with her?"

"There truly is a trio of Spanish merchant ships bound for Cádiz. Assuming they survived the storm we passed through on our way here, they should still be within easy chasing distance. But I won't lie—my motive is to stay close to her. I'm not ready yet to let her escape."

Reese chuckled. "Then you *have* fallen under her spell."

Nicholas nodded. It was true enough. If she were a witch born of the sea winds, then she had cast her spell over him.

"So if Holland agrees, I should ask for you to stay on her ship as my emissary and she could send someone to mine from hers?"

"Yes, exactly." Nicholas hoped the other man would agree. It would make things much easier. Flag signal communication was easy to do between ships staying close together.

"Well . . . my crew have been a bit bored since Dom settled down with Robbie. It would be nice to chase a few prizes."

"So you'll do it?"

"We'll do it." Reese laughed. "Never thought I would see you, a navy—"

"I am that no longer," Nicholas cut in, silencing Reese from saying anything that might get him into trouble here.

"Oh? But I thought—"

"Finding Dominic was the reason I went to sea in the first place. Now that I have, I saw no reason to stay."

As he said the words, it occurred to him that there was more truth to them than he cared to admit. The cut-and-dried morality he once believed in was far less absolute than he'd once thought, and he had trouble seeing himself continuing on like this year after year. Once this mission was done, he would tell the admiral he wished to resign his commission. He wanted to leave and return to Cornwall to start a different sort of life.

"And now you've set your sights on Holland. Well, I wish

you luck with her. Why don't we meet down at the docks tomorrow morning and I'll speak with her."

"Thank you, Belishaw." He shook the man's hand, then bid goodbye to the other sailors he'd befriended as a prisoner aboard Dom's ship, something that now felt like a lifetime ago.

He left the tavern and strolled through the village until he found what he was searching for. A drunken man lay half propped up against the wall next to a blacksmith's forge. The man's once-white powdered wig was now a dirty gray, his face was unshaven, and his clothes were covered in mud. Under one arm, he clutched a bottle of rum and hummed a bawdy ditty to himself.

"Ho there." The man's speech slurred as he spotted Nicholas looking at him. "Got a shilling for a poor bloke?"

Nicholas dug in his coat for a few coins to press into the man's grimy palm. As the coins touched the man's hand, Nicholas said, "So you can see the White Cliffs once more."

The man's drunken, bleary façade vanished, replaced by a sharp, knowing expression.

"Send word to Admiral Harcourt in Port Royal that we are to chase merchant ships at sea bound for Cádiz. I will notify him when I discover our friend's location."

The coins vanished and the keen look in the man's eyes did too. "Aye, thank ye." The man took a dramatic swig of his rum and winked slyly at Nicholas before he stumbled to his feet and wandered off.

Not wishing to linger, Nicholas took a new route back to town. As he passed by a brothel, a buxom woman waved him over. He would've ignored her, but she had an urgent, panicked look in her eyes that made him think she may be in trouble. She gestured for him to come to the back of the brothel through the kitchen, where a fat cook labored over a pot of stew.

"Miss, are you all right?" Nicholas asked when he caught up with the woman. Her face was painted white and her lips were dark with rouge, but he could tell that underneath the paint she was probably a pretty creature.

"Ye'll help me?" she whispered.

He kept his voice low. "Help you with what?"

"There's a man here, says 'is name is Buck and I know there's a reward for 'im. Will ye help me take 'im to the navy so I can collect it?"

Nicholas highly doubted Buck was here. No doubt this girl had seen some other man and assumed he was Buck. Still, Nicholas wanted to verify this for himself. "Miss, where is this man?"

"I ain't showing ye unless ye are who I think ye are."

"And who do you think I am?"

"An officer in the navy. That's what ye are, ain't ye?"

This was a dangerous game. Admitting that to the wrong person was a sure way to get himself killed. It felt and sounded like a trap, but if he was clever he could see who was involved and escape before it snapped shut. "I could take your information to an officer," he said cautiously.

She pouted and folded her arms across her bosom. "Not good enough. You'll just run off and claim it for yourself. I'll only speak to an officer."

Stubborn chit, he thought. "You'll have a damned hard time finding a naval officer here, madam, though I might know where to find one. But what makes you think I'd be inclined to do so?"

"Same reason as me, the reward. 'Tis too much to resist. I've been waiting a long time to see money in me pockets for knowing about him." She smiled slyly. "Think of how much fun we can have if you help me. I'll split it with you."

He decided to play along, if only to see what the woman's game was and who her partners might be if it was in fact some trap for unwary officers. "Very well, we'll split the reward. Show me where Buck is."

"This way, love." She led him out of the kitchen and into an alley behind the brothel. He gripped his dagger tightly, ready for anything he might face. They walked half a dozen feet before the attack came.

Without warning, he was grabbed from behind, a blade digging dangerously into his neck. If he struggled, his throat would be slit instantly.

"So, flying yer true colors at last, are ye?" an angry Scottish voice growled.

A moment later, pain exploded in his skull and he fell to his knees. Before he passed out, he heard the girl say, "Told ye I can always spot a navy man. Too gentle-like, this one. Too bad ye have to kill 'im now, eh?"

The world shrank to a single pinprick of light before darkness swallowed him whole.

CHAPTER 12

Brianna heard the commotion in the passageway outside her cabin and left her charts and maps abandoned on her table. She opened the door to find Joe and Patrick talking, and between them on the wooden planks lay Nicholas's unconscious form.

"Joe?" Brianna rested her hands on her belt, her cutlass within easy reach.

"We have a problem, lass." He nudged Flynn with the toe of his boot. "And it's him."

"What do you mean?" Part of Brianna wanted to run to the fallen man, but she didn't dare. Instead, she raised an eyebrow, waiting for an explanation.

Joe shrugged. "The lad's fine. I knocked him out is all."

Patrick gave Joe a concerned look, and Brianna knew she was going to need to be more direct about all this.

"All right. *Why* did you knock him out?"

"Because he's no pirate. He's a bloody naval officer," Joe spat.

The floor beneath her feet seemed to suddenly drop away.

Brianna couldn't process his words right away, but her body stiffened. "He's *what?*"

"He's the *enemy*, lass. We brought him here so ye could decide what to do with him before the rest of the crew finds out."

Brianna was shaking as she stepped back to allow Joe and Patrick into her cabin. "Bring him inside."

Joe hoisted Flynn up and threw him over his shoulder before he carried him inside.

"Patrick, fetch me a bottle of rum," she said, sending the cabin boy away.

Once they were alone in Brianna's cabin and Flynn was once more lying on the floor, she rounded on her first mate.

"So you think he's a spy. How can you be sure?"

Joe sighed heavily. "Because I was the one who discovered it." She could see he was taking no joy in revealing any of this to her.

"How?"

"I followed him. He made a stop at the edge of town and spoke to a man I've seen before, a man who I hear delivers messages to the navy."

"That's it? That's not enough to—"

Joe cut her off. "I hired a wench at a brothel to ask for his help, to tell him what I reckoned he wanted to hear and that she needed an officer. He told her he was one."

"A man might lie for a pretty woman's attention—"

"In Sugar Cove?" Joe snorted. "Only a fool would say that to get under a woman's skirts. No, he said it because it's true."

"Then why the masquerade? He was flogged by his own men in Port Royal, Joe. He nearly *died*."

"He nearly died for *ye*, lass. What better way to win yer trust? A man dedicated to a cause will do that, and more."

Brianna's mind was fogged with pain as she tried to understand what Flynn's betrayal meant. "Why, Joe? Why me?"

"It isna because of ye, but who ye ken."

Realization dawned on her. "My father."

"Aye. Even if they didna know ye captained the *Serpent*, if they thought ye sailed with me, they could use ye in hopes of finding Buck."

She stared down at Nicholas. Her dreams of another life withered like crops without rain. She felt as though her soul might drift away beneath the slightest breeze.

"We'd best chain him up before he wakes," Joe suggested. "I'll be back."

He left the cabin, and Brianna collapsed on her bed, staring at Nicholas's face. Assuming that was his real name. He was vulnerable, completely under her power. Any other pirate captain would kill him and be done with it. But she had too much of her father in her. She was not a ruthless killer.

Even if he was a navy man as Joe said. The thought made her shudder. She'd watched a twelve-year-old cabin boy hang alongside his crew for piracy. She'd seen homes burn with women and children inside because the navy thought a wanted pirate was inside. This entire time she'd been lulled into some enchantment by Nicholas's blue eyes, he might have been plotting her and her crew's death. The betrayal was infinitely deeper than she ever imagined anything could be.

"Traitor," she murmured. No, she couldn't bring herself to think of him that way. They had been through too much for her to simply dismiss him out of hand. She had dared to let her guard down, and now she was paying for it, *dearly*.

"Oh, Nicholas, what have you done?"

She didn't move until Joe returned. She just watched him breathe as she debated what to do.

When Joe returned, he hoisted Nicholas into a seated position with his back to the wall opposite Brianna's bed and clapped a manacle around Nicholas's left wrist. The other end was secured to a metal ring in the wall where Brianna normally hung wet clothes to dry.

"That should keep him out of trouble for a bit. I dinna trust the crew to leave him alive down in the brig should they hear why he's there."

Brianna nodded, her chest hollow. She didn't want Nicholas hurt, despite his betrayal and deception.

"Will you be all right with him here?" Joe asked.

"I'll be fine." It wasn't quite a lie, but Joe didn't press her on the matter.

"Call if you need me, lass." He gave her a regretful look, which only drove deeper the fact that she held Nicholas's fate in her hands.

And what would that fate be? Right now, she had no idea.

❧

NICHOLAS GROANED. HE AWOKE WITH PAIN BEATING A senseless rhythm into his skull. The darkness lifted from his vision to reveal Brianna's cabin. How the devil had he ended up here? The last thing he remembered, he was leaving a brothel to help a woman—

He lunged to his feet, ignoring the way the room spun around him. Brianna was perched on the edge of her bed, watching him. She wore knee breeches and a white blouse pulled in by a leather waistcoat. Her hair was tied into a queue at the nape of her neck by a black ribbon. She looked both beautiful and dangerous.

"Brianna." He took a few steps toward her and jerked to a halt. His left hand caught on something holding him fast, and he realized he was chained by the wrist to the wall. A sinking feeling took over his insides, like he was being dragged below the ocean's surface. Brianna knew who he really was.

"Why?" Brianna's voice was cold as the steel of her blade, but it couldn't completely mask the pain she surely felt.

Nicholas didn't answer right away. What could he say that wouldn't doom him further?

"Flynn, why did you betray me?"

"I didn't betray you, and I never intended to. My mission was to find Thomas Buck. Just him."

She looked away from him. "This was all about Buck? You drove a dagger into my back for that?"

He sucked in a breath, barely able to breathe. A vast weight was pressing him down, crushing him. "Brianna—"

"*Captain* Holland," she corrected. Her words hit as if she'd backhanded him.

He tried again. "Captain Holland. I was tasked to find Thomas Buck, and Admiral Harcourt thought you might . . ." He paused. "But that's not why. Not really. I did it because

Captain Waverly was going to hang you once he had what he wanted, and if he discovered you were a woman before that, things would've been infinitely worse for you. There is no controlling that man. I don't want to think about what he would've done to you."

Brianna's eyes hardened. "Oh, so this was all for my benefit, was it?"

"Admiral Harcourt wanted me to win your confidence and gain your trust because he learned you had a close connection to Buck. He thought at first you might be Buck's son, but when I told him you were a woman, he thought perhaps you were a daughter or lover."

"Is that so?" Brianna's tone conveyed nothing about how she was taking his explanation.

"Yes. Admiral Harcourt has a daughter of his own. He would never hurt a woman. This was the only way—" Nicholas's voice trailed off. He realized there was nothing else he could say to win her trust back. It was lost forever. The best he could do was stay alive and keep her safe, if she would let him. But he'd never reclaim what he'd once thought might be possible . . . to find his own kind of happiness.

"I understand," Brianna said.

Nicholas blinked. "You do?"

Brianna nodded slowly. "I understand that if I had been Bryan instead of Brianna I would be dead now. That my *only* saving grace in your eyes is my gender. Tell me, what would have happened if it had been Patrick in that cell with you instead of me?"

"Patrick?"

She got up and took a step toward him. "My cabin boy.

Young lad, barely old enough to shave. You know, the one you saved from Billy. He's never once fired a shot in anger or engaged in any actions against another ship. What mercy would you and your *admiral* have shown him had he been in my place at Port Royal?"

She was close now, close enough to run him through if she chose to pull out that cutlass of hers. Flynn looked down. He knew the answer just as well as she did, but he couldn't bring himself to say the words. It was the truth; he might not have thought about a boy like Patrick. He would have gained the information he sought and been on to his next mission, and in the back of his mind . . . he'd know the lad would have swung from the gibbet.

"I thought as much. You disgust me."

She turned and walked away from him. Somehow that hurt more than if she had stabbed him. She had laid bare his hypocrisy, and yet he still could not regret the choices he'd made.

"How did you find out?" he asked after a long moment of silence.

"How?" She echoed the word softly as she looked out the window of her cabin.

"Yes, how did you know?"

She laughed, though the sound was bitter. "I didn't. Joe saw you speaking to a man known to pass messages along to the navy. He then hired a woman to trick you into showing your true colors."

Even though his head was throbbing, he could put everything together now. He had been a fool, clumsy and far too eager to see an end to this.

Now Brianna did pull out her cutlass, though she kept her back to him. "What did you tell the messenger?"

Nicholas could lie, but after seeing her face tonight, seeing the pain in her eyes, pain he had caused, he was done with lies. What good would lies do him, anyway? He would likely end up dead one way or another. She had no cause to grant him mercy, and even if she did, her crew would have other plans. Knowing his death was imminent made him value the truth that much more.

"I told him we were planning to chase Spanish merchant ships to Cádiz and that I hadn't found Buck yet. I told them I was still searching. If the navy caught you then, I'd be able to tell them that I'd only witnessed you chasing Spanish ships, a country we are at war with. It wouldn't be viewed the same as attacking English ships."

She stared at him a long moment, weighing his words.

"That's all?"

Nicholas nodded. "There was nothing else to tell. They will be chasing ships along the route to Cádiz searching for you. Now you can avoid them easily."

She slowly turned her back on him as she walked toward the windows and faced the sea.

"I have to warn my father," she whispered, more to herself than to him.

"So it's true, then? You are the pirate king's daughter?"

"Does that surprise you?" Brianna asked.

"I've heard Buck is an extraordinary man. It's only natural his child would be as well."

She half turned her head his way and raised her cutlass at him. "Your flattery is no longer welcome, traitor. You won't get what you want. I won't let you hurt my father."

"I only wanted to protect you," Flynn said.

Brianna almost laughed. "While everyone I care about is shot or hangs? Be still, my racing heart—such gallant nobility will surely make me swoon." She sneered, and her eyes took on a wild, predatory look. She sheathed her cutlass, then unfastened the belt that held it and her pistol and tossed them onto the bed.

She approached him without fear now, and it made Flynn a bit uneasy. He backed up a step as she placed her finger on his jaw and raised it up ever so slightly.

"Besides, you shared my bed—isn't that enough?"

What the devil was she playing at?

"As if one night with you would ever be enough," he said, allowing the rogue in him to resurface. She was toying with him, like a cat with a mouse, but if this was to be his last intimate moment with her, he wished to enjoy it. He grabbed her arm and pulled her into his embrace, holding her captive to his passion for perhaps one last time.

He lowered his head to hers, and she didn't fight him. Brianna's mouth opened beneath his, and he kissed her like a man possessed. She pushed at his chest lightly, then seemed to change her mind and burrowed closer as their lips fought for dominance. He nipped her bottom lip, and she flicked her tongue against his, each sensing a sensual battle between them. Yes, he would never have enough of this woman, but luck was with him because he wouldn't be alive long enough to suffer the rest of his life without her touch or kiss.

Then, as soon it had begun, she jerked away, the back of her hand coming up to touch her lips as she stared at him in anguish.

"That is the last you shall ever taste of me. All that is left is to decide your fate." She went back to the bed and put her belt and weapons back on.

"So what is it to be, then?" Flynn asked.

"By all rights, I should maroon you. It's better than you deserve." Though she did not shout, there was anger in her words, hiding the pain he saw in her eyes.

"But you won't, my beautiful pirate queen," he said, playing the only card he had left. "For the same reason you didn't maroon your crew."

"I was going to," she countered.

"And you would have hated yourself for the rest of your days if you had. It didn't take much to convince you to show mercy, because that is what is in your heart. That same sense of mercy is what bound my fate to yours back in Port Royal. Don't allow my actions to turn you into a monster, Brianna. If they do, I'll have failed you in every way, and I truly would prefer death to seeing that." She had too much heart, too much soul to do anything so cruel, even to someone like him who had hurt and betrayed her.

Her eyes narrowed. "Damn you to the depths, Flynn," she said and left the cabin, leaving his fate uncertain.

He sank to the floor, resting his back against the wall and closing his eyes. It was going to be a long night.

BRIANNA IGNORED THE LOOKS OF HER CREW WHO WERE ON deck as she crossed to the mainmast and began to scale the rigging. She reached the crow's nest and leaned back against the mast. It was her favorite part of the ship. Few men came up here, so it gave her a chance to have some time alone and watch the sea. She also found the sway of it, noticeable even in calm seas, strangely relaxing.

They would set sail within the hour. They still had to round up the rest of the crew on shore, but once they were aboard, they would set sail for Saint Kitts since the wind was with them and the tide was going out. If the navy was prowling for her father, he had to be warned. The navy had been hunting him for years, but something felt different now. To send a spy into the midst of her crew—that was a new trick and far bolder than the navy's usual tactics. Who knew what other means they were pursuing at this moment? She had to see her father so he could make plans to escape, just in case.

The more she thought about it, however, the more she realized that wasn't the reason. It was the excuse. Buck had evaded capture for twenty years and under worse circumstances than this. No, what was different this time . . . was her.

As much as Brianna didn't want to think about it, she knew that things would have to change. Her father couldn't run from the navy forever. Sooner or later, the nets would close around him. No one could run forever. The question was, could they stop running and avoid capture? What would their lives be like without the freedom of the sea? What would *her* life be like?

She watched the sun slowly sink beneath the horizon until the last remnants of its glow faded from the surface of the sea. And with it, her heart sank deeper and deeper. What was she going to do about Flynn? The smart thing to do would be to simply kill him herself. She had brought him on board, so the burden belonged to her.

But she wasn't like that and never *could* be like that. Flynn was right. She didn't want to become a monster.

Brianna tucked her legs up under her chin. For the first time in her life, Brianna felt truly alone. Something inside her had changed, and she couldn't go back to her old self. Everything was different now. The carefree wanderer she had been, Thomas Buck's daughter, was losing her grasp on the world.

Flynn would be her ruin. She had sensed it the moment he'd walked into her jail cell, and that worry had borne disastrous fruit.

What the devil was she to do about him?

REESE BELISHAW THREW BACK THE LAST OF HIS ALE AND slammed his mug down with a contented sigh. His crew filled the tavern, and he smiled as he saw the faces of men he trusted with his life. But no matter how long he might have captained the *Emerald Dragon*, he would never be her first captain, her *true* captain. That honor would always belong to Dominic Grey.

He missed Dom. All of them did. But Dominic's path had changed the moment he'd abducted Admiral Harcourt's daughter. He'd nearly swung from the gallows before a lucky rescue had spared him the noose, but his salvation had come at a great cost. Dominic's pirate days were over. He was a husband and the future Earl of Camden, of all things, and that was enough for him. So Dominic had passed the *Dragon* to Reese, and the crew had agreed to serve under him. But it still felt strangely temporary. As if at any moment Dominic might come back aboard the ship and take over.

"Cap'n?" Chibbs, his first mate, appeared in front of him, breathless and red-faced from running from wherever he had been. Chibbs's merry, round-shaped face and lively demeanor had earned trust and affection from even the roughest of pirates.

"What is it, Chibbs?"

"It's Flynn, Cap'n. Somethin' is wrong."

"What do you mean?" Reese stood, his hand reaching for his belt where his pistol hung.

"Someone from the *Sea Serpent* lured him out of a tavern down the road and, well, hit him hard enough to knock him out. I saw them carrying Flynn off. I thought to meeself that it didn't look right. I mean, he came to us, saying he wanted us to partner with the *Serpent* not so long ago, see if Cap'n Holland would chase prizes with us. So I asked meeself, why would Cap'n Holland's first mate nab Flynn like that?"

"The first mate?" Reese echoed.

"Aye, it was Joe McBride himself who knocked him out."

Something was definitely wrong. Reese could smell it. "Has the *Serpent* left port yet?"

"Just now, the crew were called back to the ship. What should we do?"

"Send word to Dominic at King's Landing. He'll want to know. Did you find out where the *Serpent* is heading? Are they still headed for Cádiz?"

"No, sir. Word by the dock is they're bound for Saint Kitts."

"Saint Kitts . . . ," Reese began.

"Aye, Cap'n. She's headed to Buck's nest. I'd say something's got her spooked."

"But what?" Reese whispered to himself. "Brianna never risks visiting her father when there are naval frigates prowling the waters like this. She must have a damned good reason to go to him."

"You don't think . . . ?" Chibbs began, his face deepening to a dark shade of red.

"Think what?"

"Well . . . that perhaps she and Flynn got too close on her ship and now she might be in the family way? It would explain why Flynn might be carried back to the ship against his will. Mayhap she wants the old man to force Flynn to make an honest woman out of her?"

Reese chuckled at that. He supposed it was possible, but he never thought Brianna Holland would settle down. No, this felt far more serious than a wedding held at the end of a blunderbuss.

"Whatever the reason, we should follow them and find out what to do in order to save Flynn, assuming he needs rescuing. Find the crew and tell them we're going on a rescue mission for Flynn. I think the lads will agree to go."

"Aye, they will. No one would let anything happen to Captain Dom's best mate."

"No, we wouldn't." Flynn would have followed Dominic to the very end of the farthest horizon, and Dominic's former crew would do the same for Dominic's friend.

We're coming, Flynn, Reese promised himself. As he stepped out of the tavern, he looked up into the clear Caribbean skies and took a deep breath. A storm was coming.

CHAPTER 13

Admiral Charles Harcourt finished reading the letter aloud in front of the young midshipman who had delivered it to him. It had come from one of their more reliable spies in Sugar Cove. He set the letter down and weighed his options. "Interesting."

The young man who had carried the letter into Charles's office stood even straighter at attention, if such a thing were possible. "What are your orders, sir?"

"Well . . . it seems we are to sail for Saint Kitts."

"Sir?" the young man asked, confused. "But the letter said that Lieutenant Flynn—"

"Yes, our man relayed Lieutenant Flynn's directions, but he also said he'd heard on the docks that the *Sea Serpent* is bound for Saint Kitts."

"Does that mean you think Flynn lied to us, sir?"

Charles shook his head. "Flynn is our man, through and through. He wouldn't try to misdirect me, not for some pirates." Even as he said it, one worry niggled at him. Flynn had seemed to bond to the young Holland woman enough to want to protect her. Could this have somehow changed Flynn's allegiance? *Surely not.*

Then again, he had seen firsthand how a woman, especially a clever, beautiful one, could change a man's destiny. His own daughter had done that by saving Dominic Greyville, one of the Caribbean's most notorious pirates, from the gallows. Who was to say it could not happen the other way and just as easily doom someone?

The midshipman was still trying to puzzle it all out. "So Flynn didn't lie . . ."

"No, but if they are taking a different course, then the pirates may be onto him. He could very well be in danger. All the more reason for us to make haste for Saint Kitts." Charles scribbled a few letters and then handed them to the midshipman to deliver to the four captains with ships currently docked at Port Royal. Thankfully the crews weren't on shore but had recently returned to their ships within the last few hours. They would be ready to leave quickly.

They would sail for Saint Kitts within the hour. Weather permitting, they could reach the island at the same time Flynn and the pirates did. Perhaps Thomas Buck would be among them. If only luck would grant him that. He looked over his charts to consider the best possible route to take.

A few minutes later, the door to his office burst open and Captain Waverly stormed in.

"Is it true? You're going after the Holland boy?" Waverly's dark eyes blazed with cruel excitement.

Charles frowned. It was his duty to uphold the law, but there should be no thrill or joy in condemning another man to death. Souls who wandered off the path of lawful behavior were to be mourned and pitied, not salivated after like a hound treeing a terrified fox. And Waverly was nothing short of a sadist.

"We are pursuing a possible lead," Charles answered carefully, but Waverly seemed quite able to read him.

"It must be some lead, Admiral, if you are mobilizing every ship in port. I will have a contingent of my men ready to sail on your ships and lead them personally."

"Really, Captain, you need not do that. This is a naval matter, after all. We are looking into a possible sighting." Charles knew he could refuse to take soldiers, as he was the real seat of power in the fort, but refusing to let the soldiers come if they did encounter Buck could put his ability to hold his position in jeopardy.

"And if you should come across Buck's lair? If there is any fighting to be done upon the land, you will need my men," Waverly reminded him with a cold smile.

"Captain, really—" Charles started, but Waverly had already spun and walked away.

"Damnation," Charles muttered. Now he would have to worry about keeping Waverly away from Nicholas and the Holland girl. The captain had developed a personal hatred for Holland and even Nicholas. Charles would very much like to prevent whatever might occur should the two men meet again.

Perhaps if Charles found Buck, that would keep Waverly's interest away from Nicholas. He could only hope, because he was fond of Nicholas. The man was the son he'd never had, and he wasn't about to let some sadistic madman like Waverly do him harm.

SLEEPING CHAINED TO THE WALL WAS NOT HOW NICHOLAS would have preferred to spend the last two nights. He'd woken up briefly the first night to see the cabin boy remove a few of Brianna's things out of the room. The second night, Joe had paid him a visit with some questions that had left Nicholas aching with bruised ribs and a sore jaw.

Patrick was the only crew member he had seen for the last three days, aside from Joe. The cabin boy had emptied the chamber pot, and brought him food and drink as well as a sponge and water for bathing. He was talkative enough whenever Nicholas spoke to him. However, when Nicholas asked the lad how Brianna was faring, the boy flushed.

"I'm not supposed to say," Patrick said. "She's very angry."

"At me?"

Flynn chuckled wryly at the boy's wide-eyed nod.

"What—what did you say to her?" Patrick asked in a grave whisper.

"She hasn't told you?"

"No. No one knows you're in here but me, Joe, and the captain. The rest still think you're in Sugar Cove."

"So if the captain isn't sleeping here, where is she staying?"

"She's sleeping in Joe's cabin."

Flynn suddenly leapt to his feet. Had the girl moved on so quickly? With Joe? He had to be, what, twenty years her—

"Joe's sleeping on the floor," Patrick added, his voice hushed.

"Oh. So they aren't . . . ?"

"Aren't what?" Patrick asked, and a knowing look reached his face. "You think they're tupping?" The boy suddenly laughed. "Lord no, Mr. Flynn. Joe wouldn't . . . not with the captain. He's like an uncle to her, practically helped raise her. And right now they fight too much to—"

"Well, sometimes fighting leads to tupping," Nicholas muttered darkly, then paused to consider what Patrick had said. "What are they fighting about?"

"*You*, of course. Joe wants to hang you from the yardarm, but the captain won't do it. She says you're worth more alive than dead."

"How comforting," Nicholas sighed. "Can you tell me where we're headed?" He could only see endless bright blue water through the tall windows of the captain's quarters.

"Well . . . I suppose I can tell you, on account of you helping me before. We're approaching Saint Kitts."

"Saint Kitts? Why there?" He knew there were rumored to be pirates in Saint Kitts who attacked sugar-laden ships bound for England, but nearly every island in the West Indies had its pirate nests. Saint Kitts, like most of the islands around it, had a legacy of bloodshed, with the French and British massacring the Carib people who lived on the island in the middle of the seventeenth century.

"Are we docking at Basseterre?" It was the island's capital city. If Flynn had to guess, that's where he would make berth.

"Eat up, Mr. Flynn. We'll be docking soon." Patrick rushed away, leaving Flynn alone in the cabin with his questions unanswered and his food untouched at his feet. He flexed his wrist, testing the strength of the manacle that kept him bound here.

A soft voice came from the doorway behind him. "Planning your escape?"

Flynn shot Brianna a wicked grin over his shoulder. "Naturally." He was a man facing death, and he wanted to laugh madly in defiance.

"Rumor has it we're docking at Basseterre," he said, watching her face for a reaction to his guess. Her eyes widened slightly and her lips parted before she could stop herself.

"Patrick . . . ," she growled, her fists clenching. He'd heard men describe women as being in a "fine fury," and now he could understand the phrase. She was lovely—more than lovely. She still wore her snug breeches, and her shapely calves were on display beneath her white stockings. Her trim waist was molded by her waistcoat, and her long gold hair flowed behind her, loosely tied with a ribbon. She was every inch a pirate queen. He would have done anything to take her into his arms again and taste her, to feel the wild pulse at her throat as he nuzzled her neck and the warm breath of her sighs in his ears as he made love to her. Instead, he fisted his hands at his sides to keep from foolishly reaching for her.

"Don't blame the boy. He didn't say a word. I merely recognize these waters," he lied. "There's a certain shade of blue that only exists near Saint Kitts or Nevis."

She arched a dark gold brow at him. "Is that so?"

"It is." He smiled at her again, and for a second something fractured in her hard glare before it vanished. His chest tightened as he felt whatever had been growing between them, such a new, fragile thing, slip out of his grip and into the endless sea far below.

"You will remain here until . . ." Her voice faltered a little. "Until I figure out what the bloody hell to do with you."

Nicholas didn't try to beg or bargain. Whatever decision she came to would be the right one for her. That would have to be enough for him.

"Very well. I await your decision, Captain."

BRIANNA STEPPED OUT OF HER CABIN AND CLOSED THE door, locking it behind her the way she'd done every night for the last three nights. She'd come long after he'd fallen asleep to check on him, and then after she couldn't bear to watch him anymore, she'd leave. Each time Patrick left, she or Joe guarded the cabin door, but he did it nonchalantly, since his room was next door. It was still dangerous for Flynn every second that he was aboard her ship.

She knew what was expected of her, but she didn't have the will to see it through. And if the crew found out, it could mean the end of her career as a pirate. It was a damned good thing they were in her father's waters. The crew would be on their best behavior. No one crossed Thomas Buck, and no one would dare mutiny against his daughter so close to Buck's home.

Calls from the deck above told her they had reached Basseterre, but she already knew. She'd felt her ship dock by the way it had slowed to a stop, the anchor dropping giving it a little tug before it stopped. Steps from the companion ladder above made her tense a little, but only Joe appeared, not a crewman angry at being deceived. It was getting to the point where she always expected a revolt now.

"I've sent word to your father that you'll see him soon. I'll stand watch here until you get back." Joe settled in against the doorframe, gently muscling her out of the way.

"Thank you, Joe." She impulsively kissed his cheek, and the Scotsman blushed and grumbled something about "navy louts" under his breath. It wasn't often that she showed affection like that to Joe in public. It was important to always act like the captain she was, but she was bound so tight with worry for Flynn—and for herself and her ship—that she'd relied more than usual on Joe.

"I'll be back as soon as I can." She rushed up the companion ladder to the deck. Her crew were taking the gangplank down to the dock while others tied the mooring lines to the posts. She felt the entire ship's crew's eyes on her as she leapt onto the gangplank and strode confidently down to the dock. It was probably just her shaken nerves, but she had a growing fear that the crew knew something wasn't right on board, and she didn't want them to see her running to her father with her tail tucked between her legs.

Basseterre was bustling under the midday sun. With the sugar trade still booming on Saint Kitts, there were plenty of dockworkers loading crates of cargo onto dozens of ships. The harbormaster, as per agreement with her father, would register the *Sea Serpent* under a less conspicuous name.

Brianna wove her way through the docks until she reached the city, where a familiar sight greeted her. A dark-blue coach waiting in its usual spot. She rolled her eyes but walked over to the fancy conveyance. The driver spotted her and leapt down to open the door for her.

"Miss Brianna," the middle-aged driver greeted with a warm smile.

"Hello, Phineas." She hugged the driver before climbing inside. Phineas has been with her father for more than fifteen years. Her father insisted on treating her like a fine lady, which meant each time she came to Basseterre, she was expected to allow Phineas to drive her to her father's home.

"Your father will be right pleased to see you." Phineas winked at her as he closed the door and climbed back on his perch. The carriage jolted into motion, and Brianna settled back on the dark-blue velvet cushions. The home her father had built was up in the hills, but it didn't take more than half an hour to reach it. When they pulled in front of it, she opened the door and hopped out before Phineas could assist her. She started toward the veranda of the white-pillared plantation house, where she could already see her father waiting for her.

"Bri, darling," her father's booming voice greeted her. His dark hair was threaded with silver, but he was still a dashing man for his age. "Fit and fighting," as Joe would declare anytime someone asked how Thomas Buck fared.

"Father!" She laughed as he grabbed her by the waist and lifted her up, swinging her around. His eyes crinkled at the corners as he smiled down at her.

"I was delighted when Joe's message arrived." He kissed her forehead, and she laughed again as she pulled away.

"Stop it. I'm not a child," she reminded him.

"A fact I'm well aware of. Reports of your latest prizes have been impressive. You and the *Sea Serpent* have been busy." His eyes twinkled with mischievous pride only a piratical father like him could be capable of.

She was glad he hadn't heard about her capture in Port

Royal, but she was going to have to tell him sooner or later, and she'd rather it came from her.

"Yes, well . . ." She looked down at the toes of her boots, and he tucked his hand under her chin, lifting her face so she couldn't avoid his eyes.

"What is it, Brianna?"

"We docked in Port Royal for a quick supply run . . ." She swallowed hard. "Joe was recognized. I gave him time to escape, but I was apprehended."

Her father's face paled. "And I'm guessing from your tone that you were not released after offering some convincing tall tale to your captors?"

She shook her head.

Her father put an arm around her shoulders. "Come inside and tell me everything, from the beginning. Leave no detail out."

He led her to the kitchen, where Brianna told him everything. *Almost*. She left out the part where she and Nicholas had shared her bed.

"So now Flynn is chained up in my cabin and the navy should be on their way to Cádiz if they believed the message he sent them. But I'm worried, Father. This feels different than their past attempts to capture you."

Thomas stood from the table where he and Brianna had been drinking tea and paced the length of the kitchen. "Well, it isn't the first time a spy has been sent among my men. But I admit, none have gotten this close before. And that Waverly fellow you mentioned . . ."

Elida, his Spanish housekeeper, was busy kneading bread on the table. Her eyes flitted between Brianna and her father. She seemed to sense that Thomas was worried.

She had been with Buck as long as Phineas had been, perhaps even longer. Brianna couldn't remember a time when the brown-eyed Spanish beauty hadn't been in their lives.

"*Señor*, finish your tea," Elida said with such gentle affection and command that Thomas obeyed without question. He retrieved his cup from the table, sipping at it but still pacing.

"Father, what's the matter?" Brianna had never seen her father like this.

"You're right to be worried. You can never assume that the Royal Navy doesn't have the upper hand. Even if this Flynn fellow believes he sent them off in the wrong direction, it doesn't mean another spy in Sugar Cove wasn't watching your movements."

"You think we aren't safe?" She slowly got to her feet, a terrible sense of dread clenching her chest in its invisible hands and squeezing.

Her father smiled. "Darling, you of all people know that we're *never* safe. But yes, this does feel different."

"We have to leave. *You* must leave."

"Let me think a moment." He scowled, his thoughts turned inward, and then he faced Brianna again. "You said this man is an officer?"

"Yes, a lieutenant. Does that matter?"

"It might." He set his teacup down, once again deep in thought. "I want him transferred to the *Sea Hawk*'s brig at once. He will be a useful bargaining chip. If he was a simple seaman, they would probably leave him to die, but if he's an officer, he's likely to be a well-born young man. It will be a matter of honor to see him safely returned, or else they could face consequences back in England for letting the son of an aristocrat die."

"You think he's well-born?"

"At the least, he'll be a country gentleman's son. Lads who start out as midshipmen must have family connections with a captain or be of particularly high standing or influential socially."

That explained so much, she thought. Flynn was from a different world. He had a refined elegance to his manners that still showed beneath his charming roguish ways. She had thought him a gentleman pirate when she'd first met him. She'd been right about the gentleman part.

"Brianna." Her father's voice pulled her out of her thoughts. "I know you must have liked this fellow, but whatever he said to you, it cannot be true. Remember that."

He need not have reminded her. It was why everything in her world was now tinged with shades of gray. He had robbed her world of color and sparkle, and yet she couldn't hate him for it.

"I know," she sighed. "We had better leave now."

"Elida, you know what to do until I return." He pulled the pretty housekeeper to him, stealing a quick kiss. She blushed and mumbled something in Spanish before leaving the room, her eyes bright with tears.

"It's getting harder and harder to leave her," Thomas confessed to Brianna in a rough voice.

She understood now why her father wanted to settle down. He and Elida had grown close over the years, and the thought of having to leave her to face a possibly gruesome fate at the hands of the navy was a heavy weight upon him. She'd felt that awful sinking feeling when she'd first had to part ways with Flynn, and she'd only known the man a short time. Her father had shared his life with Elida for almost twenty years.

Brianna cleared her throat and caught her father's sleeve as they resumed their walk side by side through the house.

"Why not marry Elida? She's loved you for years."

Thomas looked stunned. "You would not be angry with me?" he asked.

Brianna paused, her hand resting on the front door. "Why would I be angry with you? You deserve to be loved again."

"You wouldn't feel as though I'd abandoned you?"

"What? Of course not. I wouldn't ever feel that way. What's the point of life if you only end up in the hangman's noose?" She didn't tell him that she would miss him, because until she too gave up pirating, she'd have to stay away from him most of the year to keep him safe.

At this, her father's eyes glowed. "That would mean returning to England. I wouldn't be able to stay here safely in the West Indies. It's not like the old days when Morgan became lieutenant-governor. I'd never be safe here, not even in Saint Kitts, not if I want to truly enjoy life and not hide away on my plantation."

"I know." It meant he would be leaving her alone in the islands, unless she chose to go with him.

"We have time to discuss this later. Now we must deal with your officer."

NICK WAS STANDING WITH HIS GAZE SEARCHING THE SEAS through the windows of Brianna's cabin, his legs braced and his hands behind his back in a military stance, with only an inch of slack on his chain. He didn't turn when the cabin door opened.

"All right, laddie, time to go," Joe said.

So, a decision had been made.

The Scotsman wasn't alone in the cabin doorway. Another man stood beside him. This man wore black breeches and a white shirt, had dark hair and was built more leanly than Joe, perhaps in his midforties. The man held himself in a way that warned Nicholas he was dangerous, but he was more interested in the man's eyes. They were sharp, missing nothing as they took his measure. There was only one person besides his captain Joe would open the door for, and only one man who had the gaze of a clever fox.

"Thomas Buck," Nicholas said with a small nod.

"Mr. Flynn," Buck answered just as calmly. "It seems we find ourselves in a rather difficult situation."

"It seems so."

"You saved my daughter's life. That puts me in your debt. But you also used and manipulated her to find me on behalf of the Royal Navy, something that could cost many lives. I would say that puts us on a little more even footing, does it not?"

Nicholas didn't reply.

"Since the navy is hunting me, I will take you onto my ship to use as a bargaining tool, if necessary. If we can get to England without anyone chasing my ship or Brianna's, you will be set free to return home, with the promise that you will not reveal our final destination."

"You trust I would keep that a secret?" Nicholas asked.

"*Trust* is not a word wielded easily in my world, Mr. Flynn. But I think you will keep that secret for two reasons. First, it is my intention to retire from and have no more business pirating at sea. Second, I do not believe you would willingly put Brianna in danger, and as she will be with me, that would surely seal her fate. If you agree, I will see to it you are set free. If we are attacked, I will use you however I see fit to save my daughter and my crew."

Nicholas waited a moment before replying. "I understand and agree to silence." If Buck truly planned to hang it up, then there was no longer a point in chasing him. A man like Waverly would hunt him until one of them died, but not Nicholas.

"You may unchain him, Joe," Buck commanded.

Joe unlocked the manacle, and Flynn rubbed at the reddened flesh around his wrist.

"Follow me, Mr. Flynn." Buck left the cabin, and Nicholas fell in step behind him, suddenly boxed in between Buck and Joe. When they reached the upper decks, he saw Brianna and her crew watching him from one side of the ship. He met her judging gaze, wishing he had a chance to say something.

"Holland," Buck called out. His daughter joined them at the gangplank that now connected the *Sea Serpent* to the ship next to it.

"Say your goodbyes," Buck said to her, then crossed the gangplank to the other ship.

Joe cleared his throat and stepped away. They had a moment alone, at least to be unheard. Nicholas wasn't sure what to say. There were a thousand things that hung upon his lips. But the crew was watching them, and he didn't want anyone to see something that would weaken Brianna in their minds. Every man on board had to be wondering what was happening. He too wondered what would happen once he left her ship. He was in the world of pirates now, a shark-filled sea, and he had nothing to cling to, nothing but his own limbs to keep his head above water . . . and even that would only draw danger to him that much faster.

"Your father says he will free me," he said instead of everything else on his mind.

"If he says he will, then he will." She lifted her chin, prideful and trying to bury the hurt he'd caused her. It was all his fault. He'd wounded this beautiful pirate queen beyond imagining, and he wondered if she'd ever trust a man enough to get close to her again.

Silence settled between them, and the wind rippled through the canvas above their heads.

"Brianna." He said her name softly, and her lovely eyes, such a summery green, held him fast in a warm dream that would end all too soon.

"Was—was any of it real?" she asked in a quiet voice. "You . . . me . . . what we shared. Am I mad for wanting it to be real?" There was both vulnerability and condemnation in her words. He wondered for a moment if he should lie, if it would make it easier for her if he said he'd felt nothing. It might give her a chance to dismiss the entire affair and start her life over. But his heart commanded that he tell the truth. He owed her that.

"I was never a pirate, but I helped the *Emerald Dragon* escape the navy, and Dominic Greyville truly is my dearest friend in all the world." He paused, drawing in a breath. "And what happened between us, all of that was real. Perhaps, in another life . . ." He stopped before he said something foolishly romantic.

"In another life?" she urged him to finish.

Seeing the hope burning in her eyes, the words tumbled from his mouth.

"In another life, I would've moved the heavens themselves to make you mine." Before she could respond, he crossed the gangplank to where Thomas Buck stood waiting for him. He didn't look back, didn't want the image of her sorrowful face etched in his mind. He would cling to other memories, ones where those eyes sparkled with mischief and life.

Nicholas ignored the stares of Buck's crew as he was led down to the brig. Yet another cell was waiting for him. He turned toward the bars as they clanged shut. Brianna's father made as if to leave.

"Buck!" he called out.

Buck's jaw clenched as he faced Nicholas again. "Yes?"

"You must make her leave the West Indies. She isn't safe here. There's a captain in His Majesty's army, a man named Waverly—he won't stop until he finds you and her. I got her out of the jail in Port Royal before he discovered she was a woman. But if he learns what she really is, Brianna will never truly be safe."

Buck came to the bars and leaned against them, studying him. "Why does her fate concern you so much? She is just another pirate, one of hundreds who live dangerous lives."

Nicholas knew the truth might not sit well with him, so he kept silent.

Buck's sad smile was the only thing about him that

reminded him of Brianna. They had no other features in common.

"Does she know that you love her?" Buck asked.

"Yes, but that doesn't matter. I know our fates aren't bound together. I just wish . . . I wish she had a different life, one that didn't risk her life ending with six feet of rope and three feet of air underneath her feet."

Buck gave a short nod and left without another word. Nicholas was left alone in the cell as the ship made ready to sail.

Nicholas knew he would never see Brianna again. He had become a pawn between the pirates and the navy, and he had been a damned fool to fall in love with the Shadow King's daughter.

CHAPTER 14

The bosun's whistle, calling men to arms, came too late. Nicholas had been sitting on an overturned crate and brooding when he heard the shouts of warning on the deck above, following the piercing whistle. Only a navy ship could cause such distress here.

Buck's ship was moving fast, no doubt trying to slip out of the bay next to Basseterre, but if Admiral Harcourt was in command, the man would have his fleet surround the entrance long before the pirates knew they were trapped. Both Buck and Brianna would be captured...or killed.

"Hey!" Nicholas shouted at the companion ladder near his cell. Feet thundered overhead as men rushed to open gun ports and roll out the cannons. His thoughts turned to Brianna and the *Sea Serpent*, striking him with a fear he'd never felt before. He reminded himself that she was more than capable of defending herself and her crew, but that didn't reduce his fear for her.

His fingers curled around the bars. "I need to see Captain

Buck!" he shouted again. He yanked on the iron, but it wouldn't budge. This was the second time he had been locked up during a major sea battle. It would have shamed him if he hadn't been so bloody worried. This time it was worse, because Brianna was the one in danger.

Christ, her father was right. He was in love with the woman, and if anything happened to her . . . He stopped to listen to the sudden silence on deck. Perhaps the navy didn't send too many ships and they—

Guns exploded above him, and the ship rumbled with the angry thunder of their report. Nicholas braced his legs and held on to the bars of his cell as the massive ship quivered with the force of battle. From what Nicholas had briefly seen, Buck's vessel was a fast sloop in good condition. He suspected it had been beached yearly to remove barnacles from the hull and repair any damage done during its voyages. If it could slip through the gaps between the naval vessels, it might stand a chance. Then again, if the ship took gunfire on its broadside at close range from the cannons, it would sink in minutes, taking him to the bottom and drowning him in the brig. If he drowned in the brig, he'd never find a way to get to Brianna's ship or stop the navy from firing upon the *Sea Serpent*.

"Help!" Nicholas shouted, but his voice was drowned out by the sounds of battle all around him.

He broke apart the crate that served as a stool and pushed several planks of wood between the iron, hoping to force the bars with leverage. For a few brief seconds he heard the iron groan, but it did not budge. With a curse, he kicked the bars and pressed his head against them, eyes closed in defeat.

The sound of feet on the companion ladder forced his eyes back open. Buck came toward the cell door, his face lined with concern and looking years older.

"What the devil is going on up there, Buck?"

"The navy has blocked us in. I fear the only way any of us can get out of this is if I surrender." The cold piratical look faded from Buck's eyes, and Nicholas saw a man as mortal as any other. "They won't sink us if I turn myself in, will they? Brianna and her crew might make an escape if I distract them with my surrender. Brianna . . ." He halted on her name, and Nicholas understood the fear in Buck's voice now. It wasn't for himself but for his daughter.

"It's too late. I never planned for her to be caught up in this, but now . . ." Nicholas shook his head. "She was supposed to slip free of the net before it closed around you. That was always my plan. But we both know she'd never run, not when she knows her father is in danger."

Rather than curse him, Buck's eyes lit, and he fumbled for the keys to the cell.

"It may not be over yet. I have an idea, but it requires your help and trust. Tell me, what are you willing to do to save Brianna?"

"I would do anything for her."

Buck unlocked the cell. "Then follow me. We have no time to waste."

Nicholas hurried after Buck as he moved through the chaos of his ship in the midst of battle. Every man was either at the sails or at the guns. Even the small boys known as powder monkeys were leaping about, carrying powder down the line of guns.

Buck opened the door to his captain's cabin and

motioned for Nicholas to join him inside. Through the windows at the stern, Nicholas saw the harbor of Basseterre and the chaos of dockworkers fleeing as round shots of cannon-balls launched perilously close to shore.

Buck threw open the chest at the foot of his bed and dug through layers of clothes until he found what he was searching for, an oiled leather satchel. He shoved it into Nicholas's arms.

"Inside this is the key to saving her," Buck said. "It is proof about her true family."

"What do you mean, her true family?"

"Aye, she was never *truly* mine, Flynn. I found her parents on a sinking ship not far from here. Her father was beyond saving, and her mother bore Brianna in the middle of a raging storm right before she died. Before he passed, her father gave me this."

Buck pulled out a signet ring hanging from a leather cord around his neck and held it out to Nicholas. The crest emblazoned on it was one that Nicholas had grown up knowing. He, like every young English aristocrat, had learned to recognize the crests of the most powerful families in England.

"That is the crest from the House of Essex. But how . . . ?"

"Her father was the duke's younger brother."

"Brianna is the Duke of Essex's niece?"

"Aye." Buck pushed Nicholas into the passageway. "And with that knowledge, you can save her."

Assuming he could get to her in time. Her uncle had almost as much influence as the Crown itself.

Nicholas and Buck raced up to the deck and skidded to a

stop beneath a sudden rainstorm that rolled toward Saint Kitts. The rain nearly obscured the naval ships in the distance. Bursts of white fire in the storm showed the location of the ships' guns as they fired.

"Where's Brianna?" Nicholas asked. Buck peered into the distance, searching for her ship, then pointed to another sloop farther away.

"There! They closed in on the *Serpent* when the storm rolled in." Buck cursed. "She's trying to draw them off. They think I'm aboard that ship."

"Why would they think that?"

"Before I gave Brianna command of the *Sea Serpent*, she was my ship for nearly twenty years."

Nicholas looked between the *Sea Serpent* and the naval ships, judged their speed and direction, and saw a growing opening where the *Sea Hawk* could escape, given the right conditions.

Nicholas put a hand on Buck's shoulder, forcing his gaze away from Brianna's ship and the crew that was fighting valiantly for her. "Buck . . ."

"Raise the white fla—" Buck started to shout.

"Belay that!" Nicholas shouted over him.

Buck glared at him, but Nicholas shook his head. "If you stay, you *both* die. If you run, there is a chance I can save her."

"Are you mad? She's *my* daughter. I raised her. I'll not leave her now." Buck's voice broke, and it knifed Nicholas's heart. How many times had Nicholas heard Dominic's father speak like this, never giving up searching for his missing son?

"You will see her again, but not from a hangman's noose," Nicholas promised.

Buck looked out toward his daughter's direction once more. "What about you? How will you get to her?"

"I'll need your jolly boat."

There was a moment where their eyes met, a father facing the man who loved his daughter enough to risk his life and betray his country. Buck must have seen that in Nicholas's eyes, because he shouted to his crew a second later.

"Lower the jolly!" Buck bellowed. His men raced to lower the small boat into the water, even as another volley from the enemy landed dangerously close to the *Sea Hawk*. Nicholas slung the leather satchel over his arm and climbed down the side of the ship, taking one last chance to look up at its captain. Buck stood on the waist deck of the ship, the black flag decorated with a white hawk flying high above him as he gave Nicholas a solemn nod before he and his crew made ready to escape behind a veil of heavy rain.

Godspeed to you, Shadow King.

Nicholas settled himself into the small boat and raised the sails, then headed for the distant battling ships that looked like ghosts as they dueled within the storm.

THEY WERE LOSING. CANNON-BALLS TORE ACROSS THE deck of Brianna's beloved ship. Everything seemed to happen so much slower beneath the heavy rain. Men lay on the deck, some blown to pieces, others valiantly fighting on. They'd managed to draw the fire away from her father's ship and give him an opening to get past the frigates and out into open water where the *Sea Hawk* could outrun them. But the

Serpent wouldn't be able to make the same escape. Her main-mast was down, and her crew were fighting for their very lives.

"We canna last long, lass," Joe said. His chest expanded as he sucked in a deep lungful of air. He had been up in the rigging with the topmen to handle the sails, hoping to escape their current position. But the naval ships had caged the *Sea Serpent* in.

"Where's my father?" She searched the bay and saw no sign of the *Sea Hawk*. Had he managed to escape? She could only hope so, because her crew were paying for this chance with their lives.

"He managed to slip away," Joe said. "I saw the *Sea Hawk* leave with my own eyes."

Another deafening burst of cannon fire rattled the ship. They would sink if they took another hit like that.

"Raise the white flag, Joe," she said calmly.

"Are ye sure?" he asked her.

Brianna saw men bleeding out on her deck; the cries of her crew were drowning her, along with the torrential rains.

"It's our only chance. If we raise the flag, they will cease firing and our men can swim to shore before the enemy boards us." They were close enough that most of the men who were strong swimmers could reach shore and vanish onto the island.

Joe nodded and cupped a hand by his mouth. "Raise the white flag!"

She watched the pale flag shoot up the mast and whip wildly as the wind and rain lashed against it. What felt like an eternity later, the other three ships stopped firing upon the *Sea Serpent*.

"Have our men abandon ship. Now!"

"Are ye coming, lass?"

She nodded. "You go. I'll be with you in a moment."

Joe gave the order to lower all the lifeboats they had left, and any man who could swim was welcome to go. Her men crawled over the side and jumped into the water as fast as they could, Joe following behind. Brianna raced down the companion ladder, shouting at men she saw still manning the guns to abandon ship. By the time she reached her cabin, she had but a few minutes to gather her beloved possessions—including her mother's hairbrush—and stuff them into a satchel before leaving the cabin. Booted steps on the deck above made her freeze. The voices she heard were not those of her crew. She listened to her ship groan and the waves crashing against its side, and above that, the masculine voices coming ever closer.

Blast and damnation . . . Her ship had been boarded sooner than she'd expected. Brianna ran back to her cabin and barred the door with a chair, sliding the lock into place. Her mind raced over a dozen possible ideas, but only one gave her a chance to avoid being thought a pirate. She stripped out of her breeches and other masculine clothes and hastily pulled on her red dress. She rushed to fasten the laces at her breasts and tighten the bodice. The voices were louder now, and a fist pounded on her door.

"Open up! You are hereby ordered to surrender."

Brianna briefly stared at the glass windows of her cabin, wishing now that a cannon-ball had shattered them. If it had, she could have leapt through the hole and dropped into the water and escaped instead of embarrassing herself like this.

"Break it down!" someone shouted outside the cabin door.

Cursing her luck, Brianna pulled the chair back from the door and unlocked it.

She gasped through shining tears as four men stumbled into the room, "Please! Don't hurt me! I'm not a pirate." One man was a young officer, while the other three were common seamen. The officer held up a pistol, aiming it at her chest.

"Arrest this woman."

"No! Please! I was being kept here against my will. Those pirates *kidnapped* me." Brianna broke into pitiful sobs, and the men all glanced at each other uncertainly.

The young officer lowered his pistol a little, caught off guard. "Er . . . Apologies, miss. It's all right . . . please stop crying."

One of the seamen growled, "Don't be daft, sir. She ain't innocent. She's just a pirate's doxy," and lunged for Brianna. She reacted on instinct, knocking the man down with a blow from her satchel. Unfortunately, the other two men managed to grab her arms, pinning her back on the bed. When the young officer tried to intervene, one of the men knocked him out flat with a fist. He collapsed onto the floor.

She screamed with rage and kicked out. "How *dare* you!" But her cries were ignored as she was pinned down on the bed. Brianna was strong, yet she couldn't fight the muscles of these two men as they held her.

"Let me have her first," the one she'd felled snarled as he climbed up from the floor.

"You cannot rape a woman," Brianna tried to protest. But she knew they would. Bad men were bad men—it didn't matter what flag they sailed under—just as there were good men who sailed as pirates.

One man laughed. "You're nothing but a pirate's whore. That's different."

Brianna was going to kill every one of these men in a terribly painful way the moment she had a chance, and she *would* find her chance . . .

Someone reached for her skirts, and she lashed out, kicking the face of the man who'd touched her. She felt a nose break beneath her boot, and the man screamed in pain. She laughed in triumph.

"You little bitch!" One of the others slapped her with a blow so hard it blacked her vision for a precious few seconds and she tasted blood. Rough hands were everywhere they shouldn't be. She screamed, a primal sound of female fury that in the ancient days would have called the sea to rise up to drown each man who had dared to hurt her. A pistol fired, and everyone froze.

Gasping for breath, Brianna stared at the man standing in the doorway of her cabin, black rage filling his cold blue eyes. How the devil—? Her thoughts were interrupted when her rescuer spoke.

"Unhand that woman at once," he said. "Or I swear you shall eat a bullet."

Slowly, the hands on her body withdrew. Brianna stared at her unexpected savior.

"Who are you?" the man demanded.

"Lieutenant Nicholas Flynn. I'm here under the orders of Admiral Harcourt."

"We were only having a bit of fun . . . She's just a pirate's wench, is all."

"On that you're quite wrong. The woman you just accosted is *my wife* and the niece of the Duke of Essex. He will see you punished for what you've done to her."

"What?" the man scoffed. "Her, a fancy duke's niece? What's she doing here, then?"

Brianna had but a moment to take Nicholas's clever lies and use them to shore up her own story.

"I'm here because I was *kidnapped* by pirates, you bloody fools. I was on my way to my husband when my ship was set upon by pirates and I was taken prisoner. Now you've found me, but rather than rescue me, you've *dared* to assault me." She jerked free of the men and scrambled off the bed. Nicholas held out a hand to her, and she rushed into his embrace. He caught her and held her close, still keeping one arm raised and aimed at the three men who had assaulted her. The young officer that had been knocked out came around with a groan.

"Are you all right?" Nicholas whispered so only she could hear.

"I'll feel much better after you give me your pistol and I've shot the bastards," she hissed back.

"Yes, well, that I cannot do. But play along and I might be able to save your life."

She set aside her revenge plans and gave a big, theatrical sob as she buried her face against his shoulder.

"We didn't know who the wench was, honest," one of the men protested.

"There's my clever girl," he chuckled before he kissed the crown of her hair the way only a concerned husband would. Later she would digest the fact that she'd had to play the role of Flynn's wife.

He lowered the pistol and tucked it into the belt on his waist. "The admiral would hear you plead your case. Come, my dear, let's get you somewhere safe."

Flynn ushered her up the companion ladder to the upper decks. She skidded to a stop at the sight of her remaining crew. Six of them under guard who hadn't gotten off the ship in time, their weapons lying on the deck. Her cabin boy was among them. Patrick wore a stoic expression like all the rest. None of them breathed a word as she was forced to walk past them with Flynn's protective arm around her shoulder. Her eyes burned with traitorous tears at the thought that they would protect her with their silence to their last breath, and she felt like a coward for not admitting who she was and joining them in their fate. But here, at least, she might find an opportunity later on to save them.

The admiral and a few of the captains of the other ships were clustered, speaking together.

"Admiral," Nicholas called out to him. "A word, if you don't mind?"

The admiral turned, and his eyes widened ever so slightly as he spotted Brianna.

"Of course, Lieutenant." The admiral excused himself and joined them.

"Admiral," Flynn whispered. "I need you to trust me. I can explain it all once we are safely in private."

"I trust you," the admiral replied without hesitation.

"Good. This is my new wife, Brianna Flynn, but she was born Brianna St. Laurent, and is niece to the Duke of Essex."

"Niece to the—" The admiral's brow rose. "What are you playing at, Flynn?"

"Trust me, Admiral, it's true. I will explain soon, but right now we need to protect her."

"Er . . . yes. Of course." The admiral cleared his throat and walked back to the men under his command, who were watching him curiously. He spoke to them in hushed tones, and whatever he said was apparently believed.

"This way, Lieutenant. You and your wife shall be taken aboard my ship at once."

She and Flynn walked past her crew, and she felt the weight of their stares as a lump formed in her throat. They were all going to hang. She'd run out of clever games and escape routes. No tomato-throwing or grand chases in a marketplace would save her men this time . . . or herself. She would face whatever Flynn had in store for her, and she'd do everything in her power to come up with a plan to rescue her crew.

The storm that had shrouded her father's escape had let up, and she looked out to the sea.

Goodbye, Father. She squared her shoulders, ready to face the end of her freedom with every last ounce of courage she had left. And if she had any bit of luck remaining, she'd save her men.

CHAPTER 15

Nicholas escorted Brianna into a spacious cabin on Admiral Harcourt's ship. He kept himself calm, at least as far as the other seamen aboard could see, but deep down he was so relieved he could scarcely believe he'd succeeded. He'd found her and saved her before . . . He tried not to think about what those men would have done to her. She'd fought like a lioness, but she'd been outnumbered.

He kept his arm around her shoulders and noticed she was starting to shake against him. The same often happened to him after a dangerous fight at sea. He'd shake for several minutes until the shock of it all wore off. She'd most likely be furious with him once she got back to feeling like herself again.

"Where are we?" she asked. Her voice sounded almost numb.

"One of the officer's cabins. Why don't you sit down?"

Flynn dropped his arm from her shoulders and nudged her toward the bed.

One of the officers had given up his cabin so that Nicholas's bride would have a more comfortable journey back to Jamaica. Little did the officer know that Brianna was no delicate English rose who would wilt at the sight of a small cabin. Still, after the day she'd had, she needed to rest and recover.

Brianna collapsed onto the bed, her gaze distant and her body trembling. She was soaked to the bone like he was, but Nicholas feared she might be going into shock. He closed the cabin door, setting down the satchel that Thomas Buck had entrusted to him, along with the bag that she'd retrieved from her ship. He came and knelt in front of her, his face level with her own in that position, and cupped her face gently in his hands.

"Brianna." He cupped her face gently in his hands. "Brianna. Look at me."

Her glassy gaze slowly sharpened. "Why did you save me? Why lie? I should be with my men in the brig." The loss of her ship, her father, her men, and her freedom . . . this was a woman who had lost everything. Tougher men would have crumbled from such a loss.

"I didn't lie. Well, the bit about us being married, yes, but the other part, that wasn't a lie. You see—"

A knock on the cabin door interrupted him. He cursed and checked to see who it was. The admiral stood in the passageway, eyes fixed on Nicholas.

"Come in, sir." He stepped back to allow the admiral inside before he closed the door again. At least he wouldn't have to tell the story twice.

"You promised me answers, my boy. Now, what the devil is all this?"

"Sir, this woman is Brianna, daughter of Hugh and Beatrice St. Laurent, the younger brother and sister-in-law of the Duke of Essex."

Though he was speaking to the admiral, Nicholas didn't take his eyes off Brianna. Her eyes flew wide in disbelief. He couldn't begin to imagine how his next words would devastate her. To take Buck's fatherhood away from her, only to then deliver news of the fate of her true parents. It was a blow he would wish upon no one. He only hoped that she would forgive him for what he was about to say.

"But how? He and his wife were lost at sea twenty years ago. We searched everywhere for them. I was a young captain then and tasked with finding them. There was simply no trace to be found."

Brianna mouthed the words *lost at sea*, and the look in her eyes showed him that this news had upended her entire world.

"Thomas Buck came across a ship that had struck a reef in a storm. He found only two survivors still alive, a man and his pregnant wife. She was in the final moments of birthing her child when Buck discovered them. The husband soon died of his injuries, while the wife bestowed her mother's name upon the child before she too passed."

Brianna's lips trembled as she blinked in a daze, as though this was all some rather maddening dream she couldn't wake from.

"Lady Brianna was Beatrice St. Laurent's mother . . . ," the admiral murmured as he stared at Brianna. "I met her once, years ago."

"After Beatrice died, Buck gathered the newborn child and the personal effects of her parents that he could find. He raised that girl as his own, and until today she had no knowledge of her true family or the life she would have had if her parents had not died that day."

"Is this true?" the admiral asked Brianna.

She lifted her shocked gaze to the admiral's. "I . . . I honestly don't know . . . ," she stammered.

Nicholas retrieved the bag that Buck had entrusted to him and opened it. He dug around and, after a couple of attempts, found the signet ring. He held it out so the admiral could take it.

"That is the crest of the House of Essex. My God." The admiral looked at Brianna with new eyes. "No one can know she was raised by a pirate. They may still hang her even if they know who her uncle is. We must explain how she came to be on that pirate ship."

"That is why I said she was my wife, who had the misfortune of being captured by pirates on her way here from England."

Nicholas didn't look at Brianna. He was afraid he would see something in her face that he wasn't ready to see. He had betrayed her, had destroyed her life, or at least the life she'd been raised into, and in order to save her, he was going to have to throw her into a new world she wasn't ready for. To save her, he would have to rob her of her freedom.

"You understand what you are doing? What it will require?" the admiral asked in a hushed tone.

"Yes, sir, I do." He shot a look at Brianna again, and judging by her wide, confused eyes, he knew she didn't understand the gravity of their situation. But he did, and until she'd recovered from this fresh shock, he would take care of her, just as she'd taken care of him in that cell after the lashing he'd taken to save her.

"Good. The moment we land in Port Royal, we shall make all the arrangements, but it must remain a secret. No one can know."

"I understand."

The admiral took a deep breath, as if a small part of a much larger burden had been lifted from his shoulders. "I'll do what I can to support your story here. In the meantime, why don't you both rest? We will speak again tomorrow."

"Should I resume my post on this ship?"

"No, lad. Just rest. You've earned that much." The admiral smiled sadly, then left them alone. Nicholas closed the door behind him.

"What did he mean? What arrangements?" Brianna's voice was soft but coated with suspicion. "What are you planning to do with me?"

Nicholas came back over to the bed. He eased down beside her, trying to figure out how best to break the news. "Brianna, you should rest."

"Tell me, Nicholas. You owe me that much." Pain gave a raw edge to the hard flint of her eyes.

She was right. He owed her that, and so much more.

"Once we dock at Port Royal, you and I must be legally wed. We have to make it a real marriage and have the magistrate date our certificate to say we married a year ago. It will help cover our deception until we can safely get you to your uncle in England."

A dozen emotions flashed across her face. "My uncle . . ."

"The Duke of Essex is a powerful man. He can protect

you once you're safely on his lands. So long as everyone believes that you and I were wed in secret months ago, you will be safe." He reached for her hand, which was tearing fretfully at her skirts. He'd never seen her like this, so upset and unable to settle down.

She pulled out of his reach. "I will be *trapped*."

He let out a sigh. He had expected this. "If you can think of a better solution, I am willing to hear you out. Why don't you sleep?" Sleep would give her time to process all that she had been through. He rose from the bed and made a pallet on the floor for himself.

"I can't believe he did this to me," Brianna whispered to herself. Nicholas paused by the pallet he had made beside the bed and stared at her.

"What did you expect him to do? Leave you to die? He's your father, Brianna. Sharing that story saved your life."

"A father wouldn't do that to his child. He *destroyed* my life, my sense of who I am, my past. He's not even my flesh and blood."

Nicholas once more knelt in front of her. "A good father, blood or not, will do anything to protect his child. Telling me who you really are? He knew that meant giving you up forever, but he also knew it would save you, so he did it. And he would do it again if he had to."

Tears formed in her eyes, and she wiped at them as she lay down on the bed.

"So you would have me see my friends hang while I sit in a gilded cage. I'd rather you have shot me dead and been done with it."

She rolled to face the wall, showing him only her back. Nicholas curled his fingers in frustration around the wooden lip of the bed frame as he stared down at her. Someday she would understand what Buck had done for her. Someday she would understand what Nicholas had done too. *Someday . . . maybe.*

BRIANNA WASN'T SURE HOW LONG SHE SLEPT, BUT A TRAY of food was on the table by the bed when she woke, and she was alone in the cabin. She breathed a sigh of relief. She couldn't handle facing anyone right now, especially Nicholas. She felt like she'd been bashed against a bulkhead over and over again until every part of her ached.

She didn't want to think about what he'd said about her past, or her father. The only thing she could focus on was what she would do now that her life was to be permanently tied to Nicholas's in matrimony.

It felt like some terrible dream, one that she couldn't run fast or far enough away from. Joe and most of her crew were likely hiding in the hills in Saint Kitts, but the others would hang if she didn't find a way to free them. Her father was gone, and she was to marry Nicholas and be packed off to England like a piece of luggage. How quickly everything that mattered to her had turned to ash. *I could always run. . .* The thought whispered through her mind. *Find a way to free my crew and then escape.* But the thought of leaving Nicholas tore her up inside just as much as the thought of staying and letting this sham of a marriage occur.

She gazed out the porthole of the cabin. Clear skies and a healthy wind would carry them back to Jamaica soon. She had so little time. Only her men had less of it. A shiver rippled beneath her skin as she faced the fact that Patrick and the others would die because of the choices she had made. All because she had brought Nicholas onto her ship.

"I wish I'd never met you, Flynn."

She was still taking in the sight of the sea from the small window when the door opened. She watched Flynn enter and stare at the untouched tray of food she'd left.

"Brianna, you must eat."

She turned her back on him. "I'm not hungry." If he dared try to push that food at her, she'd throw the tray straight at his head.

"Fine, but playing the martyr doesn't help anyone, especially not your men."

At this, she spun around, hungry for information. "May I see them? Will you take me?"

She wasn't sure why it was so important to her. Perhaps she wanted to reassure them that she was doing her best to find a way out for all of them. Perhaps she wanted their forgiveness, knowing there was no way out. But she'd give anything to get them free, if she could but find a way.

Nicholas checked that the cabin door was locked before he came over to her. "You can't see them on the ship. It would raise too many questions. But . . ." He hesitated. "When we land, there may be a chance for you to see them at the fort in Port Royal."

There was something he wasn't telling her. She could see it in his eyes. Was he lying to get her to cooperate?

He retrieved the bag from the floor. "Here, why don't you have this? It's yours now." She'd forgotten it was even there. She'd been so lost in grief the previous day, and only now was her mind beginning to focus on what needed to be done. She came and took the bag from him, her hands numb as they closed around the leather.

"I will have a tub brought in for you to bathe. I'm sure I can find something for you to wear once you've finished."

She glanced down at the rain-soaked red dress and swallowed an unexpected wave of self-pity. There was something symbolic in this, wearing a ragged, torn gown, one she'd once thought beautiful, one that had mattered to her because it was hers and *she'd* chosen it. And now she wondered if anything in her life would ever be her choice again.

Yes. Yes it would. Her life was her own, and no one was going to take that from her. But she needed time. Her men needed time. And so she would play the game set before her. It was something her father had taught her. Don't give in, no matter how desperate a situation might seem. *If you see a storm so great you think it will swallow your ship whole, you can either accept that fate or you can get to work, doing what needs to be done step by step, until the storm passes and you are left standing.*

"Thank you. I would like a bath and whatever clothes you can find." Since it was a ship and unlikely to carry a woman's wardrobe, she would probably end up in breeches and a shirt again. At least she would feel more like herself then.

Nicholas seemed relieved at being able to do something and quickly left the cabin. Brianna sat back on the bed and opened the bag. She removed the contents one by one, examining each item as she did so.

There was a silver comb that matched the brush she had used all her life, and a matching hand mirror. The three pieces formed an elegant set. A packet of letters tied with a dark-red ribbon, the ink faded from black to light brown was also among the contents. She stroked her fingertips over them and set them aside for later. There was the signet ring that Nicholas had shown the admiral. She'd seen her father wear it every day of his life, but she'd never thought to ask him about it. She had assumed it was his and never wanted to pry into his life, lest it was something painful. And to know he'd worn such an important piece of her past close to his heart this whole time . . . The thought made her shiver with emotions she was too afraid to examine.

She slid it onto each of her fingers one at a time, testing its fit. It finally sat only a little loosely around her middle finger. She traced the crest carved into the flat surface. Two lions surrounded a shield with the letters *EX* on it. *The House of Essex*. Her family.

She knew nothing of England, or the ancient families who held power there. Her life was here in the West Indies, on the ocean, not in some stuffy old house in a cold and dreary place halfway around the world.

Brianna almost removed the ring, but the weight of the gold was strangely comforting. She left it on her finger and dug deeper into the bag. Carefully rolled up at the bottom was a silver-and-light-blue gown. It had no undergarments with it, but it had a beautiful bodice with lace sleeves and a layer of skirts. She unfurled the silk and let out a soft gasp at the exquisite quality. She'd never seen anything so fine or beautiful in her life. Had this belonged to her mother?

It was strange to imagine her mother now as someone else, not married to her father but to this *other* man, the one who had entrusted his ring, the symbol of his family, to a stranger who'd agreed to take his child to safety. What had they been like? The only parents she'd ever known were Thomas and his housekeeper, Elida.

With care, she packed the items back into the oiled bag. With a heavy sigh, she gave in to the grumbling of her stomach. She retrieved the tray of food and set it on the bed. Unlike the hard-as-rock biscuits, salted pork, and mashed peas that were her usual fare aboard the *Sea Serpent*, this was far superior. Nicholas must have raided the larder for the food reserved for officers.

She had a small leg of roast chicken, grilled potatoes, carrots, and several slices of fresh lemons that had been baked with the chicken, which were a true delicacy. She finished the mouthwatering meal but didn't enjoy it. All she could think about was how her men were likely not eating well, if at all. The momentary reprieve from her black mood faded. She had to do something, anything, to help her men. But what could she do, trapped in this cabin?

A strapping young cabin boy dragged in a copper tub, and she was able to bathe and consider the problem. Orchestrating a breakout while at sea would be pointless. There weren't enough of them to take the ship, and even if there were, there would be too much bloodshed. If she had more time and a means to contact her father, something might have been arranged during the transfer to the prison. That only left a plan after they were locked inside, and that, to say the least, would be desperate.

Once her bath was done, she threw on the red dress again and paced the floorboards, seeking inspiration until Nicholas returned. In his arms he carried several items of colorful clothing.

"These are courtesy of Admiral Harcourt. His daughter travels with him on occasion, and she always has a spare gown or two aboard." He laid out the clothes on the bed in front of her.

"A spare gown or two?" She stared at the expanse of silks in front of her. These dresses were fine and expensive, yet the woman who owned them had enough gowns to leave these behind.

The dress was a pale-cream-and-pink striped gown that had tiers of folded fabric on the train that gave the wearer a full figure around the hips and bottom, which, last she heard, was still the style of the day. There were pannier hoops and stays. She'd never worn any of those before, and they certainly weren't suited for working on a ship. She lifted up one side of the hoops and stared at the half cage that it formed when it dropped down. When she'd been shopping for gowns in Port Royal, she'd not given much thought to the necessary underthings to hold up skirts like these.

"Do you need assistance?" Nicholas cleared his throat awkwardly. "I . . . er . . . know where all the parts are supposed to go."

"And just how do—?" She swallowed down the rest of that question. It was an invitation to a discourse she did not care to have. "I will be fine."

"Well, hurry up, then. I would like to get up on deck."

She fumbled to remove the stiff red gown and held it up to shield her while Nicholas located a chemise among the things he'd placed on the bed. She wasn't one to be ashamed of her nakedness, but things had changed between them, and she felt more vulnerable than she ever had before. Betrayal had a way of doing that.

"This first." He held the chemise out and turned his

back. She let her red gown fall to the floor and pulled the chemise down over her body.

"What's next?"

"Stays." Nicholas held up a loosely laced set of whalebone stays. There was no way she would figure this out on her own.

"I suppose I could use your assistance for this." She raised her arms, and he slowly lowered it over her. Then he moved behind her.

"I'll just tighten these ribbons," he said, his lips close to her ear. She closed her eyes, so very aware of how close he was and how she'd missed that, how she'd missed *him*. The realization left her with a bittersweet ache, because *that* version of him had been a lie. She had no idea who the man behind her was. He pulled and tugged gently at the stays until they were snug and her breasts were lifted quite scandalously upward.

"Not too tight. I still wish to breathe," she gasped. She certainly wasn't used to this. She'd spent her whole life pressing them flat against her body.

He loosened the stays, but only a little. "Apologies. It seems you and Roberta are of a similar size, but I do believe her dresses may be a few inches shorter. Not that anyone will notice—they won't be looking at your feet but at your face." Nicholas gave one last tug on the stays and then retrieved a set of panniers next. He tied one to her left hip, using the long ribbons to lash it around her waist and secure it to her. Then he did the same with the other hoop to her other hip.

After that, he draped a full-skirted petticoat over her head that covered the undergarments completely. Then he retrieved the lush cream underskirt and assisted her in putting it on over the petticoat. She had seen all these women in ports in fine gowns, and she'd never truly known what they were wearing underneath, or how much trouble it was to put on. And it was *warm*—far too warm to wear so many layers, at least on the islands.

"Now the outer skirts and bodice."

"There's *more?*"

"Oh yes." Nicholas helped her slide her arms into the sleeves of the bodice, which stopped at her elbows in a triple layer of elegant lace cuffs. Then he helped her fasten the rounded buttons up the middle of the bodice to secure it together.

"It's a wonder women get anything done like this," she muttered.

"They seem to manage somehow," Nicholas said, and as he did so their hands briefly touched. She pulled away. Determined not to give in to maudlin thoughts, she went to the mirror and stared at the effect she presented.

She looked feminine, more than she had in her entire life. She also looked like a stranger. At least in her old red dress, she had felt like herself. At least she could *move* properly.

And yet something else about her reflected image spoke to her. Spoke of a life that she might have had if one terrible storm hadn't changed her life.

Nicholas stood behind her in the reflection of the mirror. "Are you all right?"

"I . . ." She stared at herself, then at him, and the truth came to her unexpectedly. "I don't know her, this woman . . . This isn't me."

Nicholas moved around her to stand between her and the mirror and caught one of her hands, holding firm when she tried to pull free. He traced the thick calluses on her palms with tenderness. A sudden shame filled her. She didn't want to feel like this, dressed up in bows and finery. She was no lady. She—

"You are still *you*, Brianna. A dress, no matter how pretty, doesn't change who you are inside. You are the captain of the *Sea Serpent*. You grew up with the sea air in your lungs and the waves and the cries of storm petrels as your lullabies. You are a pirate queen." His eyes, such a deep blue, lulled her into a seductive trance as he held her. She tried to shake free of that hypnotizing look.

"But then why pretend? Why not let me be who I am, let me be with my crew and face the same fate as them? Why this masquerade as your wife?"

He was quiet a moment. She saw pain in his eyes, though not a pain she'd caused.

"Because your uncle deserves to meet you. He searched for his brother and his sister-in-law for years. I *know* that pain. I know what it means to live decades without answers. Don't do that to your uncle. Meet him, and then once you let him know you and what befell your parents, you can run off to sea again."

Without a ship. Without a crew. Damned to be a coward twice over. And yet . . . "I will meet him," she promised, surprising even herself.

"Good." Nicholas turned back to the bed and retrieved two stockings and a pair of beautiful pink satin silver-buckled shoes. "Try these. Come outside once you are ready. I have permission to escort you about the decks." He left her alone to stare at the closed door and contemplate her fate.

NICHOLAS'S HANDS ITCHED WITH THE NEED TO HOLD Brianna again. She looked so *lost*. In the time he had known her, she'd never been lost. A wanderer, yes, but lost? *Never*. As he'd helped her dress, she had let him guide her. If she would only trust him, he would do everything to see that she was free again and to save her crew as well. But gaining that trust might require a miracle.

The cabin door opened. Brianna stood there, a vision of wild loveliness barely contained in a genteel female disguise. The pink striped silk accented the natural rose in her cheeks, brightened her green eyes, and made her honey-blonde hair tied back at the nape of her neck glow.

She spoke to him; he saw her lips moving, but Nicholas was lost in the glorious sight of her. When he'd been helping her dress, he had been focused on the task at hand, but now he was a witness to the vision of her beauty.

"*Nicholas*." She waved a hand in front of him. "Flynn, are you listening?"

"Er . . . what? Yes, sorry." He crooked his arm toward her, and like a skittish filly, she slid her arm in his.

"There now," he whispered. "'Tis not so bad, is it?"

"What's that?" she whispered back, her eyes wide with bafflement.

He smiled at her. "Playing a lady."

Her eyes narrowed. "I'm only doing this if it means a chance at seeing my crew . . . and my uncle."

"So you will agree to see him?"

"Yes, if only to put the matter to rest and nothing more."

He had a flare of joy at the small victory. So she had listened to him and was considering meeting her uncle.

"Let's take in some fresh air on deck." He led her up to the companion ladder and paused to let her lift her skirts so she wouldn't trip. When they reached the deck, the sailors were all busy at work. Topmen were up in the rigging or astride the yardarms, tacking the sails. Others were mending ropes, and a few were pushing holystones, which were soft and brittle sandstones, along the deck to clean it. Brianna let out a little breath as she studied the ship.

"I've never been aboard a frigate like this," she said quietly. "How many crew it?"

"Two or three times the number on the *Serpent*," he replied. They paused at the railing, and Brianna leaned against it, staring down at the rich blue water.

"Lieutenant." A man's voice made them both turn. Nicholas tensed. Captain Waverly stood there in his red uniform, not a hair out of place despite the stiff breeze. Damn his luck that the man would be on this ship instead of one of the other three.

"Captain Waverly." Nicholas kept his voice calm but curt. The last thing he wanted to do was alert Waverly to the possibility that something was amiss.

Waverly smiled at Brianna. "I heard that this enchanting woman we rescued from those pirates is your wife. I had no idea you were married, Flynn." At this moment he behaved nothing like the Waverly who'd whipped him at Port Royal. He had known this kind of man all his life, a monster in an officer's uniform, who was all smiles until he decided that you were the enemy. He had served alongside such men more often than he cared to admit.

Brianna kept her head down, acting shy and timid. Hopefully, Waverly would believe the ruse.

"You heard correctly," Nicholas said. "This is Brianna Flynn, my wife. She is the niece to the Duke of Essex"

"Is she indeed? I didn't think Lord Essex or his brother had any daughters." Waverly's smile and intense gaze didn't seem to affect Brianna, but her hand on Nicholas's arm dug slightly into his skin.

"It's rather a scandal, Captain Waverly," she said demurely. "My parents died on their voyage here. I was raised by a kind elderly couple on Nevis. They decided to move back to England when their sugar crops failed. I met Nicholas while he was in Cornwall, and I agreed to marry him and follow him out here, but . . ." She paused to sigh, her voice girlish and breathless. "Pirates took our ship, and . . . *ohhh* . . ." She sucked in a little sound of distress. "Pardon me, Captain. I'm not yet over my ordeal."

She turned to face the sea, wiping at her eyes. Without hesitation, Waverly offered his handkerchief to Brianna as he joined her on the other side of the railing.

"I meant no offense, my lady," he said. "You are . . . forgive me for saying so, quite striking. Have we met in passing before? Perhaps somewhere in Cornwall? I have the strangest sense that we've met before."

Nicholas's fists curled at his sides. Waverly's smile was so natural and his concern so genuine, but part of him couldn't help but wonder if he was up to something.

"Perhaps, Captain. But if we have, I wasn't aware of it." She politely declined his handkerchief. "Thank you, but I am feeling better now."

"Of course. Lieutenant, you have an excellent lady here. I

hope you are smart enough to hold on to her."

Flynn forced a smile. "I would be a fool not to. Excuse us, Captain. But I promised to let the admiral speak to my wife." Nicholas slipped an arm around Brianna's waist, gently guiding her away.

"Lord, I hate him. I would wear his guts for garters," Brianna hissed once they were safely away.

"I hate him as well," Nicholas murmured. All their pleasant exchange had done was remind him of how unaffected Waverly was by his own cruelty.

The admiral was on the poop deck with two more lieutenants. Nicholas called out to him as he escorted Brianna up the steps.

"Ah . . ." The admiral excused the other officers. "How are you today, Lady Brianna?"

Brianna stiffened, unused to being addressed this way, but she adapted quickly.

"I am well, thank you, Admiral." She snuck a glance at Nicholas, and he gave a subtle nod of approval. His pirate queen was a quick learner.

"Good, good. Well, the wind favors us. We shall be at Port Royal in a day or so. I have told the officers that Lady Brianna is still recovering from her ordeal and that she won't attend the officers' dinner tonight. That should buy you some privacy."

"Thank you." Nicholas was glad for the admiral's excuse. If Brianna sat across from Waverly at dinner, she might be tempted to throw her knife at him, and Nicholas could hardly blame her.

Brianna's gaze moved away from the admiral to the ship and the sea. Nicholas let go of her arm as she walked to the railing that looked over the waist deck. The wind tugged playfully at her wavy honey-blonde hair as the ship cut through the ocean. Her proud and strong features were only slightly softened by the feminine clothes, and yet they suited her as well. She was no dainty, virginal woman he might meet in a ballroom in London. She was the wind and the waves, the sea and sky, a goddess from a religion too ancient for men to name.

"You had better be careful," the admiral said.

Nicholas turned back to his commanding officer, unsure what he was being warned about.

"There is no changing a woman like that, not if a man truly loves her. I know you long for a quiet life back in Cornwall, but if you tie your fate to hers, know that she will never be caged. Not that one." The admiral clapped a hand on Nicholas's shoulder, his eyes sad and his smile rueful before he turned away.

Nicholas felt he was being pulled in several different directions. Duty to his king and country lay with the admiral and a life of service. But the admiral was right—he did yearn for a quiet life back home as well. And then there was the siren's call toward Brianna and the danger and adventure that would come along with loving a woman like her.

The Caribbean sun warmed his face as he moved to join her at the rail. They stood shoulder to shoulder, gazing out at the sea as the ship flew like the chariot of a god, its white canvas sails pulling it through deep blue water as pure as the sky above.

Brianna gave him an enigmatic smile, one that was as much question as answer. As he reached over and covered her hand with his, he knew what it meant to fly.

CHAPTER 16

Brianna felt a wave of fresh dread as the ship docked at Port Royal. Nicholas stood at her side, his arm around her waist. She should have resented it, felt there was some subtle message of ownership behind it, but right now it was the only thing that comforted her enough to keep her sane.

The last three days had changed everything. She'd gone from hating him to using him to needing him. By the third day, he'd left his pallet upon the floor empty and tucked himself around her, and she'd held on to his arm wrapped around her waist as though it was the only thing that kept her grounded. He hadn't tried to seduce her into bed, hadn't suggested passing the time with pleasurable distractions. He'd only kissed her cheek, sweetly, comfortingly, before giving her what she'd needed—a sense of comfort.

But now they were at the end of that quiet intimacy and were facing something else entirely—marriage.

It was late in the afternoon when the ship docked. The

admiral arranged for a coach to take them to King's Landing, where a magistrate was waiting to perform the wedding ceremony in secret.

"Are you ready?" Nicholas held the bag that contained her new world inside it. Somehow that frightened and reassured her in equal measure.

"As ready as one can be," she replied coolly as they walked across the deck to the gangplank. Waverly was at the bottom of the gangplank, issuing orders to his men. Her crew were there too, being escorted away as prisoners.

She tensed, barely able to suppress the urge to grab the short dagger in Nicholas's belt and run at Waverly. She wanted to *kill* the man like she'd never wanted to kill anyone before in her life.

"Just breathe," Nicholas murmured in her ear before he kissed her cheek the way an affectionate husband would. It reminded her of the last three nights in the cabin where she'd felt safe. He'd been with her, holding her. Just as he was now.

She breathed. And breathed. Each breath was giving her a chance to move past the man who wanted her dead. Then they were clear of him and stepping into a coach that would carry them away.

"Where is this place that we're going?" she asked Nicholas when they were alone.

"King's Landing belongs to an old friend. The admiral sent him an urgent message the moment we docked, letting them know we are coming."

"An old friend?"

Nicholas smiled, and the expression was one she'd never seen on him before. It was boyish, happy, not simply pleasant or seductive. "Trust me, you will be glad to be there."

Brianna doubted that. She couldn't imagine why she would be glad to meet any of Nicholas's old friends. Would it be another old admiral, or some other officer?

When the coach finally stopped, she lurched up toward the door, wanting to get this over with.

Nicholas urged her back into her seat. "Just a moment."

She grumbled and crossed her arms over her chest. He had put her in another of the admiral's daughter's gowns; this one was bright green with blue-and-white striped skirts and a flower-embroidered bodice. It was beautiful, but Brianna would prefer to be back in her breeches right now. Part of her suspected the clothing was as much to hamper any attempt at escape as it was to keep up their ruse.

The coach door opened, and a servant unfolded the small steps before holding out a hand to her. Brianna stared at the servant's waiting hand and held back a sigh. Nicholas stifled a laugh as she awkwardly lifted her skirts, almost raising them up to her head, and placed a hand on the servant's palm to step down. This world was not hers, and at times like this it painfully showed.

She looked up at the grand house in front of her, which reminded her of her father's home in Saint Kitts. A young couple stood arm in arm, waiting to greet them. She recognized them at once. The young woman was the admiral's daughter, Roberta, and the gentleman was Dominic Grey, the former pirate and a dear old friend. When Dominic had retired from piracy, she'd lost track of him when he'd settled down. It was bold as brass of him to stay here like a fox among hens.

Roberta rushed down to them ahead of her husband. "Welcome, *Lady* Brianna." She clasped Brianna's hands in hers, smiling broadly, an impish gleam in her eyes that Brianna liked immediately. The auburn-haired beauty was simply breathtaking. She wondered if Roberta would recognize who she was or not. They had met only briefly once before in the admiral's office when she'd been dressed as a boy.

"Robbie, this is Brianna," Nicholas said. "Brianna, this is Roberta."

"You might as well call me Robbie. All the men do." Roberta sighed dramatically.

"Why Robbie?" Brianna was a little confused, but it only made Roberta laugh.

"I disguised myself as a cabin boy when a certain pirate captured my ship. He still calls me Robbie, and now he's got Nick doing it as well." Roberta shot that impish look at her husband as he joined them. Then she threw her arms around Nicholas, hugging him in an intimate way that made Brianna's jealousy flare, much to her own surprise.

"We're so glad you're safe, Nick," Roberta said. "Reese arrived yesterday with news that you were kidnapped by . . ." Roberta looked to Brianna. "Well, *her*."

"It was a small misunderstanding," Nicholas reassured her.

"I see." Roberta's eyes glittered with amusement.

"So, it's been a while, Holland." Dominic's voice rumbled in a laugh, and then he looked to Brianna. "Finally got caught in the naval net like me?" The former pirate grinned at her.

She managed to smile back at him. "So it would seem."

Dominic winked at her, and she rolled her eyes. It would

be easy to relax around Dominic. He was from her world, after all. She'd been a young girl when Dominic had first visited her father as part of the pirate Brethren, and he had gotten along well with her father. She'd missed him deeply in the year since he had left the life.

"Come inside." Dominic, rather than trying to take her arm, simply waved at the door, and they proceeded toward the house together. "Everyone here is former crew from the *Emerald Dragon* or a friend or family member of one. You are among trusted friends."

She let out a breath she hadn't realized she'd been holding as she and Dominic walked inside, Nicholas and Roberta following behind. To keep his crew with him at his house rather than normal servants suggested he wanted to have a crew ready to leave at any moment, for whatever reason he might find. Perhaps he hadn't left his pirate ways behind completely.

Dominic and Brianna had a moment alone as the admiral's daughter showed Nicholas some new additions to their home. He took Brianna's hand. "You know me, Brianna. I wouldn't send any man to the gallows, and I won't send a fellow comrade in arms to her doom, and that includes being leg-shackled to my best friend. I have a magistrate in the parlor." She looked up at Dominic in surprise. "But say the word, and I will sneak you off the island and send Nicholas off on a wild chase to the opposite end of the Caribbean."

Brianna wanted to say yes, but she couldn't. She was trapped. Trapped by her feelings for Nicholas, trapped by her fears for the fate of her crew and the need to know who she really was and where she came from.

"I . . . ," she started, but then shook her head at Dominic

just as Nicholas and Roberta rejoined them. Their heads were bent toward each other as they talked. They shared an easy intimacy of friendship that Brianna found herself longing for with him.

"Those two knew each other before I ever met Robbie," Dominic said. "Fate is a funny thing, is it not? When I thought I was going to hang. I made them swear to me they would marry each other. They agreed, the liars, both of them." He said all this with affection. "They promised to stay away the day I was supposed to hang, but instead they came to try to save me. They never planned to do what they'd promised." Dominic's tone held a note of bittersweet misery. "I remember seeing them standing there on the platform as it gave way beneath me. I wasn't thinking about their broken promise then, only how damned glad I was that they were so loyal and loving that they refused to obey my orders. Knowing that their faces would be the last I saw was a strange comfort." Dominic cleared his throat. "If you marry him, Brianna, he will be that for *you*. Nicholas is a man who doesn't do anything by half measures. He loves wholly and completely as a friend or lover. He will be yours until he dies, if you but give him the chance."

Other than her father and Joe, Dominic was perhaps the only person whose opinion she trusted. He was from both her world and Nicholas's, and his allegiance had not broken to either side. If he said Nicholas was a man she could trust, she would not doubt Dominic's word.

Roberta left Nicholas and came over to her, that infectious smile of hers making Brianna reluctantly smile back. "Brianna? Do you mind if I call you that? I feel like we shall be as close as sisters, now that you will be Nicholas's wife."

"You do realize this arrangement is simply to keep me from hanging, don't you?" She found her voice more bitter than she meant it to be.

Roberta eyed her thoughtfully. "To you, perhaps. But to Nicholas, this wedding is real, which means it is real to Dominic and me."

Brianna bit her lip a long moment, taking in Roberta's words before she finally replied.

"You may call me Brianna, if you wish." Brianna wondered why Roberta wanted her as a sister. She'd never given a thought to siblings before. Living on a crowded ship had given her plenty of brothers, but a sister . . . that would be such a different thing, perhaps even exciting. She could ask Roberta the sort of questions she'd never asked anyone, except Elida, but Elida didn't have the experience of an English lady. If Brianna's fate did lead her to England and she had to meet her uncle, Roberta's instructions would help keep her from being laughed out of London's ballrooms.

"Would you like to come upstairs? Nicholas mentioned you had a gown. I thought we could have it pressed and see if it might suit for your wedding tonight?"

"I . . ." She looked helplessly at Nicholas, who held out the bag that contained her mother's dress, as well as the other items from her parents. She took the bag from him, hesitant about what to do next, then remembered who she was. She was a pirate's daughter, a pirate queen herself. She wasn't about to let a fine house or a fine gown or a forced wedding rattle her.

Squaring her shoulders, she followed Roberta up the stairs to a bedchamber and set her bag down on the bed. A little embarrassed, she dug through it until she found the gown, then held it up against her body for Roberta to see. What if it didn't fit? What if her mother had been a petite woman? She was rather tall, like her father . . . Wait, had Hugh St. Laurent been a tall man? She suddenly found herself wishing she knew.

"Oh my heavens," Roberta gasped. "I've never seen a gown so exquisite in my life. Oh, it's perfect." She pulled the bell cord for a maid to come and collect the gown to press it.

Brianna reluctantly relinquished it to the maid when she arrived. "You think it is suitable?" she asked Roberta after the maid left.

"It is one of the finest dresses I've ever seen," Roberta said with no hint of exaggeration. "Your mother had wonderful taste." She offered Brianna a sad smile. "I know what it's like to grow up without a mother. Mine died when I was very young. In a way, my life wasn't very different from yours."

At this Brianna glanced up, stunned. "Really?"

"Oh yes, I sailed almost every time my father did. I've even been in a battle or two. I once helped the powder monkeys. Papa was furious when he learned of it, but later, he crowed to all the officers at dinner that I saved the day. He's such a dear." She blushed a little and chuckled at the memory.

"I did the same for my father," Brianna admitted. "Before I was allowed to join his crew officially. Powder work is hard and dangerous, but when you're small, it's the best job to do."

Roberta nodded. "When I got older, I took over helping with the ledgers of the food storage and even the ammunition. The officers were glad to leave that work to me so they could be out on deck. I wasn't allowed up in the rigging, at least while we were at sea, but I snuck up a fair bit when we reached port and learned to tie knots as well as any sailor."

"Why are you telling me all this?" Brianna asked. She sensed Roberta was trying to make a point, but she wasn't sure what.

"Life isn't as awful as you're imagining for young ladies in our position. As the wife of an officer, you'll have privileges, and when Nicholas leaves the navy, you'll have even more freedom. I run wild here at King's Landing. Dom finds it charming to see me break the rules of society whenever it pleases me. He quite encourages it."

Brianna wasn't convinced that Roberta's life was as free as it could be, but that was a discussion for another day. She focused on one thing Roberta had said. "Nicholas is leaving the navy?"

"Yes. My father said in his letter that Nicholas was resigning his commission after your marriage. I think a naval life was never what he wanted. He did it hoping to find Dominic, but now he should be free to do what he wants."

"I only wish I knew what that was," Brianna muttered, but Roberta overheard her.

"He wants a life with you, and whatever adventures that life will hold."

"He's only doing this to save my life. He's so bloody noble," Brianna argued.

Her new friend only shook her head. "He is noble, but oh, Brianna, you don't see what I see. The way he looks at you, the way he moves when you're near him. He is connected to you in a deeper way than you can possibly know. I've been friends with Nicholas for a while, and I've learned to see things in his eyes that he tries to hide. He's not even trying to hide what he feels when he looks at you. He wants to marry you because he loves you."

"Loves me?" she echoed, a sudden burning longing filling her, and yet the piratical part of herself, the part that made most of her decisions, scoffed at the idea.

"Yes. He may not have said it yet, but he does. Trust me on this. He wants a life with you."

"A life with me." Brianna suddenly dared to let herself think about what that might really mean. If he loved her . . . he would help her free her men, and he would not cage her and leave her to die a slow death as a highborn lady. He might be free *with* her. If he left the navy, they could do whatever they wished. Suddenly, a new hope lit Brianna from the inside.

Roberta embraced her, fierce and tight, and a brief sob came from her. Roberta backed up, cleared her throat, wiped at her eyes, and smiled.

"I'm sorry. I just . . . Why don't you have a hot bath, and then we'll do your hair. Your gown should be ready by then."

Brianna let Roberta take control as weddings and things ladies such as her would know to do were well beyond her element. Brianna was in deep, foreign waters with no oars and at the mercy of wherever these winds of change would blow her.

DOMINIC POURED TWO GLASSES OF BRANDY FOR THEM. "I think you need a drink," he said with a chuckle.

Nicholas sagged in the chair by the fire, a heavy weight settling over him. "You have no idea."

"So tell me, what on earth happened? One minute I hear you're off on a spy mission, the next you've been captured by pirates in Sugar Cove, and now you've shown up in desperate need of a wedding to the Shadow King's daughter. Christ, Nick, I thought you wanted a simple life. It's as though after finding me after all these years, you've been set on a mad path to adventure. Have I been that bad of an influence on you?"

"Undoubtedly you have," Nicholas teased. "But I assure you I got into this mess all on my own." He sipped the brandy. "Dom, how long have you known her?"

"Brianna?" Dom considered the question. "About ten years. Buck gave me a position on his crew, and we worked together until I was able to take my own ship as a prize."

"The *Emerald Dragon*?"

"The same. Brianna, well, she was at his side, even as a tiny little thing. Blonde curls and big green eyes, she was doted on by all the men, but she was strong, and she learned the ways of the sea alongside boys twice her age. She is nothing like the other women you've met." Dom's gaze grew distant. "You do realize that this ceremony means nothing to Brianna, don't you?"

"What do you mean?"

"Well, back home, marriage carries social, spiritual, and legal weight behind it. But Brianna is not from that world, and she feels none of that weight. To her, these are just words on a piece of paper and vows being made under duress."

Flynn frowned. "What are you trying to tell me?"

"Well, if your only intention is to offer her some measure of legal protection, then nothing." Dom took a sip and gave him a cunning look. "But if you actually wish to have her as your wife, then you are in for a grave disappointment. This contract? Simply another cage to escape. She is not someone who will become a docile wife and wait at home for you with a babe in her arms. She is more like those old Viking princess tales we heard as boys."

"Harcourt said much the same thing." Nicholas dragged a hand through his hair.

"If you wish to keep her, Nicholas, you must *win* her. You won't do that by forcing her to fit your expectations. She'll leave you the first chance she gets if you try."

"I don't want to cage her or change her, but she can't go back to pirating. Times are changing, the war with the Spanish is waning, and that means the Royal Navy will be turning their attention back to restoring order to the shipping lanes. Her father's days are numbered. As for her ship and crew . . ." Nicholas leaned in and spoke to Dominic in a hushed tone. "That reminds me. Most of her crew escaped to Basseterre during the fight, but about half a dozen were captured, including Brianna's cabin boy, an innocent lad. We must free them. I can't let those men hang."

"You want to save the lives of some pirates?" Dominic asked, his dark brows arched in shock. "Why the sudden change of heart? You once believed we were only capable of murder and mayhem."

"Let's just say my views have changed of late. Not all are cut from the same cloth." He'd spent time among the men, living with them, laughing with them, hearing tales of their raids, and Brianna was right. They weren't the sort of men who deserved to be killed. Perhaps imprisoned for a time, but death? Not her men.

At this, Dominic's eyes glinted dangerously. "You know what you're asking, don't you? To save them, we can't play by your rules. We have to play by *mine*. It means a jailbreak. Are you certain you can stomach that? It would be a direct action against the navy *and* Charles Harcourt. People might get hurt. People you know."

Nicholas let out a slow breath. "I'm aware." He took another long sip. "I believe I gave up on any future in the navy when I fell in love with a pirate queen."

Dominic chuckled at what he'd just said. "As she is the Shadow King's daughter, I do believe that makes her a princess, not a queen. Very well. I have an idea. Once you are wed, you will tend to your bride, and I will go—"

"Not alone you won't. Those men are my responsibility. I betrayed Brianna's trust, and this is only one of the many ways I must atone for that. I've been a fool for separating good and evil so easily in my mind. We live in a world where so much is painted in shades of gray rather than black or white, right or wrong. Take the navy, for example. We uphold the laws of England, and England allows slavery to continue. You know just as I do how wrong owning another man is. Yet England continues to support the trade." He paused, his thoughts turning back to Brianna. "She once asked me if I'd only saved her because she was a woman, if my compassion was limited by gender, whereas I would let a cabin boy hang. Well, I won't. Patrick is a good lad. I will save him and the others or die trying."

Dominic was quiet a moment as he sipped his drink and watched Nicholas. "There's the Nicholas I left behind in Cornwall," he said, a smile on his lips. "Brianna saved you where I could not."

Nicholas didn't argue the matter. In a way, it was true. She'd saved him from the version of him that had refused to see the areas in between, where most men and women actually lived.

"We'll wait for Brianna to fall asleep and go together," Nicholas finally said.

Nicholas and Dominic drank, perhaps a little too much for what a groom and his friend should drink before the groom's impending nuptials. They were laughing and wiping tears from their eyes as they reminisced each other with boyhood stories.

By the time Roberta announced Brianna was ready, Nicholas was seeing the world in a rosy hue. Alcohol had always calmed his nerves.

Dominic fetched the magistrate and escorted him outside into the gardens while Nicholas waited at the foot of the stairs for his future bride. Roberta came down first, beaming at him, and then she stepped aside and looked back up the stairs as Brianna emerged from the corridor. Her silver-and-blue gown was unlike anything he'd ever seen.

The evening sunlight poured in through the windows, illuminating Brianna in her diaphanous gown like she was a falling star. She glided toward him with a grace that reminded him of how she moved on the rigging of her ship. She paused on the bottom step, her hands knotting worriedly in her skirts.

"Well? Do I pass muster?" she asked.

"I . . . What? Oh yes," Nicholas stuttered. "You look . . ." He didn't have the words to finish.

"That means you look lovely," Roberta told Brianna. "When you strike a man speechless, it's usually a good sign.

Come along, bridegroom." Roberta tugged at Nicholas, and he offered Brianna his arm as they followed Dominic's wife into the gardens.

The heady scent of flowers perfumed the air, and Nicholas felt as though he'd drifted into some wonderful dream. Beside him, Brianna stared wide-eyed at the gardens and the fountains, the paradise that would soon host their union.

"It's so beautiful. I've never seen some of these flowers before," she admitted with a blush. Nicholas made a silent vow to always have flowers for her, wherever she went. But first . . . he'd have to win her heart and her trust again.

Dominic and the magistrate waited in the garden near an archway trellis covered in pale purple wisteria. Nicholas escorted Brianna down toward the magistrate. Suddenly, he realized more than ever what Dominic had said about this being a false marriage in Brianna's eyes. He didn't want that. He wanted her, and he wanted her happiness. If he had to force a marriage like this, it wouldn't be real to either of them, no matter what the magistrate said.

Nicholas turned to clasp her hands in his own. "Wait. I can't do this." Her eyes widened, but she didn't interrupt him. "This isn't fair to you, Brianna. I made this bargain with the admiral as a means to save you from the gallows. Long ago, I vowed to see you safe for saving my life back in Port Royal, and I told myself this was a means to that end.

"But the truth is, I'm doing this for the most selfish of reasons. I'm doing this because I want to marry you, for you to be my wife. You have been such an exciting part of my life, I cannot imagine going on without you in it. But at no point did I ask myself if it was something *you* wanted. And how could it be? You have been caught between the devil and the deep blue sea. I realize now that I'd rather see you free than chained. So if you wish to call this off, I will see to it that Dominic finds you safe passage wherever you wish to go."

It was true, all of it, and as he bared his soul to her, he saw something about her change. She searched his face for a long moment, as if wondering what his words truly meant, and when she saw no deception there, he saw shock behind her eyes. Her lip trembled for just a moment, before she composed herself and nodded.

"Thank you, Nicholas."

His heart sank. He turned to Dominic, ready to tell him to prepare a ship for her, only she placed her hand upon his cheek and turned his head back toward her.

"I will marry you."

It was now Nicholas's turn to be shocked. "You will?"

"You already held my affection. Now you are willing to give me my freedom. That has earned you my trust. Let us consider this one more adventure we might attempt together and see where it leads us."

Then she faced the magistrate, who, after a nod from Nicholas, began the ceremony. They exchanged vows, and Dominic produced a pair of elaborately carved gold rings for them. Nicholas noted the intricate scrollwork and how it seemed too fancy for anything Dominic would have found on the island.

"Where did you get these?" Nicholas asked suspiciously.

Dominic shrugged. "Some answers are better left ungiven." He then volunteered to sign the marriage license first, followed by Roberta, who wiped happy tears from her eyes before Nicholas and Brianna finally signed their names, Brianna as Brianna Holland St. Laurent. The magistrate then rolled up the license and offered his congratulations, pronouncing them husband and wife. The magistrate, with a look and a nod from Dominic, wrote in a marriage date one year prior to conceal the true date of the wedding.

"Husband and wife," Brianna mouthed the words. Her beautiful green eyes moved up to his, and the world exploded around him with purpose and joy, all connected to this woman and the life he wanted to lead at her side.

Nicholas felt a rush of elation at the realization he was a married man, even more so because she had agreed to it even when offered the chance to leave. And he did not have just any wife—he had a wild pirate queen who made him feel alive like nothing else in the world ever had.

"Congratulations." Dominic kissed Brianna's cheek, making her blush, before he shook Nicholas's hand. "Now, let's have a glass of sherry to celebrate. Maybe two!"

The magistrate joined them in two glasses of sherry and long conversation before he took his coach back to Port Royal.

Roberta tugged on Dominic's hand with a smile and a wink. "It's rather late. We should turn in."

"It's not that—" He stopped when he saw his wife jerk her head at Nicholas and Brianna. "Ah. Of course. Good night, all." And with that, they left the two alone in the drawing room.

"I suppose we should retire soon as well," Nicholas said, feeling surprisingly nervous. He and Brianna had slept together before, but this felt different, more *official*. It was both comforting and alarming that Brianna probably did not feel the same pressure.

"All right." She got up and led him upstairs to the room they were to share while they remained at King's Landing. He closed the door behind them and joined her at the balcony that overlooked the front of the house and the road that led to the distant town of Port Royal.

"Brianna," he said softly. She shivered as he bent to kiss the back of her neck.

She leaned into his kiss. "You meant what you said before? Before our wedding?"

Nicholas held her tight, trying to reassure her. "Every word."

"Tell me you won't cage me, Nicholas," she whispered.

"What?"

She turned to face him, her green eyes flashing like jade daggers. "Tell me I'm free. Tell me I can leave whenever I wish."

"Free? Brianna, you are, but . . . what is troubling you?"

She cursed and spun away. "I think I need to be alone for a little while."

Nicholas knew that look. She was plotting something—he could see it clearly in her eyes. She had to be thinking about her men.

"Brianna, whatever you've gotten into your head, put it aside, just for tonight. Please."

"Are the lives of my men so trivial that you would wish me to go to bed and forget them?"

"No. That's not what I'm saying. But you can't help them, not tonight." He desperately wanted to share his plans with her, but he couldn't. If he did, she would want—no, she would *insist* on going with him, and he would say no because he wasn't about to let her go anywhere near the fort or Captain Waverly. She had barely escaped being proven a pirate in Saint Kitts. He didn't have another miracle tucked up his sleeve to save her a second time.

She paced away from him, a queen of starlight as she moved about the room in her silver-and-blue gown. He'd learned tonight that it was one of her mother's gowns and he couldn't begin to imagine what it must feel like to her to wear it. She had no idea how utterly beautiful she was, inside and out. He needed to keep her distracted, at least for tonight.

"Brianna." He caught her wrist as she passed by him, and she spun easily into his arms. He held her captive, feeling her breath quicken in excitement. "You said we should consider this one more adventure we might attempt together. Let us enjoy our wedding night and see where that leads us."

Her eyes narrowed. "You cannot simply distract me from—"

Nicholas smiled wickedly as he bent his head and covered her lips with his.

Oh, but he could.

❧

BLOODY MAN AND HIS SINFUL MOUTH.

That was the last rational thought Brianna had for a while. Nicholas pinned her against the wall by the bed, and she clung to his frock coat, her hands feeling the embroidery of the fine gold stitches beneath her fingertips. He hadn't worn his naval uniform for the wedding, and something about that made her intensely grateful.

She gasped as he dug a hand into her skirts, pulling up the fabric so that his palm could reach her bare skin. His rough handling of her sent excitement shooting through her like the guns of her ship all blasting at once in a single devastating broadside. Her knees buckled, and he caught and held her up against the wall, his prisoner, his plaything, and right now she adored it. Right now, she *needed* it.

"Nicholas! Don't stop." She rubbed against his hand as he cupped her between her legs. The exquisite pressure of his touch sent zings of pleasure through her. She'd already forgotten whatever he'd said that made her angry. All she wanted right now was him touching her, pleasuring her until she was drunk and sated from their lovemaking.

"Stop fighting me, wench, and I'll give you what you need," he said as he bit her throat playfully. "Or *do* fight me —whatever pleases you will please me."

She started to laugh at his teasing but gasped in shock as he thrust two fingers deep inside her body. She loved how he could tease her sweetly in the same breath as he made love to her.

If there was one thing she couldn't resist about him, it was the way he'd mastered her body. He used his fingers to drive her into a panting, restless creature, making her feel like a tide was pulling her away from the shore. She clung to his shoulders, pulling him closer. She wanted him inside her, filling her, stretching her, and owning her until nothing was left but the pleasure she knew he could give her.

"Stop teasing me, Nick . . ."

"Oh, but I like to hear you beg me," he chuckled. "The

sound would be enough to drive a man to glorious madness. I can't wait to make you beg me for many things, little pirate."

"I won't beg," she said as she kissed him, nibbling at his bottom lip. "You can beg me, however, and I shall consider your pleas and decide whether or not to be a benevolent wife."

Nicholas's laugh sent fresh waves of hunger through her. "I think you shall beg first," he warned with a sensually wicked glint in his eyes.

"Oh, you'll be begging me before the moon rises," she promised as she moved one hand down his body to cup him through his trousers. He groaned, and she smiled victoriously as she continued to rub him until he was hard as stone beneath her hand.

He captured her mouth, his tongue boldly conquering hers until she was dizzy with the taste of him. He continued to thrust his fingers into her, driving her to new heights of excitement. Her legs quaked as her climax broke through, and he swallowed her cries with new kisses. The waves of pleasure were swift and sweet. She sucked in a breath as he moved his lips down to her throat and then covered her collarbone in gentle kisses. He held her for a long moment, letting her catch her breath, even as he continued to draw out the quivering aftershocks of her climax with his fingers still inside her.

She stared up at him, and their mouths touched, their breaths mixing as they simply *breathed* together. It was the single most intimate thing she'd ever felt in her life, like nothing outside the two of them existed. Every worry, every fear, every thought ended beyond the two of them right here and now, him holding her.

Nicholas peeled off her gown, taking his time, then turned her to face the bed. She grasped one of the bedposts as he stripped her of everything but her stockings. Then he scooped her up and tossed her onto the bed. She laughed in surprise as he nearly ripped his own clothes off in his hurry to join her.

Brianna stretched languidly back on the bed, utterly naked except for her stockings, which he now peeled off in a slow show of seduction. He kissed the arches of her feet before dropping the stockings to the floor.

"Tempting wench," he mused.

"Presumptuous arse," she shot back with a saucy grin.

He pounced on her, pinning her wrists to the bed above her head. His body pressed down into her, trapping her beneath him. Once more, that excitement for pleasure began to build inside her. There was nothing more wonderful in the world than being beneath Nicholas, his powerful body smelling of leather and the scent of flowers in the gardens drifting from the windows. It was enough to convince her she might be dreaming.

Brianna parted her thighs so he could settle between her legs. He kept her hands trapped above her head with one of his and used the other to adjust himself, aligning his shaft at her entrance.

"Well, now? Are you going to storm my decks or just stand there holding your spyglass?" she taunted with a roll of her hips.

He laughed out loud at that. "You will never bore me, will you?"

"I doubt I will, but you had better not bore me," she warned and gave a wriggle of encouragement beneath him.

He leaned down, stealing a slow, drugging kiss from her, then, with a grand thrust of his hips, plunged into her. They shared a gasp as he seated himself fully inside her. She felt full, no part of her untouched by him.

"My God," he whispered against her lips. "You feel like heaven."

He kissed her, harder this time, no longer taking his time to tease her. He was chasing his own pleasure now in addition to hers, and she thirsted for his possession, his roughness. She liked that he didn't treat her delicately in bed. There was an animal-like battle for control between them that was hard to resist, and it demanded the same from him as it did from her. She'd never let another man do that, take such control of her, and be able to give such trust to him in return. But with Nicholas, it was easy, like breathing.

He withdrew from her, but before she could protest, he'd already flipped her onto her stomach, parted her thighs, and drove back into her from behind. The new angle of penetration made her cry out in tortured pleasure. He pounded into her like a man possessed, and she encouraged him, lifting her hips to meet each thrust. Nick held on to her, his fingers gripping so tight she knew they would leave light bruises in the morning, and she didn't care one bit. This was what she needed, this complete and consuming hunger. Right now she was beyond words, beyond anything but the motion of their bodies, the feel of their souls colliding and the sound of their harsh breaths mixing in the humid island air.

Nicholas dropped down over her body, caging her from above as he slid a hand beneath her, cupping her breast and kneading it roughly. He pinched her nipple, and the blend of pleasure and pain lit her orgasm like a match dropped into a powder keg. She blew apart inside with mind-numbing ecstasy. Nicholas continued to thrust, using her limp and sated body to find his own release, and then he collapsed on top of her, careful not to crush her. Their bodies glistened with sweat in the moonlight.

For a moment neither of them spoke. Then Nicholas rolled their bodies so they lay spooned on their sides, his cock still deep within her. She trembled as small aftershocks made her inner walls clamp around his shaft. He curled one arm around her waist, holding her gently to him, and she savored the intimate sensation.

"Are you all right?"

"Yes," she replied drowsily and smiled. "I like you, Flynn. You're not bad, for a husband."

At this he laughed, a deep, exhausted, wonderful sound meant only for her.

"Not bad? Then I shall endeavor to improve my performance, wife." His teasing still held such tenderness in it that her heart, hardened by years of life as a pirate, simply melted.

She had something she had never known she wanted, but as she felt her body drift to sleep in his embrace, she wondered, *At what cost?*

CHAPTER 17

Flynn woke several hours before dawn and pulled his wife into his arms. His *wife*. He still had trouble wrapping his mind around this new reality, and yet it was as if it had always been.

Brianna chuckled in her sleep as he nuzzled her throat and cupped her breast. Whatever she was dreaming about seemed pleasant. He traced her face with his fingertips and watched her lashes flutter in response. She was so strong, brave, and beautiful, and she was going to be furious about what he was about to do.

He wanted to stay in this bed with her forever, but the fate of her men was on the line, and it was his fault they were to hang. That made it his responsibility to save them, and he wouldn't risk her life because of his failings. If he did it correctly, he could have it all: Brianna's crew free, her father out of the navy's reach, and her safe at King's Landing with a new name and a new life.

"Brianna," he purred in her ear, and she stretched

languidly, arching her back so that her breasts rose up toward him like an offering to a lustful god. He couldn't deny himself one last memory of giving her pleasure.

"I need another hour, Joe," she mumbled. Flynn laughed as he placed his lips over the pink tip of one breast. He laved at a nipple before gently tugging on it with his teeth. She gasped, coming awake abruptly.

"How dare—what?"

"Joe wouldn't do that, would he?"

The fog lifted from her and she grinned. "Not if he knew what was good for him."

Nicholas leaned over her, his hand sliding up her inner thigh until he found the delta of her wet heat. Last night he had seen her fear and worry and turned it into passion, but now he wanted to enjoy a sweet and gentle claiming, a true meeting of bodies and hearts rather than some animalistic mating. If things went badly at the fort, he wanted to carry this moment with him, no matter what.

She was still a bit drowsy as she parted her thighs and Nicholas sank into her welcoming body. He pinned her hands above her head, but their fingers laced and tightened. The connection of their mouths made him lightheaded with indescribable joy. He rode her gently, each roll of his hips drawing soft sounds from her lips, and he reveled in every moment he learned new ways to please his wife. Her eyes opened whenever he stopped kissing her, and she smiled back in a dreamy sort of way.

"Being with you is like sailing for the first time," she said. "It's like flying through a sea of glass . . . like riding the clouds of heaven."

Her words resonated inside him like someone had struck

an ancient, hallowed bell, its pure sound reverberating out from his heart.

"I love you, Brianna," Nicholas murmured as he moved faster over her, in her. He couldn't get enough of her, never enough.

She let out a soft cry and clenched around him. He breathed her name reverently as his own release followed. He'd never felt like this before, like anything was possible with her. Their hearts beat as one. Their life was just beginning and all the years before were simply a blink of history. Now he was where life truly started.

His brave pirate queen stared at him, her green eyes wide and vulnerable in a way he'd never seen before. Storms at sea that would scare any sane man didn't frighten her, but his profession of love had.

"You don't have to say anything back," he said. "I just wished for you to know how I feel."

"I love you too and will love you as long as the words you spoke to me at our wedding remain true." She seemed stunned by her own words, as though by saying them she had parted a curtain and stepped into a world so beautiful that she couldn't believe what she was seeing. He knew because he felt the same way. Saying those words was as freeing as it was frightening, just like life upon the sea.

He lowered his head to hers, and she smiled as he kissed her slowly, burning him up piece by piece like a fire on a harsh winter night. Brianna responded to him as naturally as breathing. He adored that about her, that she was so comfortable with her own desires that she could be so free with him.

"Is it time to wake up?" she asked, burrowing into his arms, her breathing slowing down.

"Not yet. Sleep a while longer," he whispered as he kissed her. Dawn was still far away.

He waited another quarter of an hour until she was deeply asleep once more. Then he untangled his limbs from hers and dressed in the clothes Dominic's valet had laid out for him. A dark shirt and trousers would help him go unseen tonight.

He met Dominic in the corridor. The house was dark and quiet, only a few lamps were lit, which cast wavering shadows on the walls, making Nicholas feel strange, as if someone had stepped on his grave.

"Tell me you have a plan," Nicholas said.

Dominic grinned. "I do. Or rather, Roberta does." He held up four bottles of very expensive wine and gave a soft whistle. Roberta stepped out of the shadows wearing a dark cloak about her shoulders, which blended with her sapphire gown. He endured a stab of guilt for not waking Brianna, but he didn't want her anywhere near Waverly or his men. She'd go straight for the man's throat and risk her own life if she got blinded by her anger.

"Ready?" Roberta asked as she took the basket of wine bottles from Dominic.

"Always, my darling," Dominic assured her. "You two go first. I'll meet you at the fort. I'll see that my ship is ready to sail once the men are free."

"Then we had better go quickly." Roberta led the way outside, where a coach was waiting for them. As a servant opened the door, Roberta turned to Nicholas, her eyes full of happy tears.

"Nick, you cannot know what today meant to Dominic and me."

"What do you mean?"

"Your marriage to Brianna. It means you've finally let go." She smiled wider.

"Let go?" He didn't follow her meaning.

"All those years you pushed yourself through a life you never truly wanted in order to find Dominic. But even after saving him, you didn't seem to accept that the struggle was finally over. I saw a different Nicholas tonight, a man who has let go of the pain within and turned his face toward a new horizon."

Roberta understood him so well. Today had been a turning point. He was no longer chasing a far horizon. He was there—he had reached it, and the view was like nothing he'd ever dreamed it could be, as he'd spoken his wedding vows to Brianna beneath the setting island sun. He now felt true peace, true joy. Brianna was the sunlight upon his skin, the light reflecting off the waves, the playful dolphins leaping in the air. She was the wind in every sail, as well as the current beneath him. She was a gift, a treasure, and he would spend every moment of his life trying to be worthy of her.

"You're right, Robbie."

"Of course I am," she laughed, and hugged him fiercely.

"But first I need to right this wrong I caused."

"Of course." She brushed tears from her face. "You might even call it a wedding present."

"I only hope she sees it that way," Nicholas said.

"She will. We had better get started, then. I'm sure her men have had their fill of Port Royal's hospitality."

He smiled and helped her into the coach, and then the

footman closed the door behind them. Roberta settled her dark-blue skirts about her body. Beside her on the bench was a basket of wine, which she patted with a grin.

"This is going to work," she promised him.

Nicholas nodded. "It has to."

❧

BRIANNA STARED AT THE SCENE BELOW HER WINDOW, NOT daring to breathe. Nicholas and Roberta were embracing in the dark, alone. The moonlight lit their faces, and Brianna saw with heart-wrenching pain that Roberta was smiling. Why were they alone? Why was Roberta hugging Nicholas and getting into a carriage with him? Where was Dominic?

Brianna stepped behind the shadows of the curtains as the coach departed King's Landing. Her thoughts whirled as she tried to come up with an explanation for why her husband would leave with another woman in the middle of the night after embracing like that.

Was this some sort of ruse? Was it possible that Nicholas had deep feelings for Roberta? Did he love her? Why else would he leave with her well before dawn? If there was an innocent explanation for this, then Dominic should have been with them, shouldn't he?

Only a daft fool jumps to conclusions, she tried to tell herself. But she needed answers. He'd said he loved her . . . Had that been only words said in a time of passion? She wanted to trust him, to believe his words, but what other explanation was there for leaving her alone on their wedding night to go away with a beautiful woman whom he valued deeply as a friend and perhaps more.

It wasn't like Brianna to feel jealous. She'd never cared about her other lovers being with other women. But this was vastly different. It was Nicholas, the man she'd confessed to loving. He was her husband, and he had convinced her that that meant something.

Numb, Brianna wrapped herself in the dressing gown Roberta had lent her. She left the bedchamber and searched the quiet, still house until she found a footman who was asleep in a chair near the front door. Most servants, as far as she understood it, were allowed to go to bed after midnight, but they would stay up and wait if their master or mistress was out.

The man blinked and straightened as he woke. "My lady?"

"Where is Dominic?" she asked, trying hard not to make it a command.

"His lordship is at the docks, seeing to matters regarding one of his ships."

"This late?"

"When you're trying to catch the tides in the morning, you need to be ready," the footman reminded her, stifling a yawn.

"Of course." She half turned to go back upstairs, but then she paused and spoke again. "And Roberta and my husband?"

The footman's eyes betrayed something, but she couldn't say what. He coughed nervously. "I'm not sure where they went."

Brianna knew the servant knew where they had gone, but she was in no mood to threaten him. She would find her own answers, even if it ripped her heart from her chest to learn the truth. It galled her to think of how easily he'd betrayed her, and the flood of fury and pain she felt nearly stole her breath.

"Please prepare a horse for me."

The footman seemed ready to protest, but her cold stare changed his mind, and he rushed off to do as she asked. Brianna returned to her bedchamber and slipped on a pair of Nicholas's trousers, one of his belts and shirts, as well as a waistcoat. They were slightly larger than she was used to, but she would make do. She went to Dominic and Roberta's bedchamber and retrieved a pair of riding boots that belonged to Roberta. Thankfully, Dominic's wife had the same size feet as her.

Once ready, she collected her belongings and stowed them in a bag and went to claim her horse, which the footman had ready on the road for her.

"I will have someone send your horse back," she said.

"My lady, where shall I tell them you have gone?" the footman asked as she mounted the powerful black beast.

"What you tell them doesn't matter," she said, and it didn't. She was leaving. Whatever she'd hoped to have with Nicholas, it seemed it wasn't enough for him. As much as she wanted to confront him, to demand answers, she would much rather protect herself from whatever the painful truth might be, and the best way to do that was to leave.

She mounted her horse and rode for Port Royal. The town was still sleeping in the early hours well before the sun rose. Only a few shopkeepers were awake and preparing for the day. She kept her distance from the fort, not wanting to be discovered by Waverly or his troops. When she reached the docks, she found a young lad kicking a bit of driftwood down a dirt path.

"You, boy. Care to make some coin?" She dismounted and let the coins in her purse jingle. The boy's eyes lit up.

"What do you want me to do?"

"Take this horse back to King's Landing. Tell them Lady Brianna promised you a reward for returning it." She removed a few coins of her own. "This is for you now, and they'll give you more when you arrive. Can you handle that?"

"Yes, ma'am." The boy grasped the reins and boosted himself into the saddle.

Once alone, Brianna continued down to the docks, studying the ships in the harbor. One she recognized—the *Lady Siren*. She almost laughed, not believing her luck. Of course the captain of *that* ship would be here, bold as brass to be so close to danger. She kept a watch out for Dominic, but she was no longer certain which ships he owned. There was a group of men loading a small rowboat, and she stopped by them on the dock.

She pointed at the distant vessel. "Are any of you headed out to that ship there?"

"Oh, aye." One man squinted up at her. "Are you wanting to see the captain?" He took in her appearance with appreciation and a little bafflement. The men behind him snickered.

"Not in the way you're thinking, ya scallywags, but your captain is an old friend. He won't mind me surprising him."

The three men exchanged glances and then shrugged. "All right, on you get," one man said.

She climbed aboard the boat and got out of the way of the rowers as they began to drag their oars through the water toward the distant ship.

When they reached the ship, she climbed up the rope ladder and was helped aboard by one of the crew.

"Is your captain aboard?" she asked the grizzled seaman who'd lifted her up.

"Not yet. Should be back soon, I reckon. We're leaving tonight."

"Excellent." Brianna left the crew to their duties and headed for the stern of the ship, where she knew the captain's quarters would be. Nothing had changed much since she'd last been aboard. The elegant bed was still in one corner, and a beautiful card table and desk sat opposite, fastened to the floor. An old masthead of a mermaid stood propped in the corner. Her friend was a sentimental sort, and the masthead was from his first ship, the *Seafoam Witch*.

She set her bag down on the table and unrolled the nearest chart, examining various routes that had been marked. It didn't matter where he was bound—she was determined to go with him, at least for a while.

Abandoning the charts, she walked over to the tall windows and took in the dark skies only just starting to recede to the faintest of light cresting over the island.

The safe haven she'd thought she'd found in Nicholas's arms had been torn apart, and with her father also gone, she felt so very alone.

"Well now, you're a sight for sore eyes, lass," a deep voice said with a chuckle. Brianna looked over her shoulder and smiled.

"Hello, Gavin."

The handsome, dark-haired pirate grinned back and closed the cabin door behind him.

WAVERLY SAT IN THE GRIMY TAVERN, BROODING IN A corner as he drank another pint of ale. Before him on the table sat a letter that he'd opened a few hours ago while in his office in Port Royal's garrison. The words then had been just as sour as the words were now. It was a letter from his wife, Regina. She rarely wrote to him, only to bring him important news of the family that absolutely must be shared with him.

His lip curled in a sneer as he read the worst of it again. *"Your father has been charged with embezzlement. He is facing the loss of his property holdings and all of his wealth, not to mention his good name—our good name. I married you at my father's request, but your father's criminal undertakings and your dishonorable behavior has done me in. If you ever bother to return to England, the children and I will be living at my parents' estate in Yorkshire. Do not come to visit. You will not be welcome."*

He crumpled the letter in his fist, unleashing his rage on the helpless paper forcing it to bend and fracture at his will. Then after a long moment, he lifted up the crumbled ball, lit one of the ends on the nearest candle, and then set it down in a silver tray to burn.

As he watched the flames burn and bits and pieces caught the wind and lifted into the air before blackening into harmless ash, something tugged at his mind, something he'd been ignoring.

He closed his eyes and replayed that moment on the deck when he'd met Flynn's blushing English bride. Something about her had caused his blood to hum and the beast to stir fretfully in the darkness of his chest. She'd turned to face him, and for an instant, he'd seen something in her eyes. What was it? He replayed the moment over and over, focusing desperately on what he could remember, and then it hit him.

Rage. Violent, powerful rage and a hint of fear.

He'd seen that once before in a pair of haunting green eyes . . . when he'd been shoving a boy's head into a water trough to kill him. The boy had known his intention then, and his eyes had given Waverly that last sweet glimpse of rage and fear seconds before the admiral had come to the boy's rescue.

What were the odds of two people with the same green eyes like that, almost like cat's eyes with a slight tilt to them? The odds were slim, almost impossible. The fact that Flynn was involved with both the boy and the woman . . . it made the conclusion quite clear to Waverly. So clear that he smashed his mug of ale down on the table and cursed so violently the men around him shifted their chairs a good few feet away.

Holland wasn't a boy—he'd *never* been a boy. Holland was a woman . . . and a pirate. And she'd escaped him again. Lady Brianna St. Laurent, the supposed niece of a duke, was a pirate, and he was going to see her hang. He threw a few coins down on the table and left the tavern. Waverly would head straight for King's Landing, where Flynn had told the admiral he and his "wife" would be staying.

Once he captured Holland and Buck, Waverly would prove to the admiral, to the entire navy, and to his wife that his actions weren't dishonorable. He'd be hailed as a hero when all this was done. For the first time in hours, he smiled.

NICHOLAS HUNG BACK IN THE SHADOWS AS ROBERTA walked up to the main gates of the naval fort, the basket of wine in her arms. The guards allowed her inside and closed the gates behind her. It was one of the benefits of being an admiral's daughter—she could walk in at practically any time with that sweet, innocent smile of hers.

A hand touched Nicholas's shoulder and he spun, dagger raised. Dominic glanced down at the knife at his throat.

"Got you," Nicholas chuckled, relieved to see his old friend.

Dominic grinned and pricked Nicholas's side with his own blade. "Got you too." The pair withdrew their blades and watched the fort's entrance.

"I take it Robbie's already inside?" Dominic asked. Nicholas nodded. Dawn was coming fast; they had only one hour to make this happen if they wanted to get away from the fort before sunrise. Striking at about three thirty would be key. Most people would be deeply asleep; even the guards on duty would be nodding off, waiting to be relieved.

After fifteen tense minutes had passed, Dominic whispered, "There she is!" and pointed toward the gates. The cloaked figure of Roberta emerged from the front gate, waving them inside.

"That was quick. How much of that drug did you put in the wine, Dom?" Nicholas asked.

"More than enough." Dominic laughed. "It's not my first prison break. Did this to the French three years ago. Let's go."

They left their vantage point and hurried toward the entrance.

"Are you sure everyone is out cold?" Nicholas asked once they were inside.

"I believe so," Roberta said. "Each of the sentries on duty thinks the others are still on duty. No one knows they all got bottles of drugged wine." Roberta's eyes twinkled with dangerous mischief. "Now let's go rescue Brianna's men." She held up a set of keys and tossed them to Nicholas. They couldn't be certain every sentry was asleep with drugged wine or even that the men had drunk enough to stay asleep. Time and fate were all that ruled their destinies now.

They were careful as they roused each man they freed, giving each one a gentle shake and holding a finger to his lips as his sleepy eyes sharpened to consciousness. They whispered instructions as to where they were to wait, made sure the plan was understood, and moved on to the next one. Patrick was the last one to be found.

"Mr. Flynn?" the boy whispered as Nicholas entered his cell.

Nicholas held a finger to his lips. "Come on, lad. We must move. Now."

"Where's the captain? I . . . I thought you were one of them." He jerked his head toward the guards asleep at the end of the hall.

"The captain is safe. I came here to free you for her."

As the boy stepped out of the cell, Nicholas got a better look at him. He was pale, and bruises shadowed his eyes and jaw. Someone had hit him, and Nicholas had a good idea who it was. He silently wished he could find a way to get his revenge on Waverly. But perhaps he already had. A mass escape like this, under Waverly's watch, would haunt and infuriate the man for the rest of his career. It would have to do.

"Let's go." Nicholas ushered the boy out of his cell. As they made their way to the front gate, he feared that one of the sentries would wake up and sound the alarm. At one point, Patrick tripped over the leg of a man stretched out across a hallway, holding the drugged bottle of wine tucked under his arm. Everyone froze and Patrick's eyes grew wide with terror, but the man slept on.

Once they had left the fort, they all headed straight for the woods. They were safe, for now.

"What's next, Flynn?" one of the men asked.

"We run. Follow Dominic."

Dominic waved his arm for them to follow him, and began to run down a path through the dense vegetation.

Dawn reached the island just as they came upon a small cove where a rowboat was waiting for them. Nicholas recognized it as a similar one he and Brianna had used after they'd escaped the fort and met Joe. In the distance Dominic's ship, the *Robbie Darling*, was waiting for them.

"Are you coming with us?" Patrick asked Nicholas.

"Not this time."

"Is the captain aboard? Is she all right?" Patrick hesitated to get in the rowboat. He looked so afraid yet brave as he faced an unknown future. Nicholas was proud of the lad.

Nicholas gently nudged Patricktoward the boat. "She's safe in King's Landing. I vow to take care of her."

"With your life?" Patrick asked, deadly serious. "She's the best captain I've ever had. She deserves . . ."

"She deserves the world, and I will do my best to give it

to her." Nicholas clasped the young man's shoulder. "Now off you go."

With everyone aboard, they rowed toward the distant sloop. Dominic, Roberta, and Nicholas waited for the *Robbie Darling* to collect its passengers. They were safe, at least for now.

"Where's your ship headed?" Nicholas asked.

"New York. We have a scheduled trade stop there to sell some tea. No one will think anything is amiss with a few new crew members."

Roberta linked her arm through Dominic's and grinned at him cheekily. "This is why I insist on planning all of Dominic's schemes. It went rather smoothly, didn't it, Nick?"

Dominic harrumphed.

"Yes, it did." Nicholas looked to his friend. "So what was your plan, Dom?"

"He wanted to blow the fort apart with cannons."

"It would have been far more fun to blow up that damnable fort than to sneak out of it under the cover of darkness." Dominic kissed his wife's forehead and gave Nicholas an evil smirk, as though imagining blowing up the fort in just such a manner.

Nicholas chuckled as Dominic and Roberta continued to argue the merits of various escape plans. "Shall we return home now? My wife will be up soon."

An hour later, they wearily trudged up the steps of Dominic's home. All Nicholas wanted was to sink into the feather tick mattress beside Brianna and sleep. Then when she woke, he would tell her the good news, and all would be well. She might be mad that he'd left her behind, but he hoped she would forgive him knowing that Patrick and the others were safe and on their way to New York.

One of Dominic's men burst out of the front door as they arrived. "Thank goodness you're back."

Nicholas saw the concern on the man's face.

"What is it, Lawson? What happened?" Dominic asked.

"It's Mrs. Flynn, sir. She's gone."

"Gone?" Nicholas echoed the word. It didn't make sense. "Gone where? How?"

The footman handed Nicholas a sheet of paper that had been folded. "She left this for you in your chambers. I didn't think it could wait."

Flynn opened it, staring at the words Brianna had written to him.

Flynn,

You broke your word to me. I can see clearly now that a life with me, a life we share, isn't something you truly wanted. Now I'm free and so are you.

Holland

"Nick, what is it?" Dominic asked.

Nicholas handed him the letter. "She left . . . She thought I didn't want her. Why the bloody hell would she think that?"

"Lawson, when did she leave?" Roberta asked.

"A few minutes after you and Mr. Flynn, my lady. I didn't know if I should stop her, but . . ." The former pirate blushed. "I didn't want to restrain her."

"It's all right, Lawson," Dominic said. "I doubt you could have.

Roberta's face was stricken with anguish. "Oh, Nick, I've been a fool."

"What do you mean?"

She pointed to the balcony that overlooked the front steps and the road beyond.

"She must've seen us, Nicholas, just the two of us before we left."

Nicholas replayed that departure in his mind, trying to see it from his new wife's perspective. "Oh. Oh no."

Dominic sighed. "We had better go after her."

"But where would she go?" Nicholas asked.

"Back to her father," Dominic replied, as if it was obvious.

"Where would that be? No one can find the Shadow King," Nicholas said.

Dominic gave him one of his insufferable grins. "He's easy to find, if you know where to look. He'll be on the island where the Brethren of the Coast gather."

"The Brethren of the Coast?" Nicholas stared at Dom. He, like every young midshipman, had secretly studied the history of pirates. "But . . . they disbanded sixty years ago. These pirates here today don't trust each other like the old ones used to."

Dominic barked a laugh. "That's just what we want you naval men to think. Buck has been the Admiral of the Black for ten years now."

"Admiral of the Black?"

"You call him the Shadow King. To us, he's the Admiral of the Black."

Dominic turned back to Lawson. "Have the men at the docks ready the *Dragon's Enchantress* for sail. We need to leave in a few hours."

"Yes, Captain."

Lawson disappeared, and Dominic took his wife by the shoulders.

"Robbie, I need you to stay here. Be as angry as you want, but we need eyes and ears on the fort and any ship movements. We need to know what they might be planning. You know who to relay messages to if you need to send word to us."

She sighed. "All right. Bring Brianna back safe, won't you?"

"We will, won't we, Nick?"

Nicholas didn't answer. His gaze was on the horizon. He was going to find his wife and explain everything. He loved her, and he wasn't about to fail her.

Wherever you have gone, I'll find you, my pirate queen.

CHAPTER 18

"Well then, what brings the enchanting and fearsome Brianna to my ship?"

Gavin Castleton was, by all accounts, one of the most notorious and rakish pirates in the West Indies. He leaned back against the closed door and grinned lazily at her like a cat who'd just discovered a bowl of cream.

She'd forgotten how darkly handsome he was. It was little wonder that she'd taken him to bed on more than one occasion. Gavin had been enjoyable enough—raw, rough, passionate—but something had always been missing between them. Whatever it was hadn't been physical, but *something* had indeed been missing.

She had never been tempted to linger in his arms, to feel his heartbeat against her cheek or whisper stories of pirate queens to him, not like she had with Nicholas. There had been something deeper about her connection to Nicholas that she didn't fully understand. She tried to ignore the ache in her chest that thoughts of him created, but pushing them away only seemed to make them stronger.

"I needed a ship," she finally told Gavin.

"What happened to the *Serpent*?" His humor faded, and true concern deepened on his face. "Did you lose her in a storm?" He knew she loved that ship more than almost anything. To lose it was to lose a part of herself.

"No, she was taken by the navy to be docked at Kingston."

Gavin pushed away from the door.

"And yet you are free. Did you abandon her?"

She shook her head. "My father and I were trying to run a blockade at Basseterre. A storm came up, and we were able to draw the navy's focus from my father so he and his crew could escape."

Gavin stared at her, his gaze the hard, appraising look of a pirate captain. "And you were taken . . ."

"Most of my men escaped, but a handful, along with myself, were still on board when the navy boarded us."

"My God . . . How did you escape?" Any other man would have thrown his booted feet up on the nearest table and leaned back to enjoy a well-told yarn of her escape, but Gavin was more serious than other pirate captains . . . and he'd professed to love her once. He wouldn't treat this tale lightly.

Gavin drew his chair closer to her and reached out for her hand. She almost pulled away; instead, she let him touch her, inwardly marveling that it didn't feel the same as when Nicholas touched her, perhaps because it didn't mean the same to her heart. Nicholas knew more secret parts of her than any other person.

"I didn't." She played with the sextant on the table as she told him how Nicholas had insinuated himself into her crew, how his duplicity had been uncovered, how her father had intended to use him for leverage, and how he had come back for her once her ship was captured. "He told the officers I was a captive of the pirates and that I was his wife."

"His wife?" Gavin choked out. "Why would he say that?"

"He felt it was the only way to save me. We were married yesterday. Everything was done secretly, and the magistrate dated the documents to show we married a year ago, of course."

Gavin gave a disbelieving snort. "Brianna, surely you were coerced. The marriage is void if—"

"I wasn't coerced." She wished she had been. But she hadn't.

"Then why am I sensing there is so much you haven't told me? We are friends, Brianna," he reminded her. It always amused her that this fearsome pirate could be so kind whenever he was alone with her.

Brianna owed him an explanation since she was running away on his ship. Once Nicholas returned to King's Landing, he would find her gone. She had left a note, but she wasn't sure if it would keep him from chasing after her.

She told Gavin everything in regards to Nicholas, even more than she had told her father. She had this desperate need to talk to someone, someone who knew her, about how she felt about Nicholas. Gavin listened patiently, his honey-brown eyes fixed on her while she spoke.

"So that's how I ended up here."

"Running away from the man you love," he added.

"I only said that to him in a moment of passion," she argued.

Gavin smiled. "Then he must have been an *exceptional* lover. You never once said that to me when we shared a bed."

Brianna blushed, but he was right. When she had lain beside Nicholas, even the brief time that she'd been with him, it had felt real to her in a way no others had because she'd been her truest self. Just herself, fully and completely.

Brianna tried to change the subject. "So, where are we headed?"

"The Black Isle," Gavin said, lowering his tone. "Your father sent word—the Brethren are convening."

Hope blossomed inside her. "You heard from my father?"

"Aye. The *Sea Hawk*'s colors were seen flying on several ships today in the port. The call he sent out was to meet at the Black Isle."

Years ago, her father had developed a system among pirates to communicate. They planted Brethren on merchant ships to act as normal seamen, unbeknownst to the rest of the crew. They could send signals back and forth between ships as they passed. Large colored handkerchiefs were used on the port side of any given ship, which her father had jokingly called the *Sea Hawk*'s colors. There were four or five different colors. Black was the signal for a meeting at the Black Isle. Word could travel fast with such a system.

"Why has he called a meeting?" she asked.

"I'm not sure. Given your tale, I'm wondering if it might be about you. He could be rallying the captains to come to your rescue."

"I haven't seen him since my capture in the harbor of Basseterre," she mused. "I suppose it's possible, but he knows I'm safe with Nicholas—or rather, I was. I thought, perhaps . . ."

Gavin leaned in toward her across the table. "Perhaps what?"

"Well, he might be considering hanging it all up." She trusted Gavin with this knowledge, whereas she wouldn't trust most others. Her father had maintained a tenuous alliance between the various pirate captains, and while they respected him, she believed they wouldn't hesitate to strike if they thought it would give them an advantage. The Admiral of the Black was a powerful position to hold.

"If that's the case, we had better make haste for the Brethren meeting. He'll need our support to have a successful change in leadership. If you'll excuse me." Gavin stood and left his cabin to give new orders to his crew.

Brianna stared down at the charts again. No official map labeled the location of the Black Isle as an actual island. Pirates, at least the ones in charge of navigation, marked the island with a black raven drawn as if it were flying.

When Gavin returned, he made a pallet on the floor beside his bed, but when she tried to take the pallet, he stared at her.

"Gavin . . . ," she said warningly. She'd never liked being treated like a delicate lady, not by men who should be valuing her as an equal.

"Bri, you're a fine lady now—"

"Supposedly," she retorted. "Fine, let's flip for it."

He was the quicker of the two to pull a Spanish piece of eight from his pocket and call his side. She called hers, he flipped it, and she caught it, laying it flat on her hand where he could see.

"Blast and hell!" she cursed and stomped toward the bed before she flung the coin at him.

Gavin caught it with a wicked grin and slipped it back into his trouser pocket. Then he took his spot on the floor.

Brianna lay there in the dark long after she'd blown out the oil lamp hanging by the bed.

"Thank you for taking me aboard, Gavin."

"Of course," he murmured back. "You'd do the same for me."

A pang stung her at how easily she wished it was Nicholas's voice she heard so close in the dark.

"If you want me, I'll be here, Brianna," Gavin said. "If you ever decide to let go of the man who holds your heart, there's always room in mine."

Once, that might have tempted her. Once, before she'd fallen in love with the enemy.

She listened to the creaking of the ship and felt the rhythmic sway that was far more comfortable to her than the land. What had she done, marrying Nicholas, trusting him with her heart? Even though she had run away, she wasn't sure she could ever let go.

It could never have worked for the two of them. She was a creature of sea and wind, needing to see every new port and chase new adventures, sometimes against the laws of England. Nicholas was a refined gentleman, one who craved a simple, quiet life with a woman who wanted the same things he did.

We were a disaster from the moment we kissed. But she couldn't regret the hurricane of passion that had existed between them, nor the infinite peace she'd felt when in the eye of the storm as she'd opened herself up to him, lying in his arms. She wouldn't let herself regret a moment of it.

But how did one sail through calm seas after experiencing such a raw, powerful storm of the heart like falling in love? She couldn't go back, but she didn't know any way forward either. She was sailing without charts. All she could do was find her father and then decide on her future.

The gold signet ring on her finger was warm to the touch. That was the funny thing about gold. It warmed against one's skin as though it enjoyed being worn. Her wedding band was the same type of gold, resting on her other finger. For as long as she could remember, she had craved the feeling of treasure pouring through her hands, feeling the gems and coins slipping between her fingers in a waterfall of riches, knowing she was going to spread it among people who needed it, but now she knew there were other treasures to desire, treasures of the heart.

Treasures to long for and be haunted by.

NICHOLAS STOOD AT THE BOW OF THE *DRAGON'S Enchantress*, one of several new ships Dominic had named yet again after Roberta. He stared into the night, the black water mixing with the inky darkness as far as the eye could see. The waning moon was a mere sliver, offering no real light. It was as dark around him as it was within him.

He should have listened to Dominic and let Brianna come with them on the rescue mission. He'd been so focused on righting the wrong that had been done against her that he'd stumbled into an even greater one.

What he wouldn't give to find her, to pull her into his arms and hold her, then get on his bloody knees and beg her forgiveness.

He sensed someone creeping up behind him and saw Dominic when he looked over his shoulder. They still wore their black shirts and trousers from the rescue, and it reminded him of their youth. How they would often dress in dark clothes and sneak about causing mischief. He smiled at the memories. Nicholas had never wanted to be a pirate, but back then he would've done anything Dominic asked him to.

"How long will it take us to reach this island?" he asked. Dominic joined him against the railing, studying the sails and the way they billowed out in the direction they were headed.

"Tomorrow evening, if this wind holds."

They were silent a long moment, listening to the sea and the wind rippling through the canvas above them.

"What will you do when you find her?" Dominic asked.

"I'll do my damnedest to explain to her what she misunderstood. I'll tell her that her crew is alive and apologize for not taking her with me. What could she have been thinking, just running off like that?"

"She was raised a pirate, Nick. In case you couldn't tell, having conversations about our feelings is not really something we are good at. Such things make us predictable, vulnerable. Those are the quickest ways for a pirate to get caught and hanged. She's doing what feels safe to her."

"I thought I was protecting her." Nicholas dragged his hands through his hair as his head dropped beneath his shoulders in defeat.

"Do you remember that hunting party Lord Faulkin had when we were ten years old? The mother fox who was shot?"

Nicholas winced at the memory. He'd never enjoyed watching fox hunts. "I do."

"We found that vixen crawling toward her den, but she died before she reached it," Dominic continued.

The sounds of the little orphaned kits still haunted him. "I remember," he grunted.

"You crawled into that den and collected those three kits before the hounds sniffed them out, and then you carried them home."

Nicholas smiled. "Mother was furious but didn't dare to tell Father about them." He had kept the kits in a basket under his four-poster bed, which, thankfully, was on the opposite end of the house so his father hadn't heard the kits crying at night. But it hadn't been easy. Saving the kits had been hard work. They bit and clawed and barked at him and only ventured out from under the bed to eat when he wasn't in the room. He'd been bloodied and scratched up in his attempts to win their trust.

Then one night, the kits had left the nest beneath his bed one by one to come and take milk from a saucer and bits of meat from his outstretched hand.

"You earned their trust. You showed them that something different, something foreign isn't always to be feared. People are no different. We fear the unknown, whatever it might be. When we reach the Black Isle, you must find your wife and show her again and again that she has nothing to fear with you." Dominic paused and considered Nicholas for a moment. "You have something that I have never mastered."

"What is that?" Nicholas asked.

"Compassion and patience. It is something that most

people go their whole lives without, and it's what makes you a better man than I. All you need to win her trust is courage and kindness." Dominic placed a palm on Nicholas's shoulder. "That was why I told you to marry Roberta if I ended up on the gallows. It wasn't because you were my best friend or that I trusted you. It was simply that you are a *good* man, the best I've ever had the honor to know. You gave up everything to find me, gave up so many years of your life, not even knowing if I was dead or alive. It's time now that I help you."

Nicholas said nothing at first, but then the emotions he had tried so hard to ignore swam their way to the surface. "I truly love her, Dom. *Madly*. Every little thing about her."

Dominic gave a wry chuckle. "That's the thing about love. One minute you're sailing through a storm so vast you think you'll sink before you reach the other side. Then, in a single instant, the winds die, the rain fades, the clouds break, and all before you is sunshine and sweet, glorious light."

Nicholas could feel the storm now. He was so weary, but if he trusted his friend, he might just feel the sun upon his face again.

"Now, come down to my cabin and let's drink," Dominic said. "It's been a long time since I've had anyone decent to play chess with."

THE SUN WAS WARM, THE SAND BENEATH HER FEET HOT BUT not too hot. It was the perfect sort of temperature to lie on the beach all day. Instead, Brianna raced down to the surf and plunged into the cool water. There was nothing so splendid as hot sand, cold water, and warm sun to make her feel alive.

Something touched her hand, and she glanced down to see a set of fingers laced through her own. She looked up, and Nicholas was watching her with that teasing smile of his that made her breath catch in her throat.

"How did you find me?" she asked.

"I'll always find you." The twinkle in his intense blue eyes made her feel both longing and heartache.

"In what distant deeps or skies.
Burnt the fire of thine eyes?
On what wings dare he aspire?
What the hand, dare seize the fire?"

BRIANNA BLUSHED. WHO KNEW HER NICHOLAS READ poetry? She'd told him once that she loved poetry but so rarely had a chance to find good poetry books in the ports she visited.

"I didn't want to leave," she said. "I didn't want to leave you." Why had she run from him? She should have stayed. Should have argued with him. Wasn't love worth fighting for? Instead, she'd run from him like a coward, but he'd still found her.

He smiled and pulled her into his arms. "I know. That's why I'm coming after you. We are two halves of a whole, my little pirate queen." He brushed the back of his hand over her cheek, and tears burned in her eyes.

"What do you mean? You're here with me now."

"You're dreaming, lass, wake up. Wake up!"

Brianna bolted up and fought hard as hands on her shoulders shook her. She swung a fist and struck someone's face.

"Christ, I forgot you were so strong,"

It took a moment to get her bearings. "Gavin?"

"You were crying in your sleep. I thought it was best to wake you. Also, we've arrived. I figured you'd better come up on deck."

She pulled on her boots and followed him up. She studied the waters as they approached the Black Isle. It was a forested island surrounded by a rocky shoreline, except for one cove that only the captains of the eight major pirate ships knew how to navigate safely.

"I see you have men manning the guns," said Brianna.

Gavin joined her at the railing. "We haven't had a meeting of the Brethren in almost three years. Anything can happen."

Anything can happen. Somehow the words filled her with a mix of dread and hope.

FAR BELOW IN THE HOLD, CAPTAIN WAVERLY LURKED IN the dank, musty darkness, biding his time where no one would come looking for anyone.

He had followed the Holland girl all the way from King's Landing, intending to grab her when he had the chance, but he'd had to steal a horse to catch up with her, only to almost miss her when she reached the docks. But he'd seen which ship she had boarded, and it was one he'd been suspicious of for some time. Waverly used the promise of the reward money for Buck's capture to hire a local ship and its crew to follow his orders. He would find a way to board the ship the Holland girl was on and have his hired ship follow them out to sea and wait for his signal to send him a rowboat whenever they reached land.

It amazed him how all he had to do was escort a drunken pirate from one of the many taverns to the docks and appropriately dress himself in sailor's togs, and then he was able to board the very ship she had gotten onto. He'd said he was a new member of the crew when one of the men had asked him his name, but other than that, none of them had been suspicious when he'd come aboard.

Then all he had to do was slip down into the part of the ship where few people ever went unless they feared the vessel was leaking. Before he'd reached his hidden vantage point, he'd lingered in the upper decks to overhear conversations. Sounds traveled well on a ship. He heard the captain and the Holland girl speaking, the flapping tongues of fools who thought themselves safe to talk. Now, thanks to those same fools, his suspicions had been confirmed. Lady Brianna St. Laurent, the Holland girl, was a pirate, and not just any pirate. She was Buck's daughter. Once he'd learned that bit of information, he'd slipped down through the ship until he'd reached the hold, where several barrels were stored as ballast, and he'd ducked behind them to wait.

He grinned malevolently in the dark. Oh yes, he would get her alone and then spirit her away. Once Waverly had Buck's daughter in his possession, he could make Buck surrender.

He would hang the pirate king, and then he would use

the man's daughter however he liked until the fire in her green eyes was gone. Then she too would hang, and he would have sated the beast inside him, for now.

Far above him, the men sang as they worked. They were close to their destination. He hummed softly along with them, and his smile widened in the dark.

CHAPTER 19

Brianna swung a machete to clear a path through the trees and plants as she and Gavin forced their way through the thick underbrush of the Black Isle. Despite the fact that she walked this path a few times each year, the plants and wildlife always grew back to conceal the entrance, as if nature itself wanted to hide the pirate haven.

Exotic birds trilled in the mist that hung like a cloak around the island. Between the mist and the forest, the island was shrouded in darkness.

Ahead of them lay a small village built by escaped slaves, known as Maroons. A few of the older pirates, like her father, had their own small houses in the village to stay in when they visited. The Black Isle was a true pirate haven in an age when most had been destroyed by navies from the great nations that still vied for dominance on the sea.

The life she'd lived growing up had been an ever-changing landscape between her father's home in Saint Kitts, this island, and on ships, which seemed on the surface so different from the life she would have been expected to lead as Nicholas's wife, yet she faced danger at every turn in every way as a woman in a world run by men. She'd grown up under the protection of her father and had then been given over to Nicholas to protect, not unlike an arrangement found in London. It was strange to think of such different worlds mirroring each other like that. Was there no path for a woman who could protect herself?

They moved deeper into the village that made up the haven. The cozy little cottages, the tavern, the small market stalls. It was surprisingly civilized, for a place listed on no maps.

There was one large hall built rather like a long cabin made of logs, a meeting place for the eight pirate captains who led the majority of the crews that made up the current incarnation of the Brethren of the Coast.

Brianna wiped sweat out of her eyes as she took stock of the villagers mingling with the pirates who'd already arrived. Dozens of people drank and laughed as they caught up on the latest news from other crews. More than a few first mates were loaded to the gunwales, with their bellies full of spirits. Only the captains would refrain from drinking—at least until the meeting was concluded. Then a celebration would follow, unless the meeting ran hot with tempers.

A familiar face in the crowd sent Brianna's heart leaping, a Scotsman who was watching the other pirates with a brooding glare.

"Joe!" she called out. When he heard his name, his ill mood vanished in an instant.

"Lass!" he bellowed, sending a number of pirates around

him scattering out of his way. He rushed toward her, arms open wide.

Brianna nodded at Gavin. "I will see you later."

"Of course. I'll be around if you have any need," Gavin replied. It was hard to miss the lustful look mixed with something deeper and more profound in his eyes. It was the kind of look that every woman longed for, even a pirate like her.

"Thank you, Gavin."

If she had only fallen in love with a pirate like Gavin, things would've been different. But she loved Nicholas, damn the man, and had no way of getting her heart back. Even now, he owned it and her.

Joe reached her and scooped her up like she was a mere child.

"How in the blazes are ye here? I saw ye were taken and . . ." His face darkened. "I told yer father I wasna sure what happened to ye. He said he let Flynn go after ye to try to save ye."

"It's all right. I'm free, Joe," she said. He set her down, but as he looked at her, his gaze focused on her fingers. She was wearing the gold signet ring and her wedding band.

"It happened," he pronounced glumly.

She touched the gold wedding band protectively, even though wearing it caused her heart to ache.

"I . . ." She fumbled for words that wouldn't come.

Joe glowered. "So ye've thrown yer lot in with Flynn."

Brianna was all too aware of the eyes of other men on her. "I can explain later. Where is my father?"

"He's in the meeting room." Joe gave a jerk of his head toward the large hall in the center of the village.

She wasted no time getting there. She opened the door and saw her father and three other captains speaking in the corner of the large room that housed the Brethren's round table. The hot, humid air of the island mixed with the smell of ale and rum filled the air of the meeting room. It was almost comforting to smell such things again.

Her father glanced up at her, nodded at the other men near him, and excused himself. He didn't embrace her or show any sign of affection until they had left the meeting-house and crossed the dirt road to a cozy two story house that had belonged to Buck for at least a decade.

Only when they were alone in the entryway of the house did her father pull her into his arms and hug her. His fingers dug into her arms as he clasped her to his chest and pressed a kiss to the crown of her hair. His breath was suddenly ragged, as though he was overcome.

"Thank God," he whispered. "These last few days have been hell. Flynn promised to save you, but I couldn't know for sure what he could manage, given the circumstances."

He pulled back, cupping her face and examining her for injuries. His face was gaunt with worry, and the gray hair streaking his temples seemed more silver than before. It was as though losing her, however briefly, had aged the mighty Thomas Buck. The knowledge that she'd done this to him left a heavy guilt upon his shoulders. Perhaps he was right, that this life was too much now for both of them. She found herself weary of outrunning the navy and fearing for her crew. Before, they'd had a merry time of raiding merchant ships, always staying one step away from the noose, but now the noose was here. Hanging her men . . . men she by all rights should be dying beside.

"When I sent him after you, I feared that . . . that he might take you to England before I could . . ." He didn't finish, but she knew what he was referring to.

"It's all right. I'm here now." She gently pulled his hands down. "But we need to talk. I need to know about my parents. Nicholas told me what he could, but I need to know more. I need to know everything."

Her father sighed and nodded, leading her into the drawing room. They sat down on a faded brocade settee together. Her father hesitated a moment and glanced instead about the decently furnished room. He'd spent many years coming here, as had she. It was almost a second home in addition to their residence on Saint Kitts. It wasn't as grand as the Saint Kitts house, but it was suitably comfortable for any nights spent here on the Black Isle. Even as a pirate, her father had always enjoyed the finest things.

"Where do I begin?" he said, half to himself, half to her.

"Tell me about them. As much as you know." Her voice had turned slightly rough. It was strange to be so affected by the thought of two people she'd never known, yet they were the people who had given her life. Right now, that mattered as much to her as the man who'd raised her.

"It was a terrible storm. We came across a ship in distress. It had crashed upon a reef, and its hull was ripped open. Most of the crew had gone overboard, and those who were left were dead on the upper deck. I held little hope for any survivors, but I had to be sure. I found two in a cabin. Your father had been severely wounded. I think he'd been trying to help those up on the deck, but he was mortally wounded when one of the masts broke.

"He was with your mother, who was laboring with you,

and he knew he wouldn't live to see your birth. He gave me his signet ring and asked me to look after you once you were born. The way he spoke about you and the way he looked at your mother, it was clear you would have been loved dearly by that man. Perhaps that's why I love you the way I do. It's as though he and your mother gave me their love to carry until it became my own." Her father cleared his throat, his eyes a little red. "You were mine to love and cherish the moment I held you in my arms."

Brianna had never heard her father speak with such emotion before. She'd known he was a man deeper than the sea itself, but he often kept much of what he was feeling from her. Now she was being granted access to his thoughts and feelings, and it was threatening to make her cry, something she rarely did.

"And . . . my mother?" The words cut straight through her as she somehow felt her parents in the room with her as she spoke.

"She stayed with us long enough to bring you forth, name you, and tell me to love you as my own. I did. I *loved* you as my child with all my heart, and I loved you for *them* too." He held her hands in his and felt the wedding band on her finger. He looked at her in silent question.

Sorrow burrowed into her heart. He had missed her wedding. Yes, it had begun as a sham, and it had ended as one, but when she'd said her vows, she'd meant them. She'd believed Flynn's words and had wanted to be married to him. And her father should have had the chance to escort her to Nicholas and see her tie her life to his.

"After you escaped, I tried to get my men off the ship. Most swam ashore without being rounded up by the navy, but we were boarded before I had a chance to escape with the last of my men. They took me captive, but Flynn arrived and informed them that I was his wife."

"Did he, now?" Buck murmured.

She fingered the gold wedding band absently, heart in her throat. She did not want to meet her father's eyes lest he see how complex her feelings had become for her husband, especially given what had happened after her wedding night.

"He told them he had sent for me from England and I had been kidnapped by pirates before reaching him. But Admiral Harcourt, Dominic's father-in-law, had us marry in secret and had the marriage certificate dated back to a year ago to cover our story."

She hesitated, but finally continued. "I don't know what to do. Six of my men are in Port Royal facing the noose. Flynn distracted me the night of our wedding when I should've been planning a rescue."

Her tone had changed, and her father eyed her suspiciously. "What aren't you telling me, Brianna? Why are you here now instead of with him?"

Brianna looked away. "I woke up before sunrise and saw him leaving with Dominic's wife. They were embracing and left alone in a coach, just the two of them. I didn't stay to listen to any excuses or lies they might give me. I just needed to . . ."

"Run away?" her father asked. His tone was one of shock, yet he had a rueful smile on his face. "Without confronting him? Without answers? I've never known you to run away from things that scare you, Brianna. What made this different?" His gravelly tone was still soft and held all the gentleness and compassion he'd had for her as a child when the darkness frightened her and her father had come to her rescue.

"I don't know."

"I think you do. Do you love Flynn?"

She swallowed hard and nodded. "I don't want to, but I do."

"And that is why you were too afraid to get answers from him. When our business is concluded here, I want you to return to him and sort this out."

"But what if I can't face him?"

"I've seen you face down frigates armed with twice as many guns as your sloop. Flynn is just one man."

Brianna suppressed a chuckle because of the dark thoughts still gnawing at her. "But what if I'm right about him?"

Buck shook his head. "I doubt Dominic's wife would stray from his bed, and I doubt Nicholas would look at any other woman but you. He didn't deny that he loved you when I asked him. He knew he tempted death at my hands, and yet he admitted his feelings freely. So you face a choice, my heart. Return to him and discern the truth, or stay away and leave yourself to wonder about it the rest of your life."

She'd done nothing but regret her cowardly act, and it stung even more now to know that she had to face up to her own stubborn foolishness.

"I suppose I do." She was no stranger to sailing in foreign waters, and yet these were not merely unfamiliar to her—they were uncharted. Her father was right. It'd been easy to sabotage her relationship by running away because it had felt safer than staying behind and facing what might come next.

"Do you want a life with him, a life with children and—?"

"Yes, but what will it cost? You know me. I could never stay home and be the sort of wife who waits for her husband to return from an adventure. I *need* more from life."

Her father raised an eyebrow in challenge. "Has *he* told you that is what he wants? That he wants you to stay at home and not be who you are? And since when must children be raised ashore? You certainly weren't."

"I don't know what he wants. But he does say that he wishes for me to return to England and meet my uncle. And what more is there for a woman in that part of the world? Where there are laws for men, there are chains for women. Here, at least, there is a chance to be free."

Buck let out a slow sigh. "All your life I taught you about the sea and sailing, but I forgot to teach you about life, about living your life with another person. Perhaps it's because I've had a hard time doing it myself. Flynn may surprise you, my heart. But it's up to you to find out. You've stormed onto armed ships to plunder their treasure; surely a simple conversation can't be that frightening."

"I wasn't supposed to find love . . ." Her voice lowered as she continued. "At least, not with a man like Flynn. I wanted someone like you, a pirate, a man who would let me have my freedom."

"True love *is* freedom," her father said. "If he cages you, then you don't really love him, nor does he truly love you. Love, *real* love, is incredibly simple. If you trust your instincts, you'll see what I mean."

She closed her eyes briefly before she opened them again. "But what if that means leaving you? What if, after all this, I won't be able to see you again?" That was one of her worst fears, that if she chose a life with Nicholas, she'd never see her father again.

He gripped her hands and gave them a tight squeeze. "I never planned on being a father, but the moment I held you in my arms and you gazed up at me with those green eyes, love was there in my heart, fully and completely. No matter what you find in England or who you become in the years to come, I will be your father, always. Time and distance won't ever change that."

Always. That word spoke of a love that could not perish. It was more permanent than the seas themselves. It was *infinite*. How beautiful it was to think that such an infinite, vast thing as love could be contained within a human heart. But that's what made love such a miracle. One shouldn't be afraid of miracles, but embrace them.

She threw her arms around her father's neck and held him, tears streaming down her cheeks as he hugged her back. This moment felt like a goodbye, and she didn't want it to be.

"No matter what happens, I will always find you, Brianna. *Always*."

She lifted her head from his shoulder to stare at him. Something about his tone frightened her. "Father?"

"It's time for the Brethren to convene. We will talk again once this is done." Buck stood and released her.

"When what is done?" she asked. "Why have you called this meeting?"

Her father smiled. "You know why. My time is at an end. A new Admiral of the Black will be chosen, and I am to retire from this life."

She'd suspected that this was what her father had

planned, but it still left her feeling strangely empty. The Brethren had their code, and she must respect what occurred today, no matter what came next.

NICHOLAS HELD HIS BREATH AS HE AND DOMINIC ENTERED the village on the Black Isle. The island was dark with forests, and the sun struggled to penetrate the fog and trees. It left him with an eerie feeling that he was somewhere very old and that power resided in this place. He had been brought ashore as Dominic's first mate to be at his side while the Brethren convened. In all his years in the navy, he'd never heard of this island or seen it on any chart. Yet here it was, an island that was seemingly unfindable, except to pirates. How was such a thing possible? There were no high peaks, and the entire island was shrouded in mist. He felt *trapped*.

"Calm yourself," Dominic murmured. "Remember, you are no navy man here."

Yes, today he was a pirate, and he was here to find his treasure—*his wife*.

"Follow me." Dominic strode toward a structure in the center of the village. When they stepped through the door they faced a large round table, one that made him think of old Arthurian legends. The room was dark, but as the light from the lamps grew brighter, he saw the room was full of men and Buck stood across from him on the other side of the table.

"Dominic, good of you to join us, if unexpected," Buck said with a respectful nod. "And Flynn," he added, his eyes betraying a flash of emotion too quick to name.

"Buck," Dominic replied, and he took his chair. Nicholas stayed standing behind Dominic just as the other first mates stood behind their seated captains. Only Buck remained standing among the captains. Nicholas searched the room for Brianna and her first mate Joe, but they weren't among the men seated here. Dominic had warned him she wouldn't be, she was a lesser captain. Only the most experienced captains qualified for a seat at this table.

"I called for this meeting to announce that I will sail no longer under the Jolly Roger. We shall vote today on a successor for Admiral of the Black, whose duties will be to lead the Brethren profitably and, it is hoped, wisely. Before we begin, each man must surrender his weapons to the table." Buck moved first, placing his short sword and pistol before him on the table. One by one, the other captains followed suit and their first mates did the same. The weapons were all within easy reach of their owners but the surrender was symbolic of the peace they sought to keep in this room.

"Upon the blood of our brothers, we are now to vote a new man in my place. Who wishes to become the next Admiral of the Black?"

There were a few glances in Dominic's direction, but he betrayed no emotion as he continued to stare straight at Buck. Nicholas realized just how powerful his childhood friend must have been in the pirate world before he'd given the life up. It still surprised Nicholas that they were even here. He must not have given it up completely. Nicholas wondered if Roberta knew about her husband's side business. Mostly likely she did, given her behavior during the prison break. But Admiral Harcourt certainly didn't know.

"No one wishes to take the role?" Buck sounded mildly surprised. Nicholas glanced about, taking the measure of the six other captains aside from Buck and Dominic.

An older Spanish pirate with a black-and-silver beard adorned with colorful beads cleared his throat.

"Buck, what if you were to name a successor?"

"Captain Encino, thank you, but I will only appoint one if the entire court of pirates requests it. You should determine your fates, not have it dictated to you by me."

"Perhaps, but you have led us well for many years and have kept us free of the noose. How could we not trust you now?" Captain Encino raised his hand and looked around at the other seated captains. "Raise a hand to have Buck choose his successor."

Every hand at the table went up, and Buck let out a sigh.

"Very well. I will make a choice, but I want no bloodshed if there are those who disagree with my decision. We have kept our peace many long years through our respect for one another."

Nicholas couldn't deny Buck's charisma as a leader, his quiet confidence and respect both given and shown by others. It was easy to see how such a man could rule from the shadows as he had all these years.

"Aye, we will respect your decision," another captain answered. "And if I wanted a sermon, I'd have stayed in the priesthood. Get on with it already!" The occupants of the room chuckled at the man's exaggerated impatience.

"Very well, then. My choice is based not only on skills at captaincy but also cunning and courage. I believe he is a man who will stand for all of you." Buck pointed at the man seated next to Dominic. "I choose Gavin Castleton to be the next Admiral of the Black."

There was a moment of quiet, and then Captain Encino reached across the table to lift the butt of his pistol and rapped it on the table in approval. The others followed suit, including Dominic, who pounded the handle of his dagger on the stout wood.

Gavin stood, and Nicholas took a moment to study him. He was of a similar height, but he was dark where Nicholas was fair-haired. He was perhaps twenty-five or twenty-six, but there was an ancient look to his face that spoke of a man who'd already done much in his life.

"Thank you, Buck. I am humbled and gladly accept the nomination."

Dominic and the other captains stood. "Gavin Castleton, Admiral of the Black," they shouted as one.

"Congratulations, Castleton," Buck said, visibly relieved his choice had been well received. "Now, why don't we all drink to celebrate?"

Nicholas joined the others for a customary bit of rum before he felt Buck's gaze on him.

"Looks like you had better go speak with him," Dominic whispered, leaning close. "Now's your chance."

Nicholas followed Buck out of the meetinghouse through a back door and continued to the edge of the jungle that surrounded the village. For a moment, Nicholas worried that Brianna's father might be ready to do him in.

"So you've come for her, then?" Buck asked. The man crossed his arms over his chest, frowning at Nicholas.

"I have, if she's here."

"She is," Buck said.

Nicholas let out a breath of relief. "Thank God." The tension in his shoulders faded, and the knot of fear in his stomach began to subside.

"She is the bravest woman I've ever known," Buck said softly, "but she fears a broken heart more than anything this world might throw at her. Whatever you did to make her run, you had better fix it."

Nicholas was suddenly overcome with guilt that he had put Brianna through all this. He had caused her so much pain trying to spare her from it.

"She's my everything, Buck. I won't fail her."

"You'd better not." Buck's gaze turned distant. "I'm leaving for England as soon as I settle my affairs here. Would a former pirate be welcome at your home, should she decide to return to Cornwall with you?" Buck's voice was calm, but Nicholas could only guess how much his answer would either destroy Buck or save him.

"Brianna's father will always be welcome at our home, wherever it may be. I am resigning my commission from the navy. I would've done it the day of our wedding, but I was preoccupied with saving her crew at the fort."

At this, Buck's eyes gleamed. "You saved Brianna's crew?"

"We did, thanks to a clever plan by Dominic's wife."

Buck chuckled. "Ah, so that's where you two went."

"What?" Nicholas asked.

"Brianna saw you run off with Dominic's wife and thought, well . . . She wasn't sure if you had betrayed her, so she erred on the side of caution."

"I see. But still, it is my fault she ever had to make that assumption."

"You'd best find her and make your explanations. Make

her see she has no reason to fear loving you." Buck smiled and left. One moment he was there, the next he had slipped into the thick foliage on some unseen path. Nicholas turned back to the village and went in search of his wayward wife.

❧

JOE JOINED BRIANNA AT THE SINGLE TAVERN IN THE village where most of the first mates and a few captains were enjoying a tankard of ale. "There. 'Tis done, lass." The tavern was now filling with the first mates who'd been present at her father's meeting, but Brianna barely noticed.

She was slumped in a chair in the corner, watching the festivities and wondering where Nicholas was and what he was doing.

"Lass?" Joe said more loudly as he sat down beside her. "Yer not even listening to me."

"What's done?" she asked as she recalled what he had said.

"Yer father retired the *Sea Hawk* from sailing under the Jolly Roger."

"I figured he would. Have they replaced him?" She wished she could have sat in with him, but only eight captains commanded the table. Those eight had been sailing together on the high seas the longest and had the most trust between each other. Her father stepping down would mean that the new Admiral of the Black would choose a new captain to take the spare chair. She and Reese Belishaw as younger captains might have a chance at earning a position at the table, but she'd have to wait and hear. Of course . . .

she had no crew and no ship at the moment, so likely she would be passed over for such a position of honor.

"Gavin Castleton took his place."

"Gavin is the new Admiral of the Black?"

"Aye." Joe tipped his head back as he took a long drink. "And yer man is here too. He stood as Dominic Gray's first mate. Reese sent word that he was surrendering his seat at the table for Dominic for the vote."

"My man?"

Joe lifted up his left hand and wiggled his ring finger at her.

"Nicholas?" She stood so quickly she knocked over her chair, and several men shot startled glances at her.

"Where is he?"

"Last I saw, he went to talk to yer father behind the meetinghouse."

Brianna was running before she even had time to think. She crossed the dirt path of the street and rounded the edge of the meetinghouse building only to find it empty.

"Nicholas?" she called out. The name echoed into the stillness around her.

The forest was quiet. No birds sang, no frogs thrummed their voices, no monkeys chattered. All was still.

Then, without warning, she took a blow to her head. All strength left her body. She crashed to the ground and only partially regained consciousness, smelling the dirt by her face and seeing a dark, blurry figure looming over her. The sound of a harsh chuckle followed her into blackness, which was far more terrifying than sinking beneath the depths of the sea.

"We meet again, Holland."

CHAPTER 20

Brianna's head throbbed, and the pain slowly forced her back to awareness. She lay on a wooden floor somewhere dark and cold. With tentative fingers, she touched her head and winced as fresh pain pounded through her skull. When she tried to move, a wave of nausea and vertigo made her head spin. After several long minutes, she finally felt well enough to move again. She got to her knees and leaned against the nearest thing to her for support, which turned out to be iron bars.

"No," she groaned as her fingers curled around the bars of the cell. *How . . . ?* She struggled to think about the last thing she could remember. She had seen her father, learned Nicholas was on the island, and—pain sliced through her head as she failed to remember anything after that.

Her eyes adjusted to the dark. From the sway of her body, she knew she was aboard a ship. Water crashed against the sides of the hull in a rhythmic pattern, and she knew that they had to be far from a port. She looked around for something, anything, to work the bars with, but of course there was nothing. Nothing to do but wait.

She sat down on an overturned crate and rested her chin on her hand. Where was Nicholas? Knowing that she'd likely never see him again left a hollow, desolate ache inside her. If only she'd found him before she'd been captured. But now it was too late.

She heard boots thud on the companion ladder nearby as someone came toward her. She flinched when Captain Waverly's face came into the dim light.

"I thought perhaps I had hit you too hard. It would've been a pity to kill you when I plan to see you hang." He wasn't wearing his pristine red uniform. He looked like a common sailor in blue trousers and a white shirt belted at the waist. Something about that worried her more than she could say.

"I want to speak to the captain of the ship. He should want to see me if I am a prisoner of the navy."

At this, Waverly laughed with dark glee.

"Oh, we aren't aboard a naval vessel. None of those captains back in Port Royal would listen to me when I insisted we go after you. So I was forced to hire my own crew."

A pit of dread formed deep within her. Marriage license or no, the admiral would not be able to protect her. Not from this man.

"What's your plan, then?" She was unable to hide a slight waver in her voice, and his face split into a wicked grin again.

"I will take you back to Port Royal and show the navy how a civilized nation deals with pirates. Then your father will hear of your impending execution, which will be stayed if and only if he turns himself in. Once Buck is dead, we'll hang you anyway."

"Buck won't come. He won't know you've taken me, and even if he learned of it, it would be too late. He's left the West Indies."

"My dear, consider where I found you. I saw every notorious fiend wanted by the Crown there, including your father. And he *will* come for you—Buck wouldn't leave his daughter to die. I left a very clear message for him." Waverly chuckled and pointed to her head and she touched her hair, finding a small lock of hair by her ear had been cut short. Her father would know what the blond hair meant if he saw it.

"He will come chasing after you, I will prove that Admiral Harcourt is a doddering old fool, and that those who are loyal to him are as misguided as he is."

She didn't dare ask Waverly how he'd discovered she was Buck's daughter. She wanted to divert his attention away from her father as much as possible.

"What do you have against the admiral?" She wanted to keep him talking. A man like Waverly should never have an idle moment; it could prove fatal for anyone near him.

Waverly's lip curled in disdain. "He's the father-in-law to a damned pirate. He is supposed to uphold the law of the Crown, and yet beneath his nose, you all sail about wreaking havoc on our trade. Mercy has no place in these savage lands until they are well and truly tamed." He touched the bars of her cell as he spoke, giving them a slight tug, and Brianna barely stopped herself from retreating a step.

Brianna knew she was staring at a madman. A zealot. Nicholas had shown her that there were good and honorable men in the navy, but this man represented everything she'd grown up despising. The iron boot on the throat of the Caribbean, taking what they wanted and giving nothing back. The *real* pirates.

Still desperate to keep Waverly talking, she prodded, "How did you get me off the island?"

"I carried you to the shore, and the captain of the ship had a rowboat waiting for me. He couldn't find his way into the cove like the other pirate ships, but that didn't matter, he knew to send a rowboat to the nearest shore which could land a rowboat. Before I came after you, I located the beach and spotted their ship and signaled with a brief fire that I put out before your pirates even noticed."

"But how did you even find the island without being followed?"

He lifted his chin with an almost gleeful sense of pride. "I followed you to the docks and boarded your ship. The vessel I hired was ordered to follow at a distance and wait for me to signal them. As for not being noticed, you forget that island is along a major trade route. All my hired ship had to do was move away frequently out of sight on the horizon when needed, and the pirate crews would believe it was just a different ship appearing and disappearing on the horizon as the ships travel the trade route. No one even guessed it was the same ship."

Brianna closed her eyes as her head throbbed again.

"You and I will have so much fun together," Waverly almost crooned. "I—"

His words were cut off as a shrill whistle sounded from above. The piercing alarm could not be ignored. Waverly stared at her for a long, terrifying second, and then without a word he rushed up the ladder and Brianna pressed her head to the bars and drew in a deep breath, trying to calm her racing heart. Waverly knew she was a woman, and he had her trapped. There was nothing worse she could have imagined than this. The only consolation she had was that he hadn't mentioned Nicholas. It gave her hope that he was still alive.

Whatever the boson on deck had seen to make him blow the whistle like that was enough for a call to arms. She only prayed that whoever was chasing them was on her side.

NICHOLAS SEARCHED THE ISLAND FOR AN HOUR BUT KNEW in his heart that Brianna was gone. He returned to the place where he had met Buck behind the meetinghouse, hoping to get others to help him search, and he found a lock of her golden hair pinned to the earth with an English military dagger. He immediately recognized it as the one Captain Waverly kept sheathed in his belt. Nicholas collected the items and ran for help, finding Buck, Joe, and many of the pirate captains still inside the meetinghouse.

"If she isna on the island, that bloody scum must've found a way to get her off," Joe said in a low growl.

"There are plenty of ways off the island," Buck agreed. "The cove is merely the best way for our ships to remain unseen, but any jolly boat or rowboat could meet a ship offshore."

Buck glanced around at the other pirate captains in the meeting room.

"Anyone who wants to aid me in rescuing my daughter is welcome, but I do not ask this of any of you, lest we face a naval attack once we leave the safety of the cove. I cannot say what awaits us out in open waters."

"You are the Admiral of the Black until midnight," Captain Encino said. "I am still at your back, old friend."

At this, the other captains added their agreement.

"Thank you," Buck said, and then turned to Nicholas. "We have no time to waste."

The cove was soon emptied as they set out to sea, and it wasn't long before the ship they were chasing was sighted. It was as Buck had guessed. Waverly was headed back toward Port Royal on the most direct route possible. Nicholas stood beside Buck on the upper deck of the *Sea Hawk*, Buck watching their quarry through a spyglass. He handed it to Nicholas, who pressed it to his eye and frowned at what he saw.

"That's no naval ship."

"No. If Waverly took a naval vessel we'd notice, but if one of our crews saw a merchant ship trailing behind them, they wouldn't think anything of it. This island is along a major trade route, and we see plenty of merchant ships in these waters. They must know we're on their heels. I wonder what the man is thinking."

Nicholas wished he could view the situation as calmly as Buck seemed to, but his fear for Brianna's safety was nearly choking him. He had seen Waverly's hate for Brianna when he had thought she was a boy. He had seen how unhinged Waverly could be. He knew how very dangerous the man was to her. Even now the captain could be torturing her. They needed to go faster.

"How are you so bloody calm?" Nicholas asked as he handed back the spyglass.

The former pirate king's face was grim. "I'm not. For the last two hours, I've planned a dozen ways to kill that man, none of them merciful."

Nicholas tried not to think of Waverly. Instead, he thought of the things he would say to his wife once she was safe in his arms again. He couldn't allow himself to think of any other outcome.

"Cap'n, we're gaining!" a sailor cried out. Nicholas tensed, desperate to make the ship move even faster with willpower alone.

Buck bellowed to his crew. In a quarter of an hour, they would be close enough to board.

"Raise the red flag! We give no quarter if we board!" Buck said, a fiery light in his eyes as he rejoined Nicholas at the helm.

"You save her. I will handle him," Buck said without looking at Nicholas.

Nicholas nodded and rested his hand on his pistol. His blood hummed with the anticipation of battle and the need to save his wife. He would not let anyone stand in his way.

BRIANNA LEAPT TO HER FEET AS WAVERLY UNLOCKED THE cell door. He held a pistol in his hand.

"Come up on deck. If you try anything, I will put a bullet through you."

Brianna did as he said. She'd felt the ship slow and knew they must either be close to Port Royal or they had stopped in the middle of the sea because the other ship had reached them. Up on deck, she may find an opportunity to escape.

She proceeded ahead of Waverly up the companion ladder until she reached the waist deck. The crew of the ship stared at her as she stopped next to the mainmast, still at gunpoint. She saw the approaching vessel and the fleet behind it. Her father's ship was in the lead and gaining on them. What if Nicholas was among them? If Dominic was there, then Nicholas had to be on one of the ships behind her father's. She couldn't help but smile.

"You won't outrun them," she told Waverly calmly.

"I'm aware," he growled back.

"That red flag means he doesn't intend to take you alive."

"I'm *aware*," Waverly growled again.

"However, if you surrender, I'm sure I can change his mind."

Waverly grabbed Brianna by the jaw and forced her to look into his wild, unreasoning eyes. "Not. Another. Word. From. You."

Then he called up to a man straddling the yardarm above her. "Drop that line down here."

A rope fell down from above to dangle and coil on the deck near Waverly's feet.

Waverly passed another seaman his pistol, and then he advanced on her, the rope in his hands. "Hold this gun on her. If she fights me, shoot her." She assumed he meant to bind her wrists, but instead he looped it around her neck, and she began to panic. Thankfully, he didn't pull it tight. The sailor holding the pistol on her trembled slightly as he watched her.

"You! Hoist her up until she is dancing like a marionette!"

"A wot?" the man upon the yardarm shouted back.

Waverly rolled his eyes and muttered, "Barbarians." Then

he enunciated clearly, "Until she is standing on her toes. Only hang her if I tell you to."

Brianna winced as the rope tightened around her throat. She dug her fingers in, trying to ease the pressure against her windpipe as she was pulled up to her tiptoes.

Waverly stood at the railing, now facing her father's ship as it slowed to shouting distance. He bellowed Buck's name and then pointed at Brianna. She drew in shallow breaths as she realized what Waverly's plan was. With her on deck, an instant from swinging her feet in the air, Waverly could keep the other ships from openly firing at his ship.

"Surrender yourself, Buck! Call off your sea dogs and she will live. Fight me and she hangs for all your men to see." The hired seamen around her murmured worriedly as her father's name passed between them in whispers. Had Waverly not told them they would be chased by the king of pirates?

Brianna closed her eyes, her heart pounding like a frightened animal before she shouted what would likely be her last words.

"Don't do it!" she screamed.

The rope on her neck tightened, and all she could do was gasp like a fish on the deck, begging for breath.

Her father's voice came to her through the haze of her blurry vision from across the water. "I'm coming! Let her down!"

"Don't . . ." The word escaped on a whisper. No one heard her but the wind.

NICHOLAS SAW THE ROPE WRAPPED AROUND HIS WIFE'S throat and lurched for the railing.

"Hold on, lad." Joe grabbed Nicholas by the arm. "We need a plan. Ye canna help her if yer dead."

Nicholas shook Joe's hold off his arm. "Buck, what's your plan?"

Buck's gaze moved over the deck of the other ship. "To surrender, of course."

"But—"

Buck held a finger to his lips and looked up toward the rigging and the yardarm above their heads.

"I will go across and surrender. Once I've done that, you will do whatever is necessary to save Brianna, regardless of my life. Do you understand? She is the only thing that matters." Buck turned to Joe. "Signal the other ships to fall back, but to wait for our sign if we need them to intervene. I want every man now on board that ship alive."

"But the red flag . . ."

"Bring the colors down." Buck's voice was cold. "I will make these men suffer for taking my child. Death is too kind for them."

"Aye, Captain."

Flynn moved quickly toward the rigging of the ship, trying not to attract unwanted attention. Thankfully, Buck's crew was extending the gangway between the two ships now, and it proved a good distraction. Flynn climbed toward the tallest sailing yardarm on the mainmast of Buck's ship. Buck had given him a mad idea that would either save Brianna or Nicholas would die in the attempt to rescue her.

As he reached the tallest yardarm, he cut free a link of rope, sawing through with his dagger. His plan was to swing from one ship to the other using the rope. He made certain one end was still securely tied to the yardarm. He glanced down as Buck stepped across the gangplank and leapt onto the deck of the other ship. Careful to keep his balance, Nicholas used one hand to hold the mast while he gripped the rope, winding it around his left arm several times to give him a solid hold.

Far below him, Waverly raised his pistol as Buck walked toward him, arms raised in surrender. Buck was saying something, but Nicholas was too high up to hear him.

Without warning, Waverly lifted his arm in a signal, and the man on the yardarm across the water raised the rope, jerking Brianna into the air to hang her. Her legs flailed and her hands dug into the rope at her throat. Nicholas couldn't wait another second. He leapt into the air, the rope the only thing holding him as he swung toward the other vessel.

CHAPTER 21

Brianna flailed as she dangled from the rope, her body fighting for any place her feet could catch hold, but there was nothing. Her father's cry of rage was loud at first but faded as her vision grew dark around the edges, and the burn of her lungs began to bother her less and less in a terrifying way.

A shadow blocked the sun above her. She blinked in a daze as a figure came hurtling toward her, sliding down the canvas sail, a knife in his hand, barely slowing his descent. When he was a few feet above her, he swung the knife to slice the rope holding her up, causing them both to plummet. She landed with an agonizing thud on the deck beside him, gasping for air as she pried the noose from her neck.

His name escaped as she gasped for air. "Nick . . ."

She started to smile, only to see a shadow loom up above him. Nicholas must have read something in her eyes because he turned at the last second, his dagger raised in defense as

Waverly swung a short sword toward him. The two blades clashed as Nicholas backed into a fighting stance.

Men charged onto the deck, fighting with sailors aboard the ship she'd been held prisoner on. Muzzles flashed as shots were fired and steel blades clanged together.

Brianna struggled to her feet, leaning against the nearest mast, trying to steady herself so she could join in the fight. Nicholas struck at Waverly like a man possessed, but Waverly fought back with just as much fury. He forced Nicholas back toward the starboard railing and kicked him the next time their blades locked. Nicholas dropped his knife as he crashed into the railing, gripping it so he didn't fall overboard.

Brianna spotted a short blade that lay abandoned next to a fallen man on the deck. She reached for it and charged Waverly from the side. But before she reached him, he spun, pulling a pistol from his belt and aiming it at her, like he'd expected this move all along.

She skidded to a halt, staring down the barrel of his gun.

Waverly sneered as he cocked the hammer. "Send my regards to the devil, *pirate*."

Nicholas leapt and shoved Brianna aside as Waverly fired. Nicholas grunted and stumbled back.

Time slowed as she watched Nicholas face her, blood spreading on his shirt, a stunned look in his stormy eyes. Red descended over Brianna's vision as she surged up and lunged at Waverly before he could bring his blade to bear. Her short sword sank deep into the man's stomach.

"Give him your regards yourself, you bastard." She uncurled her fingers from the blade's grip, which was soaked in his blood.

Waverly dropped his pistol and gripped the short sword's handle, his hands shaking violently as he tried in vain to pull it free. Blood dripped down from his mouth as his strength left him and he dropped to his knees.

Anger, fear, and confusion swirled in his dark eyes. Brianna's mind was oddly quiet, her rage fading as she gazed at the man who'd tried to take everything from her.

"I wish I could kill you a thousand more times," she hissed.

"Filthy . . . pirate . . . ," Waverly gasped as he sank to the deck, blood pooling around him.

Breathing hard, she rushed back to Nicholas. His face was pale, and he held a hand to his stomach. Blood oozed between his fingers.

"Nicholas!"

He gazed up at her, a dreamy smile upon his lips. "You really are my farthest horizon . . ."

He crumpled to the deck, and she fell with him, screaming her father's name.

Her father and Joe reached her first. All around them the fighting slowed, and the enemy dropped their weapons. The man who'd hired them was dead, and the other pirate ships were closing in around them. It was pointless to resist.

"He's been shot," she whispered helplessly.

"We must get him to Dr. Flores, Brianna. He'll do what he can," her father said.

She managed a shaky nod but couldn't seem to release her hold on Nicholas.

Joe and her father pried him from her arms and carried him across the gangplank back to her father's ship. Buck had one of the best doctors in the West Indies on board, and if

Brianna could have chosen anywhere in the world for Nicholas to be right now, it would be on her father's ship. She followed them into the sick bay, where Dr. Flores and one of the cabin boys who assisted him were already tending to a number of wounded men. At the sight of Nicholas's wound, he had the other crew make space on the long wooden table that filled part of the room .

"He took a bullet to the stomach," Buck said.

Dr. Flores, a wiry Portuguese man in his late forties, nodded without a word and pulled Nicholas's shirt up to examine the wound. Brianna gripped the wall for support as her usually strong constitution failed her. She was no stranger to death and injury, yet this was different. This was her husband, the man who'd said he loved her . . . and now he'd proven it in a way her fearful heart could never have dreamed. A guilt and agony like she'd never felt in her life threatened to drown her.

The surgeon probed the wound until he found the bullet and pulled it out. He let it drop into a silver bowl, where it clinked and lay silent.

"It's possible that it didn't pierce any organs. I did not feel anything ruptured when I was retrieving the bullet. I'll stitch him up, but fever is bound to set in. Only time will tell if he will survive."

Buck and Joe remained motionless, watching the surgeon work as he stitched up Flynn's wound. When it was clear there was nothing more any of them could do, her father kissed her temple and told her he had to see to the men. She understood, but none of that mattered to her. The only thing she cared about was the man breathing on the table in front of her.

She wasn't sure how much time had passed when Dominic burst into the sick bay, shouting Nick's name, but then he came to a halt, his face pale as he saw his friend's condition.

He stood vigil opposite Brianna once the surgeon finished his work. Then they were alone with Nicholas between them.

"I've killed him," Brianna whispered hoarsely.

"If we're apportioning blame, then it's my fault he's here at all. If I'd never been taken as a boy, he would never have gone to sea. All he did was love you. Dying for someone you love is . . ." Dominic paused. "It's terrible, yes. And yet I would not hesitate to do so for my Robbie."

"If I hadn't run away from King's Landing . . ." Brianna wiped furiously at the tears that wouldn't stop falling.

"I told the daft man we should tell you our plan. But he was dead set on you staying far away from the rescue."

"What rescue?"

"Our rescue plan to free your crew."

"But how did you manage it?"

"Roberta and Nicholas took drugged bottles of wine to the sentries on duty. I went to ready my ship for your men and then joined them at the fort."

The world around her spun as Dominic explained and she realized she had deeply misjudged her husband. She had once accused him of not caring for the lives of boys like Patrick, but he had. He'd betrayed his king and his country for her and her men. Brianna lifted one of his hands and pressed it to her cheek.

"I'm sorry, Nicholas. I'm sorry," she murmured, her eyes closed.

❧

IT WAS NEARLY MIDNIGHT WHEN SOMEONE ROUSED HER.

"We've docked at King's Landing," her father said. "We have to carry him to shore where he can heal in a clean bed with access to medical supplies."

She wiped at her eyes and stood, one hand still clutching Nicholas's.

"King's Landing? But we've only been at sea for half a day."

Her father's face softened. "You slept a day and a half at his side. Dr. Flores wants him ashore now."

Two men carried Nicholas to shore on a litter. Dominic had gone ahead to see that rooms were prepared in his home to accommodate Nicholas, Brianna and the others. As Brianna walked up the steps of Dominic's house, a strange sense of déjà vu overtook her. She'd first come here to marry Nicholas, and now she feared she would have to bury him.

Roberta came flying out of the house in a swirl of colorful fabrics. "Brianna! Thank heavens you're all right." Her mint-green gown billowed out around her legs as she raced toward Brianna. She flinched as Roberta threw her arms around her, unused to such displays.

"You look dead on your feet. Why don't you come inside?" Roberta gave her a gentle smile and led her upstairs, where Brianna's bloody clothes were stripped and carried away by a maid. A copper tub was filled with hot water for her. She was numb as Roberta helped her in and scrubbed dried blood off of her hands.

Once Brianna was clean, Roberta gave her a nightgown and a dressing gown and escorted her to another room.

Nicholas lay on a bed, also stripped and washed clean, and still alive. Brianna's lips quivered with relief when she saw his chest rising and falling with steady breaths.

"I knew you would not want to be too far from him, but you need your rest as well. You may sleep beside him, and you will feel better."

Roberta left, and Brianna went toward the bed on shaky legs. She lay down next to him, careful to not be too close lest she reopen his wound. She took in the shape of his features until she was certain she would never forget a single detail. She wrapped her fingers around his.

"You must live," she whispered. "You must. That's an order from your captain, you understand?" The fingers she held twitched ever so slightly, and her heart leapt with foolish hope. It was then she noticed the signet ring with the Essex symbol was missing from her finger. Had she lost it in the battle on the ship? Whatever happened, it didn't matter now. All that mattered was Nicholas stayed alive.

"You promised to obey me," she reminded him. "Don't you dare break that vow."

THOMAS BUCK LINGERED AT THE PARTIALLY OPEN doorway, watching his daughter. A lump formed in his throat as he knew it was time to say goodbye to the life he'd made here. Time to let go of her. There was much to be done, much to prepare for, if he was to give Brianna the life she deserved.

He stepped back from the door and felt eyes upon him. He turned and saw Dominic at the foot of the stairs, and behind him was a man in a naval officer's uniform. Dominic's face was grim as he gave Buck a slow nod. Buck nodded in return and came down to meet his fate, whatever it might be.

"This is Admiral Charles Harcourt," Dominic said.

"I'm afraid we have grave matters to discuss, Mr. . . ."

"Holland. Thomas Holland," Buck said, using the name he'd been born with, the name he'd given Brianna.

The admiral waved toward a door, which Dominic opened. "Mr. Holland, this way, if you please." The three of them entered Dominic's study. Buck and the Admiral both sat down. Dominic leaned back against the wall behind the admiral and his desk, watching silently.

"As you are well aware, we have a situation that must be dealt with," Harcourt said. "One of the army captains serving here in Port Royal has been killed."

Thomas didn't flinch. If someone had to accept the penalty for Waverly's death, he would take that blow.

"This captain, as I understand it, deserted his post and recruited a mercenary ship to chase after Brianna St. Laurent."

Thomas held his breath, unsure of where the admiral was going with this.

"Seeing as how Waverly deserted his post and attempted to murder the niece of an English peer, and he has been acting well outside of his duties, I believe that his fate was regrettable but not a punishable offense. If I may speak candidly, we are better off without men like him."

A slow breath eased out of Thomas, but he feared the admiral wasn't done.

Harcourt's hard gaze shifted to Dominic, then back to Thomas. "Oh, I recently heard that Buck, the so-called

Shadow King of the West Indies, has retired from piracy. I'm sure many men would still love to catch him and hang this fellow, but I believe that if he has truly left the West Indies, then the Royal Navy will have other pirates to pursue and perhaps Buck will soon be forgotten."

"He sounds like a fortunate fellow, if he is smart enough to stay away," Thomas said cautiously.

"He would indeed be fortunate to be given a second chance to make a new future. One that lets him be near whatever family he has."

"I imagine Buck would do that. He would be a fool not to."

"And Buck is no fool," Harcourt agreed. The two men stared at each other for a long moment, then Harcourt stood and Buck did as well. "I have letters to write. Captain Waverly left a wife and two children in England. They must be notified of his passing."

"A wife and children?" Thomas replied, hiding his shock. He couldn't help but wonder who would marry a devil like that.

"Yes, though from what I hear, he wasn't much liked by his wife or her family. It seems to have been an arranged marriage. But they deserve to know of his passing."

"I see." Thomas relaxed a little.

"Good night," Harcourt said with a nod, and then Dominic escorted him to the front door.

Buck remained in his chair a moment longer, thinking. If Nicholas survived, it would be a while before he was well enough to travel, and that gave Thomas time to send a letter of his own.

He left Dominic's study and retrieved the signet ring

from his pocket. He had removed it from Brianna's hand while she slept on the ship at Nicholas's bedside, and it gleamed gold in the lamplight now. His smile was soft and sad, his heart fracturing in his chest. He'd been given twenty beautiful years to be a father, but now he must return this gift to her true family.

"Time to send you home, my darling." He closed his fingers around the ring, holding it tight as his eyes burned with tears. Pirates did not cry . . . but he was a pirate no longer.

CHAPTER 22

Moments of his life came in slow waves as Flynn struggled to stay alive. He had visions of Dominic's sparkling, mischievous eyes as they snuck into kitchens to steal tarts, and he heard their boyish shouts as they rode geldings in the fields. Lord, he missed Cornwall, missed the adventures of his childhood before blood and death were ever a part of his life.

But all too soon, those hours of youth faded as Dominic vanished from his life and Nicholas first stepped onto a naval ship, hoping to someday find him. The pain of those first harsh months at sea stretched into long years of quiet desperation, broken only by brief periods of relief on shore and brilliant moments where the wind, sea, and sails joined in beautiful concert with one another.

Then Dominic came roaring back into his life, and with him a sense of relief that his quest had ended, only to then be eclipsed by a woman in a prison cell who changed everything.

As he relived that first moment seeing Brianna's profile and hearing her sing a pirate's lullaby, he realized he had transformed. Like a riverbed etched into a great canyon over millennia, he had been reshaped by the patterns that loving her had left behind.

He savored every kiss, every laugh, every moment that he had been at her side. The silken feel of her hair, the sound of her whispering stories in the darkness as he cradled her body against his. The feeling of belonging to her had been so strong, like coming home after a long voyage. He remembered, too, that moment he saw Waverly raise the pistol to take her life and Nicholas had risked it all to save her. He had no regrets about dying for her.

Then he felt Waverly's shot, meant for her and taken by him. In those final moments, she had come to his defense and plunged her sword into Waverly's body, her face hard and eyes fierce. She had been a goddess of war, a creature far above his reach. And when the pain of the shot had settled in and he'd lost his strength, he had known then that this was to be the end. He'd finally reached that far horizon. Now he stood on the boundary where light and dark formed a knife's edge.

Strains of an old sea ballad came back to him from a Scottish bosun who used to sing it in the wee hours before dawn on Nicholas's first navy posting. The man's low voice carried the tune well, and more than one man risked the wrath of their captain to pause in his work and listen to him. The words had been beautiful and haunting, but he had not realized the depth of truth to them until now.

"One dark and stormy night,
The snow lay on the ground,
A sailor boy stood on the quay,
His ship was outward bound,

His sweetheart by his side,
Shed many's a bitter tear
And as he pressed her to his heart,
He whispered in her ear.

Farewell my own true love,
This parting gives me pain,
You'll be my hope and guiding star,
Till I return again.

My thoughts will be with you love,
While the storms are raging high.
So farewell love, remember me,
Your faithful sailor boy.

Farewell my only true love,
On earth we will meet no more,
We will meet again in heaven above,

On that eternal shore,

I hope to meet you in that land,
That land beyond the skies,
Where parted you shall never be, from
Your faithful sailor boy."

THE SWEET HUM OF THAT MELANCHOLY TUNE VIBRATED through him; even his blood seemed to pulse with it as he sensed he was standing on the edge of that eternal shore.

"You can't disobey your captain . . . I order you not to leave me . . ."

The stern reprimand was like a ghost of a memory. The joy of that ghostly voice gave him the strength to *turn*. He turned away from the gentle, rolling waves of that eternal shore and the soft red horizon and instead faced the darkness, uncertainty, and sweet agony that was life.

FOUR AGONIZING DAYS CREPT BY AS BRIANNA KEPT VIGIL at Nicholas's side. She bathed him, forced broth and water down his lips, and held on to his hands as if only that touch kept him there, alive with her. No one at King's Landing tried to pull her away from him. They left her to pray, to grieve, to hope.

On the fifth day, she hummed an old song she'd learned

from Joe, "The Sailor Boy," as she lay next to Nicholas in bed. She was half-asleep herself, exhaustion threatening to drag her into the depths of unconsciousness, when she felt Nicholas's fingers twitch.

She raised her head and leaned over him. His dark-gold lashes fluttered, stopped, and then his blue eyes, full of storms, opened and fixed on her.

"Nicholas?" Her heart pounded wildly.

"My pirate lass . . . ," he rasped.

She raised his hand to her cheek, pressing the backs of his fingers against her skin as tears blurred her vision.

"You sound like Joe," she teased.

A raspy chuckle escaped him, and pain tightened his features.

"Don't laugh," she said. "You still need to heal. Don't move."

"I doubt . . . very much . . . I could . . . even if I wished to," he admitted.

She moved toward the table beside the bed and filled a goblet with water. She held it to his lips, and he drank deeply. With a sigh, he closed his eyes.

"Tell me a story about your pirate queens . . ." He squeezed her fingers ever so slightly.

"A story . . ." She considered for a moment. "There was once a ship sinking in a storm. A woman on board was laboring with child. Her dying husband held her hand as the storm raged and the ship began to sink ever deeper into the water. But help was coming. A lonely, noble-hearted pirate saw the ship in distress and came to their rescue . . ."

THREE WEEKS PASSED, AND NICHOLAS WAS ABLE TO SIT UP and leave the bed. With the assistance of a cane and Dominic following him about, ready to help, Nicholas once more started to feel like himself again. Everyone treated him like he was fragile as spun glass, and he was, damn it all, but soon he would be fine, and then he would demand everyone not to treat him like a babe. The only one he tolerated this from was his wife, when she hovered at his bedside and forced more food and drink down him than he could sometimes handle.

Brianna said very little, and he sensed that much weighed upon her, as it did with him. It was time they faced this thing between them together and talked.

"I should very much like to see the gardens," he said to her one afternoon when he felt strong enough for it.

She set aside the book she had been pretending to read and stood up from the chair next to the settee he'd been resting on. She wore a gown of deep and endless blue, like the ocean far out at sea. The train was tucked up in the back to keep the silk from catching dust, making her full skirts a waterfall of silk. She rustled her hands in the expensive fabric nervously, a habit she'd probably taken to when she would have rested her hands on her leather belt in days past. It would take her a while to become accustomed to wearing ladies' clothes.

"That's a rather lovely gown. Is it Robbie's?"

"What? Oh . . . no." She blushed, and that always charmed him, how easy she could be to tease. "I ordered some gowns that day I was captured in the marketplace before we met. I'd always wanted something like this, but I never got to go back for the finished gowns. I was able to have them delivered here. Do you like it?" She nibbled her bottom lip in an adorably uncertain way. Here was a fierce pirate queen, a woman who'd survived storms and battles in equal measure, and yet she was afraid he wouldn't like her dress. He wouldn't care if she wore a sackcloth—she would be perfect, no matter what clothes covered her.

"I think you have exquisite taste in clothing, just like your mother."

The smile she gave him was a gift. It filled the room as though the sun had emerged from behind the clouds. He reached for his cane, and she rushed to take his other arm. As much as the tender treatment frustrated him, he was glad for the excuse to touch her.

"Thank you, my darling," he whispered as they walked through the corridor together.

Another blush deepened the color in her cheeks. He waited until they were outside in the garden, alone and out of sight of the house. Then he pulled her into his arms, holding her against him. He felt a peace so deep fill him that it vanquished all fears of what he had to say and how she would react.

"I love you, Brianna, and I was wrong that night when I left you alone in our wedding bed. I acted in what I believed was your best interest to save your men and keep you safe. But it was wrong. *I was wrong.* I removed a choice from you I had no right to take. I promise from this moment forward, whatever we do, we do it together."

She lifted her face, tears glinting like diamond dust on her lashes. "And I never should have left. I fear little in life, yet loving you was the most frightening thing I'd ever faced. Even when Waverley tried to hang me from the yardarm, the only thing that truly scared me was losing you." She blinked away fresh tears. "You hold such power over me, Nicholas. A power that could save me or destroy me. I've never let anyone have that kind of power, not even my father."

Nicholas tipped her chin up so that she met his gaze. "I believe that is the definition of love: trusting a person with the power to hold your heart in their hands. You hold mine, my love. You have the same power over me."

"Truly?" She still seemed to doubt him. "It's just . . . I'm not some fine lady."

"And I am no humble gentleman."

"But I know nothing of being a lady, and I argue with you all the—"

He silenced her with a kiss that reminded the rest of his body that being alive was such a wonderful thing. Her lips parted beneath his, and he slipped his tongue into the sweet recesses of her mouth. She tasted like pure heaven. It took so long for their mouths to break apart that he forgot what it was they had been discussing.

"You have a few more weeks to rest, wife, and then I'll begin to claim my husbandly rights."

"Every night?" she asked with a devious giggle.

"And sometimes in the morning, the afternoon . . . just before dinner . . ." He smiled roguishly at her and then kissed the tip of her nose.

"Very well . . . I shall remember to give in to your demands, husband." She snorted out a laugh and then added, "As long as I am able to claim my wifely rights as well."

"You will find, madam, I am most eager to submit to any and all of your desires."

"Is that so?" she asked with wide and guileless eyes.

"Because I rather liked it when you were chained to the wall of my cabin. I never did have the opportunity to enjoy it the way I should have liked." She feathered a kiss along his jaw. "Can you imagine how I might've taken you into my mouth, on my knees, and you would have been chained, helpless, only able to enjoy anything that I might offer?"

Nicholas bit back a curse as white-hot desire burned through his body.

"And I imagine," he growled as he fisted his hand in her hair, which was loosely coiling down her neck and shoulders, "that I should very much like to do the same with you, my pirate queen. To chain you to our bed and pleasure you in a thousand ways until you are hoarse from screaming in ecstasy."

Brianna's breath caught, and her rebellious pirate eyes flashed up to his as she gave him that saucy grin that delighted and maddened him.

"Now that is a torture well worth submitting to. I'd better go bother Joe to find a pair of manacles . . ." She turned to leave, but he pulled her into his arms again.

"Later, my pirate wife. Later."

CHAPTER 23

Cornwall, England
Three months later

DOMINIC'S SHIP, THE *ROBBIE DARLING*, SAILED INTO A PORT off the coast of Cornwall on a clear, sunny morning in the early fall. The emerald hills, sheer cliffs, and rocky shores were the first sight Brianna had of Nicholas's home.

She leaned against the rail of the ship, taking it all in. Her bright skirts billowed around her legs and Nicholas's as he stood on the deck beside her. She peeped at him beneath her lashes, noting how the tension she had seen so often on his face had finally vanished. The sun illuminated his blond hair, and the wind tugged playfully at the long strands around his forehead. The gaunt, weary, wounded man she'd known the last three months was finally gone. He had left his cane back in Jamaica, and apparently his worries too.

Brianna nudged his arm with hers. "Are you glad to be returning home?"

He grinned bashfully at her. "I am," he admitted.

She was glad he was so happy. She had done her best to conceal her own fears until today, about whether she would find a life for herself here. But his optimism buoyed her spirits.

"There's nothing to fear, Brianna." He took her hand in his. His hold was firm and grounded her like an anchor dropping beneath the waves. She let out a breath as some of her own tension faded.

"What will your parents think of me? Surely they weren't happy to find out you'd married a former pirate, not to mention a veritable hoyden." He'd confessed to her that he'd written them a few letters and they knew the entire story of her background. She'd been horrified at first, but he'd assured her—or rather, tried his best to convince her—that his parents wouldn't care about any of that. She still wasn't sure she believed him.

"Not that it matters, but they already love you."

Nicholas seemed so sure of that, but she wasn't. "What? How could they?"

Nicholas's lips curved into one of her favorite smiles. Tender, full of satisfaction and certainty. It was the smile he gave her whenever they made love, which was almost daily. She had never known a man with such desire or stamina. Luckily for him, she was a "lusty wench," as he so adoringly put it when she demanded he bed her.

He cupped her face with his hand, his blue eyes as clear as the sky above.

"Love is simple. They will love you because I do."

Love is simple. Her father had said something similar to her what felt like a lifetime ago.

Her hand went to her stomach, a sudden need to hold her palm over her womb where the tiny life grew inside her. She hadn't yet told Nicholas he was going to be a father. She wanted to wait until the right time.

He lowered his head to hers and kissed her. "You're brilliant, brave, and beautiful. What's not to love?" Whistles and good-natured jeers from the crew made them laugh and pull apart from each other. Dominic laughed along with his men.

"Don't you all have a ship to dock?" she yelled at Dominic and his crew mockingly. It was hard to remember that this wasn't her ship and she couldn't give the orders.

She and Nicholas always seemed to lose themselves in each other in front of others.

Dominic leapt down the steps from the upper deck to where they stood as crew began to toss the lines out to the men waiting on the dock. "Are you two ready?"

Soon, the gangplank had been lowered and the crew were carrying their trunks down to a waiting coach in the distance.

Her husband turned to her, offering his arm and echoing Dominic's question. "Are you ready?" She had a strange moment of déjà vu, remembering that long-ago day in the Port Royal market with Joe when she'd imagined herself doing this very thing. Walking as a fine lady on the arm of a gentleman. Only Nicholas was infinitely more wonderful than any fantasy nobleman she could have dreamed up.

The ride to Nicholas's home was not long, and yet during that half hour in the coach, she managed to work up her nerves again to the point that she nearly ruined the fine silk of her gown as she twisted it in her strong hands. Noticing her distress, Nicholas gently freed her skirts from her fingers.

The coach rolled to a stop, and her heart began to pound against her ribs.

"There's nothing to worry about." He pulled her onto his lap while they waited for the footman to open the door and lower the step for them. "You have faced far worse dangers than this. Just imagine you won a battle at sea and now you're boarding the enemy vessel."

"Hardly. I actually want your parents to *like* me, not steal their jewels and cargo."

Damn the man, he dared to laugh in light of her distress.

"You are without a doubt the most ador—"

"If you say *adorable*, I will punch you, *husband*," she warned, quite seriously, but his smile only grew, and he hugged her closer.

"I know you will, love. Then I'll kiss you afterward to make you feel better."

His reactions to her temper always distracted her. Instead of insisting she bury her rages, he embraced them with her and promised to love her afterward. Somehow that in and of itself always seemed to defuse her anger.

"Just remember to breathe." He kissed the tip of her nose and then set her on her feet so that he could exit the coach first to assist her. Etiquette aside, she still wasn't completely comfortable in these skirts.

She held her breath again despite him reminding her to breathe. Sometimes it was quite impossible to breathe when she was worried about something else. When she finally stepped out of the coach and looked up, a man and a woman stood on the steps of the stately manor house made of gray stone. Nicholas wove her arm through his, and she let him escort her up the steps to meet the couple waiting for them.

"Nicholas!" his parents exclaimed together and embraced their son eagerly. Brianna watched with an almost violent pang of longing for her own father.

"This is Brianna, my wife." Nicholas beamed at her, and for a moment, she forgot all of her fears. "Brianna, allow me to introduce you to my father, Daniel, and my mother, Julia."

"Brianna! Oh, she's even more beautiful than all your letters said." Nicholas's mother wrapped her arms around Brianna in a warm hug before Brianna could react. Julia was a striking woman with flaxen hair and gray eyes. Much of Nicholas's fine looks clearly came from her.

"Let her catch her breath, my love," Daniel teased his wife.

"Oh, I'm so sorry." His mother released Brianna and smiled as though she was sincerely glad to meet her.

"Now it is my turn." Daniel was a dark-haired gentleman with intense blue eyes much like his son's. He came forward and embraced Brianna with far more gentleness, like a father should, warmly, all encompassing, and she immediately felt safe in this man's arms.

"Thank you for bringing our son back and saving his life." Nicholas's father said the words softly in her ear so that she was the only one who heard. Then he stepped back and said for all to hear, "Welcome to our family, Brianna."

"Th—thank you." She could barely get the words out. She was stunned by their welcoming her and even more stunned to find that she already felt like part of this new family.

"You're just in time, Brianna. Your father arrived yesterday," Daniel said.

She gasped. "My father is here?"

Her father had gone ahead to England a few weeks before them in order to look around Cornwall for a place to settle down.

"I am," Thomas Holland announced from the open doorway. Brianna's control over her emotions failed her. She rushed toward her father, and he caught her in his arms, holding her tight, and she felt that pang of longing vanish. He was here—her father and Nicholas's family were all together, and it felt . . . *wonderful*.

"We settled him on the bordering estate. Lord Faulkin died six months ago and left no immediate heirs. Since the estate was handled by his solicitor, it was quite easy to manage the sale of the house and land for your father."

"And I'm grateful for all of your help, Daniel," Thomas said. "It is exactly what I had hoped to find."

"You're truly staying close?" Brianna asked. She and Nicholas had discussed remaining at the family home until they could find their own house.

Her father chuckled. "I'll be close enough." He winked at her. "Nicholas, your father is quite the fellow. We've been out hunting pheasants and drafting new plans for the crofter cottages I've inherited with my land purchase. He's been an immense help to me."

"I'm glad to hear it, sir," Nicholas said with pride as he looked between their fathers.

Brianna had worried that the life of a country gentleman would bore her father, but it seemed that she had been wrong. There was a peace to Thomas now that was undeniable. He was ready for this phase of his life.

"Why don't you both come in? We're expecting guests for dinner this evening."

"Guests?" Nicholas asked.

"Yes. Brianna's uncle, aunt, and cousin will be staying the week with us. They arrive tonight."

"So soon?" Brianna clutched Nicholas's arm, surprised that she needed to feel him so close, but his presence always comforted her.

"Your family—your *other* family—is most anxious to meet you," Julia said. "We were worried it might be too soon, but the Duke of Essex is hard to say no to."

"Nicholas, why don't you take Brianna upstairs so she can rest and change for dinner?" Julia suggested. Brianna flashed her a grateful look. She was overwhelmed at the moment and needed to be alone with Nicholas for a short while to process everything.

Nicholas escorted Brianna through the light and airy corridors of his family home, and she was soon lost in the paintings and fine furniture.

"Not what you expected?" he asked with amusement in his eyes.

"I'd always heard Cornwall was cold, stormy, and gloomy, but this is beautiful. The house is light and so full of windows, and I can smell the sea from here."

"It can be stormy and gloomy," he admitted. "And those nights are best spent by the fire, wrapped in the arms of one's spouse. It's even better if we're naked."

She laughed at his sensual teasing. "I see."

The atmosphere here was different than on the islands.

The humidity there could often feel cloying, and now she felt strangely free. She could breathe in the air here forever.

"It smells like rain," Brianna said as she and Nicholas stopped near a bedchamber at the end of the east wing.

Nicholas chuckled. "It's England. Even on sunny days, it smells like fresh rain." He paused, resting his hand on the door handle. "Do you hate it here? Please be honest with me." He looked so worried, so uncertain, but Brianna would never lie to him.

"I've always loved the smell of rain." She nodded at his hand on the door handle. "Well, aren't you going to show me our bedroom?" She raised an eyebrow, and his face split into a grin. If she seduced her husband right now, she wouldn't have to think about meeting her family in a few hours.

NICHOLAS HAD LEARNED ONE VERY IMPORTANT THING about his wife in the last three months. She always lured him to bed whenever she desperately needed a distraction. He didn't mind indulging her desires, not when she was so tempting, but he would have to talk to her afterward about her fear of meeting her family.

They stepped into his bedchamber, and he closed the door. She walked around the room, her fingertips trailing over the coverlet and around the spindles of his four-poster bed before she paused in front of the bookshelves. Tucked between the spaces of these texts were fragments of his life. A rabbit's foot that was older than his father, a set of fishing hooks he had made himself, dozens of seashells, and other odds and ends children collected as they explored the world.

She touched each one, her smile a little sad as she finally looked his way.

"I didn't . . . I didn't have many of these growing up."

He came a few steps closer to her. "Why not?" He often wondered about her childhood and what it had been like. She said so little about it.

"My father had his home in Saint Kitts," she said after a long pause.

"It wasn't your home?"

She shook her head. "I lived there, but we so often went to sea that I grew up more on ships than in houses. There's only ever been one place that was truly mine."

He knew instinctively what she meant. "Your ship."

"The *Sea Serpent* was my world, but even then I couldn't keep too many things in my cabin. Pirates must be ready to move quickly. We can't afford to be sentimental." She chuckled softly, but the sound was also full of sorrow. She suddenly thought of the old wooden mermaid in the corner of Gavin's cabin. Perhaps she was lying to herself. Pirates were possibly far more sentimental than she'd ever wanted to admit.

"What?" Nicholas asked.

"My friend Gavin Castleton—he's sentimental, too much so for a pirate. I worry about him sometimes. His family hails from here. He left home to go to sea when he wasn't much younger than you were, and it caused a great rift between him and his brother."

"That's the fellow your father chose as the new Admiral of the Black?" Nicholas asked. "You were close to him?"

"He was one of the few men that I was able to build a friendship with, but . . ."

Nicholas didn't indulge in any jealousy. He knew how Brianna felt about him and was confident in her love, but he was curious as to what she would say. "But what?"

She turned away from the bookshelves and looked at him. "No one ever eased my loneliness until *you*." Her eyes were bright as flames, and he had the foolish desire to compose sonnets to those eyes.

"You're my home, Nicholas. Wherever you are, that is home to me," she said, and her heart shone in her lovely green eyes.

Unable to speak lest his voice break, he pulled her into his arms and held her tight, so tight he feared he might crush her, but he needed to feel her in his arms and hold the most precious gift life had ever given him.

"My life at sea has taken so much away from me. But the sea also gave me you, and that has more than made up for it. You are my gift, a shining pearl, a treasure every pirate dreams of finding. You are *everything* to me. I will go wherever you wish. If you want to live on a ship the rest of our lives, sailing around the world, then my heart leaps with joy at the thought, so long as you are there with me."

Tears soaked his shirtfront as she rubbed her cheek against his shoulder.

"You wouldn't make me stay here and play the role society demands of me? I am the niece of a duke. What if . . . ?"

"As the niece of a duke, you can do whatever the bloody hell you want," he laughed. "And I'll lay flat anyone who dares to argue otherwise."

She laughed with him, but it came out more as a sob. "I was so afraid that you wouldn't want that."

Nicholas kissed the crown of her hair. "*You* are what I want. Damn the rest."

She smiled through her tears. "Truly?"

In answer, he lowered his head and kissed her. For a long while after, neither of them worried about anything—except perhaps missing dinner.

CHAPTER 24

"They're here," Nicholas called from the doorway as he came to check on Brianna. She had decided to wear her mother's silver-and-blue gown, and her hair had been pulled up into a mass of curls and waves. Julia's lady's maid had threaded pearls onto strands of Brianna's hair, making it look as though Venus had left the sea to sprinkle the sea's treasures on Brianna's coiffure. Brianna drew in a deep breath and faced Nicholas. She prayed she looked fit to meet a duke and duchess.

"How do I look?" she asked nervously.

With a mischievous twinkle in his eyes, her husband pretended to scrutinize her appearance.

"Well, you'll have to do, but I much prefer my pirate queen in breeches and wielding a brace of pistols."

She scoffed at him as though offended and tried to march past him, chin raised haughtily. He caught her arm and pulled her back.

"You are the single most stunning woman I've ever seen," he whispered and kissed her soundly.

Lord, when he kissed her like that . . . she forgot everything whirling around in her head in that moment. There were just his lips on hers, his breath against her skin, and the feel of passion that burned like a well-kept fire.

They broke apart at the sound of a polite cough. Her father stood in the corridor, watching them with no small amount of amusement.

"Plenty of time for that later, Flynn," Thomas said.

He had been transformed into a country gentleman, wearing fine buckskin breeches, a waistcoat, and a dark-blue frockcoat embroidered with gold. At his side stood Elida in a deep-purple gown that accented her raven-black hair. Brianna had learned only a short time ago that her father had married his Spanish housekeeper and brought her to Cornwall with him. It filled Brianna's heart with joy to see them together.

"You look wonderful, Elida," she told her new stepmother, and they hugged tightly.

Elida cupped Brianna's face in the way she'd done for so many years. "So do you, darling child." She studied her with a motherly eye. "Have you've been crying?"

"Only from happiness," Brianna admitted.

"Hmm, that is well, then," Elida said with a nod. "Happy tears are good tears."

On that, Brianna agreed.

"Well, shall we all go down?" Nicholas asked. "I imagine the cook will be fussing about us attending dinner on time."

"We had better," Thomas laughed. "It isn't a good idea to upset one's cook."

At the stairs, they saw Nicholas's parents speaking with a well-dressed middle-aged couple and a younger man around Brianna's age.

The Duke of Essex and his family were here. *Her family*.

They turned to stare up at her when they heard them on the stairs, and Brianna's heart stopped.

Two pairs of bright-green eyes exactly like hers gazed up at her. Her uncle and her cousin had *her* eyes. Something about that, the connection to a lost family she'd never known she'd needed, clicked into place.

She and Nicholas came down the stairs first, and her uncle, the Duke of Essex, Michael St. Laurent, stepped forward first, his gaze sweeping over her as he swallowed hard. He was tall and quite handsome, with dark hair streaked with silver at the temples. Yet she saw in that face a man who was not to be ignored. He had power, influence, and yet there was a softness to him as well as he looked at her.

"My God," he said half to himself. "You truly are my niece. There's no mistaking it." He reached into his frock coat and withdrew a pair of miniature portraits, holding them out to her, his mouth still agape as he offered them to her.

Brianna let go of Nicholas's arms to take the portraits. Her gaze widened as she took in the likenesses of her parents' faces in painted porcelain for the first time, their features small but expertly done.

"I have large portraits of them at the Essex estate, of course, but these were easy to bring tonight. I thought you might want . . . to see them." Her uncle's voice was suddenly rough, and he cleared his throat awkwardly.

"I . . ." Brianna's mind went blank; she was suddenly unsure of what to say. She looked up into her uncle's face, seeing the likeness there so clearly between Lord Essex and her natural-born father. Then she stared at the beauty who was her mother. A shiver stole through her as she imagined, not for the first time, what her life might have been like if they had survived. As much as their deaths filled her with a deep and terrible sense of loss, she knew that if they hadn't died, Thomas wouldn't have found her, and she never would have met Nicholas. That trade of her parents' lives in order for her to find Nicholas would always be with her and remind her of how much Nicholas meant to her.

"Is it too much?" her uncle asked.

"No. I've just never seen them before, and it's . . ." She sniffled. "Thank you so much for bringing them. Would you tell me about them?" She felt incredibly shy as she asked this of the duke.

Her uncle smiled. "I would be honored to tell you everything about them. Now, I believe introductions are in order." He glanced over his shoulder. "This is my wife, Edwina, and my son, Evan. Evan has just turned twenty-one."

Her cousin beamed at her like she was a treasure found. He was as handsome as his parents, and a hint of mischief gleamed in his eyes. She knew at once that she and Evan would get along famously. She'd always had a knack for making trouble. Perhaps it was something she'd inherited from her family.

Edwina, her aunt, was a beautiful brunette with kind brown eyes. She stepped forward and embraced Brianna without hesitation.

"Your mother was one of my dearest friends in all the

world. When you came down the stairs just now, I thought perhaps she had somehow come back to us." Her aunt's eyes sparkled with tears as she paused, sniffed, and then continued. "I will tell you everything you want to know about her and your father. Everything I remember."

"Thank you, Aunt Edwina," Brianna said. Her throat grew tight as she tried not to cry.

Her uncle then turned to Nicholas. "You must be Brianna's husband?"

"I am, Your Grace." Nicholas stepped forward, and the pair shook hands.

"I admit, I'm sad to lose her to you. I was hoping to have her under my roof for a while," her uncle said. "Perhaps I can prevail upon you to come visit us often?"

With a look at Brianna, Nicholas replied, "As often as Brianna wishes to see you, we will go. I have a feeling that will be quite often."

"Your Grace . . . ," Brianna began. She'd had to learn how to address a duke in the last few hours and was still nervous about getting it right.

"Please, it's Uncle Michael to you, my dear."

"Uncle . . . Please let me introduce my father, the man who raised me in your brother's stead—Thomas Holland and his wife, Elida."

Her uncle straightened his shoulders as Thomas stepped forward.

"Nicholas has told me everything through his letters, Mr. Holland. You came to my brother's rescue and tried to save him and his wife. He told me that you delivered Brianna and . . ." Her uncle swallowed hard. "It is thanks to you that she is the woman she is today. A woman to be proud of."

Thomas shifted on his feet, and his face reddened. “She was an honor to have in my life, Your Grace. I wish every day that I had arrived in time to save your brother and his wife, but the moment your brother entrusted his child to me, she became a gift beyond all measure.”

Brianna had to clutch Nicholas’s arm again as she fought to hide such powerful emotions that she feared she would weep before all these people who already seemed to love her so much even though they had just met. Was it possible to perish from sheer, blinding joy?

“Now this, was given to me to prove who you were, and I believe, as Hugh’s child, it should be returned to you.” Her Uncle removed one more thing from this coat. Her father’s signet ring.

“How did you get it? I feared I lost it!” Brianna gasped.

“Mr. Holland wrote to me of your existence before you sailed here and sent the ring as proof.”

THOMAS STEPPED FORWARD TO ADDRESS THE DUKE. “YOUR brother gave it to me, Your Grace, and I kept it safe until it was time to tell Brianna of her birth. I didn’t know at the time who her family was. I would have contacted you years ago, had I known.”

Her uncle held the ring for a long moment before he took Brianna’s hand and placed the ring back in her palm and closed her fingers around it with his own.

“I gave Hugh that ring when he turned twenty-one. It was a gift from me, brother to brother. It is yours, my dear.”

Brianna clutched the ring to her chest and bit her lip to keep from crying.

Nicholas's mother cleared her throat. "Perhaps we can go on to dinner and hear all those wonderful stories about Brianna's parents?"

Everyone murmured their agreement. Nicholas held Brianna back a moment while they allowed the others to proceed to the dining room ahead of them.

"Are you all right?" he asked as he cupped her face in his hands.

She grasped his wrists and nodded, blinking away fresh tears.

"Yes. I'm more than all right . . ." Now was the right time to tell him. "*We're* all right." She gently pulled one of his hands down to lay it on her belly. "*We're* wonderful, in fact."

Nicholas's eyes grew round as saucers. "*We?* You mean . . ."

She laughed at his expression of shock and wonder. "Yes. The *three* of us . . ."

Nicholas's face broke into a boyish grin, the one that had made her realize she loved him all those months ago. It was like the sun breaking through the clouds and a healthy wind filling the sails of her ship . . . like a splendid day for sailing toward far-off horizons.

"We shall tell our children tales of pirate queens every night," Nicholas said.

She laughed. "Is that so?"

"Yes. They'll need to know all about their mother and how incredible she is. How she is far fiercer than Grace O'Malley."

"Flatterer," she said unable to deny the bubbling joy inside her.

Her husband just continued to grin at her, the delightful rogue.

Nicholas's father returned to the doorway of the dining room. "Will you two be joining us?"

She and Nick shared a secret smile. "Yes, we will. All three of us."

"Three?" his father asked in confusion as they walked past him.

Whatever came next in her life, Brianna would not face it alone. She had a man who loved her fiercely, and she loved him fiercely in return. She had her father and stepmother and so many new relatives that it felt as though she might be dreaming.

But no dream could be this good, this real, this wonderful. She might have been brought into the world during a storm, but the horizon before her held nothing but beautiful, endless light.

EPILOGUE

It was a fine day three weeks later when Nicholas took Brianna riding. They had been doing a lot of that lately, riding all over the nearby countryside. It was a good thing his wound had healed and he was feeling like himself again. Sometimes they walked and talked, and sometimes they rode at breakneck speed until their horses needed to rest.

Nicholas knew his wife was suffering from a restlessness, a need to keep moving, to explore rather than be confined to a life in drawing rooms and ballrooms. Once, he would have sworn that he could have returned to Cornwall and stayed there forever more, satisfied with retiring from his adventures. But that was no longer true. He understood that hunger Brianna felt to continue to sail into fresh winds and visit foreign shores. It was why he'd managed to arrange for a special gift for his wife today—not that she had any idea he was up to anything.

He guided his gelding in the direction of the port, and

Brianna kept pace with him. She wore a pair of breeches and a waistcoat as well as tall black riding boots as he did, but her hair was held back with only a ribbon. She cared not about any gossip she caused. She had even laughed and said, "If my family knows I'm a pirate and they don't mind, what's the harm in wearing a pair of breeches?"

Nicholas didn't mind. He'd much rather have her comfortable than fashionable. He was also rather partial to the way her backside looked in her snug breeches.

As they reached the port, they slowed their horses and meandered toward the docks. A dozen ships in the harbor soon came into view. He kept his face neutral as they toured the port, but secretly he was taking in every expression on her face, not wanting to miss one instant of when she saw what he was hoping she would see soon. Brianna let out a soft, dreamy sigh. Then she reached out and grasped his arm.

"Nick!" She pointed at one of the ships, and he grinned. It had been hard to keep this little gift a secret, but he'd done well. Dominic would be proud of him.

"Why not have a look?" he urged, and she leapt into motion, spurring her horse forward. He followed behind slowly, his smile widening as he finally caught up with her.

She slid off her horse and gave the reins to a young lad to hold for her while she marched up the gangplank of the nearest ship. He came aboard after her and stopped on the waist deck, admiring her as she examined the ship from stem to stern before she turned to him, a hopeful question unspoken in her eyes.

He answered with a nod.

She ran toward him, and he caught her in his arms,

twirling her about as she laughed in joy. The *Sea Serpent* and her captain had been reunited at long last.

"Oh, Flynn!" she breathed in a husky whisper. He nuzzled her nose with his, adoring how she called him Flynn. It had in the last few months become an endearment rather than an admonishment.

"Happy?" he asked. He could see from her face that she was, but he wanted her to understand in this moment what this ship meant, not just to her but to the both of them. They both belonged together, and that meant the sea was to be a large part of their lives. His pirate queen's story was far from over. Someday, they'd tell their own child stories of their mother's legendary life, and that child, boy or girl, would grow up with waves and the cries of storm petrels as their lullaby, just as Brianna had.

"Yes. But how did you find her?"

"Some arrogant arse who owns King's Landing bought it after the navy acquired it during a raid. He thought it might make an excellent wedding present for you. Since I am best friends with said arse, I agreed."

She stared at him in equal parts wonder and gratitude. "Dominic rescued my ship?"

"Of course he did, my darling. He knows how important a captain's ship is. He would never let the *Sea Serpent* stay long in enemy hands."

She gave him a delightfully sinful look. "Well, *I* ended up in enemy hands, and I can't say I'm complaining."

"Oh? Like being in enemy hands, do you?" He chuckled and stole a kiss that made him forget they weren't alone, and he couldn't resist cupping her bottom and giving it a generous squeeze that made her moan against his mouth. Several sailors started to whistle at them.

Half a dozen men were staring at them, their tasks on the deck forgotten. Patrick, Brianna's cabin boy, fresh from New York, was among them, and he grinned at the pair. Next to him, a taller, older seaman who was new to the crew blinked owlishly at their behavior.

"That's our new captain? Bit of a rogue, ain't he?" the man asked Patrick.

"Oh, *he* isn't the captain," said Patrick. "*She* is. He's the first mate."

Brianna, with a gleeful grin at the man beside Patrick, said, "Don't worry, I'm tough but fair." Then she turned to Nicholas. "We had better test out the captain's bed. Come, Flynn. Time to do your duty." She sauntered past the crew, leaving more than one man's mouth agape at her swaying backside in those tight breeches.

"Yes, Captain," Nicholas called out after her and went to do his duty *most thoroughly*.

Sometimes it was good to be Flynn.

EIGHT MONTHS LATER

Gavin Castleton wasn't sure he would survive the night. As the storm pounded the rocks where his rowboat foundered, he stumbled wearily from the boat and sank hip-deep into the icy water near the shore.

Teeth chattering, he forced himself to keep walking along the rocky beach toward the cliffs that hid a dark passageway.

It was his only refuge, his only chance to survive, if he could but reach it.

He braced himself against the wind as he finally reached the hidden entrance. Then he was inside, safe within the natural shelter of the stone passage. The wind and rain died away but still howled angrily in the distance, as though furious he'd managed to escape their wrath.

He had to make it just a little bit farther . . . A bit farther, that was all.

His cold, numb hands trailed along the walls of the passageway as he found his way in the enveloping blackness. The floor beneath him slowly angled upward, and at last he found the door handle that he sought and tugged on it.

The ancient oak door gave way, and he stumbled into a dusty, darkened room that was nearly as black as the passageway he'd just left. Shivering violently, he frowned at the cold hearth of the forgotten bedroom. Lord, he wished someone would have lit a fire. Not that anyone had expected him here in this room, especially not tonight.

He dragged his aching feet across the room until he reached the next door and opened it. The corridor outside the room was dark, not a single lamp lit. Lightning from the storm flashed outside, illuminating his family's ancestral home through the windows. He hadn't been back in more than a year, but he would have known this old manor house's halls even if he had been blind.

Pain radiated from his shoulder where he'd taken a knife wound. His blood-and-rain-soaked clothes were starting to stiffen around him, dragging him down and choking him.

Gavin bit back a groan as he fought to ignore the pain in his body and counted the doors as he moved. He had to find his brother, Griffin. When he reached the third door on the left, Griffin's bedroom, he fell against it as he turned the handle. The door swung open beneath his weight, and he staggered toward the sleeping figure in the bed.

"Griffin," he groaned, and grabbed his brother's shoulder, shaking him awake. "Griff . . . help . . ." Gavin slid to his knees, too weak to do much more than collapse onto the floor.

A woman's frantic voice broke through the haze in his mind. "Who are you?" He looked up to see a woman light a taper and bring it to a lamp at the side of the bed. Golden light softened the room, and he stared in shock at a beautiful brown-eyed young woman in a filmy chemise.

"Where's . . . Griffin?" His words came out breathless.

"Griffin? You mean Lord Castleton?"

Gavin winced. *Lord Castleton* . . . The name that was his by birthright, but he had turned his back on it.

"Aye, bloody Lord Castleton," he gasped. At last his body surrendered to exhaustion, and he fell back onto the floor.

The young woman's voice grew faint as he began to lose consciousness. "Oh heavens! You're injured!"

Her warm gentle hands touched his chilled skin, and he stared into the most beautiful woman's face he'd ever seen. Then he blacked out.

THANK YOU SO MUCH FOR READING *IN LIKE FLYNN!* The next book Devil of the High Seas will be about Gavin Castleton and Dominic's little sister Josephine. Get it HERE!

Made in the USA
Columbia, SC
01 January 2024